The Adventures of
Brother Arcadius and Pangur Ban

The Adventures of Brother Arcadius and Pangur Ban

11 Tales

by
Margaret Nagel

WITH DRAWINGS
BY THE AUTHOR

Evanston, Illinois
NEVERWERT PRESS
2016

Cover design by Bonnie Mutchler Covers
https://bonniemutchlercovers.wordpress.com

Book formatting by eBook Pioneers
http://ebookpioneers.com

Printed in the United States of America.

ISBN: 978-0-9970633-2-5

10 9 8 7 6 5 4 3 2 1

The Adventures of Brother Arcadius and Pangur Ban, 11 Tales
Neverwert Press, P.O. Box 6519, Evanston, IL 60204
www.neverwertpress.com

This is a work of fiction. Names, characters, places, and incidents are either products of the author's imagination or are used fictitiously. Any resemblance to existing persons, events, or institutions is entirely coincidental.

For my children,
Mary, Sarah, and Milton,
and my sister, Doris,
with love and gratitude

Contents

Author's Note

For the purposes of this book, the name "Pangur Bán," which is correct, is given as "Pangur Ban."

The Adventures
of Brother Arcadius and Pangur Ban

PROLOGUE

In which Pangur Ban and Brother Arcadius join
forces and travel far, but not quite far enough

AD 898

He hadn't meant to be traveling with a cat, but now he had one, so now what? And where was the party he was supposed to be traveling with? At a loss for what to do, he stood where he was on the shore, looking about him with anxious expectancy.

It was a very wide and unpromising world here, that was for sure. The view went on and on in every direction, but so far there was nothing in it that gladdened his heart. The sun shone bleakly down through a haze of thin clouds. Gray waves washed the litter of tidewrack forward and back all along the strand. The boat he'd come in on was now just a dwindling speck on the rim of the sea. There weren't any people in sight except for one. Some distance away still, an old lady, as wide as she was tall, almost, was hobbling steadily closer over the sands. She had a bunch of baskets, it looked like, slung on a rope over her shoulder. Would she know where his party might be? Should he try to ask her?

The cat mewed in his arms. He hugged the poor creature closer. Pangur Ban, he was going to name him. That was a good Irish name and it signified whiteness, so it was just right. Pangur had come up from the cargo, a stowaway, when the boat was maybe an hour out of Dublin, so he had to be Irish. And he was white—or he would be, when he'd been cleaned up. Just a kitten he still was, wasn't he, barely half grown. And the sailor'd been going to kill him! Well, was a person just supposed to keep on vomiting from seasickness over the side and do nothing about it? No, a person wasn't. So he'd paid off the sailor with one of his pieces of money, and he wasn't supposed to be spending his pieces of money.

He shifted from one foot to the other, wishing the sun would shine a little warmer. There hadn't been any dock for the boat to pull up to. The gravel spit he'd waded to shore on hadn't been much above water, most of the time. His robe was still sopping wet from the waist down. And his little bundle of things had fallen into the water back there and sunk out of sight. He hadn't been able to hang onto Pangur and grab for it too. *Grow up*, he told himself. *Don't you start sniveling.* After all, he'd been sixteen years old for a whole month now, ever since the day after the first day of spring. People who were sixteen years old weren't supposed to be sniveling. And he was Brother Arcadius of Dublin Monastery, born Tammis the brickmaker's son. And soon enough—if he ever got there—he was going to be Brother Arcadius of Spiritus Sanctus monastery, far away over still another sea, and up and down rivers and this way and that over land, and then up an actual mountain, so it was said. But with people to travel with all the way, or so it had been arranged...to Spiritus Sanctus, where they had five hundred books in the library. To Spiritus Sanctus, where he was going to be assistant librarian.

Coming along step by step, the basket lady took stock of the solitary figure in her view. Now there's a darling little monk if ever I saw one, she said to herself. Just off that smuggler's boat from Dublin, I do believe. Why, the wind could blow him away! And my! Those pretty curls peeking out from that hood! Red, aren't they. Look at him standing all alone there, clutching that cat. He'll want a basket.

She hitched her rope of wares higher up on her shoulder and hobbled faster. Brother Arcadius kept covert track of her approach. He tried to make it seem as if he hadn't yet seen her. His six grown-up brothers, his Mam, the monks at the Dublin monastery—they'd all cautioned him about falling in with strangers. Even his two younger sisters had cautioned him, as if they'd know. But this was just an old lady, and what harm could she do him? Anyway, he had to stop pretending he didn't see her. She was coming straight at him now, and waving into the bargain. Making good headway, too, considering. Closer she came and closer, steadily closer, until she was right before him, panting and smiling.

"Sell you a nice stout basket, dearie?"

What sort of talk was she talking? It sounded like Saxon, maybe? A safe guess, because he was in Saxon country now, or Angle-land as some people called it: King Alfred's lands, in Wessex, across the water from Ireland. He knew Latin, Greek, Hebrew, and Irish, but he didn't know Saxon. Or Anglish, or whatever it was. But maybe she'd understand him? If he kept it simple?

Simple, and—it went without saying—very polite. He framed his thoughts in his mind, and then said them in hopeful Irish. "Ma'am, have you seen a big party of merchants? Merchants on mules? Somewhere around here? Ma'am?"

No, she didn't understand him. He repeated himself, this time in Latin. She said nothing in answer. She pointed instead at her biggest basket, a tall willow basket with a lid, and rope handles. She pointed to Pangur Ban. She held up five fingers. That must be the price. His pieces of money were tens, so he'd get five back. And he would need something to carry Pangur in, that was for sure, and he'd do everything he could to make up for the cost. He nodded and gave her the money. She gave him the basket. Pangur liked it and snuggled down in it. But where was the five that he ought to be getting back?

Very worried now, he held up five fingers himself, as she'd done just moments before.

She held up ten. "King's costs, dearie."

He didn't understand what she'd said, but he did understand that she didn't mean to give him anything back. She was hobbling away now. What should he do? Shout at her? Run after her and block her way? He couldn't imagine doing anything like that. Forlornly, he watched her hobble out of sight. He told himself that he'd guard the rest of his money like nobody's business. Pangur Ban was curled up napping at the bottom of the new basket. That was good. As for the people he was going to travel with....

His brothers and his Mam and the monks had said that he might have to wait a few hours for them, but they would be coming along. But if it seemed he'd missed them, there was a good, safe inn some four miles away, and he should go there, because that's where they planned to be spending the night. But he didn't think he'd missed them. If they'd been by here, there would have been footprints and hoof prints all over the sand. And mule dung and such. Better wait a bit longer. Because what if they'd changed their plans and weren't going to the inn at all?

When it was one o'clock by the sun, the party arrived. They came in little by little, riders ahead, baggage mules and their handlers plodding behind—thirty merchants and their servants, many of them very well armed. The merchant in charge of the party agreed straight off that there'd been an agreement, and that letters of credit and such were all in order. Safe now and hopeful among the baggage handlers, he walked on to the inn. Skipped supper and slept in the courtyard, to start making up for losing two pieces of money. A stableman slipped him a hunk of bread and a mugful of watered beer, a kind thing to do, and he was glad of it. Pangur came out from the basket, and caught a mouse and ate it, and lapped up rain water from a puddle, and contentedly purred. Went back to his basket, too. A good, sensible cat. Imagine anyone ever trying to kill him.

The next day they all went on twenty miles to King Alfred's port. Brother Arcadius passed the time by reciting—silently, in his mind only, so as not to bother the baggage men—all the beautiful poems he knew. Psalms, mostly, but also those poems in Latin from the long ago, the bits of them that were still known in Dublin. He'd loved the sound of the old, old Latin all his life. At the port they waited for the weather to clear. Then they took a boat across another sea called the Channel Sea. The waves leaped up and down and he got seasick again. But the merchants all got seasick too, so he didn't stand out. After they made it to shore, they went north seventy miles. That was out of their way, but they had to avoid the Danes, who were raiding the coasts to the south. And after that they were in the Frankish lands known as Francia, and it was rivers and boats, and land and marching, and rivers again, and land, and for a good fifty miles he got to ride on a mule, holding Pangur one-armed in the basket.

And Pangur did not especially like it. But Pangur was such a very sensible cat, and caught food for himself and drank from puddles whenever he could. And Brother Arcadius shared food and drink with him otherwise. And skipped food and drink for himself a good part of each day. Even so, his pieces of money were being used up fast. Just as with the basket lady, everything cost more than it seemed at first that it might. There were extra charges for king's tax, count's tax, duke's tax, boat tax, road tax, even cat tax...and cat tax, oddly enough, was the highest of all. The letters of credit had paid for taxes ahead of time, but not enough, so it seemed. And of course no expenses for cats had ever been thought of. He skipped more meals. But every day Pangur Ban was more and more of a friend—not just a sensible cat but a sociable cat. And all the while Pangur and he were getting closer and closer to the end of their journey. All the while they were getting closer to Spiritus Sanctus.

To Spiritus Sanctus, with its five hundred complete and entire manuscripts, as well as parts of manuscripts—and maybe some of them would have poems in them.

To Spiritus Sanctus, and the work they'd be having him do, and the life he'd be living.

To Spiritus Sanctus, where if they didn't want cats, then what would he do?

A long journey, true, and risky, sure enough. But staying in Dublin was risky too, what with the conquering Viking Danes who'd taken it over. And now the journey was almost over and no mistake. If they kept on as they were, they'd be reaching Spiritus Sanctus in just one more week, said the merchant in charge of the party.

And they did keep on as they were, and hour by hour the week dwindled down into days. In just four more days they would be there. In just three more days they would be there. In just two more days they would be there. And then—and then!—*tomorrow* they would be there!

The long, long journey would be over, over at last. Not for the merchants, for they were going on across the mountains to Italy, but for him, and for Pangur. It had seemed sometimes as if it would never happen, but now it finally had.

Brother Arcadius slept only in snatches that night. He was wide awake well before sunrise, wishing he could rouse the whole party and get it started, wishing that he could just run on ahead—wishing sometimes with a lurch of the stomach, that he'd never left Dublin. He told himself to stop thinking childish things.

But what were these odd, odd words that the merchant in charge was saying, with the sun just up? The words that had to be wrong? The words that now he was saying all over again?

"You'll be able to find your way from here without any trouble."

Find his way? What did that mean, *Find* his way? There was a chancy, worrisome sound to it. "You were supposed to take me right to there? The agreement said?"

"Just to the turn-off, that's all," said the merchant in charge. "This is the turn-off."

"But where's the monastery, then?"

"Up the trail, just up the trail," the merchant said. "Just fifteen, sixteen miles as the crow flies. Maybe a little more. Day's march. Young man like you. Just stay on the trail and keep going in that same direction. What you'll come to first thing is a village, five miles or so on."

"More like ten, I think," somebody said.

"Or ten," said the merchant. "When you get there, ask them the way. Maybe one of the villagers will want to go with you. Make sure he keeps going due south. You'll come to a pine woods—"

"More like a forest, I think," somebody said.

"It thins out in these parts," said the merchant. "It's a woods. The monastery's right on the other side of it. So goodbye, young man. Stay on the trail and there won't be anything to it."

"Does he have any money on him?" somebody said. "He'd better not, in the forest. I mean, the woods."

"Hadn't thought of that, but you're right," the merchant said. He held out his hand. "You'll be at the monastery in no time. You won't need it. We'll send your family a note of credit for it."

There wasn't much money left anyway. Not knowing what else to do, he passed it over. His heart had started pounding against his ribs. He wished it wouldn't. The party chirruped to their mules and went on their way. Once they'd rounded a bend up ahead and were out of sight, it still took a while for the sound of their passing to die away. But when it did, then there was mostly silence. Pangur Ban was curled up sound asleep in his willow basket. The south-going trail meandered up a rise. There were pine trees up there, all right...quite a number of them. His heart was still pounding a little from the surprise, but what was he? A cowardly weakling, or what? All he had to do was just stay on the trail. Find the village. Stay on the trail.

Brother Arcadius, future assistant librarian of Spiritus Sanctus monastery, fixed his mind on the beautiful poems he meant to recite. He adjusted the willow basket, with his cat in it, more comfortably into the crook of his arm. Then he squared his shoulders and headed toward the rise.

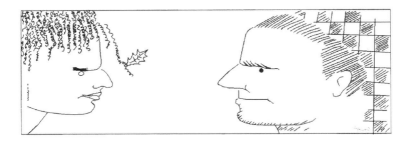

THE RUNAWAY WITCH

In which Brother Arcadius wishes that a giant eagle would fly him back to Dublin, and Pangur is forced to settle a burning question

AD 898

Brother Arcadius limped toward the monastery gate in the early dark. Sometimes he staggered, but mostly he limped. Limping or staggering, he took care not to drop the big willow basket he held in his arms. The monastery walls were thick and high and blurry, with a watchtower built into them near the gate, and now and then the walls and the tower waved slowly back and forth. There was a watchman in the tower, looking down and raising a blurry hand. A blurry door opened beside the huge and blurry gate, and all of that was very good and very promising—much better than the pine woods, and the swamp, and the ravine, and the other two ravines, and all of that.

And now he was limping across a wide courtyard with a tall blur walking beside him, and there was another door, and then a long room with candles, and a chair which he sat in, and he set the willow basket carefully down on the floor before him, and the room revolved slowly around him, so that it was almost like being seasick all over again, and he told himself not to mind it.

Three blurs came in from somewhere and stood before him. He made himself sit up very straight and attend to them. They were probably very important, he told himself dimly. Father Julian, head of the monastery. People like that. Whoever they were, one of them seemed to have very dark eyes that weren't blurry at all. "Get Salix," that one said, but not to him. The middle blur hurried out. "Sixteen? Looks more like fourteen," the third one said. "Wind could blow him away." What did that mean—"Get Salix"? Wind could blow whom away? What looked more like fourteen? And what did fourteen look like, anyway?

Brother Arcadius had no time to ponder these conundrums. Questions were coming straight at him. Trying not to cling too much to the arms of his chair, he strove to come up with good answers. Pretty soon now, he knew, he'd have to address the matter of the willow basket. But for right now he'd better just guard against any mistakes in his Latin, and make sure there wasn't too much of an Irish sound to it, and tell these blurs what it seemed they wanted to know.

Their voices went in and out and he couldn't always hear them, but he answered their questions as best as he could. Oh no, he said. He hadn't been alone on his travels most of the time. It had just been those last three days. The woods farther down had been maybe...a little thick. The place where the trail became four trails had been a little confusing. The helpful villagers had maybe misunderstood where he wanted to go. The two nights in the forest...the woods, rather...had not been all that alarming, no, really not. The cries of wolves that he'd heard had seemed quite far off, generally speaking.

Once again he straightened himself in his chair, for he'd started to sag. He was very glad, he said, that now he was here at Spiritus Sanctus. He was looking forward to getting at his work and doing it well. He could start working right now if they wanted him to.

Just as he spoke those last words, the matter of the willow basket took care of itself. The lid wobbled up and down. Two white paws appeared. A white head—a grubby white head—peered warily out. The blurs gave their full attention to this new sight. It was very clear that they wanted an explanation. "He was on the boat," Brother Arcadius stammered. "The sailor fellow was going to kill him! I had to bring him!" Then all his resolve gave way to a great spinning blackness, and he commanded his eyes to stay open, but still they closed, and he grabbed for the arms of his chair, but still he pitched forward....

...And unexpectedly breathed a breath of air with a fresh breeze in it, and it smelled of all sorts of wild grasses, and of herbs, and of...pine? Was he still in the woods after all, then? Brother Arcadius opened his eyes and gasped in shock. The face looking down at him was the most dangerous-looking face he'd ever seen, and growing up in Dublin among the conquering Danes, he'd seen many. Lean as a knife's blade, fierce in gaze, this was the face of a killer getting ready to strike. "I don't have any money!" he cried. Memory jogged him. "And where's my cat?"

"I don't have any money either," the fearsome man said in a distracted murmur. Then, more attentively, he said, "Your cat is being well cared for, in the kitchen." His voice was husky and matter-of-fact. "And you're at Spiritus Sanctus monastery, and I'm Salix, the medicus here. That's Brother Hyssop and Brother Miklas over there. Our goat-keeper, and one of our stonecutters. They know who you are of course —our assistant librarian."

Reason was slowly returning. Brother Arcadius could see now that this long room, with its basins and crucibles, its fireplace, its four beds and its open arched windows, had to be an infirmary, not a robber's den. And yes, two other men were in the room. Over there by the fireplace, a monk in a chair was soaking one foot in a basin of water, and trying not to stare at him. A second monk over by the doorway was pressing a damp-looking cloth to his jaw, and also trying not to stare. Brother Arcadius nodded politely to them. They nodded slowly back, as if they weren't sure they wanted to nod at all.

He raised himself up on his elbows. "I'm ready to get to work now, and see to my cat," he said. Lying around in broad daylight like a good-for-nothing—that was no way to start out in a person's new home. He needed to get up and just blend in with everybody else. It seemed that a start had been made in that direction. His tunic and breeches were clean and so was he, and his tonsure had been restored. His hair was no longer standing straight up like a wild man's, with brambles and burrs caught in it. His cuts and bruises had stopped hurting, and those big blisters, the purple-streaked ones that had throbbed and oozed so alarmingly, now seemed to be dried-up sore spots and nothing more. But how could all that have come about so soon? He sat up, shakily. "It was last night I got here, wasn't it?"

The medicus was giving directions over his shoulder to the monk by the doorway. "Keep that poultice pressed tight to the jaw," he said. He turned back to Brother Arcadius. "You've been lying there dead to the world for five days," he said. "Exposure, exhaustion, insufficient food and water for too many days—your vital forces have been severely taxed. You did some talking, though. Who's Pangur Ban? Or what?"

"That's my...." Think before you speak, Brother Arcadius admonished himself. Monks weren't supposed to think in terms of *me* and *mine*, or make a fuss about cats and suchlike things. "The cat I brought—that's his name. It's Irish. It signifies that he's white."

"So you brought this cat with you all the way from Ireland?" asked

Brother Salix. A wooden spoon lay on a nearby stand, with a stone flask next to it. He picked up the flask and pulled out the stopper.

"Not all the way, no," said Brother Arcadius. "Just some of the way." It didn't seem the right time or place to spell out the details. The sea, the spinning boat, Pangur peering up from the cargo, the sailor's roars, the money being offered—offered, and taken. And he wasn't supposed to be spending that money until much later, but what could he do? "I'd better go and make sure he's not bothering anybody. Then I should go and see what the librarian wants me to do. And I— shouldn't I?—see if Father Julian wants to see me. I'm all right now, I don't need to stay in bed any more."

The medicus appeared not to hear this. With swift movements, he poured some sort of liquid from the flask into the spoon. The liquid, whatever it was, smelled like a mixture of pine sap, honey, and fish oil. "Take this," he said.

Brother Arcadius swallowed obediently. The stuff didn't taste too terrible, all in all.

"Now then," Brother Salix said. He frowned and looked more than ever like a killer. "You're not leaving this room today. And you won't be seeing Father Julian for a while. He's away on family business. Left the day after you arrived. Says you're to take your instructions from his assistant until he returns. Or from the library." He turned back to Brother Miklas, by the doorway. "I'll refresh that poultice now. We'll pull if we have to, but it's too soon yet to decide."

Brother Miklas nodded miserably.

Brother Arcadius, not meaning to do so at all, went back to sleep....

And woke up to a sound of distant voices and cattle lowing, or maybe oxen, and a far-off ringing as if of hammers on metal, and sipped some broth that the kitchen had sent over, and got up and wobbled about the room.... Brother Miklas and Brother Hyssop were gone, so he didn't have to worry about their opinions.... And he sipped more broth, for broth was all he could have, Brother Salix said....

And he slept....

...And woke up the next day with everything very much different. The broth was thicker, and his robe and his battered sandals had been cleaned and repaired and given back to him, and he walked around the room without wobbling at all. "Well, the Irish are tough," said Brother Salix. "You'll stay here nights for the rest of the week, but you can go to the kitchen now and visit that cat, and after that you can go to the library."

The medicus opened the infirmary door, disclosing a view of a grassy expanse set about with cindered paths and stone buildings. One of those buildings was very large. The others, in various sizes, were quite a bit smaller. He gestured toward the large one. "That's the refectory," he said. "That's where you were the first night you got here. The kitchen connects to it. Go in through that door you see there and follow the corridor. You'll come to a door on your left and you'll hear a commotion. That's the sound of the gang of them, cooking. Follow the sound to the kitchen, and ask for Brother Marcus. He's the one in charge. You can have more broth there. Marcus knows what to give you. After that, you can see Brother Silvanus at the library—that building right alongside the infirmary here. I want you to come back here in an hour or two. As I say, I want to keep an eye on you for a few days yet."

So Brother Arcadius emerged hopefully into the daylight world of Spiritus Sanctus. He didn't like the idea of having an eye kept on him, but it was good to be out of bed, and good to be on his way to see Pangur Ban! The air was fresh and keen and alive with birdsong, and, from afar, a bleating of goats, and a mule's sudden nicker. Sunlight sparkled on the stone buildings—long, low buildings, for the most part, not grand at all, but solid and in good repair. It was all very different from the half-wrecked monastery in Dublin. No cruel Danes had ever come here, that was the reason why. No people were in sight, but far-off sounds made it clear, once again, that plenty of work was going on somewhere in the distance.

Reaching the refectory, he tugged the great door open and went inside. The corridor was dim and wide and silent, and seemed to go on forever. His sandals padded softly against the stone floor. He hoped that Pangur Ban would remember him. He told himself that maybe he shouldn't expect to be remembered. He passed arched niches set into the wall, one after another all along its length, with unlit oil lamps in them. Thin shafts of daylight came down from small windows high above his head. And halfway along, a picture chiseled into the stone showed a stone king kneeling, with stone beams of light streaming down. He didn't stop to study it.

All right, here on his left was another heavy door. Brother Arcadius passed through it into a huge room of ten long tables that had benches on either side. These furnishings were arranged in two columns that slanted toward another table and a chair on a dais. Up there would be where Father Julian most likely dined. He was just as glad that Father Julian was gone, for now. His old abbot back in Dublin really had been old—seventy, it was said. And he'd been as gentle and kind as he was old, for sure. Father Julian was younger than that, supposedly. He'd turn out to be all right, like Brother Salix had—most likely.

Or not.

"Or not" wouldn't be so good. But his Mam had always told him never to borrow trouble. Thinking about "or not" would be borrowing trouble. The clatter and thumping that now he could hear must be the commotion that he was supposed to follow. There were three doors up ahead, widely spaced—two smaller doors with a large heavy one between them. The sounds were clearly coming from behind the large one.

For the third time that morning, Brother Arcadius opened a heavy door. A blast of noise and hot air almost rocked him back on his heels. The room looked to be as huge, almost, as the dining hall, and every inch of it seemed to be in motion. A leaping flame was dying down to embers in a vast fireplace. Three men were frantically working. One of them was pounding a slab of meat with a mallet. One of them was cleaning fish in a cloud of scales. One of them was stirring away at three monstrous kettles as if his life depended on it, rushing from one to another. Could these be monks? They weren't wearing robes, but only short breeches and tunics. They had rags tied round their heads like a bunch of pirates. And there was a great steaming fragrance of, well, fragrance. Of fine sizzling olive oil, and garlic, and onions, and parsley, and maybe mushrooms...and another wonderful smell that he couldn't place. Brother Arcadius's mouth started to water, and it wouldn't stop. He suddenly realized that he was hungry. Unspeakably, indescribably, amazingly, astonishingly *hungry*.

A fourth man was coming at him, waving a knife and beaming, and motioning to him to stay where he was. If the other three men looked like pirates, this was the chief. So he must be Brother Marcus, like Brother Salix had said. Dressed like the others in breeches and tunic alone, and barefooted into the bargain, he was as broadly built as Salix was narrow, with a sweating red face and big chest and a grizzled gray tonsure that his head-rag failed to hide.

"You're Arcadius, right?" he roared over the thuds of the mallet. "I've been watching for you. I'm Marcus. Head cook. Stay right there while I fetch you that broth."

He strode off. Brother Arcadius was glad to stay where he was and keep out of the way, but where was Pangur Ban? Was he hiding away from the racket and the commotion? This frenzied kitchen didn't seem like any place that was right for a cat. But Brother Marcus clearly took the frenzy for granted. Brother Arcadius watched as the broad-built cook got waylaid by the man who was cleaning fish, held a long conversation with him about something or other, stopped by one of the big kettles to stir it himself for too many long moments, then finally came back with a steaming, entrancing-smelling mug of broth—somewhat smaller, that mug, than Brother Arcadius had hoped for. "We're going out to the kitchen garden," Brother Marcus said. "Follow me."

He led the way through the kitchen to a small back door. Brother Arcadius fought back an unmonklike desire to seize the mug from his hands and gulp the broth down. Instead, of course, he meekly followed Marcus into a long garden that seemed to go back and back, with stone walls enclosing it, and benches to sit on here and there. The lettuce, kale, and cabbages of springtime still flourished in well-tended beds, but summer's bounty was beginning to ripen all around. Tall basil formed a background for a mat of low-growing thyme. Other herbs were starting up in crocks to keep them from spreading: rosemary, catmint, sage. Half-hidden among their leaves, the garden's cherries, crabapples, and plums were not ready for picking yet, but they would be, as would the young berries on their bushes, and the melons on the ground. White butterflies moved through the fragrant air in their step-wise flight. A thrush sang urgently from a chestnut tree. A willow basket with rope handles lay on its side over there by a cluster of burdocks—a willow basket that Brother Arcadius knew well. A white shape came scrambling from it. It launched itself into Brother Arcadius's arms. Brother Arcadius forgot his hunger and everything else, and matched Pangur Ban's welcome with his own.

Brother Marcus sat down on a nearby bench. He set the mug down beside him, the mug that at this moment didn't matter at all. He pulled off his sweaty head-rag and fanned his brow. "That's a very unusual cat you brought us," he said.

"I think so too," cried Brother Arcadius. He inspected Pangur carefully from head to toe. It was not an easy thing to do, for Pangur was weaving about him in ceaseless motion. But the bright eyes, the glossy whiteness of the fur, the glistening whiskers, the straight-up tail, the fact that the ribs no longer showed as much as before—all of this proved that Pangur had been very well cared for in Brother Marcus's kitchen. Yet whose arms had he just jumped into? His first friend's, that's whose! A warm glow kindled in Brother Arcadius's heart. He'd never been able to offer Pangur such fine living. Yet he'd not been forgotten.

"Unusual," said Brother Marcus again. His Latin was the broken-down kind that was common everywhere these days, almost not like Latin at all, but his words were welcome. "It's like he's part dog, almost. Rushing up to you like that, letting you know straight out that he's glad to see you. And the way he sniffs things out like a hound, sometimes, instead of just using his eyes and ears like cats usually do. And the way he acts around catmint—that's unusual too."

"I don't know how he acts around it," said Brother Arcadius, still glowing inwardly. He'd made it to Spiritus Sanctus against so many odds, and Pangur had too, and here they were in this peaceful garden, with this benign-seeming monk who was not a pirate. "I don't think we came upon any on the way here."

"He won't go near it!" said Brother Marcus. "Can't tempt him with it, either. Strange thing. Anyway, I'm glad you brought him. Our old mouser died last Thursday, so he came just in time. But he's better already than our old mouser ever was, and he's not even grown yet."

"He always hunted a lot on the way here," Brother Arcadius said. It was unmonklike to boast of things, but truth was truth. Birds, very young rabbits, beetles, even a fish, once, had all fallen prey to Pangur's flashing attacks. "So it wasn't so hard to feed him."

"I heard you had a bad time of it," Brother Marcus said. "Heard you got lost."

"Only a little," Brother Arcadius assured him.

"Well, you got here, anyway," said Brother Marcus. "But here! We're forgetting your broth!" He handed the mug over to Brother Arcadius, who realized again how very hungry he was. He took a first sip and savored it on his tongue. It outdid every one of the broths he'd already had, and they'd been very good. "There's a spoonful of goat cheese stirred into it, and a spoonful of parboiled partridge, minced very fine," the cook said, nodding. "There's a spoonful of elderberry wine in it, too. Brother Salix says the bit of partridge and wine won't hurt you. He says you can have six helpings of it today. This would be the first."

"It's delicious," Brother Arcadius murmured with feeling. In Dublin, under the Danes, there'd hardly ever been any fancy cooking.

16

He forced himself to slow down and make each sip last. He wished he could have a big hunk of bread to go with it. Or five or ten big hunks of bread, or even more. With five mugs of broth, or more, for each piece of bread. Such thoughts were unseemly. He did his best to ignore them.

"Yes, it's one of my best broths," Brother Marcus said. "But it's nothing compared to my fish paste and my herbed game stew. You'll love them. They're famous. Everybody loves them. Whitey does too." He beamed down at Pangur, who'd ceased his weaving and settled himself close by.

"His name's Pangur Ban," Brother Arcadius told him. He hoped he sounded informative, not contentious. It seemed right to let people know Pangur's proper name.

But Brother Marcus wasn't appreciative. "Pangur Ban!" he cried. "What kind of lingo is that?"

"It's Irish," said Brother Arcadius, pressing on. "It's just like calling him 'Whitey,' because it means that he's white."

Brother Marcus shook his head firmly and waved a broad hand. "Well, I'm not Irish, so you call him Pan, er, whatever you want, and I'll call him Whitey, all right? We'll know who we mean." Clearly pleased that he'd settled that question, the cook spoke on. "Anyway, like I said, he loves my cooking. We keep him out of the kitchen, daytimes, because it's too busy. He's a very sensible cat, and I think we could trust him, most times, to stay out of the way. But if he ever forgot, he could trip somebody, and there could be trouble, do you know what I mean?"

Pans of boiling water spilling, somebody falling, Pangur in trouble, cooks getting hurt, Pangur getting hurt.... "I do," said Brother Arcadius.

"So here's what I do for him," Brother Marcus said. "First thing in the morning, when it's just him and me in there and his mousing is done, I give him a little bowl of my best cooking. Oh, does he love it! Oh, did he love it this Friday and Sunday, when he got a taste of my fish paste and my herbed game stew! That was one happy cat! If his treat doesn't come first thing, he lets me know. Sits there and meows like you wouldn't believe. But he never runs after me to beg for it, or gets up on the tables. I suppose he would if he ever got really hungry, but like you said, he dines on what he catches. A grand, grand cat. He —"

"Marcus!" came a shout from the kitchen. Pangur leaped up,

startled, and the cook shot to his feet. "I guess they need me in there," he said. "Done with your broth yet? Good, hand me the mug then. Where are you supposed to be, now?"

"The library," said Brother Arcadius. He gave the mug back. Pangur Ban stretched mightily and prowled off through the burdocks in search of something to catch. The reunion in the peaceful garden had come to its end. It was time to get on with the day, time to get on with the work he'd come here to do. He stood up. "It's right next to the infirmary, I know that. I guess I just go back through the refectory?"

Brother Marcus pointed to a door in the garden wall. "Go through there. It takes you back behind the refectory. It's a shorter way." The shouts of *Marcus!* increased. The cook hurried off.

The door in the wall was wooden and arched and sagging, and there was moss growing on it. A few easy tugs got it open, and revealed the long, low, stone infirmary in the near distance, with the long, low, stone library just south of it—the library, where Brother Arcadius would prove himself as a good librarian...or not. Here was another thought to keep hunger at bay.

Very serious now, determined to do his best, Brother Arcadius took the nearest path across the grassy way. The refectory with its heavy door was there on his left. The foursquare stone building to his right would be Father Julian's residence, most likely. The slightly larger building adjoining it was surely the church. The small building behind the church would probably be the charnel house, where the remains of deceased brethren peacefully awaited resurrection. The very small building that stood off by itself and looked like a tool shed was probably...a tool shed.

It seemed like an odd location for a tool shed, though.

Brother Arcadius walked more slowly, composing himself. Reaching the library, he wiped the soles of his sandals carefully on a nearby patch of emerging plantains, disturbing a spider. He smoothed his robe and swiped a hand over his lips to make sure no traces of broth were visible. He reminded himself that he was sixteen years and two months old now, and three weeks beyond that too. He went up the single stone step, swallowed hard, and rapped at the library door.

"Just come in," called a voice that was reedy and thin. He did so, diffidently. He saw a long table, and a man rising up from a bench on its farther side—an elderly-seeming man, although not very much so. He was short and slight, barely larger, in fact, than Brother Arcadius himself—a good thing to see. His face, thought Brother Arcadius, was a sparrowhawk's face, you might say—a small beak of a nose and gray-green eyes with an odd and chancy expression in them. His robe was rumpled and slightly askew, as if he'd napped in it, or flung it on in a hurry. "Now tell me," he snapped, "what made you choose the name 'Arcadius'?"

"I—" Surprised halfway out of his wits, Brother Arcadius fumbled for a reply. In Dublin he'd heard about poems, that was all—old Latin poems, long gone, that told of a beautiful, peaceful place called Arcadia. He'd daydreamed sometimes that he might go there with his Mam and his brothers and his sisters and the monks and all. So he'd wanted that name, and the monks said that yes, he could have it. But explaining all that to somebody else, to a sparrowhawkish person who had snapped at you and was going to be in charge of you, especially when your stomach was suddenly starting to growl....

Wanted more broth, it did, but it couldn't have it....

"*Arcadius*," said Brother Silvanus—it had to be Brother Silvanus like the letters had said—"was a notably young and notably foolish emperor of the Romans. He ruled, or misruled, the eastern half of the empire some six centuries ago. Or maybe you knew that?"

"I didn't," said Brother Arcadius. His first moments on the job, and he already felt as if he were back in the forest—the woods—trying to decide which trail of the four to follow.

"At any rate, *Caesar*," said Brother Silvanus sternly, "I trust that you do not intend to emulate your imperial namesake in your work here. And is obedience really your first nature, as the letters commending you to us constantly said?"

"I don't know," said Brother Arcadius. He tried to speak the words in a manly way, but they came out in almost a whisper. He'd always tried to be obedient, he knew that, but then there was the matter of the two pieces of money....

"The answer had better be yes," said Brother Silvanus. "A keen pair of young eyes, with useful things like legs and arms attached, trotting quickly about, obeying my every command: that's what I hope we have in you—Arcadius." Looking sterner than ever, he snapped, "Why aren't you sitting down?"

Brother Arcadius sat down in a hurry, across from him.

"And why are you not asking questions?" Silvanus went on. "You've been here so long that you don't need to ask any questions?"

Questions—of course he had questions. Having a voice to ask

them with—that was another matter at the moment. But Brother Arcadius was starting to think that all of this snappishness was maybe not what it seemed...that the head librarian might be teasing him, maybe. The stern face...maybe...seemed to be holding back laughter. And this was no night-time woods, with wolf howls that sometimes seemed to be getting nearer, but another long pleasant room with stone arches, and arched open windows that let in the breeze and the light, and cedar cabinets that were open and held many, ever so many....

Brother Arcadius found his voice. "Are there really five hundred books here?"

"Complete ones, yes," said Brother Silvanus, rubbing his hands briskly together. "We have many more in various stages of ruin, alas. And there's a trunkful behind you of very interesting bits and pieces of all sorts of things, collected from all over. I've never had time to take a really good look at them. I hope to start doing that, now that you're here." Instead of being unsettling and bewildering as before, the librarian was now simply informative—and suddenly, very serious. "Your monastery has lost most of its books, your abbot writes."

"The Danes like to burn them," said Brother Arcadius. "They threw a lot of them in the river, too."

"It had more books than we have here, not that long ago."

"It only has seventeen now, and they're all in bad shape."

Brother Silvanus shook his head in dismay. "Rampaging ignorance," he said. "It hurts to hear of such things. We've got Danes over here too now, raiding our coasts. Some of them have come over from Ireland, or so we're told."

Brother Arcadius nodded. That was true. Some hundreds of Dublin's Danes had gone off in search of new realms to conquer. So life had been a little easier there, these last two years or so. All the same, at the back of his mind, always there was a fear for his family there—for his Mam, with her hair half red, half gray, and her dear face creased into a thousand wrinkles of thought, concern, and laughter. And for his six grown-up brothers, quick-witted and stalwart. And his two younger sisters, red-headed like him and their Mam, rambunctious and gawky. They'd all said that he had to come here to this place of five hundred books and be their pride. And they wouldn't take no for an answer. So he was here. And he wanted to be here, true, but still...but still....

Brother Silvanus's next question echoed his thoughts. "Your family makes bricks, I understand?"

"Makes them and lays them too," said Brother Arcadius. "I mean, that's what my brothers do, and my Mam helps out. My sisters too. We make excellent bricks. The Danes get theirs free."

"I'm sure they do," said Brother Silvanus. "And I imagine you've had to pull in your belts. And you, did you like the business?"

Pulling in belts was right. Life had always been lean and hungry under the Danes. "I've never been any help with the business, because I was put to being a scholar when I was five."

"I see," said Brother Silvanus. "And your father, your head of house...the letters mentioned that he's been long deceased...."

Brother Arcadius squared his shoulders manfully. The memory burned like fire, even now. "He stood up to the Danes to help our neighbor, and he got struck down. When I was five."

Brother Silvanus rose slowly from where he'd been sitting. He went to a window and leaned against the broad sill. "I'm over-inquisitive sometimes...Caesar. You'll have to watch that in me. I like to claim that it's the librarian in me, but I don't know. If I'm not careful I'll end up like Brother Marcus. He always has to have his ear to the ground. Since he's a cook, not a librarian, I don't know what his excuse is. But we're monks, anyway, and we're supposed to keep our minds on our work and our prayers, so—" He smacked one hand against the other. "Getting back to the library and the monastery, I'm sure you do have other questions, so ask away."

Brother Arcadius emerged from rueful thoughts of his brave and long-dead Da, the deep voice, the broad shoulders, the horseback rides on those shoulders around the brickyard. "I was wondering, um, when everybody comes in to read." One or another monk, back in Dublin, was always poring over one or another of those seventeen half-ruined books.

"The answer to that, Arcadius," said Brother Silvanus, "is that almost nobody ever does. We're very much out of the way here, as you know, and our charter is very peculiar. Charles Martel, Charlemagne's grandfather, was our founder, back in the year of our Lord 730. That's why his image is in the refectory, cut into the corridor wall. Maybe you've seen it: Charles Martel, kneeling, and receiving inspiration from the Holy Spirit."

"I saw it," said Brother Arcadius, "but I didn't know who it was."

"He started building this place as a fort, as maybe you've heard," said Brother Silvanus. "But he changed his mind halfway through. So, taking the advice of one of the Julian family—an ancestor of Father

21

Julian's, that would be—he founded Spiritus Sanctus instead. But perhaps I'm telling you things that you already know."

"You're not," said Brother Arcadius. He leaned forward to hear more.

"Well then, there are two things that we're supposed to do," Silvanus continued. "We're supposed to collect and preserve every piece of writing that we can, whether it's an entire book or just half of a sentence, hoping that more of that sentence will somehow turn up. The learning and lore of the past, the learning and lore of the present —it's our duty, by charter, to hunt it down and keep it safe in these troubled times. But it's also our duty by charter to provide for our bodily needs with our own hands, with almost no help from outside, and that entails a good deal of very hard work. Therein lies the library's problem, as I'm sure you can see."

"People don't read much, here? They're working too hard?"

"Correct. Most of our monks can't read, or can, but see no point to it. They are simple people, generally—not stupid, I don't mean that, but simple. Very simple and very unlearned," Brother Silvanus said. "They'd prefer a good collection of holy relics to any library. The scholars generally go to other places. Father Julian is a formidable scholar, of course. I have some learning myself, I'd say. Brother Salix is learned in matters concerned with healing, and is often in here combing our collection for things pertaining to that. And there's you. And we have a handful of brothers who come in and read when they can. But our library, at present, doesn't get much use. When Father Julian comes back, he and I—and you also, Arcadius—will be working on ways to change things for the better. Tomorrow I'll tell you about some of the ideas I have."

From some distance away there came the clear sound of a bell. "That's the call to the midday meal," Brother Silvanus said. He opened a cupboard and took out a bowl, a mug, a knife, and a spoon. "I keep them here in the library during the day. It saves going back to my cell. Come, let's walk together to the refectory."

"Um...I'm not supposed to," Brother Arcadius said. "I'm supposed to go back to the infirmary and just have broth."

"There you are!" cried Brother Silvanus, suddenly smiling. "Obedience! Truthfulness, too! The letters weren't lying!" He was teasing again, maybe, but in a way that anyone could see was very friendly.

Now there came days of quietly settling in. Within a week Brother

Arcadius was taking his meals in the refectory like everyone else, and eating what everyone else was eating, to his great relief. And he had his fill at last of Brother Marcus's delicious cooking—the regular stews, the breads, the cheese dishes, the savory sauces. The famous fish paste and herbed game stew rounded out the week. They were foods that the angels might vie for, and that was a fact.

Also at last he moved into his own cell, third over from the main door, north side, of a low stone building that at first he'd thought was a stable. Eight of these buildings comprised the monks' lodgings, and his was the one that was closest to the library. It had a surprised-looking sun's face chiseled into the stone arch over the main door, and a placid-looking moon's face over the rear door, and he liked that. His cell had a cot, a trunk, a shelf, a pail, and pegs on the wall, exactly like all the others, a very good thing. But along with all that it afforded a close view of a cherry tree that grew right outside his window, and he liked that, too.

The general plan of the monastery became fixed in his mind—the part he already knew, and the farmlands and pastures and workshops and things he hadn't yet seen, though sounds from them were forever in the air. The building he'd taken for a tool shed on his first walk across the grounds was no tool shed at all, but a prison.

A prison...

That was unsettling to think of, but Brother Marcus said that only fractious travelers had ever been locked up in it, no more than five or six in a hundred years. Brother Silvanus agreed that this was so —"Although we might put you in it, Caesar, if we depose you," he said. He went on to say that a book in Father Julian's residence gave the history of it and of the whole monastery, along with the rules that everyone here had to follow. It was as old as Spiritus Sanctus itself, that book, and it was bound in the costliest leather, embossed and gilded, a marvel to look at, and brought out on solemn occasions. Or so Brother Silvanus said, and he didn't appear to be teasing.

It would be a solemn thing, all right, to have to go to prison, thought Brother Arcadius. But it would be a fine thing indeed to see that book. He wondered if someday he might.

The placement of the monastery in the larger world became fixed in his mind as well. Off to the north were the Frankish and Saxon lands. He'd passed through parts of these on his way here, so they weren't all that strange to him. But to the south, beyond the giant snow-capped mountains that loomed on the horizon, lay Rome, much reduced from her former glory, but still important because the pope lived there. Far to the east the mighty river Danube flowed, and the strange and remote city of Constantinople reared its towers beside the Black Sea. Far to the west lay Spain, and if you went mostly west and a bit to the north, and if the Danes didn't get you, and you crossed all that water, you'd come to Dublin.

But all of that was so far away from Spiritus Sanctus. Much closer in, toward the west, there were some hamlets, and the hunters who lived in them brought in the game for Brother Marcus's kitchen. Less than a mile to the south, a lake of fine waters teemed with silvery, thriving fish, and monks caught those fish and brought them in also to Brother Marcus's kitchen. Due north, at a distance of ten or twelve miles, lay the place where Brother Arcadius had asked for directions and ended up in ravines and who knew what all. It consisted of three huts only, and Spiritus Sanctus didn't regard it as a village at all. But twenty miles away or so, off to the east, there stood a real village, with a watermill and a forge and a church and all. People from there passed by once in a while, and there was some trade now and then. But mainly, as far as Spiritus Sanctus was concerned, it was like the prison —nothing that played a part in daily life.

The days grew warmer. The first fruits of summer ripened little by little.

Brother Arcadius bent to his work in the library. He found it absorbing and very enjoyable.

He was kindly allowed to write a letter home. "Thirty words at the most, Arcadius. Parchment is costly," Brother Dietrich said. Father Julian's assistant was trim and polished beyond the ordinary. His hair was always just so, and his robe never showed the least wrinkle. How he stayed perfect like that was a mystery. But his manner was pleasant. "Tell them you got here safely," he said. "That's really all you need to say."

Brother Arcadius wrote his letter. He sped it along in his mind as he followed the daily routine of work and prayers and meals. Spiritus Sanctus adhered to the Benedictine rule pretty much, he learned from Brother Silvanus. There were differences, though. Father Julian didn't call himself "abbot" but rather just "head of the monastery." And he wasn't elected, either. Like all of his predecessors back to the time of the founding, by charter, he'd been appointed by some sort of group of nobles or something, somewhere in the beyond. And by charter, they always appointed a Julian. The monks had the right of refusal, but they hadn't refused him, or any Julian before him. So the great book with gilded covers said.

The time of kale and lettuce came to an end. The last of the season's first cabbages were sliced and salted and laid away to make a tasty pickle.

It came about that Pangur Ban would have to be neutered. Father Julian had left that directive, and Brother Salix, Brother Marcus, and Brother Silvanus all concurred. Brother Arcadius was not happy about it, but he understood that unneutered tom cats did yowl, and did spray, and did get into terrible fights with other such toms—there were plenty of those in the monastery barns, it seemed. So Brother Salix did the deed, and it turned out to be nothing. Pangur, made very calm by some sort of powder, stared at a tiny incision for a moment or two, had fish paste as a reward, spent two days in the infirmary under Brother Salix's fiercely watchful eye, then went on his way.

"That's Salix!" said Brother Marcus. "Nobody like him. Sick horse, sick cat, sick me, he has the cure. We were in an army together, you know, before we came here. Never could figure out whose army. It always kept changing. But we were way south in Spain, and he picked up all sorts of lore from the Arabs and Jews. Won't have to worry about Whitey. He'll be just fine."

And Pangur was fine, and there was another worry out of the way.

But other worries came along right behind it. Brother Arcadius told himself that they were not that important, really—that thinking about them would only be borrowing trouble, just like his Mam had said. All the same, day in, day out, and more and more as the days went by, he felt the unsettling force of them and wished he didn't.

First of all, right from the very beginning, he'd wanted to just blend in with the monks around him, and not stand out. He'd hoped that as time went by, that would be happening. Instead, it wasn't.

Brother Marcus and the kitchen crew, Brother Salix, Brother Silvanus—he felt at home with them, and it was good. Brother Kongro and Brother Sifari, the day watchmen in the courtyard, were mild mannered and agreeable with everyone. And sleek, trim Brother Dietrich was always busily pleasant. But with the others, it was a different story. He didn't see much of them except in church and at meals, and monks weren't supposed to chatter about things with each other, or slap each other on the back, or visit with each other in their cells, or anything like that. But the eyes that glanced his way remained, well, guarded. And the nods that were nodded at him still seemed cool and reluctant. It made him uncomfortable and no two ways about it.

Part of it, he supposed, was that he worked in the library, although Brother Silvanus seemed to be well accepted. Then too, he was the youngest monk in the monastery by a good ten years, or so he'd learned from Brother Marcus. And he was the smallest and shortest, too, except for little Brother Zossimus the woodcarver, who was *tiny*. And nobody else had come from Ireland or anywhere near it. He supposed that none of this helped. But what he could do about it he couldn't imagine.

There were two hulking fellows who went beyond reluctant and guarded. The largest monks at Spiritus Sanctus by far, they scowled at him darkly whenever they happened to see him, tying their foreheads almost into knots with their frowns. He hung back after supper one night to ask Brother Marcus about them—the cook had come out from the kitchen for a breath of cool air. "Huge fellows?" asked Brother Marcus. "Head taller than anyone else? Always lugging boulders and tree trunks around? Always together?"

Brother Arcadius nodded. Those were the ones.

"Well, that's Brother Atalf and Brother Ziegmunt," Marcus said. "They really are brothers, too—blood brothers, I mean. Hatched in the same nest. Saxons, so I hear."

"There are Saxons in King Alfred's lands," Brother Arcadius said. The lady who'd walked off with too much of his money, hadn't she been a Saxon? He figured she was.

"Oh, these aren't those Saxons. These are Saxons from way, way east of here. East, and north. Atalf's the older, and Ziegmunt just copies whatever Atalf does. If Atalf picks up a giant rock, so does Ziegmunt. If Atalf frowns at you, Ziegmunt will too. They're great workers, though, the two of them. Won't find many to match them anywhere. Strong as twenty oxen is what they are." The cook lowered his voice and added more words in a mutter. It almost sounded as if he'd said, "And almost as smart." But monks were not supposed to insult each other. So what he'd probably said was, "And also, they're smart."

Brother Arcadius suppressed an anxious sigh. It was past time for him to head back to his cell. He was glad to hear good words spoken of the two big fellows, but that wasn't what he wanted to ask about. "I can't think why they'd dislike me," he said. "I've never done anything to them, as far as I know."

"Well, I don't know that they do dislike you," Brother Marcus said genially. "When their brows are knotted all up like you say they are, most likely they're thinking. It just takes Atalf a while to get used to things, that's all. If you'd been here already when he and his brother arrived, then you'd belong here, see? He'd be all right with you then. If he ever does get used to you, in about fifty years, then Ziegmunt will get used to you too. It's not a problem. Don't worry about it."

"All right," said Brother Arcadius determinedly. And he set about dismissing his second worry, too, or was it his third.

Father Julian.

The head of Spiritus Sanctus was expected to be returning very soon.

When he did return....

Well, for one thing, Brother Arcadius would be taking lessons with him. That was the plan that they'd laid for him back in Dublin. He'd be working to bring his Greek and his Hebrew up to the highest standard that he could reach. Even his Latin, maybe, might call for improvement —they hadn't thought so in Dublin, but he wasn't so sure. If he fell short of Father Julian's expectations, worse things might happen than just some frowns and distant glances.

Those dear, kind monks back in Dublin, learned though they were, had been ordinary folk. His own people, Mam and all, they were ordinary folk. He'd never had to have dealings with a high-ranking person.

Father Julian was a very high-ranking person. Everyone here seemed to hold him in great regard, and there was no doubt that the monastery was well run. But monks didn't sit around discussing their superiors. Nobody said what sort of a person he was.

From remarks dropped here and there, mainly by Brother Marcus, he'd learned that Father Julian was said to be blood kin in all sorts of direct or very complicated ways to counts, dukes, queens, and kings, and various popes. Blood kin in fact to almost everybody of any renown, present or past—even to the forebears of Julius Caesar of so long ago. Julians hadn't just founded Spiritus Sanctus with Charles Martel, they'd been there behind the scenes at every important event before and since, secretly counseling, guiding, smoothing things over, arranging things—*blending in*, but not in the way that assistant librarians did. *Uncle, a word with you*, said to some king. *Nephew, let's look at it this way*, said to some pope.

It made Brother Arcadius feel gloomy and weighed down just to think of it. Of course, he fought against feeling that way, but even so!

Here at Spiritus Sanctus, Father Julian lived, as far as he could tell, in a fairly humble way. The room of state in his residence was said to be bare of much adornment, aside from a very magnificent latch on the door. Behind that room, his own quarters were said to consist of merely a regular cell. He ate and drank what the monks did at every meal. The rock crystal goblet he drank from and the silver service he ate from were marks of high office merely, handed down from Julian to Julian, so that the monastery would not look mean and shabby in the eyes of others. But nobody ever said, "Oh, he's a good fellow! You'll find he's very kind!" Or, "Father Julian? What a twinkle there is in his eyes! How he loves to laugh!" Or, "Brother Arcadius, he'll be a second father to you—and what a great pet he'll make of Pangur Ban!"

The day came when he arrived. Not long after the midday meal, Brother Kongro on the courtyard walls raised up a great cry of "In view! In view!" A party of travelers, well guarded by armed men, was approaching over the grasslands to the west. Before long the courtyard bell was ringing incessantly. "They wouldn't ring it like that for anybody else," said Brother Silvanus to Brother Arcadius. "We'll see him tonight at supper." They bent their heads once more over their work.

Brother Silvanus was right. At supper that night, in the great dining hall, up on the dais, seated at the high table laid out with the monastery's rock crystal goblet and silver service, there he was, the man of great family, the head of the monastery. Brother Arcadius studied him out of the corner of his eye, glancing up quickly when he thought nobody would notice. He saw a man of perhaps forty, a little over average height, not thin, not fat but, it might be said, solidly built —good-looking in a dark-browed, rather jowly way, and with the dark, dark eyes that Brother Arcadius had last seen the night he'd arrived, on that blur who'd peered down at him and then said, "Get Salix."

Dark within dark was what those eyes looked like. Was it kindly or cold or what, that darkness? Brother Arcadius couldn't say. His hurried glances showed that Father Julian did indeed eat and drink what everybody else was eating and drinking. The only different thing came about when supper was almost over. Then Father Julian opened a book lying near his plate, not that grand book with the embossed and gilded covers, but something very small and ordinary. In a quiet voice that filled the hall all the same, he read out a tale of Saint Christopher, guardian of travelers. After that he asked if there were any questions about Saint Christopher, and there were some, and he answered them.

And that was that.

The next day, though, Brother Dietrich appeared at the library door and said, "Arcadius, Father Julian would like to speak to you now." Then he turned and strode back to Father Julian's residence. Brother Arcadius followed along behind. He tried to ignore the sudden chill that had settled in his heart and in his stomach. There was no need for any such chill. He was trying his best to blend in, although so far he hadn't. And if Brother Silvanus didn't like him or his work, wouldn't Brother Silvanus have told him? On the other hand, when Brother Silvanus made teasing comments about the long-ago, inept, imbecilic Emperor Arcadius, maybe he wasn't really teasing at all?

"Don't knock, just go right in. He's expecting you." Settled behind his well-ordered desk again, Brother Dietrich gestured to the inner door, the one with the latch. It really was magnificent, that latch—iron-work lilies and laurel leaves spreading out in all directions, and a crown in the middle, maybe for Charles Martel. Brother Arcadius pressed the thumbpiece down and went in. Went in and stood there, while Father Julian studied him with those dark eyes. Brother Arcadius himself studied the floor. There was a red rectangle of woven fabric there, with a silken sheen to it. It had a curious design of various shapes and curlicues all over it, and a fringe at either end. It was maybe two paces long by one pace wide—regular paces, not Atalf's and Ziegmunt's paces. Brother Arcadius recognized this as a carpet, although he had never seen any such thing before.

"Arcadius...." said Father Julian. He was seated on an ordinary chair at an ordinary table. There was another chair next to where Brother Arcadius was standing.

"Yes, Father," murmured Brother Arcadius. Would he be asked to sit down now, or what?

"I want you to start your studies with me tomorrow. Your monastery in Dublin writes that you're advanced in Greek, but somewhat less advanced in Hebrew. They feel that you need no further studies in Latin. Do you agree?"

"I do, Father."

"Needing no further study" was not the same as "not needing any improvement." Brother Arcadius lifted his eyes a little. The striking thing about the room was its absolute bareness. Aside from the carpet and the table and chairs, the only other furnishing was a single bookshelf on the wall by the door that probably led to that cell. A very large book stood on it, embossed and gilded—the grand book of

Spiritus Sanctus for sure, with all the monastery's rules and its history. Oh, and there was a small stand in the corner, too.

"We'll proceed on that basis, then," said Father Julian. "We'll start tomorrow night, directly after supper. Your work in the library won't be interrupted."

"All right, Father." There was a, a what, a game board on the stand, marked off in squares, with odd figurines standing on it. Brother Arcadius studied the carpet again.

Father Julian leaned abruptly forward. "Do you play?" he asked.

Startled, Brother Arcadius took a step backward. "Father?"

"Chess," said Father Julian. "Do you play chess?" He stood up. He moved the stand with its game board away from the corner.

"I um...I don't...." *Chess?* Brother Arcadius had never heard such a word before. Chess! Was it Hebrew, or what?

"It's not all that well known here, true," said Father Julian. "Bring that chair over here and sit down, and I'll show you how it goes."

So Brother Arcadius carried the chair over and sat down. He was baffled. He was dumbstruck. He was suddenly eye to eye—he tried not to be, but it couldn't always be helped—with the head of Spiritus Sanctus monastery, across a game board. It was soon very clear that this game was not to be played for fun. These were pawns, and they moved like so, and like so. These were bishops, and bishops moved this way and that. These horsemen moved two squares forward, and one square to the side. These castles did such and so. The queen moved like this and like that. The king....

The object, it seemed, was to trap the poor little king. The king appeared to have almost no powers at all, like a second Emperor Arcadius. Father Julian put the figures back in their places. "We'll try a few moves," he said. "I don't expect you to play well immediately."

Or ever, thought Brother Arcadius. Guided by Father Julian's pointing finger, he moved the squat pawn in the middle one square forward. "That's a good standard move for beginners," Father Julian said. All right, but what should beginners do next? The finger stopped pointing and waited, expectantly. Through a haze of bewilderment, Brother Arcadius tried to puzzle things out. Taking turns with the man of great rank sitting darkly across from him, he moved a few more pawns forward. He boldly swooped a bishop five squares ahead. He hopped a horseman toward the center and then, on his next move, hopped it back again. "Check," said Father Julian. "Mind your king." He minded his king. A malevolent queen was unleashed from the other side.

"Mate," said Father Julian. "No, don't move again. The game's over." He stood up. His eyes had gained another layer of darkness, it seemed, or perhaps it was just a trick of the light. "We'll add chess and lessons in reasoning to your studies, Arcadius. They are both good for the mind," he said. "We'll meet twice a week for your lessons in Greek and Hebrew, and once a week for your exercises in thought. I'll see you here tomorrow night after supper, then. You may go."

So Brother Arcadius went. On the way back to the library, he tried to clear his head and reassemble his thoughts. He hadn't been told that he was no good in his work, or that he'd be sent back to Dublin if he didn't improve. He hadn't been told that Brother Silvanus thought ill of him. He hadn't been told anything at all to his discredit, or, Heaven forbid, to Pangur Ban's discredit. But on the other hand....

There'd been no reassuring words of welcome. No *Glad that you're here*. No *I understand that you're doing well in the library*. No *I hope you've recovered from the deprivations of your journey*. No *Please come to me if you're ever in difficulties*. No *Brother Marcus thinks highly of the cat*. There'd only been those dark, unreadable eyes.

And that so-called game, which seemed likely to become a torment.

Chess.

Lessons began. Brother Arcadius made swift, sure, happy progress with his Greek and Hebrew, or so it seemed to him, at any rate. He blundered his way miserably and determinedly through chess and reasoning. Chess turned out to be all about thinking far ahead—farther ahead than ever seemed possible. Reasoning involved a great deal of Aristotle and premises and deductions and *If X's are Y's*, and who knew what all. Father Julian spoke no words of praise, and no words of reproof. He simply corrected mistakes and then moved on—or not. With chess and reasoning, he mostly went back and explained things in new ways.

"Well, Caesar," said Brother Silvanus, "I wouldn't worry about making mistakes in chess. Brother Dietrich and I, and two or three others—Salix, Kongro, Malachi—we play against him too, when he asks us to. Two, three quarters of an hour.... That's the most that any of us ever last against him, and we're fairly good players. You're just a beginner. So don't be hard on yourself."

"I'll always be a beginner," Brother Arcadius said. He tried not to say it bitterly, but still! He wasn't used to being an absolute fool in his studies. From birth on, almost, he'd always been Tammis Scholar, maybe no great prodigy like people were always saying, yet always well able to learn. But in chess and in reasoning he felt as if he were back on that boat out of Dublin, tossing about on the waters, spinning helplessly round, or as if he were coming up out of the pine woods again, with all the world just a blur.

True summer came in. The midday meals were graced by bowls of cherries.

Pangur Ban excelled as a mouser more and more. More and more too he appeared at the library during the working day, leaped lightly onto a window sill, leaped lightly in. A few mews of greeting, and then he'd go back outside or curl up in a corner. Never did he interfere with anyone's work. Brother Silvanus made him welcome from the first. It was very pleasant to have him nearby so often. And he was growing amazingly, too. No more a mere half-grown kitten, he showed every sign of becoming a very big cat.

A storm struck, with a night of much thunder and lightning and high winds into the bargain. A murmured joke made the rounds of the monastery: that it was a wonder the assistant librarian hadn't been blown right back to wherever he'd come from. And somebody'd said that there wouldn't have to be any storm—a breeze could do it. And getting hurt feelings about it was just giving way to the demons of pride and self-love, and he knew he shouldn't. But still!

Cherry time ended, and the time of plums began. Days of fine rain mingled with days of sunshine, and new abundance sprang up from the ground. Bees droned in the clover along the pathways. Father Julian remained an alarming mystery. Chess games were routs.

One evening, when Brother Arcadius went into Father Julian's room of state for his lesson in Greek, an unexpected—a startling!—sight met his eyes. Brother Atalf and Brother Ziegmunt—they were there too! They were standing over there by the chess board, pressed against the wall and staring, arms held tight to their sides. They barely seemed to be breathing. Only their lips were moving, as if they were rehearsing something to themselves. And their brows were knotted in the way that might mean thought. Or dislike of assistant librarians. Or who knew what. "Sit down," said Father Julian to Brother Arcadius. Then he turned to the two hulking brethren. "You say you have a request concerning Brother Arcadius," he said in his even-toned way. "Speak it now, in front of him."

"Uh..." Brother Atalf swallowed hard. He looked at his brother, and his brother looked back at him. "Uh, Father, my brother and me, we think..." His voice was a low rumble, from deep in his chest. Brother Ziegmunt nodded earnestly. Whatever Atalf's thought might be, he would think it, too. "Uh, my brother and me, we think, Father, that Brother Arc...uh...Arcaperus...*him*.... I mean, he's been here a while, and he ought to start working more, like around the grounds. Uh...that's what we wanted to say."

"That's fair!" cried Brother Arcadius before he could stop himself. It *was* fair, and besides, he felt he ought to atone for thinking evil of these two brethren—for thinking, sometimes, that they looked as mean as Danes. It would only be right to help them, they worked so hard. If, for instance, the two brothers each took an end of one of the big logs they carried so often, he was sure he could hold up the middle.

Father Julian appeared not to hear this interruption. His dark gaze was trained on Brother Atalf alone. "Then you also think that you should do library work with Brother Silvanus, and take up studies in languages and reasoning with me."

The two brothers stared at him in horror. "No, Father," gasped Brother Atalf. "No, we don't think *that*."

"If it is true that Brother Arcadius should work like you," Father Julian said, "then it must be true that you should work like Brother Arcadius."

"Uh, we don't...we can't...." Brother Atalf stopped speaking and just stared, his mouth working. Brother Ziegmunt shrank back from the books on Father Julian's table, as if they'd suddenly come to life and might force him to read them.

"Your request is unreasonable, then, and I must deny it," said Father Julian pleasantly. "You may go." The two hulking brothers bowed frantically, then all but tripped each other hurrying out the door. Without saying a further word about what had just happened—without affording a chance to think about it, even—Father Julian turned to Brother Arcadius. The unreadable look in his eyes had never changed. "You are not to start working outdoors," he said, "but you are to start taking your walks."

"Father." It was Brother Arcadius's turn to be all at sea. First Atalf and Ziegmunt, now this. His walks! *What* walks? Walks where?

"Brother Salix is adamant that you need to get out every day and take exercise," Father Julian said. "Walking is what he feels is best for you. We recommend anywhere that's not too close or too far away. You're not to go beyond the sound of the courtyard bell. You will walk for a quarter of an hour to begin with, and increase the time to an hour as you grow stronger. Brother Salix says that this is the key to your continued good eyesight and good health." Father Julian's dark eyes darkened further, or maybe they didn't. "You'll be no use to us here if you turn sickly. We'll work out the details tomorrow. Now, if you will, please translate into Greek the following passage...."

Brother Arcadius turned to his lesson with an inner moan. He was the youngest monk here by ten years, the smallest except for one, breezes could blow him away, people weren't used to him yet, and now he'd be walking. Walking, when monks like Atalf thought he ought to be working. Walking an hour a day, when no other monk ever went walking at all. Walking, when he'd had more than his fill of walking on the way here.

Well, he wasn't going to have any choice in the matter. And it wasn't his way to question his elders, either. Obedience really was his first nature and always had been. So, hating every moment of it, feeling like a fool doing it, scorned by just about everyone for doing it...

Still he would walk.

It turned out not to be so bad after all.

He decided right away that he'd mostly walk in the pine woods, at least for now. His memories of those woods were not at all pleasant, but up here by the monastery the trees really were spaced farther apart. Yet there were plenty of branches to screen him from other people's eyes, so he wouldn't be right under the noses of his laboring brethren. Brother Kongro, up in the watchtower or on the courtyard walls, would catch glimpses of him sometimes, but amiable Brother Kongro seemed to take people for what they were. As for the others....

Brother Atalf and Brother Ziegmunt weren't knotting their brows at him any more these days. Instead, they seemed to flinch, almost, at the sight of him and quickly look elsewhere, or hurry slowly off in their ponderous way. That was no improvement, but at least it meant that their eyes wouldn't be on him, much. And they rarely had work in the pine woods, as far as he knew. Whenever they did, he would simply walk where they weren't. And most everyone else spent their days on the farther grounds, on the farm, in the workshops, in the mill, in the stables, and so forth. Maybe they wouldn't even realize he was taking these walks. Various low-voiced jokes did begin to circulate concerning librarians who had to build up their muscles just to lift up a book, but he was unaware of them. Before long, he did begin to feel stronger, even larger. He measured himself hopefully against the wall of his cell every night. His height didn't seem to increase, but he felt that soon it might.

Another good thing was that Pangur Ban had taken to coming with him. Up and down the path that had once seemed so steep, so hopelessly difficult, the assistant librarian walked with increasing ease, laughing to see how Pangur frisked and cavorted, bounding in circles around him.

All of this was so pleasant that one day Brother Arcadius decided to leave the path and force his way like a hero of old through the woods themselves—not that there was all that much forcing to do. If he kept going northward, and perforce downhill, he would come within less than a mile to the actual wild, wild woods where each step was a struggle, but he wasn't supposed to go that far, and did not want to. Once was enough! But just going off the path a ways was a different matter. So forward!

With Pangur leaping in small arcs just ahead of him, he plunged into the shady tangle that stretched along the narrow path on either side. Ten steps, and the monastery buildings were hidden from view behind the clustering pines. Between the trees, and held in place by ropy roots that stretched along the surface, the ground descended in a series of shallow ledges, slippery and fragrant with pine needles, toadstools, mushrooms, and various humble plants that Brother Arcadius could not name, for they weren't like anything that he had ever seen around Dublin. All he knew was that it was great fun to gather up the skirts of his robe, clutch them to his side with an elbow, and then skid down like somebody on wheels, grabbing at pine limbs and mottled, rough-textured trunks to steady himself on his way.

If he hadn't been a monk and a scholar, and if he hadn't cared about blending in and not being different, he would have shouted for joy, it was so much fun. But suddenly he pulled himself to a halt. Up ahead, something had flashed across the way and out of sight again—something quite large, but not a deer. And Pangur Ban had followed this creature, whatever it was, and was now peering intently at a tangled pile of wind-blown, fallen branches, tall enough for even Brother Atalf or Brother Ziegmunt to hide behind.

If some dangerous beast was hiding there, something that could leap out and rip a cat to pieces.... Stepping cautiously, so as not to alarm Pangur and make him hard to seize, Brother Arcadius moved forward to catch him close and bear him to safety. But Pangur was purring, of all things, and whatever was hidden behind the branches was breathing in great sobbing breaths that didn't sound like an animal's, and in the next instant a human girl slid out from behind the branches and stood there before him, gasping for breath.

For a moment Brother Arcadius could neither move nor speak. All he could do was stare at this apparition. She was maybe older than he was and taller, too, but not by much. Her tangled mop of dark brown hair had leaves and twigs caught in it. Her nose was commanding. Her dark brown eyes—not as dark as Father Julian's and not unreadable, either—flashed with some sort of furious purpose. Except for shoes on her feet, she was clad—or unclad, rather—in a single garment, a linen shift that didn't even reach as far as the knees and revealed all sorts of curves beneath, the kind of curves that monks should not attend to, so Brother Arcadius didn't. Well, she was in some sort of trouble, that was for sure. He found his voice. "Are you lost?" he stammered.

"Oh, it is worse than that!" she said. Her voice was low and throaty, with a catch in it. Her eyes bored into him. "I must get to Spiritus Sanctus monastery. Isn't that where you're from, little monk? How do I get there? What's the quickest way?"

Little monk! What a way to address a person you'd only just met, a person of sixteen and more who really was not all that small, no matter what people said. Even so, people who were in trouble had to be helped. "The monastery is right up there," he said, pointing. He spoke with formality and dignity, to forestall any repetitions of "little monk." "There's a path off to your right, just past those trees. I will take you —"

The apparition didn't let him finish. Even as he spoke she was striding toward the path, pushing her way past the trees, and then climbing upward. And keeping pace right beside her, as if dear life depended on it, went Pangur Ban. Girl and cat were moving fast, and Brother Arcadius hurried along behind. It would all be sorted out up there at the gate, he told himself. The watchmen—Brother Kongro, Brother Sifari—would not let this person pass through in the state she was in. They'd send for a robe, most likely, and find out who she was, and then call for Brother Dietrich to take charge of her. And Brother Dietrich would ask Father Julian what he should do, and Father Julian would tell him. And he himself would reclaim Pangur Ban and the day would go on. But he'd better be up there to help explain things to the watchmen. Otherwise more "little monks" were apt to be said.

He pushed himself to climb faster, but in his haste he kept

stepping on the hem of his robe, or slipping on stones underfoot, or getting slapped in the face by small branches that swung back at him from where they'd been pushed aside by the girl ahead. When they all emerged from the woods, he was still behind. And when she gained level ground, the girl started running. And Pangur Ban ran with her. So he himself had no choice but to start running too. And Brother Kongro looked down from the watchtower, his mouth agape, and made wild motions to Brother Sifari, there on the ground, and Sifari opened the door beside the main gate, and the girl ran through, and so did Pangur Ban, and he did too. "In view," croaked Brother Kongro, as they all passed through.

And always, always the courtyard was empty at this time of day, with even Brother Marcus caught up in his cooking, but today....

Today, it was crowded and much, much worse than crowded. *Father Julian* was over there by the kitchen door, deep in conversation with Brother Marcus and Brother Dietrich, while a good thirty monks or more stood waiting to talk to him. But when the girl, no longer running, came striding in, with Pangur Ban frisking along beside her, all thoughts of monastic business were swept away. The conversation by the kitchen door halted. Every eye was on just three things. The girl. The cat. The assistant librarian.

"Where is your abbot?" the girl demanded of Brother Sifari, who was staring at her goggle-eyed. "I must speak with your abbot." Her haughty voice carried across the courtyard. Brother Marcus gave Father Julian a quick glance and hurried into the kitchen. Father Julian came forward, with Brother Dietrich behind. The girl strode toward them. Pangur Ban followed her like a four-legged, cavorting Dietrich.

It would have been a wonderful thing at that moment to be snatched up by the likes of a giant eagle, as in a tale, and carried back to Dublin, but there was no rescue in sight. Squaring his shoulders, Brother Arcadius walked past the dumbfounded gaze of Brother Vitus the miller, Brother Henriz the latrine master, Brother Atalf, Brother Ziegmunt, and all the rest. He tried his best not to slink. Father Julian's dark gaze raked him briefly, and he braced himself to answer the questions that now he'd be asked. But Father Julian spoke to the girl instead. "Who are you?" he asked in his usual level tones. "And what is the matter?"

"My name is Beatrice, and wicked people are pursuing me, that's what's the matter!" said the girl. She spoke imperiously, as if to a servant.

"How many people?"

"Three!" cried the girl. "And I am in peril, and you must grant me asylum!"

"Where are those people?"

"Somewhere back there in the woods! I know they're coming!"

Brother Sifari, red-faced, had drawn near to apologize. "Father, we wouldn't have let her in, but she was with Arcadius there, and they were running, so—"

Brother Arcadius wilted further, but Father Julian merely nodded. "You did the reasonable thing," he said to Sifari. "But ask me before you let anyone else in today." He turned to the girl...to Beatrice. "Follow me," he told her. "Dietrich, Arcadius, you come along too." He didn't ask for Pangur to be taken away. He'd decided, it seemed, that the cat's presence was of no importance.

"But—" the girl began, with her regal air. Her name was Beatrice, then, but Beatrice what? Countess Beatrice? Duchess Beatrice? Princess? Queen? She couldn't be any of those. If she were, she'd be kin to Father Julian, and he would know her. But why did she think she could speak so rudely to people? Assistant librarians were one thing, but Father Julian, head of Spiritus Sanctus, was quite another. *She'll end up in trouble*, thought Brother Arcadius darkly.

At the moment, though, she subsided and said nothing more, and if Father Julian was annoyed, he gave no sign of it. Turning, he led the way past clusters of staring monks into the nearby refectory through its courtyard door, and then into the reception room, the long, bare room across from the dining hall. The last time Brother Arcadius had seen that room, it had been a revolving blur. It almost looked that way again, so great was his consternation. But he managed to calm himself and take it in.

It didn't look like a room that ever did much receiving. Stools of various sizes were piled up at the farther end, along with empty storage baskets and suchlike things. But five chairs and a small serving table stood near the doorway. Here Brother Arcadius had sat in his first moments at Spiritus Sanctus. Here those three blurs had stood, looking down at him—Father Julian, Brother Dietrich, Brother Silvanus, as he now knew. He'd been the center then of all their gazes. Now he edged behind one of the chairs, hoping that in all the commotion he'd just be forgotten—hoping too that Pangur Ban would soon come to his feline senses and just leave.

Ignoring the smitten cat purring there at her feet, Beatrice threw herself unbidden into one of the chairs. Her flashing eyes fell on Brother Marcus, who'd come hurrying in from his kitchen with laden arms. He carried bread, cheese, dried fruits, and a sausage, all in a basket, and a jug of water and a wooden cup besides. Before he could set even one thing down on the table, she'd snatched the sausage out of the basket, and consumed a good third of it in hurried bites. Father Julian sat down across from her. "I'm in danger!" she said again, between mouthfuls. "You have to give me asylum!"

A murmur arose from outside. The monks left behind in the courtyard hadn't stayed put. Like so many straws drawn to amber, they were peering in through the windows—six arched open windows down the room's long length, with a cluster of five or six faces at every window. Contrary to every monastic rule of behavior, they were jostling each other aside for a better view. "Robe," murmured Father Julian to Brother Dietrich. Brother Dietrich nodded briskly and hurried away. "All right, explain things," Father Julian said to the girl. "Who are you, first of all, besides just 'Beatrice'?"

The girl Beatrice drew herself up proudly. "I am the daughter of Rodolfo of Aventinus, a master arrowsmith in the service of King Charles of Francia." The monks outside traded glances of guarded approval. Master arrowsmiths were quite important people, and well paid, too.

"Why are you not with him now?"

"I am not with him now because he is dead," cried Beatrice with a sob in her throat. Her next words poured forth in a torrent. "Dead and buried for this past week! I was his only child, his beloved daughter. His housekeeper, too, for my mother died many years ago. He had leave from King Charles to go to Rome to see about a legacy there, for my father was Roman by birth—and so am I."

Her haughty gaze swept the room, from Father Julian close at hand, to the piles of stools and baskets at the farther end, to Pangur Ban at her feet, purring and gazing up at her with adoring eyes. "Roman, I say," she repeated with emphasis, as if everyone within hearing distance had better bow down. But for Brother Arcadius, at least, her haughty manner now was clearly explained. He'd heard from the monks back in Dublin that Romans were turbulent people who put on airs, even though Rome itself had fallen long, long ago. "My father wished me to go with him on his journey," this proud Roman continued. "Along the way we stopped at that village down there, that accursed village off to the east of this accursed mountain, to see an accursed cousin of his or sort of a cousin, who has an acc—"

Father Julian held up a restraining hand. "There's a village about twenty miles from here in a direct line," he said. "Is that the one you mean?"

"There isn't any direct line," snapped Beatrice, tossing her mop of hair. A dislodged leaf fell to the floor. "But that is the one. We stopped there and stayed with that cousin, and she has a son—no real son of hers, but the son of her second husband of years before. He is a tanner, that son, and his name is Gaspard. I spit on it! And neighbors came by the first day we were there, and one of them happened to mention this monastery. And my father asked many questions about it, many, many! He asked just how to get here, over and over! And I wondered why. And that night my father said—"

Beatrice smote her breast with a clenched fist. "He told me he felt ill, very, very ill! It was pains in his chest, he said, a feeling like some huge hand was squeezing him there, an old complaint, but much worse than it had ever been before. And he feared that his cousin's son was after me, me and the legacy! He said we should leave in the morning and come straight here, and stay until he felt well enough to go on to Rome. He drew us a map on a piece of old leather. And then he died! And yes, it is true, the son is after me! And you must give me shelter and asylum, and help me get to Rome, for my uncle lives there, and he is a very important master weaver, with a hundred people working under him, and—"

Father Julian cut her short. "So you are being pursued by this Gaspard?" he asked.

"Yes, I'm being pursued by this Gaspard," answered Beatrice through gritted teeth.

"And it took you how long to get here?"

"I left the village at three this morning," Beatrice told him. "I never stopped to eat, and I drank from streams. I got my bearings from the sun and the stars in the sky and the moss on the trees, as my father taught me. And I used the map he made, which I have here." She reached beneath her shift and pulled up a pouch that hung from a drawstring around her neck. "My money is in here too, a gold piece, and the address of my uncle in Rome." She let the pouch fall back out of sight. Brother Arcadius, listening intently, told himself it was no wonder that she'd come through her twenty miles better than he'd come through his. She'd had a good map, and she hadn't started out hungry, and she'd been taught about moss and the stars, not the sun alone. Also, she hadn't been carrying a cat.

Not that it mattered. Monks weren't supposed to get into contests about things. But still! If she went on to say, "And then I met that little monk in the woods," that would be painful and no two ways about it. There were things that even monks found hard to take.

But Father Julian was speaking again. "So Gaspard the tanner is pursuing you, so you think, to claim you by force as his bride, and thus take control of the legacy."

"No," snarled Beatrice. "Gaspard the tanner is pursuing me to burn me alive. When he gets here, that's what he'll say you must do."

Burn her? Burn her alive? The monks outside stared at each other. "Explain—" began Father Julian, but just then Brother Dietrich returned with the robe he'd been sent to get. Beatrice shrugged herself into it with no word of thanks. Her curves were now decently concealed, but not one monk left the throng outside the windows. Everyone crowded closer to hear more. Father Julian resumed his questioning. "Gaspard the tanner wants you to be burned because...?"

"Because he *did* plan to take me by force and *did* plan to get his filthy hands on the legacy," cried Beatrice. "But I never would have married him, never!" She seized a handful of dried cherries and swallowed them rapidly down, glaring at Father Julian all the while. "My manners right now are not good because I am hungry, very hungry. But he, he's a pig, I tell you, a pig! He slobbers up food like a pig and it runs down his chin, and gobs of it stick to his clothes and his hair. Oh, it's disgusting! Revolting! You'd turn your eyes away from the sight!"

Beatrice shook her head vehemently, dislodging another leaf. "For that reason alone I could never marry him. But that's just the least of it. As bad as his manners are, his soul—oh, it's a hundred times worse! And I am a woman of Rome and he is a gobbling, guzzling pig, and here we sit talking, talking, and he will be coming! He and those two friends of his that he always has with him! They will tell you bad things about me that you mustn't believe! You must give me asylum, I tell you, and help me get safely to my uncle, to my uncle in Rome!"

"You have not yet explained why he wants you to be burned alive," said Father Julian. He spoke evenly, but Brother Arcadius, looking on and listening spellbound, thought that all at once there was a difference in him, a new darkness growing that hadn't been there before. People didn't get burned alive at Spiritus Sanctus, of that he was sure. But Roman or not, this Beatrice ought to ask for help more politely. Rudeness was wrong, that was the way of it. It wasn't a crime, but still it was an annoyance. It seemed likely that Father Julian really was getting annoyed. And maybe he had his doubts about Beatrice's tale.

"Like I told you, he came at me!" Beatrice answered. "As soon as my father was buried, then he came at me! And those two friends of his were right beside him. And my father's cousin said I'd better give in, for she is a coward like everyone in that village. They all fear Gaspard. But I am a woman of Rome, and—"

"Explain the burning," Father Julian said quietly.

"I *am* explaining it," Beatrice cried. "Gaspard threw himself upon me, but I got hold of his thumb. And I tried to bite it, bite it to the bone! But he pushed me away, so I couldn't. And then he started howling and roaring and shaking with fear, and he said that good women don't fight back when men want to take them. He said if a woman fights back, that means she's a witch. And I—I did fight back, so he claims I'm a witch!"

A witch! A gasp of real horror arose from the monks outside. Instead of trying to press in closer, they now stepped hastily back, treading on toes and pushing others aside as they did so. This strange young woman with her haughty and imperious air...this young woman from who knew where...this stranger who came before them, unabashed, in just a shift.... If she were indeed a witch, that would explain her.

"And you claim you are not a witch," Father Julian said.

"Of course I claim that I am not!" answered Beatrice in almost a shout. "I am an innocent woman of Rome, and a master arrowsmith's daughter, and an orphan too, and you must send Gaspard away and not listen to him, and help me get to my uncle's, and—" She paused for breath.

The murmurs and mutterings outside the windows grew louder. This Beatrice person should not get asylum if she was a witch. She ought to be tested to see if she was a witch! Spiritus Sanctus should never, never give aid to a witch! Father Julian listened to the muted uproar for the briefest of moments, then turned back to the girl. "So the tanner charges you as a witch because you tried to bite him," he said.

"Because of that, yes," cried Beatrice, "and because of the cats, the cats in the house where we were, because they all liked me and always wanted to be near me, like this cat does here!"

She pointed downward, and all eyes shifted to Pangur Ban, purring his loudest there at her feet. "Cats have always liked me very much," Beatrice continued. "I don't know why, and I can't help it. When I try to shoo them away, they just come right back, and so I ignore them. I don't do anything to be friends with them, and I don't go into forests with them and summon up devils, like the monster says."

Father Julian shook his head. "You say that Gaspard and his friends and the entire village were ranged against you, and yet you escaped. I find it hard to see how you managed that."

The monks outside nodded fearfully at each other. A woman who was just a woman could not have gotten away against such odds. But a woman who was a witch....

"I'll tell you how I escaped!" cried Beatrice. "After I tried to bite him, then he feared me, like I said, and wasn't sure yet what he ought to do with me, but he and those friends of his dragged me into a room and locked the door. They said they'd burn me in the morning because a witch's power is weaker when it is day. And then they got drunk and fell asleep. But the shutter was loose on the window, so I got out. I hurried into the forest to make my way here. I left my other clothes in a pond, because I knew they would hamper me if I wore them. And I thought that Gaspard and his dear friends might think I was drowned and not come after me. But I heard them calling to each other behind me at midday, so I know they're coming, and you must protect me and give me asylum and—"

"I would need to hear their side of the story too," said Father Julian calmly.

Beatrice pushed back her chair and stood up. Her nostrils flared, her eyes glared. "Their side is all lies!" she cried. "I'm telling the truth! So stop wasting time with your stupid, foolish questions and give me asylum and help me get to Rome!" And she stamped her foot, stamped it at Father Julian!

Stamping her foot at Father Julian! Telling him that his questions were stupid and foolish! That settled the matter. "She's a witch," moaned a deep, deep voice from outside. It was Brother Atalf. "A witch," moaned Brother Ziegmunt, after him. Now the dreaded word was on everyone's lips, no longer spoken in doubt, but in certainty. Then Brother Kongro's voice rose up from the courtyard. He was talking urgently to someone. Within moments came his cry, "In view! In view!"

"Father!" Brother Vitus, the miller, came hurrying through the doorway. "Brother Kongro's spied some men through the trees, down on the lower bend on the pine woods path, coming up pretty fast. He can't tell how many there are. Just two or three, he thinks. He wants to know if they should be let in when they get here."

"If it's only two or three, they should be let in," said Father Julian. He turned back to Beatrice, and all at once he was unreadable no longer. Cold fury was in his eyes. His voice was a voice of chill iron. "Witchcraft is a grave and evil offense and peril," he said. "I cannot and will not expose my monks to such danger. I offer you no asylum, Beatrice. But neither will I assume your guilt in advance. You will stand trial, and you will stand it here, when everything has been made ready. Until then, you will be shut away from the good monks here, lest by some evil spell you do them harm. If the trial shows that you are not a witch, you have nothing to fear. In the meantime—"

With a finger-snap like the crack of a whip, he summoned Brother Atalf and Brother Ziegmunt back to the window from which they'd shrunk away. "You, Brother Atalf. And you, Brother Ziegmunt," he said. "I want you to take this woman to the prison house. It's only a short way there, so have no fear. Make sure the cell is completely bare. She must have no bedding, no chair, nothing that she might use to cast a spell. No further food or drink. She should have a pail, so that she won't defile the floor if she has certain needs. Keep watch through the night, though from a safe distance. In the morning you'll bring her to her trial, securely bound in many chains."

"You're sure she can't hurt us, Father?" faltered Brother Atalf. The big man had turned almost green with fear.

"In the short time that you actually need to touch her, she can do you no harm," Father Julian said. "And she'll have nothing to work with while she's locked up. Come in now and take her away. As her guards, you will not convene for vespers or supper tonight, but your meals will be brought to you, and our prayers will be with you." He raised his voice so that everyone could hear him clearly. "May woe betide those who aid witches," he said. "Here at Spiritus Sanctus we'll do no such thing." The monks outside whispered relieved amens.

Brother Atalf and Brother Ziegmunt came trembling in. Father Julian unfastened two keys from the ring on his belt. He handed them over. "The larger one is for the prison door," he said. "The other is for her shackles in the morning." The brothers took deep breaths and then seized Beatrice. She'd stood through all of this in wide-eyed silence. All of her rudeness and fight seemed to have left her. She threw one quick and imploring glance at Father Julian, and then her burly escorts rushed her effortlessly through the room and out the door. Pangur Ban stared after them, fur bristling slightly. Then he came over to Brother Arcadius as if seeking an explanation.

"Good," said Father Julian. "Pick him up, Arcadius, and make sure you don't let him go."

Brother Arcadius complied with dread in his heart. Whatever was about to happen, he feared it. Pangur stirred restlessly in his arms. The cat's claws were unsheathed, just slightly. He was being polite to his friend, Brother Arcadius, but at this moment he didn't much want to be held. Nor did Brother Arcadius want to hold him. He wanted to shoo him away from whatever was coming.

"Don't let him go," Father Julian repeated. He turned to a cluster of monks at the open doorway. Now that the witch was gone, they'd ventured, a courageous few, to come in from outside. Father Julian beckoned to one who was at the forefront. "Brother Helmuz," he said. "If you will—"

"Yes, Father," said Brother Helmuz, alarmed but ready.

Father Julian pointed to the far end of the room. "Brother Helmuz, quickly. We need to secure the cat for the trial tomorrow. Go get the willow creel that's lying back there, the largest one, with the lid, and bring it to Brother Arcadius. He'll put the cat in it and keep the lid shut. You'll go to the kitchen cellar. They always keep rope down there. Fetch a good length of it, enough to secure the lid so it can't come off." Brother Helmuz dashed off, hurried back with the creel, and then sped away to the kitchen.

The creel was a good deal larger than Pangur's regular basket, and the weaving of the sides was thick and tough. There were plenty of spaces where air could flow in and out, but they didn't give much scope for damage from tooth or claw. "Put the cat in it, Arcadius, and close the lid," said Father Julian. Heartsick, but not knowing what else to do, Brother Arcadius did so. Instantly there were alarmed and indignant yowls from within, and the sides rattled as Pangur clawed at them, seeking release. Brother Marcus, still standing alongside the little table, looked unhappily away.

"Keep the lid shut," said Father Julian sternly. In total dismay Brother Arcadius complied with that order too. He felt like the wicked betrayer in the songs about Charlemagne's hero Roland. He felt like bursting into tears. He felt like seizing the creel and running back to Dublin with it, with Pangur inside. But all he did was hold the lid down with his entire strength, until Brother Helmuz came back from the kitchen with the rope.

He'd brought enough rope to tie up a hundred creels, or so it seemed to Brother Arcadius. In moments the lid and sides were secured so tightly that even a witch's cat could never get out. In any case Pangur's efforts were already flagging, from weariness, maybe, or from discouragement. Or was he gathering his strength for one more heroic try? A try that surely must fail, and would lead to no good if it succeeded, but still, but still....

"Brother Helmuz," said Father Julian, "take the cat to your cell and guard him through the night. Don't let him out of that basket for any reason. Keep your cell door shut. You will bring him to the trial in the morning. From this instant on he must have no food or drink of any sort. As with Brother Atalf and Brother Ziegmunt, your supper will be brought to you and our prayers will be with you. Is all this clear to you, Brother Helmuz?" Helmuz nodded a firm yes. "Then go now," said Father Julian, and the rope-bound creel was lifted up and carried away.

One last plaintive yowl floated back from the creel as it went through the door, but new sounds eclipsed it. Beatrice's accusers had arrived at last. As poor Pangur was carried off down the corridor, in they came, guided by eager monks who were showing the way. First in came a broad-shouldered, barrel-bellied, heavy-chinned man, almost the equal of Atalf or Ziegmunt for size. He towered over the two sly-faced men who were with him. Father Julian stepped forward. The big newcomer dropped to his knees and bowed his head. "Holy Father," he said, in whimpering, oily tones. His voice did not accord with his size at all. "Holy Father, Gaspard is my name. I am an honest tanner and a godly-minded man, and I have come—"

"I believe I know why you have come and where you have come from," Father Julian said. His rage had subsided, it seemed, at least for now, and he spoke in his customary voice. "I welcome all who show respect for religion and true fear of witches, for witches indeed are a great peril. The woman you accused of witchcraft has told her dubious story and has been jailed. A cat who may have assisted her has been locked away also. You need have no fears for your safety. Please rise."

The big man eagerly did so. He and his companions were disheveled from their long trek, but they hadn't been starving. Their food-stained packs showed they'd had plenty to eat. The tanner, in fact, had been chewing as he came in. Father Julian seemed not to have noticed the packs, or the chewing. He turned to the cook, standing glumly there by the little table. "Brother Marcus, these good men have traveled far in pursuit of justice," he said. "We must grant them our best hospitality. I will lead them to the dining hall. Bring proper sustenance to them—indeed, bring them the very finest of whatever you have, and in plenty. Your fish paste, if any is left from yesterday. Your herbed game stew—It's Saturday, so it must be almost ready."

"It needs to simmer until tomorrow, Father." Ordinarily, Brother Marcus was eager to talk about cooking, but Pangur's plight had taken the joy away. His tone was respectful, but somber. "It won't be at its best if I serve it now."

"But I ask you to serve it now," Father Julian said. "It may fall a bit short of what it might be, but I doubt it will be by much."

The cook nodded and went off to his kitchen. Father Julian led the three supplicants across the corridor to the dining hall. Brother Dietrich, on the alert for any new task, followed them with quick steps. Brother Arcadius, not having been dismissed, trailed miserably along behind. Soon Brother Marcus and two of his kitchen crew hurried into the hall with bowls, knives, spoons, and goblets, all of silver—the service that was reserved for honored guests. They laid the table silently and headed back to the kitchen to fetch the food.

"Brother Dietrich!" Father Julian turned to his assistant. "Brother Dietrich, tell those who've been listening outside to come quietly into this hall and sit down, not for a meal at this time, but to serve as witnesses. Then bring me the book of rules."

Brother Dietrich sped off again. In moments monks began filing in. The witch-girl and the worrisome cat had been safely stowed away at Father Julian's very comforting command, but many of them were still uneasy. One by one they took their places to await events. While they waited, they bowed their heads in silent prayer. They did not look up even when the kitchen crew came in with fragrant platters and bowlfuls of splendid fish paste and nearly perfect herbed game stew.

Whatever faults she might have, and whatever she might be, Beatrice had described Gaspard's gross manners correctly. By the time Brother Dietrich returned with the great book of rules, the tanner had gobbled down three huge helpings of both fish paste and stew, using his hands more often than his silver spoon, wiping those hands again and again on his layers of garments, instead of on the fine linen napkins the monks had provided, dropping gobbets of food down his front as well. Father Julian's dark eyes remained steadily on him, never registering disapproval or disgust. Rather, they showed concern and sympathy. This was not a pig at a trough, but a soon-to-be-proven (most likely) victim of witchcraft—a poor, simple man who was seeking redress from evil.

The feasting seemed to go on forever, but at last Father Julian raised his hand for attention. "Gaspard Tanner," he said, "now that you've refreshed yourself somewhat from your journey, please tell us how the accused witch came to attack you. We have heard what she says is her story. Now we need to hear yours."

"She's a witch beyond any doubt, Father," simpered the tanner. "I had my suspicions about her from the very first. We have cats in our house, and when she arrived with her father, they went rushing up to her and purred and meowed and carried on like they never had before, not for anyone. When cats act like that, it's a sign that you're dealing with witchcraft. I speak as an honest man."

"And then she attacked you," Father Julian said.

"Yes, she did, Holy Father!" The tanner waved his thumb in the air for all to see. "She seized my thumb and did her best to bite it! The marks haven't gone away! It was after her father died. She said he died of an old complaint, but you have to wonder. There's a legacy, and who knows what a witch will do to make herself rich?" The listening monks cast dark looks at each other. Who knew, indeed?

"But my friends here will tell you I'm no coward," the tanner continued. "What happened first was I went to pay my respects to the dead like a decent man should, even though I'd seen how the cats behaved and I had my misgivings. And that's when she came at me. She came at me snarling, Father, with her claws out to get me! It was like she'd turned into a cat, a giant cat, with her fangs closing down on me, ready to drink my blood! That's not how real women behave, Father. That's how witches behave! But before she could cast a spell I fought her off—thank God for my strength. Then I came here for help from you, Father. And to help you too, because I knew she was heading your way. It's a good thing you locked her away, but she mustn't go free. She's a witch, and she has to be burned."

The listening monks shuddered in terrified agreement, but Father Julian stood up and motioned for silence. "However," he said, "according to the rules of Spiritus Sanctus, there must be a trial before there can be any burning."

"Oh yes, Holy Father! Of course there must be a trial" The tanner picked up his bowl and sucked at the stew within. His spoon lay unused before him. Rich gravy dribbled down his ample front. He seemed unaware that his elbow was in his fish paste. He put his bowl down and nodded matter-of-factly. "Will it be the one where she stands in a tub of water, and if her feet get wet it shows she's guilty? I've heard that's a good one."

"No," said Father Julian. "We'd use that test if she'd been casting spells with water, but we must fit our proceedings to the circumstances. It is by the behavior of cats that you recognized the woman Beatrice to be a witch, and it is by the behavior of a cat that her guilt will be affirmed—a cat that has already shown her uncommon friendliness. Thus we are told to do in our book of rules."

He picked up the great book of Spiritus Sanctus with its gilded covers, turned to a page near the back, and began to read. Sonorous and laden with doom, the Latin words filled the room. The accused would be brought to the test exactly at sunrise. The accused would be wound about with chains. Accuser and accused would stand twenty paces apart. The testing beast would be carried in and placed between them. The person the cat ran to was guilty, and must be burned. So be it. Father Julian closed the book and looked down at the tanner. "Did you get the gist of that?"

"I tried my best, Father," said the tanner uncertainly.

Father Julian gave a quick explanation. Then he added, "Again, I assure one and all that none of us here is in danger. We can all sleep tonight without fear. We will assemble at the testing place half an hour before sunrise. After the trial, the regular business of this monastery will continue as always."

"You'll burn her right here, won't you, Father?" put in the tanner. "I think that would be best."

"We will make that decision after the trial, my son. But you, Brother Arcadius—" Father Julian raised his voice again. "You, Brother Arcadius, lest you be tempted to come to the aid of the cat you brought to this monastery, and which is now instrumental in tomorrow's great test of witchcraft, I command you to go to your cell now and stay there until the trial, not emerging for any reason until then. And to insure that temptation does not overcome you, I appoint Brother Yarnas to keep watch outside your door."

Brother Yarnas stepped willingly forward. He was one of the monks who'd always seemed most unfriendly. Until this moment, Brother Arcadius hadn't even known his name. The new precaution pleased Gaspard the tanner immensely. "Thank you, Holy Father," he cried. "Thank you for being so careful about everything!" Amid murmurs from every side, Brother Arcadius went off shame-faced and shocked to his cell.

Four hours later full dark had fallen. The monks of Spiritus Sanctus had convened at the church for vespers—all of them but five. Brothers Atalf and Ziegmunt were on guard at the prison. Brother Helmuz was on guard over Pangur Ban. Brother Yarnas was on guard over Brother Arcadius. Brother Arcadius paced in his cell, four strides forward, four back. He'd been given an ample ration of bread and water, but he hadn't touched it. It made him sick to think of touching it.

It made him sick also to think of that toolshed prison. How many times he'd walked by it, and how many times he'd been glad that only a few fractious travelers had ever been locked up in it! For all intents and purposes he was in prison now, and Pangur Ban was in prison just as surely as Beatrice was in prison, and who had been fractious? Who? Beatrice had been rude, but had she ever been *fractious*? The distant chanting of his brethren rang hollowly in his ears. He listened for cries from Pangur Ban, but heard none. Didn't expect to hear any, actually. Pangur's jailor lived in the farthest building from his.

Four strides over to the farther wall, four strides back to the cot, try to calm the heart that felt close to bursting, try to think what to do.... Brother Arcadius couldn't put a name to all his feelings, but none of them were good. So obedience was his first nature, was it? Well, people had their second natures too, and his had come to the fore. By now he'd searched the length and breadth of his cell a hundred times, trying to find a place where maybe, by determined scrabbling, he might break through the stonework. He had measured and re-measured himself against his one window, to see if somehow he might slide through it the way Pangur did in the happy days—gone forever now? —when he came visiting. Opening the sliding panel in his door—all cell doors had one here—he had asked and re-asked Brother Yarnas to go and tell Father Julian that he, Brother Arcadius, had to talk to him.

Brother Yarnas had looked pleased, each time, to refuse him. "Father didn't tell me to do that."

"No, but just ask him."

"If I go ask him, I won't be here. He said to stay here."

"I promise you I won't leave."

"Stop talking to me. You're not supposed to."

Although the cell window was much too small for even assistant librarians to climb through, and even though the branches of the cherry tree that grew nearby blocked some of the view, the outside world wasn't entirely shut away. Looking out in despair, Brother Arcadius could catch clear glimpses Beatrice's two hulking guards in the moonlight. They were staying well back from the prison, but patrolling it round and round. Whether they'd figured it out for themselves or someone had told them, Atalf was facing one way, Ziegmunt the other, so that no side was left unwatched for very long. They'd been joined by one of the tanner's sly-faced companions. Brother Arcadius strained to hear what they were saying.

"She turns into a cat, she tries to kill him," Brother Atalf rumbled. "She's a bad one, all right, as bad as they come."

"Couldn't be worse," said the tanner's companion. "That trial had better come out right tomorrow. Look, I saw some catmint in your garden. You ought to rub a lot of it into the grass over there, where she's going to be standing. Just to make sure the cat goes right to her, you know? So justice will prevail."

Yes, do it! For just a moment, the heart of Brother Arcadius leaped in hope. But then it sank again, for Atalf was saying, "No, with that cat it wouldn't work. It hates catmint. Won't go near it."

"Well, that's a shame," said the tanner's companion, aggrieved.

The voices faded away as the men went by. Brother Arcadius wrung his hands and gnashed his teeth. He felt that the ground beneath him was crumbling away. Yes, Beatrice's shocking rudeness had been sorely provoking, and yes, Father Julian had to protect his monks from witches. But what about Aristotle? What about X's and Y's and deductions and premises and conclusions and all of that? Was Father Julian, deep down, a man who could not think clearly?

Brother Arcadius went back to pacing again. He was the one who had trouble with clear thinking and logic. He was the one who struggled with premises and conclusions. He was the one who bungled his X's and Y's. But even he could see that this trial made no sense. Would a real witch struggle through miles of briars and brambles and whiplashing branches to seek asylum in a monastery? Would a real witch let herself be chained up in a prison? Would a real witch have let this Gaspard Tanner come at her in the first place? No! A real witch would have turned Gaspard Tanner into a toad, or worse, and then flown away to the devil, wildly laughing. Why couldn't Father Julian see that? Were premises and conclusions useless when it came to real life?

Girls who stamp their feet at holy fathers are witches.

Beatrice stamped her foot at Father Julian, who is a holy father.
Therefore Beatrice is a witch.
That was nonsense.
Girls who are accused by tanners are guilty.
Beatrice was accused by a tanner.
So Beatrice is guilty.

That was nonsense too. If you started out with nonsense you'd end up with nonsense, no matter how many rules of thinking you followed. Worse than nonsense, when lives depended on the outcome. For the fact was that with his own eyes, Father Julian had seen Pangur Ban making up to Beatrice in that very foolish way, not like a sensible cat at all, but almost like a cat drunk on catmint. And Father Julian had to realize that there was every chance that Pangur would act that way again, at the trial at sunrise. And if Pangur did, than Beatrice would be declared to be a witch, and if she was declared to be a witch, then....

Brother Arcadius sat down and buried his head in his hands. He didn't like Beatrice very much, but he didn't want her to be burned alive, either. He just wanted her to get to her uncle's in Rome and live her life, well away from the monastery and Pangur and everything. He'd seen people get burned alive. The Danes had done it in Dublin. Just for the fun of it they'd put a torch to a place sometimes, and laugh at anybody who got trapped inside. He'd known some of those people himself. He'd seen what remained of them in the smoldering wreckage. This would be like that. There'd be a girl with a rude tongue and curves of the sort that monks should not attend to. Then there'd be the fire. And after the fire there'd be this blackened lump.

No! He, Brother Arcadius, could not let that happen. He'd be released at sunrise for the trial, wouldn't he? The instant they let him out, he would make Father Julian see that Beatrice was no witch, that Beatrice should stand no trial. If they didn't let him out, he would shout *No Fair! No Fair! No Fair!* through his window until they had to listen to him. And if the worst happened anyway—

His face settled into grim lines. Then somehow he would collect Pangur Ban and leave this place where such a thing could happen. Somehow or other the two of them would get back to Dublin, to the monastery there, or go back to the brickyard, no matter what his brothers thought, and his sisters...or even Mam...and beg to be taken in. He could be helpful there. He would put his mind to it. He would do his best. Or he and Pangur would somehow find a home in some wilderness far from here, and live on dew and leaves and whatever they could catch. Because they could not stay in any place where such terrible and witless and cruel injustice could....

Oh.

Brother Arcadius sat bolt upright. "*Oh,*" he whispered again on a drawn-out breath. Out of nowhere, a whole new thought had come to him, a wondrous thought coming up like sunrise inside him. It was a thought that turned all the nonsense around and made sense of it. It was a thought from which everything could properly follow, link upon reasonable link. He stood up and began to pace again, back and forth, back and forth, bright hope rising, back and forth, back and forth, the wondrousness growing.

Be true, he whispered to himself. *Please be true.* And he thought it must be, because it made everything so right. If it were true, there would be great justice instead of injustice. If it were true, there would be no vile and disgusting death. If it were true, then there was no petulant rage at a girl's rudeness. Instead there was rage at something else altogether, good, sensible, justified rage...if it were true. But the proof would only come at dawn, and so much would have to depend on....

He paced the night away, turning ideas this way and that in his mind, but he was not tired in the morning. A while before sunrise, his cell door opened and he was able to join the monks assembling outside for the trial. "I just did as I was told," said Brother Yarnas. He did not sound regretful, and Brother Arcadius gave him no answer. The grounds sloped up somewhat around the place of trial, and at Father Julian's orders, the monks took their places on this higher ground, between his residence and their own cells, with the prison off to the side. They assembled in silence. There were no murmurs, no glances from one to another. A heavy seriousness had settled upon them all. Brother Arcadius, thinking ahead, found a place to stand where he could see everything clearly, and where he wouldn't be blocked off if after all he had to make a plea for common sense and mercy.

A hint of light shone on the horizon. "Let the accuser step forward and stand here," called Father Julian. The tanner strode over to a whitish rock that had been placed on the ground, most likely by Brother Atalf or Brother Ziegmunt. Brother Arcadius tried not to frown too fiercely as the tanner raised that thumb of his into the air and waved it about.

The light grew. "Bring forth the accused, and bind her well with chains," called Father Julian. Brother Atalf, trembling, opened the prison door. Visibly gathering up all his courage, he went inside. He reappeared moments later with Beatrice. She made no sound but stood there motionless in her borrowed robe, head bowed, chest heaving. Ziegmunt stepped forward now with an armload of chains. Atalf doggedly wound them about her until she all but disappeared beneath them. Then Ziegmunt locked them tight and the two brothers led her forward. Sagging under the weight of her shackles, step by slow step she reached her place of trial.

Father Julian stepped aside. The sun came up. The radiance of morning filled the world. Brother Helmuz appeared. He was carrying the rope-bound creel that held Pangur Ban. Unearthly yowls were coming from it. Another stone marked the midpoint between accused and accuser. Here Brother Helmuz set the creel carefully down. It rocked from side to side as Pangur strove to be free. Helmuz began to unwind the rope that held the lid shut.

There were knots to undo and loops to untangle, and the unwinding seemed to take forever. But after uncountable heartbeats the lid was free. Brother Helmuz lifted it just slightly and then stepped back. The creel stopped rocking, but otherwise nothing happened. Even the yowling ceased. The silence, the nothingness went on and on. Murmurs arose from the monks. The witch! Had she made the cat vanish? Had she cast a spell after all? But then, little by little, the lid shifted. Little by little, a small white head came into view. A white paw followed. A moment later, the other paw appeared. Then Pangur Ban emerged in his entirety. He looked this way and that, uncertainly. He looked up at the monks assembled on higher ground. The sight seemed to bother him, for he looked away. He looked over his shoulder at Beatrice in her chains...looked harder...turned toward her and looked harder still....

"*Oh please, no,*" prayed Brother Arcadius. "*Oh please, oh please no.*"

And then, as a sudden breeze stirred the mild morning air, Pangur Ban wheeled around. His nose went up, his flattened ears scooped forward. He aimed his nose and his eyes and his ears at Gaspard the tanner. His gleaming gaze was on Gaspard the tanner alone. And now he was running—running to Gaspard the tanner. He was running to Gaspard the tanner as if to a long-lost friend.

"Get it off me!" shouted the tanner. Unmindful of the thumb he'd been waving about, he made a meaty fist and swung it hard at Pangur's ribs, then drew his leg back to follow through with a kick. But the grass underfoot was soaked with dew, and he slipped and fell instead. And

Pangur Ban pressed his whole self close to the fallen man, the fallen man whose clothes smelled so promisingly of fish paste and just-about-perfect herbed game stew, and nuzzled and nuzzled those clothes, and meowed for all of the mice that he hadn't eaten the night before, and for his morning treat.

Father Julian strode forward. "Gaspard Tanner!" he called. "This cat has made its decision in formal trial. By your own standard, you yourself are the witch, and the accused woman Beatrice is innocent."

"Damn you, no!" howled the tanner, struggling up onto an elbow. A great cry of sheer outrage rose from the monks. Consigning Father Julian's soul to eternal flames! That girl's shocking rudeness had been nothing compared to this. True wickedness had been caught out and brought into the light! Shrinking in terror no longer, Brother Atalf and Brother Ziegmunt and many others now surged forward with their own fists clenched, ready to pound the tanner into the ground. Maybe they were getting used to having witches among them. Maybe witches who were tanners were not as alarming as witches who were women of Rome. Whatever the reason, their fury outweighed their fear.

Father Julian raised his hand in a calming motion. "Brother Marcus," he said, "The cat has given full judgment and served us well. I ask that you take him away to the kitchen and feed him. Keep him safely there until we conclude this business." Brother Marcus, beaming, bustled down to the place of trial, whisked Pangur Ban away from the fallen tanner, and carried him off to the kitchen at a fast trot. "Stand up now, Gaspard Tanner," commanded Father Julian. "Your village serves Duke Ulrich, does it not?"

The tanner scrambled glowering to his feet. The pitiful wronged man had vanished, and the bully stood there. His teeth were bared. "We serve the duke, but he's gone off to Spain," he snarled.

"That is no matter. He's a kinsman of mine. I'm always able to reach him. I shall send him quick word of all that has happened here. He will decide how best to deal with your burning. My monks and I have no wish to breathe the smoke of you, or to bury your ashes in our good ground." Father Julian pointed to where a small door in the wall stood open, just past the library. "Go now, and take your wickedness with you. Do not ask us for provisions for your journey. As you know, it is forbidden to feed a witch."

The tanner gaped at him for one brief moment. Then he whirled about and set off in a stumbling run toward the door. His comrades followed him. They went through the door one by one, into the pine woods. The receding thud of their footsteps soon died away. "Release the innocent woman from her chains now," Father Julian said to Brother Atalf and Brother Ziegmunt. Then he raised his voice in a psalm of praise. With a roar of approval, all the monks joined in, except for one. Seeing that not a soul was looking at him, that everyone seemed to have forgotten his very existence, that for once he had really blended in—with the background, if not with his fellows—Brother Arcadius did not even wait to see Beatrice set free. Light with relief, and as quietly as a shadow, he sped to the kitchen—to the kitchen and Pangur Ban.

* * *

"We'll want to get her to her uncle's as quickly as possible, Dietrich," said Father Julian. "Malachi and his crew are taking that load of goods to Sancta Eudocia convent. They can escort her as far as there. My cousin the abbess will see that she travels in safety the rest of the way. I'll write up some letters of introduction and letters of credit. If our orphan is safely united with her uncle, I trust that his Roman blood will be a match for hers."

* * *

"Goodbye, you horrid monks," cried Beatrice. A spare tunic and a pair of breeches had been found for her, so now she was decently clad. She still wore the robe that Brother Dietrich had brought her as well. Her face peered out furiously from its encircling hood. A plump pack of good things to eat was slung over her back. "I told you from the start that I was innocent, but would you listen? No, you had to have your little trial, and torture me with hunger, and thirst, and chains, and fear. I hope I never see you again!" Brother Malachi urged his mule forward and clucked to hers. It lurched into motion. Beatrice hastily centered herself, more or less, in the saddle. They rode off.

* * *

"The cat was put off by all those chains around her," said Brother Salix. "Cats are put off by anything out of the way."

* * *

"I know that book and its rules inside and out, and there's nothing about cats or witchcraft in it," said Brother Silvanus.

* * *

"A sensible cat, like I've always said," said Brother Marcus. "He was starved, and he could smell all the fish paste and the herbed game stew soaked into those clothes, and he couldn't smell anything good from the other direction, so of course he chose the likeliest path to a meal. Wouldn't you?"

* * *

"You wouldn't think it to look at him, but *he* was the witch, that tanner," said Brother Atalf to Brother Ziegmunt for the twentieth time. "The cat figured it out. It came here with that Arcaperus, but it's still a smart cat."

* * *

A week later it was, and Brother Arcadius still felt like dancing a wild, wild dance with a lot of leaping and flinging of arms and spinning around in it. The trial had worked out! The trial had worked out! But monks didn't carry on in any such way, and he was a monk who happened to have a cat, and here was the cat. With dignity, not dancing at all, Brother Arcadius scooped up the sensible, sociable, unusual, and very wonderful cat Pangur Ban and thought about all that had happened.

For one thing, Pangur didn't seem to miss Beatrice at all, now that she was gone. He'd been under her spell for a while, that was for sure. But it had been no witch's spell, and now it was over. For another.... "We've come to a good place, Pangur Ban," Brother Arcadius murmured. "Orchards, vineyards, fields, mountains, pastures, no Danes...no burnings...." And a man in charge who, hearing the demands of a very rude but very put-upon girl, somehow had figured out what should be done, and how to do it.

Brother Arcadius shook his head in sheer wonder. In the flash of an eye, Father Julian must have seen that Beatrice was no witch. In the flash of an eye, he'd understood that he had to prove that, somehow, to his frightened people. In the flash of an eye, he'd invented all that business about the trial. In the flash of an eye, he'd figured out how to make sure that Pangur would run straight to Gaspard Tanner and not to Beatrice. Flash, flash, flash, flash...it had all gone off like a game of chess, played by a master against...well, against an Arcadius. Or like one of those examples of correct reasoning, from the lessons—well, sort of. *It is wrong to want to burn anybody alive. Gaspard the tanner wanted to burn Beatrice alive. So Gaspard the tanner is wrong, wrong, wrong, wrong.*

Or something like that.

"I will study my lessons in reasoning even harder than I'm studying them now," Brother Arcadius told himself. "Because I do not understand Father Julian, and I never know what he's thinking. But his thinking is good, that's for sure. So I ought to learn whatever he thinks I should learn. And if he wants to play chess..." Brother Arcadius squared his shoulders and faced the future. "I will do my best to want to play chess, too."

"Meow," said Pangur Ban.

THE USELESS CHILD

In which an anguished search comes up against a stone wall

AD 899

"In view! In view!" From high up on the broad stone walls of Spiritus Sanctus monastery, the watchman's cry floated out over the land, a signal that travelers were approaching. Brother Arcadius quickened his pace on the rutted path he was ascending—a cold path, where patches of ice and snow had lingered on into April. If he hurried, maybe he'd get to see these people and hear what they had to say. That would make an agreeable end to his daily walk.

It was something he took under orders, that daily walk. At barely seventeen, Brother Arcadius had been assistant librarian at Spiritus Sanctus for almost a year, but he was still the same undersized person that he'd been when he first arrived from Dublin, so far away. The monastery's medicus, Brother Salix, had decreed that he needed to walk to build up his strength and maintain his health. So he walked.

Until just moments before, he hadn't been walking alone. Sometimes ahead of him, sometimes behind him, sometimes darting off to the left or right, but never once getting underfoot, the monastery's champion mouser, the white cat Pangur Ban, had kept him company most of the way. Pangur's main work took place at night in the monastery kitchen, when the hurly-burly of cooking ceased for a while, and mice felt emboldened to come out and forage. It was Pangur's duty then to leap upon them and kill them, or send them flying. He did this every night with unflagging zeal. In the daytime, though, there was too much going on in the kitchen for safe mousing. Then Pangur was free to prowl about the monastery grounds, or curl up for a good rest in some comfortable corner, or catch a hapless bird or two if he felt like doing so, and generally enjoy the day. Enjoyment usually included coming along on the walk, because Pangur Ban and Brother Arcadius were fast friends of long standing.

A year before, seasick and wretched on the cold, lurching boat taking him away from Dublin, Brother Arcadius had been amazed despite his misery to see a scrawny, wild-eyed, half-grown, and very damp and grubby white kitten, a bewildered stowaway, emerge from a huddle of cargo with a yowl of despair. A cruel sailor, as mean as one of the murderous Viking Danes who had conquered Dublin, had snatched the poor creature up and made ready to kill it. Brother Arcadius had pleaded. He'd argued. When none of that worked, he'd finally given the sailor one of his pieces of money, and he was supposed to be saving his money for urgent needs only, but this was urgent. And when things had calmed down and the kitten was in his charge, he'd given him the Irish name of Pangur Ban, signifying whiteness. He'd then safely carried his new ward and companion in a willow basket (bought with still another piece of money) the long and risky way to Spiritus Sanctus monastery, where Pangur was quickly welcomed as a mouser like no other. To Brother Arcadius, though, he was far more than a mouser. He was a person, almost, a smart, odd, fascinating *person*, and also a friend.

But now that person Pangur had run on far ahead. A sensible cat, but also a very sociable and inquisitive cat, he'd been drawn forward, perhaps, by the watchman's cry. Brother Arcadius pushed on. The tiled roofs and squat stone towers of Spiritus Sanctus appeared through the stand of pine trees that flanked the monastery walls, and there went the watchtower bell, ringing just once. The travelers, then, would be staying at least for the night, but they'd be regular people, on foot and few in number. The stablemaster would not have to find accommodations for any mounts. The kitchen would not have to come up with extra food. Father Julian, head of the monastery, would not have to come out and greet anybody in person.

The final turn in the path brought the monastery into full view, and Brother Arcadius saw that, indeed, only the small door into the courtyard was open, not the big gate, and that Brother Sifari, the watchman on the ground, was just ushering in a shabby band of wayfarers. He'd paused at the threshold to exchange words with the last of them, a person who appeared to be a peddler, judging from the sacks on his back and the sack he was eagerly opening. Sifari was clutching the waxed tablet and the stylus that he used to take down the names of people who were staying overnight. He did not look particularly happy. Brother Kongro, his fellow watchman, the one who'd called out "In view!" and rung the bell, was not in view himself, oddly enough. He was neither in the watchtower nor on the walls. But Pangur Ban had settled himself on an overhanging branch nearby, and was amiably grooming himself and surveying the scene.

Brother Sifari had now managed to get the man with the sacks to come through the door. Brother Arcadius followed at a courteous distance. Reaching the door, he came to a hesitant stop. Sifari and the others were only just paces away. Going on would mean that he'd have to push right through them or say, "Excuse me," and interrupt the proceedings. Sifari already seemed very bothered by something. It would be best to wait to be noticed, and then go on by.

"No, no, these others, they're not with me," the man with the sacks was saying. He waved a hand at the people who had gone in ahead of him and were standing by: a squat, scowling, bulldoggish-looking man, a singularly rat-faced woman, and two sullen lads who appeared to be in their early teens—an unpromising group for sure, at least at first glance. Brother Arcadius had to remind himself that books should not be judged by their covers. "Never saw 'em before in my life until just now. Now look, I've also got a good stock of buttons. Horn, copper, brass, bone, wood, all sorts. You ought to just take a look—" Yes, this was a peddler for sure. A determined one, too.

"We don't use buttons here," said Brother Sifari. He gave a meaningful tug to his belt. His expression, usually cheerful in a muted way, was set and stern. Yet he was making no effort to hurry things on. Almost he seemed to be waiting for something. Would that be Kongro, or what?

"Or beads," the peddler was saying. "Copper, horn, bone, wood, tin, clear glass, colored glass, all sorts. You want beads here, don't you?"

"This is a monastery, and everyone here is a monk," said Brother Sifari.

"Yes, I know, but you use beads to pray with, don't you? Don't you want to pray with nice new—"

The scowling bulldog of a man who'd been standing nearby now found his voice and stepped forward. He cut through the peddler's talk with a chopping gesture. "I don't think much of your hospitality here," he said to Brother Sifari. His voice was a snarl. Brother Arcadius decided that he'd been right to linger. He might have to go running for Father Julian. "One night free, and then we pay? When you monks got treasure in your cellars? Heaps of gold?"

Nothing could be further from the truth. Spiritus Sanctus was well run, certainly, and had its farm and its vineyards and orchards, and its lake of clear waters and fine fish. In living memory, at least, it had never run short of the basic needs of life. But heaps of treasure were there none, only an excellent library. However, Brother Sifari did not argue. "One free night is the rule," he said quietly. "We make exceptions in cases of hardship."

"Well, what do you call this?" snarled the man. He pointed to his shabby clothes and bare feet. "Is this hardship, or isn't it?"

"That is for Father Julian to decide."

"Father what?"

"Julian. Head of the monastery. Talk to him if you have a complaint."

"He'll just side with...."

The peddler edged to the front again. "You should just take a look at the beads—"

Ignoring him, the scowling man spoke on. "This Father What's-it —He's a monk and who's he going to side with? Monks, not me."

"May I have, your names, please, one by one?" Brother Sifari tapped his waxed tablet determinedly. "I can't do anything for you if you won't give your names." His eyes flicked toward the doorway. "Arcadius, you can go on in."

"Oh yes, *names*," spat the scowling man, but he'd stepped back again, behind the peddler. He gave no sign of getting ready to do anything other than growl and rail. Eyed momentarily by the peddler, but clearly found wanting, Brother Arcadius edged around everyone into the courtyard. Then he stopped short. Somehow until now he'd overlooked a sixth person. Standing some feet away from all the others, over there where the wall was undergoing repairs, pressed to it as tightly as if he wished to melt into it, there stood another boy, a little boy perhaps five years old.

Was he the peddler's boy, or the scowling man's, or the rat-faced woman's, or whose? They were shabbily dressed, those others, but this child was in rags. His face was pinched. His arms and legs were sticks. The others might or might not be in want, but he was in misery, with not so much as one thin cloak to shelter him from the day's chill.

Those others, what were they thinking of, to let a little boy stand here like this? The peddler was pulling open another sack, and the scowling man was still snarling his grievances. They barely looked round as Brother Arcadius walked past them. He tried to make it seem that he was just crossing the courtyard, but he let his path take him slowly toward the boy. He felt Brother Sifari's eyes on him and looked his way. The watchman glanced upward just briefly to where Brother Kongro would usually be standing. Then he mouthed the word *Salix*.

Ah, so that's where Brother Kongro had gone! Brother Arcadius nodded back, greatly relieved. Proud too that his brethren were taking quick action in this matter. Brother Salix, the medicus, would find warm clothes for this child and attend to his hurts—yes, his hurts. For drawing closer, he could see now that the twig-like arms and legs were covered with welts and bruises. One side of the pinched little face was also bruised, almost up to the eye. As Brother Arcadius drew closer, and then closer still, the child did not so much as glance at him. His brown eyes, very large and very round, seemed fixed upon something that no one else could see.

Did this section of wall seem to him like a place of refuge? It was a stretch that had been poorly built to begin with, in earlier times. For whatever reason, the builders then had used quite a few faulty stones that this year had started crumbling away. Yesterday Brother Mishel, the master stonecutter, had come with his crew and they'd pickaxed a whole course of rotten stone away from the stone that held true. Now there was a gap that Brother Arcadius could have walked into, if the wall's inner core of dirt and pebbles hadn't been in the way up to shoulder height. Dislodged by all the pick-axing, the core above that height had cascaded out and formed a high pile, whose uneven contours offered many places where a very small boy might sit down. Brother Arcadius wondered if he should ask this particular small boy, this silent, shivering, small boy, if he would like to do so.

Pausing near the child, but not so near that he might seem alarming—or so he hoped—Brother Arcadius got down on one knee and pretended to tighten a shoe strap. He mulled over the various things that he might say. The peddler's pleas and the scowling man's snarls continued. There was no sign yet of Brother Kongro returning, with or without Brother Salix the medicus. Instead, a lithe and inquisitive being had leaped down from its pine-branch perch to the wall below.

Pangur Ban.

The big cat—he'd grown much in this past year—was picking his way delicately forward along the walkway on top of the walls, now and then leaping over a gap in the paving, now and then pausing to look up at a passing bird, or consider a shadow or maybe an ant, but mostly coming straight on. Tail aloft, ears pricked, whiskers alert, he was heading right for where Brother Arcadius was kneeling, and where the little boy was standing. If he leaped down and made up to the boy, and let himself be held and petted, that would be a good thing—a warming and comforting thing.

Back there by the courtyard door, Brother Sifari had made some headway. The scowling man was finally snarling out a few straight answers, with no good grace. "Name's Oghrin, then, if it's so important to you. It's Oghrin, see? And she's Ulka. And these two are my boys. Names're...."

Oghrin...Ulka.... Brother Arcadius didn't care much about the rest. He closed his ears to it. The interest lay in what was happening before his eyes. Pangur Ban in his slow approach had reached the place where the wall overlooked the pile of rubble. Now he measured his distances. Gathered himself. Leaped down, and settled himself on a handy pile of broken stones by the little boy's elbow. The child flinched as the white shape swept from above down beside him, but then his mouth fell open and he stared at the cat as if at some wondrous thing come down from the heavens. Pangur Ban stared back. He mewed once, softly. Then, very slowly again, he reached forward with one velvet paw, claws sheathed. Lightly, lightly as a petal might drift to mossy ground, he rested that paw on the bony little forearm nearest him. The child's wide eyes grew wider still. Even the day seemed to be holding its breath.

Brother Arcadius ventured at last to speak. "He's a very friendly cat," he said in his quietest voice. "He won't hurt you. I can see that he likes you. His name is Pangur Ban. That's Irish. It means that he's white. You can pet him if you want...."

The child said nothing, but continued to stare at Pangur Ban, and at Pangur's soft paw, with very solemn, very round brown eyes. "You can pet him," Brother Arcadius said again, coaxingly. Did the child speak a different language from the men he'd come with? Did he not understand the words? Or was he just with that rat-faced woman, and did the two of them not talk like the others? She hadn't spoken at all yet, come to think of it. The two big boys hadn't said a word yet either. Well, the watchmen or the medicus would find out the way of it. Brother Arcadius reached out to stroke Pangur's smooth flanks himself, and nodded encouragingly. "He loves to be petted. Or get

66

scratched behind the ears. If you do that, he'll purr."

"You're wasting your time with him," snarled a sudden voice from behind him. The scowling man—Oghrin—had come over to see what was what. To see what was going on, and—judging by his tone—to take charge. So the child was his, most likely, yet gave no sign that he knew the man was there. "He's a dummy, see? Can't hear. Can't talk. Never could. But he can eat." Oghrin snorted derisively. "Oh yes, he eats."

He reached down, grabbed the small shoulder, and pushed the child roughly forward. With a startled meow, Pangur Ban leaped out of the way. Brother Arcadius rose in indignation and tried to find the words that would send shame straight into this bad man's heart. But before the right words came to him, Brother Salix appeared at the refectory door, with Brother Kongro behind him, took in the scene before him with his usual fierce-looking gaze, and came swiftly forward. "I believe," he said, "that this is the boy I need to see."

The peddler came forward too, all but running across the courtyard. "Hold on there!" he cried. "Are you in charge here? I've got bone needles, every size...."

"What do you mean, 'need to see'?" roared Oghrin to Salix. Brother Kongro, scarlet with pent-up outrage, roared back. Brother Sifari hurried over with words of his own. He too had been sorely tried and was having no more. The medicus, ignoring Oghrin, bent over the boy. Brother Marcus the head cook, drawn by the uproar, came to the kitchen door. He and the medicus had been soldiers together. If Oghrin tried to make trouble, there were plenty of able people to keep him under control. There was no place in all this for an assistant librarian, one who'd now delayed too long getting back to his work.

Brother Arcadius went off to attend to his afternoon duties...attend to them with half of his mind. Get him away, that's what we've got to do, he told himself. Get him away, that's what we will do. Father Julian will have to see that we have to do it. Brother Salix, Brother Kongro, Brother Sifari, all of them, won't they all see that somehow we have to do it?

Bent over the work that he loved, but at this moment not always seeing it, Brother Arcadius planned and plotted ways and means of carrying out the rescue. He did the same in church all during vespers, although he struggled mightily not to. He shouldn't be plotting and planning, he should just be praying. Help would come through prayer, wouldn't it? Not through any miserable efforts of his own. Yet still he planned and plotted on and on, even though it seemed to him that the two watchmen and Brother Salix would surely agree that they had to rescue the boy. After all, Brother Sifari had sent for the medicus in the first place, and Brother Salix would have seen those welts and bruises. He would not be inclined to send that little boy off with that snarling Oghrin, that rat-faced Ulka, and those two surly clumps of lads. Would Father Julian agree, though? *Could* he agree? What if his hands were tied by some sort of law?

After vespers, Brother Arcadius went back to his cell, as always, to collect his eating gear—his bowl, mug, knife, and spoon. In the nineteen other cells in his building, and in the seven other buildings in the monks' quarters, his brethren all around him were doing the same. On a quick impulse, Brother Arcadius opened the small basket of special possessions on the shelf at his bedside, took out the one thing in it that he prized most highly, and smoothed it out for the hundredth time. There was not enough daylight remaining for him to actually read it, but he knew what it said by heart.

"IV days aftr asenshn day dir Tammis yul be suppriz...."

His Mam—his *Mam*!—had written him a letter and sent it off over all those miles and miles and miles of land and water, and it had reached him! He'd had it for five weeks now, and he still couldn't get over the wonder of it. The wonders, really.

"—yul be suppriz yir old mam lernt hir lettrs nevr too old to lirn ha ha but i mus tell yu we ar not at the old plaiss now yir broders...."

How had she learned all this, and learned it so quickly? That was the first wonder. Back in Dublin, the monks remaining there could read and write. His brothers could read and write too, in a limited way, in matters concerning the family brickyard, but in nothing else. If she'd gone to the monks for help, most likely the hardest words would have been spelled correctly, especially words like "Ascension" and "surprise." Maybe she and his brothers had puzzled the whole thing out together. He had a feeling, though, that she'd been learning her letters in secret, keeping her eyes open, thinking things through, for a long, long time. She must have been hard at it even while she was getting ready to bid him goodbye forever—even while he was spinning around in that boat on the cold sea, rescuing Pangur Ban.

"Yir broders ar all in king alfreds survis now he pais good and keps the danes behind ther own line we ar all at baorham in wessex so rit us ther lov frm yir mam and all"

His brothers, all in King Alfred's service? There was the second wonder. How on earth had that happened, and what sort of service was it? Had King Alfred developed a sudden great need for bricks? He wished she'd added some words of explanation. Well, maybe it was all too complicated to explain. Anyway, it was an immeasurable relief to know that his whole family was now in King Alfred's kingdom of Wessex, as safe from marauding Danes as it was possible for anyone who lived in those regions to be. Or at least that's where they'd been at the time the letter was written, months before. Like all letters sent by common folk, it had simply been passed from hand to hand in a long chain of happenstance: "Are you going that way? Would you carry this along?" In the time it had taken the letter to reach him, anything could have happened. All the same, the love it expressed would never change.

The silent little boy had no family like that. No kind, brave Da who'd given his Tammis horseback rides on his broad shoulders, before dying a hero's death in a great altercation against the conquering Danes. No smiling big brothers, as kind and brave as Da. No chattering, joking, hilarious younger sisters. No Mam who kept everything together with her hard work, and learned her letters into the bargain. It was just all very sad.

But it was also going to get better. Squaring his shoulders, Brother Arcadius filed with his brethren to the refectory, eating utensils in hand. He could see the watchmen, off duty now, and the medicus some distance ahead, but he didn't call out to them or hurry to catch up with them. That would have been unheard-of behavior indeed. He'd do his best to sit near one of them at supper.

He kept an eye out for Pangur Ban as he walked along, but the sensible cat always stayed out of the way at mealtimes. After he'd spent a night destroying mice, and sometimes even rats, in the monastery kitchen, he would be given his own special bowl of good things to eat by Brother Marcus, the grateful head cook. Otherwise Pangur dined on the delicacies he caught himself, from mouse to songbird to cricket. There was no need to brave hundreds of shuffling monkish feet and general confusion.

There was less confusion tonight than there might have been. It was one of the many times when the monks who labored on the land or in the workshops wanted to stay with their duties later into the night, and have their meals brought out to them in the kitchen wagon. So the kitchen would be short-handed and instead of food being laid out on the dining hall tables tonight, there'd be a serving line instead. It was selfish to be glad that the line was conveniently short, so Brother

Arcadius wasn't. He did note that he barely had time to count to thrice a hundred before he was carrying his bowl of gruel, his bread and cheese, and his mugful of well-watered wine toward the benches and tables. These were arranged in two columns, five tables per column, which slanted toward the dais where Father Julian, and notable guests if there were any, dined in state.

The general plan was of a giant capital A without a central crossbar. Tables for common guests occupied the space where that crossbar would have been. Tonight there was only a single table there, and only six guests: the peddler, the mean and scowling Oghrin, and his family, if family it could be called. Disappointingly, the little deaf-and-dumb boy was still in his rags. No warmer clothes had been found for him, after all. That was a sort of surprise, and also a worry. Salix, Sifari, Kongro—didn't they care that this child might be feeling the cold?

There was a place to sit down quite near the little boy and the other travelers. Brother Arcadius felt he might as well take it, because the watchmen were tables away and those tables were full. Considering how the two of them had ended up shouting at Oghrin in the afternoon's uproar, it was just as well that they weren't sitting closer to him. Salix the medicus now was nowhere to be seen. Well, he'd have to be found and appealed to right after supper. He and Kongro and Sifari, trusted men who'd been at Spiritus Sanctus for years and years—they were the ones who should speak to Father Julian, and make him see, if he didn't see it already, that Spiritus Sanctus needed to rescue this boy. But if they didn't want to speak to him, then what? It would be up to him then, that was what.

"Arcadius." A voice he'd been hoping to hear broke into his thoughts. Brother Arcadius looked quickly round. There was the medicus right behind him, lean and intent, with his knife's-blade gaze that seemed to see through to the bone. "Can't talk now," he said. "Wait for me in the hallway, after supper." He moved away with his usual silent swiftness. Brother Arcadius sat down.

In the hall. After supper.

This had to be about the little boy. Had to be.

It was hard to be calm, with so much to think about and hope for.

Hard to be calm, while Father Julian took his place at the high table.

Hard to be calm, with Oghrin and the others so near. The peddler, although he didn't count in this. The rat-faced Ulka. The two young louts—well, they certainly looked like louts. And the little boy. And it was hard, very hard, not to cast mean glances at Oghrin. The man was a bully, that's what he was. He was cut from the same cloth as a certain bullying tanner who'd caused trouble at the monastery some months before.

The little boy.

There he sat, so close by and yet out of reach, staring straight ahead, barely moving. Oghrin and the others—the peddler too—were shifting about in their seats impatiently. Not having brought eating utensils of their own, they hadn't been able to join the serving line. They'd have to wait until food was brought to them. In the meantime, they looked this way and that around the big room, casting quick sidelong glances at the monks at their tables around them, and at Father Julian there on his high dais, with his silver dishes and his rock crystal goblet, set in a silver holder—not his own property, but a mark of his high office, and handed down from one head of the monastery to the next, over the generations. The peddler doubtless hoped that Father Julian might feel the need for a bead or two. Oghrin was brooding and sullen.

"Look at him lording it up there," he growled. "It's a treasure house here like I said, didn't I tell you? Look at what he's eating off of. Pure gold, eh?"

"Silver," muttered Brother Arcadius to himself. Candlelight might be giving Father Julian's table service a yellowish gleam, but any reasonable person could see that it was just silver. He gave an emphatic tap to his own bowl. It was made of tin, and had his name scratched into it, as did his mug, spoon, and knife, not to show that he owned them, but because Brother Salix didn't want eating gear to be shared. Maybe Oghrin thought that all these were made of gold too.

"Eating peacock's tongues and honey cake, and we get gruel," Oghrin snarled to the air.

"We all get gruel for supper every night," Brother Arcadius answered him in thought. "Father Julian too. So just...so just shut up, all right?"

Hard upon this unmonklike and very uncharacteristic thought, the guests were served, Father Julian said grace, and everyone fell to eating. Everyone except the little boy, who took two or three hurried, timid spoonfuls of gruel, and one or two equally hurried sips of wine-water, and then resumed his staring. Oghrin turned to the peddler, who'd just asked him something that Brother Arcadius couldn't quite hear.

"Where are we going?" he growled. "To Duke Ulrich's lands, weren't you listening out in the courtyard? I guess you were too busy trying to peddle those beads, eh? We're going to the duke's lands. There's work there and plenty of it. We go where there's work. I turn my hand to anything, you know? I slave, you know? Every day of my life, sunrise to dark, I slave. And Ulka here does her bit, and my boys—"

He pointed across the table at the little boy, who stared past him and did not move. "He's not mine," he said. "Were you listening when I said that? He's my wife's that died. He was deaf and dumb—still is—but I married her anyway. Then she died and dumped him on me. He's useless to me. Can't give him away. Nobody wants deaf and dumb. Asked the monks back where I came from, every monastery I came to, but they said—" He raised his growling voice to the semblance of a nasal whine— "'This lamb of God is your responsibility, dear son.' And Lord Gold-Cups up there will sing the same song when I ask him tomorrow, you'll see." And with that, as casually as if he were reaching up into a tree for a crabapple or a cherry, Oghrin reached across the table, seized the little boy's bowl of gruel, and emptied it into his own.

There was a stir of indignation among the monks who were close enough to see what was happening. Even the peddler gave a squawk of protest, and Brother Arcadius half rose, not knowing what he was going to do next. But Father Julian was already rapping for attention. "You there, Master Oghrin," he called. "We do not, at this monastery, help ourselves to other people's food. Give the boy back what you took from him."

Red-faced and scowling, Oghrin poured a bit of gruel back into the child's bowl.

"You had almost finished your serving, and his bowl was almost full, was it not?" asked Father Julian. Brother Arcadius and the other monks sitting nearby all nodded vehemently. So did the peddler. "Give him back as much as you took, then, please," called Father Julian.

"He won't eat it," snarled Oghrin under his breath. But all the same he complied, and the little boy sat unmoving, staring ahead, and in due course the meal came to an end, and Brother Arcadius hurried into the corridor to wait for the medicus. His heart was pounding with anger, fresh resolve, and new hope. So Oghrin wanted to give the little boy away! There'd be no trouble from that end, then. All the monastery had to do now was decide to take him. Would Father Julian alone decide? Would it be put to a vote? Would—

Good, here was Brother Salix, beckoning him over and already speaking, low-voiced, the most welcome words in the world. "We're taking him. Brother Sifari thought you'd want to know. He said you were showing concern out in the courtyard."

"I was!" said Brother Arcadius. His heart was singing. And it was good of Brother Sifari to think of him. "I saw the bruises on him, and nothing warm on him."

"He's been very badly treated," Salix said. "It's all too obvious, isn't it. We offered to have a warm cloak cut down for him, but the answer was that he doesn't feel the cold and didn't need it. But at least they allow him a name. It's Keti."

Keti. They were going to rescue Keti. "So Father Julian agrees and all?"

"I went straight to him this afternoon, after I'd checked the boy over."

"Oghrin wants to sell him anyway, did you hear?"

"I gathered as much from listening to him in the courtyard."

"Then are we going to take him now? When do we tell him?" Brother Arcadius was beside himself with impatience for things to proceed. He hoped he'd be allowed to be there when the purchase was made—that is, if there'd be a purchase. Maybe the monastery would just take Keti by right? In any case, he hoped he could be there when the child was brought into safety, no matter how. Brother Salix's next words pulled him back to earth.

"We're not approaching Oghrin about this at this moment," the medicus said. "A good-sized party of merchants will be coming later on. We just got word about that while the watch was changing. We intend to pay Oghrin off with a good sum of money, but we don't want to bargain with him. There's that to consider. Also, we have to do it in proper form. We don't want him to pretend to have claims on us later on—or on the boy. Father Julian and Brother Dietrich are drawing up an agreement, and we'll have some of the merchants serve as witnesses. If it was just our word against Oghrin's, there could be trouble later on. We'll approach him just before dawn, and settle things then."

"I want to be there," Brother Arcadius told him. He could see why things had to be done properly, but still! "Would it be all right?"

"I don't see why not," said the medicus. "Just come out to the travelers' quarters in the courtyard. If Father Julian doesn't want you there, he'll tell you." He moved swiftly off.

Brother Arcadius finished his night's duties in a storm of thought. If the merchants didn't arrive after all.... If greedy Oghrin decided to bargain, and made impossible demands.... If...if...if.... Oh, so many things might go wrong. But if they went right....

He could see in his mind's eye how it would be. He could see Keti safe and warm in the kitchen, dressed in a monk's robe cut down to fit his size, eating good food that no one would snatch away from him. He could see the welts and bruises healing. He could see himself, in time, teaching Keti his letters. It might be hard for a deaf and dumb boy to learn to read, but Brother Arcadius was sure that it could be done. They'd start, maybe, with just the word "cat," and go on from there.

He wished it were happening now. But he was grateful indeed that he hadn't had to brave speaking to Father Julian about any rescue, and grateful also that none of his lessons with Father Julian were set for tonight—the lessons in advanced Greek and Hebrew, at which he did well, or the lessons in reasoning, with Aristotle and chess and all of that, at which, strive though he might, he remained, well, a bungler. Given all the excitement, he might even bungle his recitations in Greek or Hebrew if he had them tonight.

He forced himself, finally, to lie down and try to sleep.

After an hour or so, he did sleep fitfully.

After another hour, a clamor in the courtyard woke him and told him that the merchants had arrived. Thank Heaven for it! It was the sweetest music to hear the confirming clatter of hooves as tired mules were led away to the stables. The party's servants were being directed to the barns, where they could sleep in the haylofts. The merchants themselves were going to bed down in the travelers' quarters along the western side of the courtyard, where the peddler and Oghrin and everyone—Keti included!—already slept. Or didn't sleep, more likely, given the racket and general disturbance. It was a great commotion and confusion, sure enough, but it was also a reassuring lullaby that helped Brother Arcadius fall back into a semblance of sleep. But then, sometime before dawn, the bell in the courtyard watchtower rang and kept on ringing.

How long had he slept? One hour? Two? Brother Arcadius sat up groggily, smoothed out his tunic, reached for his robe, put on his sandals. The ringing continued. It was the sort of ringing that signaled trouble, that called for Father Julian to come on the scene. Further sleep was out of the question. Brother Arcadius hurried to see what was happening. Other monks who were of the same mind were already emerging from their cells. Full of questions but wasting no time in talk, they converged on the courtyard in a silent stream.

It was dank and cold and very dark out: no moon, and layers of clouds that threatened chill rain. Brothers Sifari and Kongro, the usual day watch, had already arrived and taken over their duties. They, or more likely the night watch, had lit the hanging oil lamps that cast some light upon the dark scene. The light picked out the questioning faces of the merchant travelers who'd been called out by the sound of the bell. It fell upon Father Julian, who was just arriving. It fell upon the courtyard gate and door, both of which were closed and barred. It fell upon the furious face of Oghrin, who stood as if at bay with his rat-faced Ulka and his loutish sons beside him. Nowhere, nowhere did it fall upon Keti.

"Father," called Brother Sifari. "This man Oghrin arrived yesterday with three boys. Now he wants to leave with just two."

"I have to leave," snarled Oghrin. "I'm on my way to get work. He's sneaked off, I can't find him. You'll make me pay for another day. I don't have anything to pay you with. I can't find him. I didn't do anything to him. He just went off. You find him. Send him after me when you do. Let me go."

"You will not have to pay for another day, but you will not leave until we find the boy," said Father Julian.

"Well, where is he?" shouted Oghrin. "Where is he? Tell me that!"

"Perhaps you can tell us that," said Father Julian.

"I can't, and you can't make me stay here," snarled Oghrin. "You don't have any authority over me. Open the door and let me go."

"The question of authority will be settled later," said Father Julian evenly. The monastery's two biggest and strongest monks were now on the scene—the hulking Atalf and Ziegmunt. As Oghrin was to Keti, so, almost, were they to him. "Take this man to the prison house," Father Julian told them. "He is not a prisoner, so do not chain him. Give him whatever he needs for his comfort that is reasonable—blanket, pillow, bread, water, straw to lie on. Brother Rolfus and Brother Corvin, once he's been locked up, I want you to guard him. He must not be let loose until I give my permission."

"Not a prisoner?" screamed Oghrin. "You lock me up and say I'm not a prisoner? And what about her and them?" He pointed in fury to Ulka and the two boys, who were standing open-mouthed and shrinking back fearfully.

"They'll be given shelter in the kitchen," said Father Julian. "It's a comfortable place. And perhaps, after a while, they'll tell us where the boy Keti might be. Or perhaps they'll tell us now?" Ulka and the two boys stared mutely at him, then shook their heads. He shrugged. "All right then," he said to Brother Atalf and Brother Ziegmunt, and events unfolded swiftly. Struggling and shouting, Oghrin was taken off to the prison house that stood beyond Father Julian's residence. Brother Marcus, as cook, herded the three others into the silent kitchen, where Pangur Ban would still be mousing. The merchant travelers were asked if they'd seen a little boy. They looked at each other and shook their heads. Boy? They hadn't seen any little boy. They'd arrived in the dark, and they'd been tired.

"Well, we will have to search the grounds," said Father Julian. "We should start with the most likely places: the guest quarters, the kitchen which is both inviting and nearby, and then, I would say, the dining hall. All of these would be easy for the boy to get to and to hide in, and two of them he already knows. We must remember that he can neither speak nor hear. Therefore we had best search in silence, listening for any sound that he might make. Brothers Marcus, Salix, Embrosi, Mishel, Rosha, Adrianus, Arborius, head up groups, please, and decide among yourselves where you will search. Send someone after those who are still in their cells, and can help."

He spoke on, but the monks, although listening intently to his directions, were already forming groups in silence. For the most part, they went with the men they worked with every day. Brother Arcadius and his friend and fellow worker Brother Silvanus, the head librarian, found each other in the throng and went in silence over to Brother Marcus, who with three fingers in the air was signaling that he wanted three search groups for the kitchen and its storerooms and cellars. The silence, the orderliness overlaid great dismay.

Brother Sifari put into words what many were already thinking. "Father Julian," he said, "I wasn't on duty when the merchants came in last night, but you know how it is when a party like that arrives. It's all noise, confusion, commotion. The main gate is open, and the doors all round are open, and there's mules going this way and that, people milling around, unloading baggage, asking questions, getting lost, making demands—not to insult anybody, but that's just how it is. You just can't keep track of who's going where." He paused. From the prison house there now came a bellow of furious protest, and then another and another. "That fellow Oghrin could have come out and gone just about anywhere, and if—and if—"

"If the boy were dead, and Oghrin wrapped up the body and carried it like any bundle?" Father Julian's voice was very steady.

"That's what we have to think about, Father. He could have slipped outside and slipped back in again, and never be caught. He could have gotten as far as the pine woods, even."

As if in answer, more bellows of protest came from the prison house. The words were indecipherable, but guessable. "I didn't do it! He sneaked off! Let me go!"

"What you say is all too true, Brother Sifari," said Father Julian. "All the same, let us begin with the immediate area."

And so they did, but an hour later no boy had been found and no body. Brother Arcadius, weary, and as sick at heart as he'd ever been in his life, came up dusty and cobwebbed from his futile search through the kitchen's cellars, shelf by shelf, barrel by barrel, sack by sack. In the kitchen itself he'd seen Oghrin's family sitting like so many lumps in the corner, with old Brother Philippi keeping a pouchy eye on them. And he'd caught a glimpse of Pangur Ban, who was prudently tucking himself out of the way of all of this unaccountable activity. But there had been no trace of Keti, no small footprint in the cellar dust, nobody shivering in a shadowed corner. How bitter now to think that they'd waited all these extra hours to arrange Keti's rescue. They should have taken him into safety then and there at the dinner table—no, in the courtyard, the moment he'd arrived.

Pausing a moment before he joined a group searching elsewhere, Brother Arcadius stared out from the kitchen doorway into the courtyard, which by now should have been gilded with the first rays of the rising sun. But under the cloud cover above, everything was still dark, gray, chill, dank—barely lighter than it had been an hour ago. Squinting into the grayness, he could make out the figure of Brother Kongro, over there by the broken stretch of wall where Keti had stood the day before. Kongro was feeling around in the dark and yawning gap where stones had been removed and where so much of the inner core of rubble had fallen out. He was stepping back now and shaking his head. No boy, no body, nothing.

He saw Brother Arcadius watching. "Well, we can rule that out," he said. "A lot of the core has shifted around in there, and there's places he could have crawled into, but there's nothing. Seemed like a good place to look, though. He'd only have to get out of bed and sneak across the courtyard and climb in. He could've done that. Father Julian thought so—very much thought so. But Atalf, Ziegmunt, Miklas, Malachi, Bruno...they've all looked in there, and they've all come up with nothing. But I thought I'd give it another try. So where are you heading?"

"We've done the cellars, and we're going to search the kitchen garden again and the refectory again. I'm waiting for Brother Marcus to decide which one we should do first. He's pulling his crew off from the search to start the day's cooking."

"I guess he has to," said Brother Kongro. "People are going to need to eat breakfast." He moved on toward the courtyard door. "Well, good luck to you."

By now the area of search had long since widened. Brother Silvanus took over as Marcus's replacement. He and Brother Arcadius and the others who'd been with them, minus the kitchen crew, joined the monks who were combing the outside perimeter of the walls. The peddler and even some of the merchants had joined them and were searching just as intently as everyone else. Meanwhile, the bellows from Oghrin did not cease. The monks who were guarding him had been ordered to report immediately if he gave any clue to what might have happened, but as yet no clue had come. Maybe no clue could come. Maybe Oghrin really did not know what had happened to Keti. Maybe Keti had slipped out and run into the woods, and met disaster there in a fall, or in the cold, or who knew what.

Three hours later, with darkness persisting, but no chill drizzle yet falling, Brother Arcadius returned to the courtyard. He'd helped search the grounds as far as the fields and vineyards. He'd helped search the woods in the areas he was familiar with, the areas he knew from his walks. The areas of search were beginning to seem more and more improbable. The searchers, after returning in groups for quick mugfuls of breakfast gruel, had gone back to the fields and woods to search again, but with growing hopelessness. Standing alone in the silent courtyard, Brother Arcadius felt that he was coming close to his wits' end. Where to look next?

Where to look next?

He'd gained one thing, if not a thing else, from his lessons in reasoning with Father Julian: the simplest solution was most likely to be right.

Simplest.... Then what was simplest?

The kitchen was warm and inviting, but the living Keti had never been in the kitchen. The living Keti had been in the huge dining hall. The living Keti had been in the guests' quarters, which consisted of one big room with few places to hide in. The living Keti had stood by the scattered stones and the pile of rubble. The living Keti had stood by that gap in the wall. Atalf, Ziegmunt, Miklas, Malachi, Bruno, Kongro...six monks had searched in the gap with the utmost care. They'd reached in as far as the space allowed. They'd carefully felt this way and that for whatever might be there besides pebbles and earth. They'd listened for sounds of breathing, or sobbing, or anything that might be made by a living creature.

Where could his own arms reach, and what could his hands find, that theirs hadn't? What could his ears hear, if theirs had heard nothing? What use could a seventh try be, if six had failed?

A seventh try might be hopeless, but would it be worse than no seventh try at all?

No, another few moments of useless search would do no harm, but he dreaded finding a body. Dreaded finding the silent wreckage of a life wrongly taken. Couldn't believe, now, that there'd be anything else to find. Berating himself for being a chicken-hearted coward and no son of his brave brickmaker-warrior Da, Brother Arcadius moved toward the pile of rubble and the gap in the wall.

He felt ready indeed to burst into tears over anticipated failure—there'd be nothing there to find, or there'd be heartbreak—but he felt something else, too: soft fur and sprightly whiskers brushing across his bare and search-scratched ankles. "Pangur," he murmured. *Yes, chatter to Pangur to try to keep from weeping.* "Was it good mousing last night? Do you wonder what's going on? Shall I take you back to our cell for the day, so you won't get trampled when the search pours back here again? I'll take you there soon, all right?"

Pangur Ban was paying no attention. His tail had risen straight up, and his ears had become scoops to catch the faintest scritch or sigh that might be made by a mouse, or a bird, or.... He was trotting toward the broken wall, and he was leaping onto a ledge halfway up the pile of rubble, and his whole body seemed to have turned into a question.

A mouse, a nesting bird, or just pebbles shifting.... Why was he listening like that, what had he heard? Heart pounding, Brother Arcadius caught up with him. Maybe it was not a question of hearing, but rather of sensing. *Let there not be a body. Just let there not be a body.* He held his breath as Pangur peered up into the dark gap and mewed softly, once and then again. From within came a sliding and rattling of earth and pebbles. Pangur mewed a third time. The sliding and rattling increased. Something in there was scrabbling its way upward and forward. Something in there was whispering the smallest of whispers. Was scrabbling upward and forward and whispering, "Pangur...Ban."

And the whisper came again, and the small white face of Keti came into view. "You're *alive*," stammered Brother Arcadius. "You can *talk*!"

Keti flinched and drew back.

"And you can *hear*." Brother Arcadius could hardly speak himself. The lost was found. The lost was safe and alive. In one blinding instant, everything was different.

Keti shook his head and drew back farther.

Brother Arcadius came to his senses. "It's very, very safe to come out now, Keti," he said. "Oghrin is in prison, and can't get at you. And Pangur Ban wants you to come with him to the kitchen. Pangur Ban wants you to have a nice bowl of food, and we are going to keep you here where it's safe, and you won't have to go off with Oghrin when we make him leave. Or with Ulka and those others, either. Won't you come out for Pangur?"

He held his breath. Keti inched forward, but very hesitantly. His gaze was now fixed solely on Pangur Ban, who was sitting there, one paw upraised, the picture of expectation. For just a moment more, Keti hesitated. If the presence of Pangur seemed to be drawing him forward, fear of the world was clearly pulling him back. Then the core of rubble crumbled away beneath him. In a stream of pebbles and earth it shot him forward, straight into Brother Arcadius's arms. A small, chilled, shivering bundle of boy it was that he held there—a wonderful bundle!—grimy and sodden with piss, because it had been a long, cold, fearsome stretch of time to be hiding away and hearing Oghrin's roars and shouts and bellows, without knowing that Oghrin was locked up safe and sound.

Ringing the watchtower bell to call off the search.... Let others do that, others who didn't have Keti to hold. In joy too great for his belief, Brother Arcadius carried his prize toward the warm kitchen, with Pangur Ban leading the way. "Ulka and those big boys are in there, Keti," he said. "But we're sending them away with Oghrin, so don't worry, all right?"

Safe in his arms, Keti said nothing.

* * *

Father Julian's rare smile lit up the day. "So you can both hear and talk, Keti," he said.

Keti shook his head.

"It seems that you can."

"For Pangur," whispered Keti. "I can...for Pangur." It was a whisper that clearly was not used to being used. He was washed and warmly wrapped in a mound of spare blankets, and under Brother Salix's fierce gaze he'd been given careful spoonfuls of nourishing broth. Pangur Ban was purring in his arms. Ulka and the two loutish boys had been taken away to join Oghrin in the monastery prison, to share a meal of bread and cheese before being paid off and sent on their miserable way.

"Can you tell Pangur why you hid?" asked Father Julian.

"He told her...." whispered Keti.

"Oghrin told Ulka?"

"He told her...he told her in the bed...." Keti's whisper became deeper and rougher. He was being Oghrin, repeating what he'd heard Oghrin say. "He told her, 'Wait till the scrubland, all right? Then I'll kill him.'"

"And Ulka, what did she say?"

The whisper grew fainter. "She said, 'Good.'"

"So you hid," said Father Julian.

Keti said nothing.

"That was very wise and good of you, Keti. You heard that last night, I suppose, in the guests' quarters."

Keti said nothing, again.

"You got up then bravely in the night, and found a very good hiding place indeed, and we are all glad that you did so," said Father Julian. "But you don't have to hide again, because...do you see all these good monks standing around you? Brother Atalf there, and Brother Ziegmunt, and Brother Arcadius, and the rest? There's a lot of them, aren't there? And quite a few of them are much bigger and stronger than Oghrin besides. You will stay here with all that protection until you are bigger than Oghrin, even—and even beyond that, if you wish. In fact, you can stay here forever, if you care to, and we will keep you safe. Do you agree to that?"

For just a moment Keti stared around the kitchen in wonder. Then he bent his head lower over the cat in his arms. "Pangur *Ban*," he whispered.

* * *

"He's obviously an uncommonly intelligent boy," said Brother Salix. "A hardy one, too. Feigning deafness and dumbness all those years at his young age, and surviving that treatment and that night in the wall. It will be interesting to see what he makes of himself, won't it."

* * *

"Fact is," said Brother Marcus, "the boy was scared stupid just being around that wicked gang. It's no surprise that he couldn't talk or hear or hardly even move. He was stiff with fright, like a rabbit when it's cornered by the fox, eh? But he's thawing out. In the kitchen yesterday he spoke five words, and they weren't just 'Pangur Ban,' either. He's taking to kitchen work, too. Little jobs, but they do help out. Don't know what he'll want to do when he gets older, but I'm happy to have him as my kitchen boy for now."

* * *

"The boy was not in the wall," rumbled Brother Atalf. "But then the cat worked magic, and the boy formed, like, inside there, and Arcaperus found him. It was all magic, see?"

* * *

"Well, if you like those," said the peddler, "how about taking these too?" He reached into another sack and drew out a handful of buttons, his best glass buttons. The merchant nodded and smiled. The peddler smiled back. They'd become fast friends during the search for that little boy, so fortune was shining. He'd be riding double behind his new friend when they went on their way. It just went to show that good deeds sometimes got their rewards. Those wicked folk would be trudging along on foot through the wildlands, and if he rode by them, he'd thumb his nose at them, too. How Oghrin managed his family was Oghrin's business, but killing children was really going too far!

* * *

"There is no cat like you, Pangur Ban," said Brother Arcadius. "No cat in all the world. Keti would never have come out from that wall for any human being, Pangur. He came out only for you. He came out for you because, thank God, you called him. And do you know what I feel like these days, Pangur Ban? I feel like a big brother. I feel like—I practically feel like a Da. So thank you, Pangur Ban! Thank you for such a gift as Keti!"

"Meow," said Pangur Ban.

IV Days aftr asenshn day dir Tammis yul be suppriz

THE VISITING SCHOLAR

In which there are beautiful designs on a traveling
bag, and designs on other things, too

AD 899

At dawn, right after first prayers, Brother Arcadius, assistant librarian of Spiritus Sanctus monastery, joined his monastic brethren in the long, silent, shuffling line that was moving toward the kitchen doors and the morning's ration of gruel. As always, he nodded respectfully to the people around him, and did his best to blend in and not stand out.

That was not easy. Besides being only seventeen, the youngest monk in the monastery by a full ten years, he'd only been there for little more than a year. Most of the hard-working monks of Spiritus Sanctus —farming monks, stonecutting monks, goat-tending monks, latrine-shoveling monks, tree-felling monks—still didn't see the point of a scrawny, wide-eyed, redheaded person who hung around all day in that library *assisting* or whatever it was that he did, spoke in that finicky, *different* kind of way, and looked as if it wouldn't take much of a wind to blow him back to that place he said he'd come from...Dublin, or whatever it was. They didn't quite see the point of the library, either, but no matter. Spiritus Sanctus had always had a library, and it had always had a librarian. That was the normal and natural way of things. But two librarians....

Just as it always did, day in, day out, the line moved steadily along. Midday meals and suppers were more leisurely, and people ate them sitting down in the dining hall. Breakfast was a time to eat quickly and start the day's work.

"Pax vobis', Frars. Bon' gyoorna." Brother Marcus, the head cook, had come out himself, as always, to help serve the line. He was passing out bread and wishing peace and a good day to all his brethren in the fractured and melted-down Latin that was common now throughout the Frankish and even the Italian lands, the former Roman heartland. (Spiritus Sanctus stood more or less midway between the Frankish kingdoms to the north and Italy to the south.) Marcus was a broad-beamed, gravel-voiced, hospitable fellow who didn't care if people were short or not, newcomers or not, or librarians or not, as long as they liked his very excellent cooking. Brother Arcadius certainly did like it, so he'd had a friend in Marcus from the very start.

As always, Marcus was dressed for a long, overheated, clamorous, frenzied day in his beloved kitchen. Standing there robeless in his tunic and short breeches, with a clean rag wound about his head and stout sandals laced firmly up to his knees, he looked more like a pirate chieftain than a monk. When he saw Brother Arcadius coming up the line, he nodded and winked and mouthed the word "twenty." Brother Arcadius nodded back in full understanding as he took the bread that Marcus was offering him. Pangur Ban, the master mouser of Spiritus Sanctus, had killed twenty mice in the kitchen overnight.

Twenty was a very good tally, but not unusual in the least for Pangur Ban. Brother Arcadius took proper satisfaction from it, while making sure that he didn't give way to the demon of pride. The year before, on the long way from Dublin to Spiritus Sanctus, he'd stopped a cruel sailor from murdering a wretched, homeless half-grown kitten, and he'd brought that kitten with him to the monastery, and he'd named him Pangur Ban, a good Irish name that signified whiteness—not because Brother Arcadius favored whiteness particularly, but simply because Pangur happened to be white. No, there were no grounds for pride in any of that—there should not be grounds for pride in anything, really—but nonetheless it was pleasant to think about.

Pangur had become a hefty creature in the year since his rescue, wide of chest, big of paw, tireless in his pursuit of marauding mice. As Brother Marcus said every day, it was a marvel that the kitchen had ever gotten along without him. But he was not the only being who'd found refuge here. Just weeks ago, the whole monastery had turned out to save a little boy whose step-family aimed to kill him. Assistant librarians might not find a ready welcome from everyone, but small children in mortal danger were a different story. Everybody was very glad the boy was here, and now he was Brother Marcus's well cared-for kitchen helper and Brother Arcadius's own beginning pupil, and a very fine learner he already promised to be. At the moment, though, the solemn little fellow was nowhere to be seen. "Where's Keti this morning?" asked Brother Arcadius.

"Helping up a storm in the kitchen like he always is," said Brother Marcus, "when he's not practicing his *femina, feminae, feminineriniumerum* for you." Proper Latin endings and suchlike things held no interest for Marcus. Dismissing grammar with a wave of his hand, he leaned forward and lowered his voice. "So—how about that 'You Know What' at the library?" he asked.

"What 'You Know What'?" As far as Brother Arcadius knew, everything at the library was just going on as always, like the breakfast line.

"Oh, so you haven't heard yet? Then I can't tell you." Still beaming, Brother Marcus turned to greet the next monk coming up the line. "Peace to you, Brother...."

The library, a 'You Know What' at the library.... Mildly perplexed, Brother Arcadius went on down the line with his portion of bread. He held out his mug to Brother Alvas, one of the kitchen helpers, who filled it with breakfast gruel, a runny mixture today of mashed turnips and beans with dried berries. He swallowed this concoction in three gulps, knowing that there'd be tastier dishes later in the day. Walking on, he cleaned his mug to perfection with his piece of bread. He ate the bread while Brother Sandro, another kitchen worker, refilled his mug with a mixture of water and wine that was mostly water, the usual thing. He drank this quickly and headed off to the library, carrying his mug with him. There'd be time to take it back to his cell later on. As for that library thing that Brother Marcus knew about and he didn't....

Brother Arcadius shrugged. If it were some kind of trouble, Brother Marcus wouldn't have been beaming. Most likely it wouldn't be anything at all. Brother Marcus enjoyed hearing things first and then passing on hints about them, things that were very trivial more often than not. It wasn't proper monklike behavior, but nobody minded. A few faults could be overlooked for the sake of the cooking.

But all that was by the way. Here was the library, long and low, with its tiled roof and walls of gray stone. The sun came out in full strength as Brother Arcadius went up the single step and unlocked the door. He went in, leaving the bright day behind him for the moment. Then one by one, he unlocked the window shutters and drew them back. Sunlight streamed in. Brother Arcadius felt peace and contentment settle upon him. He loved his work at the library as much as Brother Marcus loved cooking or Pangur Ban loved mousing, and he loved the very sight of the place itself, outside and in. He saw no sign of anything different as he looked about him, no 'You Know What,' whatever that might be. There was only the usual room, the room he was glad to be in.

It was about twenty moderate paces long and thirteen wide, this wonderland of his, solidly built of stone. The two long sides were divided into bays or alcoves, five to a side, separated by stone pillars and arched windows, each with its close-fitting shutters of sturdy oak. Each alcove held a cabinet of fragrant cedar, with doors that locked at night but opened to reveal five shelves inside. Each cabinet could hold a hundred manuscripts, more or less. So the ten cabinets together, if and when they were ever wholly filled, would hold the astounding total of a thousand books. This number had not yet been achieved.

It probably never would be, thought Brother Arcadius. Attending once more to his tasks, he unlocked and opened the cedar cabinets to reveal the precious manuscripts inside. Over the years, Spiritus Sanctus had managed to accumulate five hundred complete and undamaged books, well bound in good black leather, and that was a lot. But getting five hundred more would not be easy. One more book, even, would be a cause for rejoicing. Was that what the 'You Know What' was, another book?

Brother Arcadius daydreamed briefly of a new book for the shelves, with poetry in it.

In the long, long ago there'd been thousands and thousands of books in the world. So he'd been told, although he could barely imagine it. Thousands and thousands of books of all different kinds. Poetry, and plenty of it. Every last word of great works like the Iliad and the Odyssey, whose fame had come down through the ages, but that now were said to exist in bits and pieces alone. And geographies, and books about the skies above, and books about adventurous journeys, and books of nature, and much more. But Rome had fallen and most of those books were lost. They'd been destroyed in burning buildings, or floods, or wars. They'd been ripped up and used as kindling by uncaring people, or to stop up chinks in walls. Abandoned, forgotten, they'd been consumed by gnawing creatures, or worms, or beetles, or been covered with mold....

But many, it was thought, were safe and sound in the far-off city of Constantinople, which had been Rome's partner and yet had never fallen. It was still a magnificent city, so it was said, and very likely it still had many, many thousands of books. But people didn't just go strolling off to Constantinople. It was worth your life to get there and if you did, you were treated like a pest and an intruder, and kept dangling for days and months or even years, and were then just sent home without even glimpsing a book. Or so the few people said who had ever been there. There were many books and much learning in the lands of the Arabs and the communities of the Jews too, so it was said, but there again the problem was to get there, and be allowed to come away with books if you did get there, and then get them safely home.

And there'd never, for hundreds of years, been the peace that was needed to sit down and make new books, either, at least not in great numbers. To think of what to say in the first place, and then write down all the words, letter by letter—all that took time. And there weren't many schools, like there'd been in the long ago. People didn't have much to read, so they didn't much care if they had schools or not. Even kings, or a great many of them, didn't know how to read. People learned what they needed to know by word of mouth. Old or new, books were hard to come by, and that's how it was.

Brother Arcadius took the library's feather duster down from its peg. Tenderly, carefully, he dusted the books and their shelves, getting things ready for the head librarian—formerly the only librarian—Brother Silvanus, who'd be in before long. He dusted the library's several different accounts of the life and doings of Charlemagne, and its several copies, with some contradictions, of Charlemagne's laws. He dusted Saint Augustine's *City of God*. He dusted the very thrilling and very agreeably long poem about the heroic death of Charlemagne's paladin Roland. He dusted the ten fine copies of Aristotle's various works. He dusted row upon row of saints' lives, and many volumes of the deliberations and deeds of the Fathers of the Church. Nine cabinets in all he dusted, inside and out, along with the books that they held. Then he turned to the tenth cabinet.

He hadn't even unlocked it yet. He did so now. It contained a single book. Just as he did every day before touching this book, he took a clean rag from a nearby basket and wiped his hands carefully again and again. Only then did he let himself touch the miracle that lay there. It was a copy of the Book of Genesis. Sometime in its unknown past, it had lost its cover and been rebound in ordinary black. But the original cover must have been one of those bejeweled, gold-clasped things that mighty lords like the late Charlemagne liked to carry about with them, whether they could read the words within or not.

That the cover had been magnificent was made clear by the pages themselves. A great, great artist, now unknown, had spared no effort and no expense to make them a glorious riot of design and color. Gold leaf, silver leaf, lapis lazuli, crimson, ultramarine...the text itself ran down the middle of each page in a single narrow column, in scarlet, and each penstroke was a marvel. But beyond even the beautiful penstrokes were the pictures—tiny, perfect, gleaming pictures of God creating the world; of the stars, the planets, the comets, the clouds, the trees, the flowers; of the creatures of forest, field, stream, ocean, and sky; of a spry little Eve peering saucily out from behind an exquisite capital A, apple in hand; of the Ark careening on a surging sea, the waves curling, fishes leaping, seabirds frolicking—

A small bundle of living gold hurtled in through the window behind Brother Arcadius: a frantic goldfinch, with Pangur Ban in close pursuit. Brother Arcadius shooed the bird back out the window and scooped up the cat. Pangur struggled briefly in protest, then accepted a petting. "Good morning, Pangur Ban!" said Brother Arcadius. "What brings you here besides birds?"

"Mrrow," said Pangur Ban.

"Congratulations on the twenty mice," said Brother Arcadius. ("Mrrow.") "Or it could be more, eh? Maybe Brother Marcus didn't find all the bodies. Could be you ate some. And for sure you've had your morning bowl of cheer." Even before poking up the kitchen fires in the dawn light, Brother Marcus always started the day by giving Pangur a small bowl of delicacies, to reward him for the night's mousing—on weekends, he filled the bowl with the kitchen's famous fish paste, even, or equally famous herbed game stew. "Do you need to eat birds too, Pangur Ban? I don't think so."

"Mrrow." Pangur stretched and yawned and padded off to a favorite corner. Brother Arcadius took up another clean rag, a very soft one, and whisked invisible dust away from the beautiful Genesis. Even feather dusters, he thought, might damage it. Then he locked it away again. Maybe someday Brother Silvanus might find a safe way to share it with the rest of the monks at Spiritus Sanctus. In the meantime, it had to be kept away from well-meaning fingers that might do it harm. Father Julian, head of the monastery, knew of its presence, of course. But nobody else did...not even Brother Marcus.

Now Brother Arcadius turned to his next task of the day, the main one. A fair number of his brethren could read, but didn't much like to.

Brother Dietrich, Brother Salix, Brother Kongro, little Brother Zossimus the woodcarver—these few and a handful of others came to the library quite regularly of their own accord. The rest stayed away. Father Julian and Brother Silvanus had decided that it might help if each book had an index, a handy guide to its contents. Readers who didn't like reading might like it more if they didn't have to thumb through pages that didn't interest them to find pages that did, or wait for a librarian to look things up for them. There'd be less wear and tear on the precious books as well.

There were hundreds of these guides that had to be made. Brother Arcadius had started a new one the previous day. His basket of supplies was there on the long reading table that few people ever read at, but maybe soon that would change. He sat down and took out the book he'd been working on. Its cover was just like the cover of every other book in the library, plain black with no words on it. Keeping it in the basket allowed him to find it at once when he needed it, without having to search around. Telling one book from another was one more problem that hadn't yet been quite solved. With so few readers asking for books, though, that problem could wait.

Pen, ink, a dish of sand to help dry the ink, yet another rag to wipe his hands on, the half-finished index on its piece of parchment— Brother Arcadius arranged these things before him and bent to his task: "Saint Regulus, born, page XI; Beheaded, page XII...." Pangur Ban, purring gently and rhythmically, jumped back onto the windowsill and curled up at ease there, so he could keep one eye out for more birds. Brother Arcadius noted the relocation approvingly. It was a great part of Pangur's goodness that he never interfered with a person's work, but always stayed so neatly out of the way.

"Walks to Rome with head under arm, page XIII...."

"Hail Caesar!" called a dry voice from the library door. Brother Arcadius set down his pen and turned to greet his mentor and immediate superior, Brother Silvanus. Brother Silvanus greatly enjoyed reminding his young assistant that in the latter days of the Roman Empire there had been a disastrous emperor named Arcadius—young also, but degenerate and basically witless. A rumpled-looking, generally unsmiling, tender-hearted sparrowhawk of a man, Brother Silvanus also enjoyed pretending to be exasperated by the people he treasured most: Brother Marcus the cook, Brother Salix the medicus, and Brother Arcadius himself. Father Julian, head of the monastery, was the exception. Brother Silvanus treasured him, yes, but would never dream of *pretending* anything with him. None of the other monks would, either. But young Arcadius was fair game. "I see you managed to find both your mug and the library this morning," Silvanus now said. He moved briskly into the room.

"I did," said Brother Arcadius. He was used to Silvanus's jokes now, and was able to mostly ignore them. He went straight to the thing that had been at the back of his mind most of the morning. "Um, Brother Marcus said—"

"I can guess what he said," said Brother Silvanus. He sat down at the other side of the table. "If that man doesn't stop putting his ear to the ground, it's going to get stepped on, eh?"

"Well, he didn't actually say anything straight out, but he hinted, as you might put it, that—"

"He probably gave you a hint that there's going to be a surprise, and he's quite right. We're getting a visitor, Arcadius. A visitor who's going to be with us for thirty days. A visitor from Sancta Onafria monastery. Master Tullius."

Brother Arcadius sat bolt upright. "Master—"

"Tullius, yes," said Brother Silvanus calmly. "That's why it took me so long to get here this morning. Father Julian wanted a word with me about it. It seems that there's a large party of merchants who plan to pass by here on their way to somewhere in the northwest—some sort of deal in wool is involved, I believe. They're traveling with a large contingent of hired guards for security. So Tullius is taking advantage of that to travel with them and stop here a while. He wants to see how we do things here in the library. When they head homeward again a month from now, he'll go back with them. Sancta Onafria, of course, would have no trouble providing guards on its own, so this arrangement will be some sort of a money saver." Brother Silvanus's eyes narrowed, but they glinted with humor. "As if they aren't rich enough there already."

"And they have a *thousand books*," said Brother Arcadius with awe. It was the one and only place he knew of that had that many. And Master Tullius was a scholar of such secure renown that he could assume the family name of the mighty Cicero of long ago—Tullius— and not be criticized or ridiculed by anyone.

"A thousand more or less," said Brother Silvanus. "I wouldn't be surprised if they had more by now." He gave his unnerved assistant a dry but kindly look. "But we have a fine library too, wouldn't you say? I'm sure he can learn at least something worthwhile from us. We'll start preparing for the visit tomorrow."

Brother Arcadius found it hard to sleep that night. Thoughts of Sancta Onafria with its thousand books, and Master Tullius with his awesome reputation, kept invading his thoughts and his few scattered dreams. Sancta Onafria was located three hundred miles away, in the Italian uplands. It had been founded perhaps eighty years before by the Scarpia clan, for the primary purpose of saying masses for their souls. Those masses had been much needed. Back then, the Scarpias had all been ruthless, brutal, steely-eyed mercenaries—the worst of the worst, or the best of the best, depending upon one's point of view. For hundreds and hundreds of miles around in those days, no ruler with enough money to pay them went to war without hiring Scarpian mercenaries—in fact, for years, wars throughout the region had been mainly a matter of pitting Scarpias against Scarpias, not the actual family members, necessarily, but the troops they trained and armed.

Having heaped up riches by swimming uncaringly through seas of blood, the Scarpias then made an equally huge success of every aspect of the indispensable olive oil business—producing olive oil, storing it, vending it wholesale, transporting it, everything. Washed clean, so to speak, by oil, they had become respectable, richer than ever, and welcome in the courts of the mighty, many of whom depended on Scarpian loans to get by. In fact, it was very likely that a Scarpia would become pope within the next decade or two.

In other words, the Scarpias were well able to pour immense wealth into their monastery and make it a leader in everything: in coined money and notes of credit and in accumulated actual treasure, glorious things of diamonds and gold; in holy relics of awe-inspiring lineage; in the splendor and sincerity of its masses; in its library. They were still more than able to protect their holdings at sword's point, too. Everybody knew that, and everybody conceded that what the Scarpias had, barring acts of God, the Scarpias were going to keep.

However, the doings of the monastery were kept strictly separate from the doings of war and the oil business. While "Onafria" was indeed the name of a saint (an imaginary or invented saint, some people unkindly said), it was also the name of the Scarpia clan's founding matriarch. For the sake of her honor, and the clan's honor, the purity and holiness of everything pertaining to her had to be of the highest order, well shielded from the nasty details of getting and keeping. After all, the clan had its finer feelings too, and those feelings had found refuge in Sancta Onafria's beautiful and peaceful monastery.

It was unlikely indeed that Master Tullius had the slightest contact, even mentally, with what might be called the business end of things.

"Did you ever meet him face to face?" a sleep-starved Brother Arcadius blearily asked the head librarian, next day.

"Never did," said Brother Silvanus. "We were students at the same time, of course, if that's what you're thinking. But when I was in Paris, he was at Rheims, and vice versa. All I ever knew about him was what I kept hearing: superb this, superb that, astonishing command of detail, overpowering orator, and so on. The rest of us were always in his shadow. 'You're no Tullius, Silvanus'—I heard that a thousand times if I heard it once. Except that he didn't go by the name of 'Tullius' as a student. He was just plain Primus Candidus then. But that wasn't his real name either. His actual name was Frankish, or so I've heard, but he never used it. So I can't tell you what it was." Brother Silvanus clapped his hands briskly. "Anyway—*Caesar*—what do you think we should single out for his attention when he gets here? What books should we show him?"

This was the sort of testing question that Brother Silvanus enjoyed asking. Brother Arcadius pulled himself together. His sleepless night had not been entirely a waste of time. "Well...church history is his main interest, isn't it? He'll naturally want to look at everything we have on that, which is a lot." A lot for Spiritus Sanctus, anyway; maybe not for Sancta Onafria. "And he ties church history in very much with the proper reading of the fixed stars and the five planets, so we ought to bring out what we've got on that from Aristotle and Ptolemaeus. I don't imagine we can show him much on that score that he doesn't already know."

"I agree with you on all points," said Brother Silvanus. "Now, what else?"

"I think we should show him our Genesis," Brother Arcadius said firmly. "Our beautiful Genesis."

"The Genesis, yes," said Brother Silvanus. "I believe we'll make Tullius jealous. Anything else?"

There was the trunkful of single pages and pieces of pages. "I'd like him to see some of the fragments, too. It would be so good if he could shed some light on them...."

The days that followed both raced and crawled by. Raced, because there was so much to do. Crawled, because there was so much to anticipate. But at last—at last!—the cry of "In view! In view!" went up from Brother Kongro in the courtyard watchtower, signaling that the travelers were in sight. The cry was hardly needed: the dust raised by so many plodding hooves and trudging feet was signal enough. Father Julian went out to the courtyard. Brother Silvanus and Brother Arcadius followed, as representatives of the library. The courtyard gate was opened, the first mules came through, the first merchants dismounted. Brother Bruno, the stable master, was pointing out the way to the pasture to the party's servants. Weary mules were being led away. Everything was dust, controlled commotion, questions, answers, bustling busyness...

And then he came.

He rode in on a handsome white mule, dismounted easily, and stood in the sunlight, hands on hips. Father Julian went forward. Host and guest clasped hands and exchanged greetings. Brother Arcadius hastily revised the picture of Master Tullius that he'd had in mind. He'd imagined that the great scholar would be mild, abstracted, otherworldly, on the small side, maybe, like Brother Arcadius himself, or Brother Silvanus. Instead, Tullius stood a good half-head higher than Father Julian, who was not immensely tall, true, but not short either. The scholar's shoulders were broad, his nose long and arched, his eyes hooded, his smile confident, his teeth all there and blazing white. His ringing voice was...it was what a crow's might sound like, if a crow were speaking human words in long, complicated Latin sentences, with touches of Greek thrown in. But assistant librarians were not supposed to be staring at their betters, or eavesdropping on their conversations. Brother Arcadius pulled his attention away from the man, and concentrated on the man's accoutrements instead.

His robe, for instance. Plain gray though it was, in weave and cut it was finer by far than anything that Father Julian ever wore. His sandals boasted no rich tooling, but were clearly crafted from the very best leather and had silver clasps. The crucifix around his neck, although also very plain, appeared to be a masterpiece of ivory and pearl. His traveling bag....

The traveling bag was a wonder. Master Tullius now unslung it from his shoulder in an easy swoop and set it on the ground. It was made of *carpet*. Brother Arcadius knew that carpets abounded in the courts of kings and so forth. He himself had seen only one in his life, the small one that belonged to Father Julian's room of state, but not to Father Julian in person: it went with the office, not the man. Brother Arcadius had always admired that silky red carpet with its elaborate multi-colored figures, but the carpet comprising the bag of Master

Tullius seemed silkier and more elaborate in design even than that—and yet it was a traveling bag!

A large one, too. The sides stood straight up without giving a hint as to what might be inside. And the cover folded straight down over one side, and was lashed tightly shut by what looked to be silk cords passing in complicated ways through silver loops. It would take some time to fasten the bag properly, no doubt about it. Once it was fastened, though, the contents would be secure from even the heaviest downpour. But what contents? One of the party's servants was now standing behind Master Tullius with a neat bundle of the great man's belongings. So did the carpet bag hold—might it just possibly hold?—a choice book or two from the Sancta Onafria library? To be read, discussed, and maybe even *kept*?

But now: "Brother Arcadius, our assistant librarian," Father Julian was saying. With mingled distress and elation, Brother Arcadius emerged from his hopeful thoughts and stepped forward to be noticed by the great man.

The notice lasted for the merest flick of time. "Arcadius, yes," said Master Tullius in his cawing voice. He gave a single swift nod and then his hooded eyes went straight to Brother Silvanus. "This will be the *head* librarian, I believe?" he said with his confident smile. "My fellow student, Silvanus? We meet at last?" His eyes peered warmly down at Silvanus. Then they peered farther down still, and the warmth went out of them. There at his richly sandaled feet, a white shape had materialized out of nowhere with a soft, questioning cry of "Mrrwr"—Pangur Ban! Alight with interest, the big cat was laying inquisitive paws on Master Tullius's traveling bag and sniffing at it intently.

"Arcadius...." Father Julian rarely raised his voice and did not do so now. He didn't have to. Red-faced, Brother Arcadius already had Pangur Ban in his arms. Pangur, who had always been a cat of such tact and courtesy! Pangur, who could be counted on not to be a nuisance! Pangur, who probably should have been shut up for this great occasion! Brother Arcadius stammered an apology.

"It is of no matter," said Master Tullius, but he swept the carpet bag back over his shoulder anyway. "No matter at all. I believe that in Book Five, chapter seven, line ten—at least in the Onafria edition—of his treatise on the animal kingdom, Aristotle tells us that animals' desires are not controlled by reason, and therefore we must not blame them for what they do." He turned back to Brother Silvanus. "Now, as you were saying, dear colleague?"

That evening, still mortified, Brother Arcadius carried Pangur to the kitchen to begin the night's mousing. After more than a full year of mousing duty, Pangur knew the routine and all the ways to the kitchen by heart and usually trotted there on his own. Tonight, though, Brother Arcadius felt in need of a down-to-earth word or two with the cook, in a nice warm place with tantalizing and comforting smells all around him. The cook did not fail him.

"Oh, I saw the whole thing from the kitchen," Brother Marcus said matter-of-factly in his gravelly voice. "Happened to be just looking out. Snubbed you, didn't he."

"I wouldn't call it snubbing, exactly," said Brother Arcadius miserably. He'd been battling the demons of wounded pride ever since Master Tullius had dismissed him with a single glance. There was no reason, after all, why a scholar like Master Tullius should give any thought at all to an assistant librarian, was there? Of course there wasn't!

"All right, don't," said Brother Marcus. He glanced fondly down at Pangur Ban, who was already slinking along the walls, listening, peering, sniffing even, for foolhardy mice. "And then our Whitey put himself forward and caused a little upset, too. Was Father Julian annoyed?"

"You can't tell with Father Julian."

"And Silvanus?"

"He just made a big joke out of it, later on. You know him."

"So why the long face, Arcadius?"

"I don't know why," said Brother Arcadius untruthfully. He'd had a different picture of how things would go, that was all. And he did wish—he always wished—that the cook would call Pangur Ban by his proper Irish name and not by "Whitey," in his atrocious Latin—"Alpi." But was it right to take his hurt feelings out on the cook? It wasn't! He forced a smile. "I'm all right..."

"That's the spirit," said Brother Marcus. "Here, hold out your hand and I'll give you some raisins, all right? Tomorrow's another day!"

And indeed it was. Master Tullius, needless to say, was not in the line for breakfast gruel. Visiting grandees breakfasted in seclusion with Father Julian, and stayed in comfortable quarters next to his own. The merchants had been put up, of course, in regular guest quarters where comfort was not a prime consideration, any more than it was in the monks' own cells. The merchants, in any case, were eager to be on their way, had their own food supplies with them, and were already assembling in the courtyard prior to setting off.

Brother Arcadius swallowed his gruel, bread, and watered wine even more quickly than usual. When he reached the library, he was grateful to see that Brother Silvanus was already there before him, opening the cabinets and the shutters. He looked up at his assistant's approach. "Good morning, O Mighty Caesar."

Oh, piffle on "Mighty Caesar." Brother Arcadius had weightier things on his mind. "Should we try to keep Pangur Ban out of here today?" he asked with dignity.

"How would we do that?" asked Brother Silvanus.

"I could keep him shut up in my cell, I suppose." The very thought put Brother Arcadius on edge. He could just imagine Pangur Ban's wildly active indignation. The cat was used to coming and going through the window, just as he pleased.

"Let's not do anything like that unless we have to," said Brother Silvanus. He paused and frowned. "You're not still brooding about that bag, are you, Arcadius? As our scholarly friend said yesterday in his own way, or rather Aristotle's way, cats will be cats. Put it behind you. Nobody except you thought twice about it. Let's get on with our work."

They did so. In due course, stately footsteps were heard on the path outside and Master Tullius appeared at the door. His cawing voice rang out. "Eureka! I have found it! Right at the end of the walkway, as Father Julian advised me." He entered and peered around, ducking his head as if in close quarters—the ceiling was a good two feet above that head, but no matter. "How would you like me to spend my day, Silvanus?"

"In any way you please, Tullius," said the head librarian. "But my fine young assistant here and I *both* thought you'd like to start by having a look at our books on church history. Brother Arcadius has chosen a few for you. Please do sit wherever you'll be comfortable. Outdoors even—there are benches—or in your room, if you'd prefer."

Master Tullius nodded graciously. "Most perceptive of you, Silvanus. I would indeed like to start with your church histories. But I can sit right here at this table, no problem at all." He settled himself on a bench. "Bring out your choices, and I'll lose myself in the world of our noble Fathers." He glanced up. "By any chance would you have some spare parchment for notes?"

"We take notes on waxed tablets, usually," said Brother Silvanus. Parchment was expensive, and never "spare."

"Of course, of course!" cried Master Tullius. "Of course! I apologize for not thinking of your circumstances! I can make do perfectly well—I believe—with a waxed tablet, only hoping that the words will not be effaced by heat on the way back to Sancta Onafria."

It was a valid point. At the head librarian's somewhat vexed nod, Brother Arcadius brought out five sheets of parchment, along with pens and ink, and set them down beneath the scholar's gaze. He set down the books he'd chosen, too. Then, selecting a place for himself at the farthest end of the table, he got back to work.

"Saint Alecticus, born and executed, page CIV; miracles, pages CIV-CVII, carried to Heaven by angels..."

Across from him, Brother Silvanus got to work on an index also. Master Tullius leafed through one book and then another, frowning, barely reading, taking—so far, so good!—not a single note on a single sheet of precious parchment. Except for the turning of pages and the scratching of pens, the room was silent. From outside came birdsong and the distant voices of monks, but otherwise there was nothing to disturb even a great scholar's concentration. But then a large bee zoomed through a window and out again. Master Tullius gazed after it as if with uncomprehending eyes. Didn't bees come through library windows at Sancta Onafria?

Master Tullius lay down his pen. "Silvanus," he said, "where are your other assistants?"

"There are no others," said the head librarian. "It's Arcadius here, and myself."

"Can that be true?" murmured Master Tullius. He smiled faintly. Brother Arcadius glanced up from his index, then down again. Master Tullius's smiles yesterday had been wide, gleaming smiles of confidence, or something like confidence. This smile was different, and Brother Arcadius couldn't put a name to it. The glum thought came to him that trying to do so would probably keep him awake that night, too.

"It can indeed be true," said Brother Silvanus.

"And your copyists? When do they arrive?"

"The copyists are here," said Brother Silvanus. "Arcadius, and myself."

"Can you be saying that out of, what, 150 monks on these premises, you have no copyists?"

"Yes, that's what I'm saying. Whether it's growing our food or copying books, we monks do all of our own work here. We do get our olive oil from outside sources—from *your* sources, I believe...." Brother Silvanus paused and raised his eyebrows. The name "Scarpia" hung unspoken in the air. "And local huntsmen bring in the game for our cook's famous stews. But our monks' own hard toil takes care of most everything else. There are no extra hands to be spared for the library."

Master Tullius said nothing, but his mysterious smile did not fade. He paged again through the books that lay before him. Then he rose and went over to the third cabinet. "There is more church history here, you say?"

"That cabinet and the ones on either side are all church history," said Brother Silvanus. "As you know, those books are easiest to come by."

"May I help myself?"

"Certainly you may help yourself."

Master Tullius went back to the table with three more books, opened one, read a while from it, and then carefully wrote one brief note. "I will not waste the parchment," he assured Brother Silvanus. "I realize that I am not at Sancta Onafria."

Silence fell again. Brother Arcadius added a new saint to his index. It was hard to keep his mind on his work, though. His thoughts kept straying back to Master Tullius's traveling bag and the gift of books that it might contain. That it *ought* to contain, an unmonklike voice whispered inside his head. A month's hospitality surely warranted a gift, library to library. Wasn't that so? His thoughts also kept returning to Pangur Ban. It would be pleasant for sure to see him come in right now, and give him a morning hello, and scratch him under the chin and behind the ears. But if he came in, then there'd be that odd smile and those cawing comparisons of Spiritus Sanctus with Sancta Onafria, not in the former's favor. *Stay away awhile, Pangur, all right?*

"Mrrow."

As if thinking about him had summoned him out of thin air, Pangur Ban appeared on his favorite window sill. He paused there a moment, head cocked, scrutinizing Master Tullius up and down with what appeared to be friendly interest. The great man paused in his work, pen uplifted. Brother Arcadius stood up of his own accord and made ready to scoop up the cat and carry him away, before any breech of courtesy occurred. But Pangur merely poured himself down to the floor, glanced once over his shoulder at the new man sitting there, then ambled over to the nearest pillar, stretched up, and kneaded his forepaws against the stone.

"It enters the library then," said Master Tullius faintly. His brows met in a frown and his nostrils flared. He eyed the cedar cabinets narrowly, no doubt seeking out claw marks. Well, none were to be found, and none ever would be! Master Tullius cleared his throat. "Does it not...spray?"

"He's neutered, Tullius," said Brother Silvanus easily. "He keeps the library free of mice, you know. We call him Pangur Ban. How do you keep mice out of your library?"

"Our servants make sure that there is no way for vermin to enter. Interstices between stones are promptly sealed."

"That's excellent," said Brother Silvanus. After one last searching, inquisitive look at the perturbed scholar, Pangur withdrew to the far end of the room and curled himself up in a corner. Work resumed, the day went on, the work day ended.

"Exactly what are you working on these days, Tullius?" asked Brother Silvanus the following morning. "Or would you prefer I didn't ask?"

"Of course you may ask," said Master Tullius. For an hour now he'd been restlessly taking books on church history from their shelves, glancing through them, making an occasional note, setting some books aside for another look, reshelving others at random. "Although I must interject that I am afraid I am disrupting your shelving arrangements. I have been unable to determine what those might be, and have not wanted to interrupt your work, Silvanus, to ask." He glanced at Brother Arcadius, then away. There was no point in asking *assistant* librarians for any information whatever.

"As I thought I'd already indicated," said Brother Silvanus, "there are no particular shelving arrangements. Of course there should be, and there will be. But one thing at a time. As long as books go back to the right cabinets, we don't worry much. As I said, we don't get many readers in here at present. Arcadius and I are always able to track down any book, given a reasonable amount of time."

"At Sancta Onafria," Master Tullius began. He shook his head briefly, as if to resettle his thoughts. "But you asked about my work." He leaned forward intently. "As I'm sure you'll agree, Silvanus, nothing is more important than the history of our Church. No detail of that history should be left unexplored. My own focus is on the great Council of Nicaea, in the year 325, where so many crucial decisions were made. My aim—and perhaps it is presumptuous—is to recreate accurately the appearance of the heavens above at the time and location of the council: the positions of the five planets in particular, and their relationship to each other and to the sun and the moon and the zodiac."

"How would you do that, Tullius?" Brother Silvanus looked puzzled, wary, perhaps impressed. Brother Arcadius himself did not know what to think.

"By minutely examining the decisions of the participating Fathers, Silvanus, as attested to by reliable authorities. When each decision is thoroughly understood, one can then work out the planetary relationships that must have brought that decision about. It ties one's brain into knots, Silvanus, believe me," said Master Tullius proudly. "But I believe that, if I persevere, I shall contribute greatly to human knowledge. Of course, as I said, I must be careful to use only authorities that can be absolutely relied upon. Which leads me to ask, Silvanus, what might be contained in that trunk over there. Iron-plated, always locked—might that be where you keep your choicest volumes?" He glanced unfavorably at the book that lay open before him.

"No," said Brother Silvanus. "We keep no volumes in there of any kind. That trunk holds just pieces of things, collected from everywhere, mere sentences, often, or parts of sentences—badly damaged, hard to read, often even harder to understand."

"Oh, such things would never do," said Master Tullius. "I hold that it is essential to work from whole, undamaged sources, perfect, as the heavens are perfect—as the sun and the moon and the five planets describe perfect circles in their paths around the earth: so Aristotle and Ptolemaeus assure us in their wisdom. A damaged thing obviously has not found favor with God Almighty, and must at all costs be avoided. At Sancta Onafria, we do not accept *fragments*."

"They can be very interesting, though," said Brother Silvanus. He went to the first cabinet in the row behind him, and held up a battered piece of parchment. "I put this aside the other day as something that might fascinate you. Arcadius here and Father Julian also agreed to the choice. It's a scrap of what appears to be a dialogue between a young woman and a ruler. She pleads with him on behalf of her dead brother, who died out of favor and whose body has been denied proper burial. She appeals to the gods to hear her. The ruler remains unmoved. It's only those few lines, but one feels the power and tragedy of it, Tullius. Father Julian believes it may well be a fragment of a lost drama by Sophocles of Athens, who is mentioned so often in the old sources: not in his own hand of course, but written by a copyist who was surely closer to his time than we are."

"She appeals to the gods?" asked Master Tullius, eyebrows aloft. "Then it is pure paganism, and should be completely destroyed, instead of merely partially. The pagans we can trust and learn from are already known—Aristotle and Cicero, of course, leading the way. The others, Silvanus, are beneath our notice, or worse. They are likely to be *anathema.*"

"I thank you for your learned opinion, Tullius," said Brother Silvanus. He went to the farthest cabinet in the row and brought forth a black-bound book—*the* book. "Here is something that is slightly damaged, but I doubt we could say that it is not favored of God." He set the beautiful Genesis down in front of Master Tullius, and stepped back to see the effect. Frowning, Tullius turned to the first page, then the second, and the third. He tightened his lips and narrowed his eyes. He scanned a fourth page, and a fifth. Then he closed the book and set it firmly aside.

"The word of God itself, of course, cannot be damaged," he said. "When I reject damaged sources, they are earthly sources, human sources. Nonetheless...if you will, I would like to keep this book by me for further inspection, for already I see that it contains notable imperfections in translation: 'moved forward,' for instance, instead of the more elegant 'advanced,' and 'spoke' instead of the more sonorous 'uttered.' Biblical translations should be done in the highest style, would you not agree?" Master Tullius nodded affirmatively to himself, and put the offending Genesis aside. His lips curved slightly once more in that perplexing smile.

Lying on his narrow cot that night, Brother Arcadius dreamed fitfully that he was Noah, frantically trying to keep the Ark from dashing to pieces on the rocks. Terrified elephants and hippopotami—cats too—were lunging back and forth across the deck, out of control. A bird at last appeared in the sky, but it was a cawing crow with a mutilated black book in its beak, not a cooing dove of peace with an olive branch. A rainbow formed, then turned horribly upside down.

The dream presaged trouble. "Arcadius," said a cawing voice next day. Brother Arcadius looked up in astonishment from his work. Yes, it was true. Master Tullius was addressing him, not Brother Silvanus. He realized immediately that this was out of necessity. The head librarian was not to be seen, and must have stepped out for some reason. "Yes, Master Tullius?"

"Father Julian said that I should take the matter up with you. It pertains to the cat."

"Oh."

"The cat was lurking outside my door this morning. When I emerged into the corridor, not knowing the cat was there, it tried to get in. It was very difficult, Arcadius, to make it go away. Is this sort of thing going to continue?"

"Certainly not, Master Tullius. He's never entered that building before. Really he hasn't. I'll do everything possible to make sure it doesn't happen again."

"I cannot accept 'everything possible,' Arcadius. I can only accept the complete absence of the cat from outside my door."

"I understand, Master Tullius." Brother Arcadius bent again to his work, but a whirlwind of thoughts stormed in his dream-battered head. How, how to keep Pangur Ban out of trouble? The obvious solution occurred to him at last. The same herb that attracted most cats like straw to amber caused Pangur Ban to back quickly away, who knew why? The answer probably lay in Aristotle somewhere. In his first free moments that day, Brother Arcadius hurried to the kitchen garden. Catmint abounded there, in pots so that it would not spread all over. Some of the pots were small enough to carry. "I'm taking some of these," Brother Arcadius shouted through the kitchen door. Brother Marcus nodded and asked no questions. The cook probably already knew about this latest trouble. "Take all you want."

"Was everything all right this morning, Master Tullius?" Brother Arcadius asked diffidently the next day.

"I did not see the cat." Lips compressed, the scholar turned back to his study of the Council of Nicaea and his reconstruction of the heavens above it, six hundred years before.

"I've been thinking," said Brother Marcus that night in the kitchen. Pangur Ban, all innocence, gave Brother Arcadius's cheek a delicate pat before jumping out of his arms to begin the night's slaughter. "It's a simple fact that Whitey has never gone into guest quarters before—not the ordinary quarters, and not the quarters for notable guests either. Something in your scholar's room is drawing him. It could be there's a mouse in there, but I don't think so. I think it's that traveling bag."

"I think so too," said Brother Arcadius, mainly to be agreeable. He was sick of the whole business, and just wanted Master Tullius to go away and take his life's work and his strange smile and his sneering ways with him. It was too bad that the great visit had come to nothing.

It was just too bad!

"It's a bag from the East," Brother Marcus continued. "And I think it came from there not so long ago." He looked dreamily into the distance. "Salix and I were in some army or other together in Spain, like I've told you. And we met lots of people there who had Eastern connections. Some of them had these wonderful calming powders. I know for sure that Salix came away with some. I don't ask him about it. It's his business. But he uses them in his work, I am sure of it. Once pinch and you wouldn't care if he cut off your leg."

"Well, people who've had some would talk about it, wouldn't they?" Brother Arcadius wasn't aiming to be argumentative. He just wanted to have things set straight.

Marcus snorted. "He doesn't say, 'Now hold still, I'm going to give you something from the East that will make you forget that leg.' He just puts the smallest dab on your tongue, or mixes it up in a drink, and then you're all set. It's wonderful stuff. He gave Whitey some powder when he neutered him, don't you remember?"

Brother Arcadius did remember that Pangur had been given an almost invisible speck of white powder and after that hadn't minded a thing. "Was that from the East?"

"I'm just about sure of it. It would have to be. And that's just one of the things that they have there in the East. They have lots and lots of other amazing things too. To tell you the truth, and it's not much of a secret, I have spices from there that I use in my cooking. That's part of the reason why my cooking tastes so good—I don't count gruel as part of cooking."

"Did Brother Salix bring your spices back too?"

"No, Father Julian just sends for them in the regular way," Brother Marcus said. "Anyway, Arcadius, to get to the point, that traveling bag, in my belief, lures Whitey on with the aromas of the East. You know how he is with smells. You'd think he was part dog, that cat."

"Well, I hope the catmint will keep him away from Master Tullius's door. I don't want any more trouble for him," said Brother Arcadius. "But...if Pangur Ban is so drawn to aromas from the East, why doesn't he try to get into the infirmary, then?"

"Salix keeps his medicines sealed up and locked away," Brother Marcus said. "Just like I do my spices. There's nothing left lying around for Whitey to smell. But if you say a word about Salix's remedies to anyone, and I mean anyone at all, Arcadius, I'll poison your gruel."

"I don't carry tales," said Brother Arcadius.

"I know you don't," said the cook. The glint in his eye showed that he'd just been joking. "That's why I told you about it."

Whether the catmint was doing its job, or Eastern aromas held no further allure, or whatever the reason, Pangur Ban was not found lurking outside Master Tullius's door in the days that followed. In fact, he was rarely seen anywhere on the grounds these days, or in the library. He did his kitchen work each night, then spent his days hidden away from the world, or at least the part of the world that cared about him. However, Brother Marcus was able to testify each morning that the mouse count was properly high, and that the cat looked very well.

Master Tullius, as his thirty days of visiting drew toward an end, began to take his suppers in the refectory along with everybody else, just as Father Julian always did. He did not share the monks' invariable evening menu of gruel (a better gruel than the morning one), along with greens, fruit, bread, and cheese, however. Instead, at his stately and confident request, the kitchen prepared special fare for him each day: eggs in cream, grouse in wine sauce; a small roasted rabbit stuffed with a mixture of bread crumbs, chopped pheasant, venison sausage, garlic, and parsley. Or something of the sort. "I like that in him, Arcadius," Brother Marcus admitted in passing. "If every monk ate like that every day, we couldn't afford it. But I wish that Father Julian did. I get to use my abilities."

Along with graciously sharing his presence at supper time, Master Tullius began to share his ideas then, too. Monks never chattered at mealtimes or at any other times, Brother Marcus to the contrary. So the scholar's cawing tones rang out clearly in the general silence as he spoke of the night skies above the mighty council at Nicaea, of Jupiter opposing Pluto, or vice versa, in the seventh House of something or other, with epicycles in counter motion to cycles and Venus joining Aquarius to cast a benign light upon every decision.

"You can see how the very skies assure us of the holiness and rightness of our Fathers' decisions," he said. "At Sancta Onafria we have always suspected as much. But I feel that in its own small way, my work is starting to confirm it."

Most of the monks continued eating in stolid silence, thinking thoughts of their own. A few ate more slowly than usual, listening with all their might, not skeptical at all, but plainly feeling out of their depth. A further few were wildly impressed and radiant with admiration. Among these few was Brother Zossimus, the white-haired, wispy little man who carved and painted wooden figures of saints, which sold every once in a while to passing travelers.

Brother Zossimus was modestly proud of his work, but he was in raptures about that of Master Tullius.

"His learning, his unbelievable learning!" he said in his wispy little voice to Brother Arcadius, as they filed out of the refectory with the others after supper. "And his mind! That anyone could think of such things, and understand them, and figure them out! Oh, what it must be like to be near him every day! How I envy you!"

Brother Arcadius tried to force his lips into an appropriate smile, but it was difficult. He himself did not really shine in the lessons in reasoning that he took from Father Julian once a week, at the latter's firm request. The subject was not close to his heart and that was all there was to it. Still, he had at least learned enough to wonder about Master Tullius's ideas. They were all very profound and complicated and over his head, but something seemed wrong with them all the same. He'd been waiting for Father Julian to show a hint of impatience with them, to cough, or shift position, or frown, or *something*. But no such thing happened. Master Tullius's odd smile might be unreadable, but it was nothing compared to the unreadability of Father Julian's whole self, day in and day out.

And so they went on: the days, the cawing voice, the night sky beaming down upon the Fathers of Nicaea, the catmint outside Master Tullius's door, the general absence of Pangur Ban from every one of his usual haunts except the kitchen at night. Master Tullius began to show clear signs of wanting to leave. In the library, all day long, he pulled books restlessly from their shelves, leafed through them, sometimes carried them to his room for further dubious perusal, brought them back within an hour or so, took others, returned the parchment—"It seems that I have not needed to take many notes, after all"—and paced back and forth between his room and the library with impatient strides.

The two librarians had long since stopped trying to find books that he would like. It was impossible. They'd opened all the shelves to him, even the trunk of fragments, but they'd also stopped trying to anticipate his needs or track his doings. They even gave up on the beautiful Genesis. He was still, now and then, combing through it for faults of translation, taking it off to his room, bringing it back, then setting it down, half the time, where it didn't belong. Even with this, there was no point in raising objections. He was taking due care not to soil or damage the books that he handled. He was taking far more than due care with the Genesis. Order could be restored when he was gone.

"There'll be no present for us, either," Brother Arcadius told himself with a touch of unmonklike malice. "Unless he gives us another speech about the planets over Nicaea, at the end."

And suddenly, the end was there. Suddenly the party of merchants was pouring back into the courtyard, exactly when they'd said they would. Not only had they been able to follow their travel plans to the letter, but they were insisting that they meant to leave first thing the next day, with no delays. At supper that night, Master Tullius was all graciousness during Father Julian's speech of farewell. But afterwards he stepped hard on Brother Arcadius's foot in his haste to leave the hall. He made no apologies for it, but just went on. And he made as if to pull away from Brother Zossimus when the little woodcarver came toward him to bid him goodbye, but for a moment he couldn't. Zossimus was determined to say what he wanted to say.

"Master Tullius," he whispered tremulously.

"Yes." Master Tullius was already turning away and attempting to move on.

"Master Tullius, there will be..." In his eagerness and awe, Brother Zossimus practically stood on tiptoe to whisper the next words. "Father Julian says I should tell you..."

"Oh, this is about Father Julian?" Master Tullius was suddenly attentive.

"He says to tell you that there can be a, a *presentation* tomorrow! Not to detain you! Outside your door in the morning, first thing!"

Master Tullius looked both intrigued and gratified. "A presentation will be most welcome, of course," he said. Then he strode away.

"It's one of my carvings, Brother Arcadius," Zossimus whispered. "I'm giving him my very best. The paint is almost dry. I must go now to keep breathing on it...there can be no delay...to think that he'll take it to Sancta Onafria, and look at it sometimes while he writes his great work...oh my...." He hurried off without waiting for a response from the assistant librarian, which was a good thing. The assistant librarian would not have known what to say.

So morning came and with it, the morning's ration of breakfast gruel. Brother Arcadius stood in the line impatiently. By now, Brother Zossimus's idol had probably received that carving. It had to be hoped he'd at least pretended to like it. And it was still to be hoped that maybe, just maybe, he meant to make a presentation too, the presentation of a wonderful book to the library.

Brother Marcus's hoarse whisper invaded these thoughts. "Psst, Arcadius! Why wasn't Whitey in the kitchen last night?"

"Why wasn't—what, didn't he show up?"

"Never did. Not a mouse caught. Not there this morning for his treat. Where is he?"

"I don't know," said Brother Arcadius frantically. Now what was he supposed to do? Father Julian had told both him and Brother Silvanus to be in the courtyard to say their formal farewells. Well, surely the farewells would go quickly. He could tell from all the clamor that the mules were being led from the pasture already. Packing, saddling, bridling, was proceeding apace. The merchants would stand for no delay. Master Tullius would be gone, and then he himself could figure out where his cat might be. With a sick feeling of worry in his heart, Brother Arcadius sped out the door and into the courtyard.

Father Julian and Brother Silvanus were there ahead of him, calm and composed amid the commotion, with Brother Salix the medicus nearby. They beckoned to him to join them and looked askance at his agitated appearance, but there was no time to explain. Here came Master Tullius, striding from the doorway. The magnificent carpet bag was slung over his shoulder. Its silken cords were loosely knotted around just one silver loop. It bumped against his shoulder more heavily than it had when he'd arrived. No doubt it was the hurried way he'd had to pack—or was Brother Zossimus's carved figure extraordinarily large? Zossimus was over there, waving goodbye. Master Tullius's eyes were on the fine white mule that was being held ready for him. He was not going to wait for fine speeches, that was obvious. Was not going to open the bag and present a book. Was....

From the depths of the lurching carpet bag came a muffled meow.

Master Tullius stopped dead still, stared in horror, unslung the bag, fumbled at the silken knot.

"Meow..."

"Pangur Ban!" shouted Brother Arcadius. Oblivious to everything, even to Father Julian reaching for him to hold him back, he raced to the rescue of his cat, his own cat, his cat that was trapped in Master Tullius's bag. "Pangur Ban!"

Master Tullius was bent over the bag now, trying to reach inside it with one hand, while keeping the cover shut with the other. What was wrong with the man? Why hadn't he simply thrown the cover back? Just as he'd done on that lurching boat from Ireland, Brother Arcadius found strength beyond his means. He pulled the bag away from Master

Tullius. He flung back the cover and from within lifted a groggy, bewildered, limp white cat. "Pangur Ban!"

Belatedly, he realized that someone else had joined him and was ready to help—Brother Salix the medicus, Heaven be thanked. Brother Arcadius wanted nothing more than to hand the distressed cat over to him. But Pangur's hind claws were caught in some sort of cloth, some long, winding piece of silk that was uncoiling from the bag as the cat was lifted carefully higher...uncoiling, and revealing a partly opened something that lay within...something whose flashes of gold leaf and crimson and lapis lazuli and ultramarine the assistant librarian knew well.

Every demon of rage and outrage and indignation that Brother Arcadius had ever fought conquered him now. Part of him saw clearly that Pangur was now cradled in Salix's arms, and was looking around with something like his old spirit. The other part was blind to everything except sheer fury. Shaking with rage, he pulled the Genesis of Spiritus Sanctus out of the depths and brandished it in the air. "It's our book!" he choked. "You're stealing our book!"

"Arcadius—" Father Julian's hand fell restrainingly on his shoulder. He didn't care. He pulled the coil of silk entirely out of the bag to give a clear view of what else was in there. "And our books!" he shouted. "Our *books*!"

And it was so. Brother Silvanus was at hand now, and he was taking books from the bag one after another, counting them off as he laid them carefully on the ground. There were twelve in all, not including the Genesis. He nodded grimly. "They're ours."

Brother Arcadius got to his feet. He was able now to take a second glance at Pangur Ban, still safe in Brother Salix's arms. "He's fine," the medicus murmured. "He just needed some fresh air."

So Brother Arcadius turned his eyes back to Master Tullius, and indeed, all eyes, even Pangur Ban's, were upon the man. The scholar's cheeks were flushed and his eyes were narrowed, but he was smiling his confident smile. Brother Zossimus, however, was not smiling. "You're a thief!" he cried. "I don't want you to have my carving."

"I don't have it," said Master Tullius easily. "I left it behind, and glad to do it."

Father Julian stepped forward. "Master Tullius," he said, "it appears that you overlooked a few things in your haste to pack. You were, of course, caught short by the need to hurry."

Master Tullius stood taller, and looked around the courtyard from face to face to face. "I overlooked nothing," he said. "The books I selected are at least worth a careful perusal, if only to smile at their flaws. I had to salvage *something* from my time here." His smile of confidence faded. His other smile appeared. Brother Arcadius realized that there was no mystery in it after all. It was a smile of pure disdain.

"Are you folks finished here?" called the merchants' trail master. "Could we get a move on, please?"

"You may," said Father Julian.

"And good riddance!" shrilled Brother Zossimus.

The master scholar reached for his empty bag and slung it back over his shoulder. He whisked the strewn silk wrappings out of his way with the point of his toe. Then he mounted his lordly mule and joined the others heading for the gate.

* * *

"Well, we found it," said Brother Mishel, the chief stonecutter. "There's another way into that room from outside—hole got patched up with plaster years ago, not in my time, and the plaster fell away. Big enough for a cat to crawl through, but you wouldn't spot it if you weren't crawling. The grasses hide it. Come on, I'll show you."

* * *

"So here's what happened as I see it," said Brother Marcus. "Whitey can't get through the front way because the mint is there, see? But he's drawn by the smell of the bag, the lure of the East. So all those days we don't see much of him, he's crawling around through the grasses, looking for a way in. And then he finds it, and he's in the bag, and the poppy dust or whatever's in the seams there lulls him to sleep on top of the books that Tullius has already packed. And Tullius doesn't notice him, because Tullius is in a big hurry. And Tullius doesn't lash the cover shut when he should, because he expects to be getting that 'presentation.' Probably expects he'll be getting gold or something. Foolish fellow. I don't see how he got to be a scholar. Anyway, morning comes, he gets Zossimus's saint, the merchants are yelling at him to hurry up, he's wild to get away before he gets caught, and you know the rest. I may have some of it wrong, but that's the gist of it, I'd say."

* * *

"Taking our books just to smile at their flaws? What a lie," said Brother Silvanus bitterly. "He was aiming to give them to Sancta Onafria. Maybe that's how they've built up their whole collection, eh? When he was shuffling our manuscripts around, and pulling them off the shelves and putting them back—supposedly putting them back— he was stealing them, period. Whatever he may be by blood, he certainly is Scarpian in spirit, counting on us to trust him and not keep track of what he'd taken and brought back. That's why he'd smile whenever we'd tell him that it's just you and I in the library, Arcadius, doing the work ourselves. Well, next time we'll know better."

* * *

"Pangur Ban, there'd better not be any next time," murmured Brother Arcadius. It was a wonderful thing to just sit there and stroke his revived cat, and to know that Master Tullius was gone for good. "You caught him just in time, you smart, smart cat! If he'd carried the books back to Sancta Onafria, I don't think we could have done anything about it. Pin the blame on him if some of our manuscripts were missing? Couldn't be done. Our word against his. Had to catch him on the spot, which you did."

He hugged Pangur closer, and Pangur let him. Then he smiled a dismissive smile of his own. There were better things to think about than conceited scholars with larcenous aims! "I'm sure there are much, much better cats than you at Sancta Onafria, Pangur Ban," said Brother Arcadius in a gentle murmur. "But I'll take you."

"Meowr," said Pangur Ban.

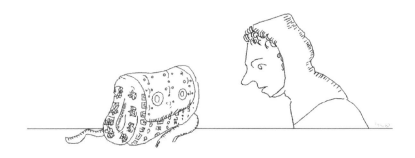

THE DISTRESSED MAIDEN

In which Brother Arcadius and others become very confused,
and the animal kingdom weighs in with strong opinions

AD 899

T he grand new mule of Spiritus Sanctus monastery trotted splendidly this way and that in the pasture. Muscles rippled beneath his coat of rich plum brown. The big splotch of white on his left hip, shaped like a giant hand with splayed fingers, gleamed like the snows on the far-off mountains. Put him in with a hundred others, and the eye would go to him immediately.

Brother Bruno, the stable master, slapped the pasture gate in delight. "Father Julian will get to the wedding all right on that one, won't he?" he said. "And back again too."

"That he will," said Brother Arcadius. He was the monastery's assistant librarian and no expert on mules, but anyone could see that here was a really fine creature.

"A good buy, Father, I told him. A bargain at ten times the price, I said." Brother Bruno squinted into the sunlight, tracking the mule's swift progress across the field. "Look at the haunches on him! Look at his gait!"

"It's really smooth," said Brother Arcadius. On his long and difficult journey to Spiritus Sanctus the previous year, he'd ridden a mule for fifty miles or so. At the time, being only sixteen and with a sixteen-year-old's notions still in his head, he'd wished sometimes that he was riding an actual horse—or rather, not just a horse but a steed, the kind you heard about it tales. But mules were just as good-looking as horses in their own way, and could be just as fast, and—the main thing, really—were much more sensible and more sure-footed. Father

Julian, the head of Spiritus Sanctus monastery, would be traveling a hundred miles to his niece's wedding within a week or so. He often had other long journeys to make on monastery business. It was good that he'd have this excellent creature to ride on.

"I just wish Father Julian would get a really good-looking saddle and bridle, to show off the mule," said Brother Bruno. "But he told me, 'Bruno, fancy trappings will serve no purpose.' I don't see why, do you? It's his niece's wedding. High-class weddings are supposed to be fancy, aren't they? But that's Father Julian. He's high-class, but he doesn't like to show it. Wouldn't use monastery funds to pay for the mule, either. Took the money out of his own purse."

Brother Bruno turned to go back to the stables, where more mules awaited his attention. "Have to get back to work, Arcadius. You'd better get back to that library of yours, too. Wind's picking up. Wouldn't want it to blow you back to—where was it you came from?"

"Dublin," said Brother Arcadius shortly. He nodded farewell to Brother Bruno and walked on. After a year at Spiritus Sanctus, jokes about Dublin and getting blown away by the wind had worn rather thin. Not that he minded them, really, but still! Blown away by the wind! Did people always have to harp on that same theme? He was the youngest monk in the monastery by a full ten years, and the shortest and slightest also, except for little Brother Zossimus the woodcarver, who was *exceptionally* short and slight—but did people always have to be bringing that up?

And the way that Brother Bruno always said things like, "That library of yours," was wearing thin too. Like people everywhere, generally, from kings to serfs, most of the monks at Spiritus Sanctus couldn't read and had no practical need to do so. Plowing, planting, harvesting, shoe making, weaving, stone cutting—that sort of work was essential, and wasn't learned from a book. It was learned face-to-face from skilled and experienced people, that's how it was learned, not by deciphering all sorts of strange little marks. So Brother Arcadius's brethren, for the most part, looked upon the library with uninterested and sometimes baffled eyes. The idea of an assistant librarian was especially baffling to some of them, and was a call for more humor. "How many librarians does it take to lift up a book? Two of 'em, heh heh."

Walking along the rutted path away from the pasture and back to the monastery, Brother Arcadius told himself firmly to dispel the demons of self-love and injured pride. There was no harm in Brother

Bruno, and anyway there were other things to think about. Things like the big wedding coming up. And things like the visit. Father Julian's niece, Lady Somebody Something de Something, was going to spend some time at the monastery with her uncle before the wedding. She and her father and their escort of guards were expected to come in some time today. The bridegroom would arrive a few days later.

The visit wouldn't last long. When it was over, they all would make that hundred-mile journey to the bridegroom's castle for the wedding. The bride was thirteen, the groom was said to be a good deal older. That's how it went with those high-class weddings. Lands and treaties and things like that were mixed up in them. Maybe something like that accounted for the bride and bridegroom coming up here, way out of their way, for no apparent reason, only to go back for the wedding a few days later.

Brother Arcadius looked up as a flash of white crossed the path up ahead. Here was another diversion from hurt feelings and gloom. "Well, good day to you, Pangur Ban," he said, as the monastery's grand mousing cat came bounding toward him. *His* cat, if you wanted to overlook the monastery rules about not owning things. Even the new mule, paid for with Father Julian's own money, would be thought of as monastery property, held in common. But who had rescued Pangur, a homeless stray, from a murderous sailor on the boat out of Dublin? Who'd given him his good Irish name that signified whiteness, because he happened to be white? Who'd brought him here to Spiritus Sanctus, the whole long difficult way, over seas and lands, and down rivers, and up this mountain? Brother Arcadius, the assistant librarian, that was who.

Well, here was the demon of self-love, creeping back again. Brother Arcadius bent down to give Pangur a good petting, and Pangur circled and twisted about him, and brushed his soft flanks against him back and forth, signaling true friendship. It was friendship, too, that had brought him so close to the stables, and the barns that adjoined the stables—to barn-cat territory, in other words. Pangur, a sociable but also a very sensible cat, had no desire to tangle with uncouth barn-cat savagery. He'd never been especially fond of mules, either. On the mule-ride portion of the journey to Spiritus Sanctus, he'd never really settled down in Brother Arcadius's encircling arm.

Mules, nieces, cats, weddings, library business...yes, there was plenty to think about today, and no mistake.

Librarian and mouser went on to the monastery.

The bride-to-be and her party arrived late that night, when Brother Arcadius and most of the other monks were in their beds. Since the party was expected, the monks standing night duty in the courtyard raised no alarms. There was simply a brief, hushed clatter and commotion out there on the pavement that roused Brother Arcadius for a moment. Would he get to see her? he dimly wondered. And if he did, what would she look like? Briefly, he imagined a small Father Julian in a fine lady's fancy clothes—dark, intense, and commanding. Then he pulled his covering tighter around him and went back to sleep.

"No, we won't get to see her." In the breakfast line at dawn Brother Marcus the cook was very firm on that point. "Great ladies of that sort stay secluded, especially when they're not married. She'll come and go sight unseen, take my word for it. By the way, Arcadius, Whitey killed thirteen mice in the kitchen last night. Same number as the lady's age. Must be a meaning there somewhere, eh?" He grinned to show that he meant this as a joke.

"Oh, for sure," said Brother Arcadius with mock pomposity, joking too. Keti, the little kitchen boy and his own apt pupil, had just come trotting up with more loaves of bread, and there was even a glint of mirth in Keti's solemn eyes. For it really was funny, although certainly not respectful or proper, to count the lady's years in terms of mice. But *Whitey*.... After an entire year and more, it was clear that Brother Marcus was never going to call Pangur Ban by his proper Irish name. No, with him it would always be "Whitey." Still, it was nice to be told each day that Pangur had killed a goodly tally of mice the night before. He was not one to sleep on the job, that cat! Keti and Pangur Ban, both bright as, well, buttons!

Brother Arcadius glanced about for a glimpse of Pangur Ban as he headed to the library for his own day's work. He caught no sight of him and didn't expect to: Pangur liked to go his own way first thing in the morning. He showed up at the library, usually, an hour or so after dawn at the earliest. Brother Silvanus, the head librarian and Brother Arcadius's mentor, would not be around yet either. Although he liked Brother Silvanus very much, the older man's penchant for arriving late suited Brother Arcadius down to the ground. He loved the library, and he loved being the first to open it each day, loved pushing back the shutters to let in the light, loved unlocking the cabinet doors to reveal the books, loved the hour or two when the fine old place was his alone, with nobody there. He unlocked the door and stopped short.

There was somebody there.

Someone short and small was standing there in the shadows, a shadow herself in the dark room. "Brother Arcadius, surely?" asked a silvery voice. "I'm Lady Aurelia de Bogardu, Father Julian's niece. He thought it would be all right for me to spend the morning here. He let me in through the back way and told me you'd be here soon. I hope I didn't alarm you." The silvery voice was speaking excellent Latin, almost one hundred per cent correct.

"Oh no...not alarmed...welcome...." stammered Brother Arcadius. "Just do what ever you..." Never, never in his life had he talked to a lady of rank or even seen one, except from a distance when he and Pangur Ban were making their way across the Frankish lands. In fact, aside from yesterday's random thoughts, the subject of *ladies* had never once been uppermost in his mind. And yet here he stood face to shadowed face with one—one who said she'd be here all morning! Now what should he do? Well, just be polite and wait for Brother Silvanus to come and take over, that's what he should do.

Through the shadows he saw the lady reach out a small hand. He had no choice but to touch it, though he did so as briefly as possible. It was very smooth and soft, with quite a few rings on quite a few fingers. "I love libraries, Brother Arcadius," she said. "And I love learning. My Uncle Julian says that you do too. My chaperone—" Her voice faltered, but then she went on. "My chaperone said that it's unheard of for a lady to spend all morning alone in a library, betrothed or not, and my father said she was right—but Uncle Julian told them that you are an agreeable young man and that spending time with you could not possibly compromise my reputation. Those were his very words. He also said that another librarian would be joining us soon. So they said I could have this morning. Part of it, anyway."

"Um," said Brother Arcadius. *Uncle* Julian! None of the many words he knew, whether Latin, Greek, Hebrew, or Irish, seemed to fit the occasion. In lieu of words, and with some desperation, he turned to his usual morning task of getting the library ready for use. Ordinarily he would have opened the shutters first, but in his confusion he started with the cabinets that held the five hundred intact and bound manuscripts of Spiritus Sanctus. "Oh, so many books!" cried Lady Aurelia. "Rows and rows of them! Just like my uncle's always told me! You'll let me see some of them, won't you, when we have light?"

"As many as you please," stammered Brother Arcadius. "And sit where you please.... Please." He nodded toward the benches at the long reading table in the center of the room. "There are benches outside, too, in the fresh air, if you'd rather." He hoped she would rather, and stay out there until rescue came in the form of Brother Silvanus.

"I had better not sit outside," said Lady Aurelia. "My chaperone thinks I'm terrible enough as it is. Can I help you with those shutters?"

Brother Arcadius, who had gone from opening the cabinets to letting light and air in through the windows, shook his head. His panic was subsiding. He'd been taken by surprise, that was all. Hadn't he spent plenty of time with his sisters, his younger sisters who were so far away now over the cold and lurching arms of two distant seas? New levels of politeness would be needed here, of course, but otherwise, could dealing with this lady be that different? Two somewhat reassuring thoughts were taking shape in his mind. First, he was four years older than Lady Aurelia, after all. Second, he was a good few inches taller. "They're not hard to open....I'm almost done."

But then, as he pulled open the last two shutters, the sun broke through the morning mists and flooded the library with light, and his burgeoning calm left him. No, Lady Aurelia was not like his sisters. He'd always thought of the two of them, beaky, wiry, red-haired and somewhat rowdy though they were, as fine-looking girls. But Father Julian's niece was...

She was as beautiful as the most perfectly carved and painted and gilded young saint in a grand, grand church—he'd peered into one on his way across the Frankish lands to the monastery, the year before—as beautiful as that, but *alive*.

Yes, her features were Father Julian's, unmistakably, but a Father Julian who'd been transformed. In no way could the head of Spiritus Sanctus monastery be called beautiful, good looking though he was. His hair did not escape in soft black clouds from beneath a richly colored scarf of fine, thin something or other. His eyebrows were not perfect little arches, his eyelashes were not long and silken, his lips most definitely did not make a person think of rosebuds, nor were his teeth like pearls. And whereas Father Julian's eyes were pitch dark, and often rather alarming in expression, hers were a magical, tender smoky blue, with tawny glimmers in them here and there, like gold dust, and they were looking straight into those of Brother Arcadius, the one and only librarian—indeed, the one and only person—on hand at this time.

There were dark shadows under them, though, as was all too plain, and the perfect face was much too pale and set.

But this niece—this vision—was not just gazing. She was saying something. Had been saying something. Arching her eyebrows a bit higher, she said it again. "But what is your name, Brother Arcadius?"

He stared at her, completely lost.

"I mean the name you were born with."

His name? The name he'd been born with? "Why...why, it was Tammis. *Is* Tammis. That's what it is."

"Oh!" cried Lady Aurelia. "That is a beautiful, beautiful name! But Tammis what?"

"My Da was a brickman," Brother Arcadius said. "We had a brickyard, and he made bricks and laid them too."

"Which is why you have red hair," said Lady Aurelia, softly laughing.

"They were brown bricks, mostly," he told her. "Or yellowish. But very good bricks, all of them. People thought highly of them." If they were going to talk about just bricks, and then go on to books, that would not be so bad.

"So you'd be Tammis Brickman, is that so?"

"Sometimes. Or Tammis Brickmaker or Bricklayer, or Bricker, or sometimes just Bricks. Or later on, Tammis Scholar. Because my Da died fighting the wicked Danes"—Lady Aurelia gave a soft cry of sympathy—"and then my Mam let the monks bring me up to be a scholar. Because I had a taste for that, and my brothers were doing fine with the brickyard. They're all older than me by a long stretch."

"Tammis Bricker...Tammis Scholar.... Oh, all of your names are lovely! Although maybe I love 'Tammis Scholar' best!" cried Lady Aurelia. "And does your family still have the brickyard?"

"No, my brothers all found service with King Alfred," Brother Arcadius said. "So they and my Mam and my sisters all crossed the water over to Wessex, and that's where they are now, God willing." Letters took a long time to reach their destination. What they said might not still be true when they arrived.

"King Alfred!!" The expression in Lady Aurelia's eyes changed upon the instant from tender and magical to intense. All of a sudden, except for the color, they might have been Father Julian's eyes boring into him. "I happen to be very interested in King Alfred. His stepmother was my own ancestress, did you know?"

"Well, no...I didn't," said Brother Arcadius.

"Her name was Judith," said Lady Aurelia in a silvery murmur. Her voice caressed the name. The look in her eyes became soft and faraway. "She was fifth cousin to my own grandmother, and so Judith is one of my names. It's a name that I'm very proud of, Tammis

Scholar—I mean Brother Arcadius. She was a great beauty, so they say, and descended from a line of great beauties—and people who knew her say that I look just like her. Not that I mean that *I'm* a great beauty, Brother Arcadius! When people compare me to her, I'm sure they've forgotten how beautiful she actually was! I mention her only because— Do you know her story?"

"I don't," said Brother Arcadius. Perhaps he should go to the shelves now and start selecting books for this lady to look at. Perhaps he shouldn't be just standing here and talking to her. Although the way of it was that she was talking to him, and he didn't know how to stop her. Wouldn't just walking away seem very rude? But if he stayed here and listened, would that be compromising her reputation? What should he do?

"It's a famous story," Lady Aurelia said. There was something new in her voice, some kind of a...would it be *trembling*? "She was Charlemagne's granddaughter, you know, and when she was twelve, King Aethelwulf of Wessex came looking for a wife because his own wife had just died. And Judith's father, Charles, King of the Franks, wanted him for an ally. So he married her off to King Aethelwulf, who was already fifty. *Fifty*, Brother Arcadius! And Aethelwulf had four other sons besides Alfred, who was still just a little boy, and two of them were already grown. And just two years later he died, King Aethelwulf died, and then his oldest son made her marry *him*. Her own stepson! Think of it! Think of the scandal!"

Brother Arcadius thought of it. It sounded scandalous, all right. But the carryings-on of kings and suchlike folk, and the church laws and rules and regulations pertaining to such, had never been part of his study. What was polite and right for a person to say? He went to the bookshelves. Saints' lives. Everybody liked saints' lives.

But Lady Aurelia was going on with her story. He turned to show he was listening, so as not to seem rude. "It was not Judith's fault that she had to marry her stepson," she cried softly. "She was still just only fourteen and he was far older, so what could she do? But after two years he died too, and her father made her come back home. And he locked her up as if *she'd* been the one causing trouble, and he started looking around for somebody else to marry her off to. It wasn't fair, Brother Arcadius! It wasn't fair! But then came the beautiful dawn!"

"That's very good!" said Brother Arcadius with feeling. If there'd been a happy ending for Lady Aurelia's grandmother's fifth cousin, maybe now they could just talk about books. If so, he'd be glad of it, and that was a fact.

"Yes, the dawn!" said Lady Aurelia. She clasped her ringed hands to her heart and spoke in a rush. "You see, Judith had a wonderful big brother, who loved her very much. And his very best friend was Count-to-be Baldwin of Flanders, a great hero, who was also known as Iron-Arm, because of his strength. And he was in his twenties, a very proper age, and although Judith was locked up and guarded, her brother and Iron-Arm found a way, and they rescued her, and she and Iron-Arm fell in love, and they married!"

"That's very good," Brother Arcadius said again. All right, heroes. Maybe she'd like to read about heroes. There was that very long and very exciting poem about the great hero Roland, although it was sad....

"Oh, better than good!" said Lady Aurelia. "Better, better, *better* than good! But doesn't something strike you about all this? Doesn't something just make you wonder?"

"I—" What should have struck him? What was it he ought to wonder?

"She never had children!" cried Lady Aurelia. "Four years of marriage, two husbands, and she never had children! I'd like to know how that came about—wouldn't you?"

The Genesis! The library's beautiful Genesis, with the wonderful pictures! Brother Arcadius hastened to take the book from its special shelf and set it down on the table. Too late, he remembered its saucy picture of Eve. But five pages past Eve, there was a picture of Nimrod the Hunter. Nimrod would help change a subject that had better be changed.

But the alarming moment was already over, or at least he fervently hoped so. Lady Aurelia was just speeding on with her tale. "Judith's father was furious with her for running away with Count-to-be Iron-Arm. He tried to get them excommunicated, but he failed. All he could do was refuse to attend the wedding—a very frightening threat, I'm sure. So my ancestress Judith and Count Baldwin Iron-Arm lived happily together in Flanders for the rest of their lives, and had *many* children, and it makes me very, very happy and proud to bear her name as one of mine—to be Lady Aurelia Rotruda Himeltrud Hildegarde Adelheid Pamina *Judith* de Juliani et Bogardu!"

"This is our library's copy of Genesis, with many fine pictures in it, and here we see Nimrod the Hunter—"

"Brother Arcadius," said Lady Aurelia earnestly, "I came here to look at books, and I will look at books. The cycles and epicycles of the heavenly bodies circling the earth—travel books with sightings of unicorns—these things interest me greatly. But if only you knew how much I need a brotherly ear! If only you knew! Can you just listen to me a bit longer, Brother Arcadius? Can you just please?"

"Well, um, I...."

"Oh, thank you, Brother Arcadius! Thank you, thank you! You see, Judith's story is not just her story. It's.... My father says that it was disgraceful for Judith to elope. It was my mother who named me after her. And whenever my father said that the name Judith was not a proper name for a girl of noble birth to have, my mother would always tell him very politely and pityingly to '*Try* to stop being *utterly* stupid, Bogardu.' She was my Uncle Julian's elder sister, you know, and had that same air. And she had no little friendly names for my father, either. She never became reconciled to their marriage, I know perfectly well. I've heard it said that it was my grandfather Julian's one miscalculation, that marriage. But anyway—"

"Um, won't they be sending for you pretty soon?"

"I'm sure they will," said Lady Aurelia. There was a bitter edge to her voice now. "So I'd better put my story in order, the way I was taught, if I want to tell it. And I do want to tell it! Tell it to you, Brother Arcadius, because you listen so kindly and so beautifully." She pressed a delicate finger to her forehead. "All right, Aurelia. Analyze, categorize, summarize, organize!"

Lady Aurelia assumed an orator's stance, posture very erect, feet slightly apart for balance, finger uplifted. She cleared her throat. "Now then. First I should say that when my mother was alive, she also made my father let me have an education. I learned reading, writing, and some ciphering also. I learned music and proper Latin, and the art of speaking too—the art of declaiming, you know, so as to hold people's attention, as I must now. Oh, it was wonderful! I loved every moment of every lesson, Tammis Scholar—I mean, Brother Arcadius! My tutors said that I drank up learning as if it were the elixir of life, and that is true. I did."

Lady Aurelia shifted her orator's stance and clasped her hands to her heart again. "Second, I should say that like Judith, I have a dear brother. And my brother's best friend is the son of the man they're making me marry: my father's neighbor, Count Remba. Are you starting to see a picture?"

Brother Arcadius thought that he was, even though this whole thing was none of his business. It was Julian family business and out of his realm. He'd best put it out of his mind.

"Third," said Lady Aurelia, "my brother and Count Remba's son have always been very dutiful to their fathers. Dutiful and sincerely respectful in word and deed. Yet my father has convinced himself that they're plotting against him and Count Remba."

"What sort of plot would that be?" asked Brother Arcadius, in spite of himself. The story was none of his business, but still.... Would asking a question or two do any real harm?

"It's no sort of plot!" said Lady Aurelia. "It's no sort of plot at all! My brother and Count Remba's son are both men in their twenties, and have their own castles and lands to the north of their fathers' lands, bequeathed to them by their mothers. My father believes that they are scheming to imprison him and Count Remba, or worse, and annex the lands of their fathers to their own. He says that down through the ages, sons have always plotted against their fathers. He uses King David and David's son Absalom, in the Bible, as an example."

"Well," said Brother Arcadius, "I don't think I ever would have plotted against my Da. And I know my brothers never did either."

"Well, that's just it!" cried Lady Aurelia. "The whole thing is...utterly stupid! But the upshot is that I have to marry Count Remba, so that the two fathers' lands will be legally joined by marriage! And I'm to have children one after the other, so that the dynasty—the dynasty, mind you!—will be secured! And I'm not to study anything, or have books to read, or go anywhere, or do anything, except just have Count Remba's children, and embroider! Because they think that doing anything else will give me *ideas*! It's a nightmare! And I counted on my Uncle Julian to help me! He did last year. He rode down and stopped my father from marrying me to Count Remba when I was just twelve —like Judith. He just got him alone and somehow talked him out of it. But now that I'm a year older he says he can do nothing for me! My fate is sealed!"

The library's back door led directly to Father Julian's quarters, and the quarters of notable guests like Count Bogardu. Brother Arcadius went back and opened it. He decided to stay by it, too. He did not intend to be caught prying—well, seeming to pry, because he wasn't actually prying—into Father Julian's business. Or Count Bogardu's. Or anybody's. But he did feel sorry for Lady Aurelia. He wouldn't want to be her. Things did sound grim. "I remember that Father Julian was away for quite a while last year, right after I came," he said. "Um, maybe you'd better stand over by the window, just in case anybody's coming, like your chaperone." Coming from a different direction, not through the back door.

"You are right, Tammis Scholar," said Lady Aurelia. She went over to the window. "There. Now I have a good view if they come this way. And the last thing I'll say about this, because I really do want to see the books—please believe me!—is that I always thought I could depend on my brother if worst came to worst, that somehow he'd work out a plan of something to do, like Judith's brother did. But the king has called him into service, and he's gone off with the best of his armsmen, I don't know where. And also...."

Lady Aurelia was suddenly struggling to speak. "Also...also...Count Remba's son, Count-to-be Rodhrighu de Rembarian.... Have you heard of him, Brother Arcadius?"

"We're off the beaten track up here," he said in apology. Lady Aurelia now looked as if she might cry, and he hoped she wouldn't.

"He's just like Judith's Count Iron-Arm—a hero. Count Remba himself is nothing, my father too, and everyone knows it—I mean no disrespect. But my brother, and Rodhrighu! Rodhrighu's known as Bold-Heart for miles and miles around, and he's gallant and good and — Oh, if you heard the call of his hunting horn on a frosty morning! It's thrilling! He blows three short notes very fast, and then a long one. It's as if the horn is saying *Suddenly Oh! Suddenly Oh!* And if he blows nine short notes at a time, which he sometimes does, it sounds like *Suddenly Suddenly Suddenly Oh!* It takes you right out of yourself, Brother Arcadius. It carries you truly away!"

"It sounds exciting," Brother Arcadius agreed. He tried to imagine himself galloping—on a steed, not a mule—over frosty fields, blowing a hunting horn.

"And all my life," Lady Aurelia said, very softly, "all my life, growing up, and he was our neighbor, and I saw so much of him—I couldn't help thinking that there was something between us. It was the way he would look at me sometimes, or help me onto my pony, or put a special cut of meat onto my plate, or ask me how my lessons were going—always so kindly and tenderly, although he was so strong. And nothing was ever said, and there were no promises, but I felt...I felt...I thought that maybe...that he and I were like my ancestress Judith and her Iron-Arm. That there was a, a, a sort of...understanding between us, that someday...."

For one horrible moment, Lady Aurelia's voice broke up

completely. Her chin wobbled, her nose turned pink, and tears coursed down her cheeks. She dashed them furiously away with the end of her scarf. "And now he's married! He went off to Brittany, and got married! He sent word back to Count Remba, and Count Remba told my father, and my father told me." Lady Aurelia took command of her features again. She looked sternly into space with half-closed eyes. "I am very happy for him," she said. "The bride is very rich, whoever she is. That's what he wrote to his father, and he wouldn't lie. I hope that they have a beautiful life together and—oh!"

Lady Aurelia stepped back in surprise as a white shape appeared on the window sill. "What a beautiful cat! Is he yours?"

"He's the monastery's cat, really, but I brought him here," said Brother Arcadius. Heartfelt gratitude at Pangur Ban's timely arrival diminished just slightly as the cat brushed straight by him and leaped lightly into Lady Aurelia's arms. Young women of any sort were hardly ever seen at the monastery, but when they were, Pangur Ban always took a shine to them, the prettier the better. With Lady Aurelia, the purring, snuggling cat bade fair to make a fool of himself.

"Oh, I love him!" cried Lady Aurelia. "I just love him!" Pangur Ban leaped coquettishly out of her arms again, and she knelt down to be near him. Purring and preening, he circled around her. "What is his name?"

"Pangur Ban. It's Irish. It signifies that he's white."

"Pangur Ban, Pangur Ban," crooned Lady Aurelia. "Oh, his dear whiskers—and how he purrs!" She brushed away another tear. "Oh, how I would love to have a cat just like him. They may not let me have books to read, but surely they'll let me have a cat?"

"I'm sure they will," said Brother Arcadius firmly. He hoped so, anyway. No other cat could ever match Pangur Ban, but maybe Lady Aurelia would find one that came close.

"Oh, I hope so!" cried Lady Aurelia. "Oh, I do hope so!"

Just then a call of "Good morning!" came from the door. At long last, Brother Silvanus had arrived.

"Oh!" cried Lady Aurelia again. She scrambled somewhat ungracefully to her feet. Even ungracefulness looked good on Lady Aurelia. The end of her scarf was still obviously wet, and her nose was still slightly pink, but she showed no real signs of having been pouring her heart out. Well, she was Julian on her mother's side, after all. She smoothed her skirts and held out her hand. "Is it Brother Silvanus?" she asked. "I am Father Julian's niece, Lady Aurelia. Brother Arcadius and I have been talking, and I am just about to choose some books to take back to my room to read."

Brother Silvanus took her hand. "When choosing books, it is always advantageous to have the help of a cat," he smiled.

His smile faded at the sound of a flurry of footsteps and a sudden call, or squawk, outside the back door. "Lady Aurelia!" The chaperone came through the door fast and was breathing fire. Brawny and tall, she made four of Lady Aurelia and no mistake. "Lady Aurelia? Lady Aurelia! Aren't you finished here yet? Your father is worried about you!" The chaperone's eyes darted from Arcadius to Silvanus, from bookshelf to bookshelf, from table to cat, and back to Arcadius again, suspiciously. "The idea of you staying here so long!"

"I was given the morning," said Lady Aurelia with dignity. She tucked the wet end of her scarf farther back, under her curls. "Or so I believed. And I have not yet chosen my books."

"Well, choose them and be quick about it," the chaperone said. "Those are your father's orders. And just bear in mind, please, that as a married woman you'll be needing no books—or getting them, either."

That night, and not at all to his surprise, Brother Arcadius could not get the morning out of his head. With great dignity Lady Aurelia had put in her request for books about cycles and epicycles and unicorn sightings. Brother Silvanus had pulled the library's best books on travel and the heavenly bodies from the shelves, and piled them into the chaperone's brawny arms with a subdued snort of extreme dislike. Then he'd courteously escorted Lady Aurelia back to her quarters, with the chaperone glowering behind. He'd returned with a few choice words of indignation about *haughty ignoramuses*, and Brother Arcadius had added some of his own.

But what good were words of indignation? Brother Arcadius turned this way and that on his narrow cot. Lady Aurelia…*securing the dynasty*…. Now that he wasn't face to face with the lady in question, Brother Arcadius gave thought to the situation. He had not grown up wrapped in fleeces. He remembered shivering in a neighbor's hut while his own Mam gasped and grunted—and once in a while, moaned—her way through the birth of his first younger sister, and then, a year later, the one after that. Then afterwards he'd heard whispers that she'd ripped something up inside there and couldn't have any more. It all sounded like a tough, tough process to him. His Mam put a lot of stock in her own constitution. But what sort of constitution did Lady Aurelia have?

Of course, Brother Arcadius had also grown up among the conquering Danes, in Dublin. He knew that you didn't have to be in childbirth to have calamity happen. With Danes you had to expect the worst, even though it might not always seem so. One moment they'd be peacefully plowing their (stolen) fields, or trying to cheat you in the market place like any ordinary trader. Next moment they'd be burning your house down with you in it, laughing and whooping and herding you back inside as you tried to escape. Or they'd have you down on your back with your chest slit open neck to navel and your ribs pulled back on either side, chuckling grimly at the pretty design you made as you lay dying, spread out there on the ground. So Lady Aurelia was not the only person in the world with troubles, was she? But still....

But still....

Even if she turned out to have his Mam's constitution, it was sad to think of her being hauled away to be married.

Sad that her brother wasn't around to cheer her up.

Sad that this Bold-Heart person had gone off to Brittany and married another.

Sad, if that chaperone and that father of hers wouldn't even allow her to have a cat.

There was no sign of Lady Aurelia anywhere on the grounds the next day, or the day after. She was being properly secluded and no mistake. But her father was much in evidence. He paced about the grounds, he sat beside Father Julian at the midday meal and at supper. Although doing his best not to yield to ill will and spite, Brother Arcadius did not like the look of him. An inch or so taller than Father Julian—in other words, fairly tall—Count Bogardu couldn't be called plump in any way, and yet there was something soft about him. His face was very round, his eyebrows were very thick, and his mouth was always turned down as if he'd just suffered a severe disappointment. Pacing ceremoniously about the grounds in his long black tunic that reached smoothly from neck to toe, he made Brother Arcadius think of a long black moving ink stroke with a circle on top.

Brother Marcus the cook had a thought or two to share about him after supper that evening. Marcus could be counted on to find out all sorts of things, and pass them on if and when the time was right. "I wouldn't say this to anybody but you, Arcadius," he said. "And you shouldn't say anything either. But this niece isn't going to be bringing anybody any big dowry, and she's not going to be key to controlling any big territory. Her father's not an important count, not at all. The bridegroom isn't either. It's partly them and it's partly where they live. They're like us—out of the way, out of touch. The big players don't think they're worth bothering with. By the time the king's message comes asking for help, the war's over." Marcus chuckled. "Myself, I don't see that as a problem. But this Bogardu stalks around as if he's the center of the world. And it looks as if he's got Father Julian in on it too. What're they planning for, anyway? An invasion of Saracens, or what?"

An invasion of Absaloms, maybe? Count Bogardu might be expecting his son to come back out of nowhere and lead some sort of attack. Or being suspicious by nature, maybe he'd come up with something new to be scared of.

It did seem that he was leaving nothing to chance regarding the journey to his neighbor's castle, and that Father Julian was in on it. Whenever Brother Arcadius glanced out the library windows these days, there were the count and Father Julian giving things a close inspection. According to Brother Marcus, they'd tested the courtyard gate for ready action in opening and closing, and they'd counted the paces down to the edge of the pine woods, where the trail began that led to the lands below. He'd also heard that they'd been down to the mule pasture repeatedly, giving the new mule a thorough going-over, almost hair by hair, each time. This was uncustomary behavior for Father Julian, but it continued day by day.

Another unusual thing was that all of Brother Arcadius's lessons were canceled, along with his daily walks. Father Julian gave these unexpected orders in his usual level tones. "It's just for the time being, Arcadius," he said. "Lady Aurelia's military escort will be gathering to take us safely to her wedding. Best to keep out of the way. And I'll be busy." He gave a brief nod of dismissal and went his way.

The escort, so far, consisted of Bogardu's own men, the ones who'd arrived with him: ten stern and resolute-looking retainers, well armed with swords and battle-axes and stout clubs, too. They camped outside the monastery walls, next to their tethered mules. Ten men did not seem like a large escort for a count, but Remba, the bridegroom, would be arriving with more. How many would he bring? wondered Brother Arcadius. A hundred?

One or another of Count Bogardu's men took turns standing guard outside a window that had to be Lady Aurelia's, in the quarters reserved for notable guests, alongside Father Julian's own rooms. Unlike the plain, unbarred windows in the monks' lodgings, these guest windows boasted elaborate grills in intricate designs. Never daring to actually stare, but with multiple brief glances, Brother Arcadius now and then saw a pale face pressed against the grillwork of the guarded window. And more than once a flutter of small fingers greeted Pangur Ban, for the cat had discovered the whereabouts of the lady he thought so much of. More than once each day he came trotting up with his tail aloft and his ears pricked alertly forward, only to be sent flying by the stampings and shoutings and arm-wavings of the guard. Yet sooner or later he always came back again, a compassionate cat giving comfort to a friend in distress. It made Brother Arcadius feel proud, but also a bit worried. Let Pangur like Lady Aurelia, but not like her so much that he'd pine for her when she left....

These unusual days had one more puzzle to offer. Heading back to the library after prayers and supper, Brother Arcadius was very surprised to have a fellow monk come straight up to him and stop him in his tracks. "Arcadius!" It was Brother Carolus, a monk who was part of the night guard, there in the courtyard—the one who was usually up in the watchtower, or on the walls. Brother Carolus had never said as much as ten words to him before. Yet here he stood with a question on his lips. "Arcadius, you spend plenty of time with Father Julian, don't you?"

"Only for lessons," said Brother Arcadius. Lessons, and that weekly board game that Father Julian made him play—that indeed he wanted to play, for Father Julian's sake, but otherwise no. *Chess.* No matter how many knots he twisted his brain into, his king always got hopelessly trapped within fifteen moves.

"Well, could you tell me, please, why Father Julian and that count went off together last night in the dark, off the paths, into the scrublands? Why would they go there?"

"I don't know," said Brother Arcadius, mystified.

"Well, I know we've taken our vows not to meddle with things that are none of our business, but it bothers me," said Brother Carolus. "They stayed out there a long time. I was on the walls and I saw them go. It was hours before they came back."

"Watching the stars, maybe?" said Brother Arcadius. It was the best—the only—thought he had to offer.

"There weren't any. Clouds." Carolus frowned distractedly at the path for a moment. Then he hurried back to his post in the courtyard.

Count Remba arrived the day after. He too brought an entourage of only ten men mounted on mules. They also were armed with battle-axes, swords, and clubs. They joined the others outside the walls, and Remba joined Bogardu and Father Julian at their table in the dining hall at suppertime that night.

Along with every other monk, Brother Arcadius studied the newcomer from the corner of his eye. So this was the bridegroom. Remba's son might be the glorious Bold-Heart, but Remba himself resembled nothing so much as a goblin, a funny little goblin. He had a small body and a big bald head with a tuft of white hair on the crown, and another tuft of white hair on his chin. He was bowlegged too, and seemed half stupefied by everything around him, and miserable into the bargain. Now and then he cleared his throat with a resounding "grrrk." Having already decided that he didn't like Count Bogardu, Brother Arcadius strove hard not to pass any more judgments. But a farther cry from heroes like that Bold-Heart could not be imagined. He hoped that Lady Aurelia would at least end up with a very excellent cat.

After supper, he went back to the library and let himself in. Brother Ormun, three cells down, had actually asked if he might borrow a book—a saint's life, he wanted, with a good deal of traveling and fighting in it, so he hoped. Brother Arcadius had found just the right book for him, but hadn't wanted to bring it to vespers or supper. He went back for it now. He had set it right there on the table and could find it by touch...or maybe he couldn't? He eased open a shutter to provide some light.

"Grrrk!"

The reverberant noise from outside made him jump, and then stay very still. A sound came of footsteps approaching, and then they stopped. Count Remba and Count Bogardu were right out there beside the darkened library. He could have reached through the window and touched them. Count Bogardu was speaking now, as if to a backward child. "Calm your fears, dear Count Remba, and kindly listen to me. Yes, just as you say, it's a long way up here, and yes, just as you say, in a short while we'll all go back down again, and yes, just as you say, I could have brought my daughter straight to you without this detour— but I didn't, and that is the point."

"Grrrk!" Count Remba cleared his throat again, tremendously. "I don't get it! God's eyes!"

Opening one's ears to such blasphemy was unmonklike and wrong, but now Count Bogardu was speaking. Brother Arcadius leaned forward and listened harder. "My friend, why would you need to understand it? You are the bridegroom in this, and I am the planner—

the military strategist, if you will. We each have our part to play, and we'll play them well. But I will explain. First, our coming up here will confuse our sons, and confuse them we must. They will not know where we might go next from here. They will not know where to best deploy their forces. Do you see? That is strategy. Serving with the king's army or not, married to heiresses or not, our sons will still be aiming to upset our plans...to steal Aurelia away and marry her off to some minion, and gain control of our properties that way."

"If I didn't have to have her, I'd let 'em," whined Count Remba. "God's eyes! Another damned marriage! God's eyes!"

"But you do have to have her," said Count Bogardu. "Do you want your son Rodhrighu to be your heir? After the insolent way he's behaved with you? I do not speak of my own son, or my own interests in this matter."

"God's eyes!" rasped Count Remba. "The way he swaggered up to me! And looked down at me! And said I could just sit back and *rest* now, because he'd be so glad to *help* me manage everything. God's eyes! Glad to help himself to everything I've got, that's what he meant. Never could trust his mother when it came to property—she hated bed, didn't have to worry about her that way—and I don't trust him. Smooth-talking snotty know-it-all, that's what he is."

"I had a Julian," brooded Count Bogardu. "You should have tried living with a Julian."

"I will be living with a Julian! God's eyes!"

"A young Julian, Remba. That makes all the difference. Mine was already twenty and steeped in pride and willfulness when I got her. It took everything I had to keep her under control—everything. And then she gave me a son who's the living image of her, Julian through and through. But I say this to you, Count Remba: no Julian will ever play the haughty master with me again!"

Remba stirred uneasily. "That shutter's open a little," he said. "Maybe somebody's listening."

Brother Arcadius, listening spellbound, shrank further back into the darkness.

"The monks are all in their cells now," Count Bogardu said. "Nobody's in there. Getting back to my two-pronged strategy, the first prong is diversion and confusion, as I just said, and the second prong —I must say, Count Remba, that even though there's no need in the world for you to understand it, it does help me clarify my thoughts to talk it out loud to a listener, namely, you. So it's probably for the best that you voiced your doubts. But before we consider the second prong, which is even more important than the first, let me give you a father's advice about dealing with my daughter. You have to be firm. But all the same, it helps to be kindly, too. You can do little things now and then to cheer her up."

"What things?"

"Why...if there are certain colors she likes to embroider with, see that she has them, if they're not too hard to come by. Or you might get her some ribbons for her hair, or a little dog to cuddle. Most ladies like dogs. My wife never did, but—Don't I recall seeing your wife with a little dog in her arms? Or was that somebody else's wife?"

"A little dog?" Count Remba sounded all at sea. "A little dog! God's eyes!"

"Yes," said Bogardu. "Ribbons, a dog, anything of that sort. But now let's get back to the second prong of my strategy. In a word, by coming up here and dealing with my brother-in-law Julian face to face, I've succeeded in getting protection for us beyond our dreams. We're going to be guarded by Scarpian mercenaries!"

"Scarpian mercenaries! God's eyes!"

"You may well say that, my friend," Count Bogardu exulted. "My brother-in-law has always let people assume that he travels with mere groups of merchants, but I've always doubted that. So when he came to my castle last year to scuttle my first plans for my daughter's marriage to you, I faced him down. 'You keep Scarpians on retainer,' I said to him. 'Admit it,' I said. 'The merchants you say you travel with are Scarpians in disguise.' And he didn't say I was right—that is not the Julian way—but by the look in his eyes I knew I had him. Then, for a year, I've been after him by letter, keeping all this a strict secret from you, to hold things secure. Not that I don't trust you, dear friend, but castle walls do have ears. I've been after him by letter, I say, assuring him that if he hires protection like that for himself, he can very well hire protection like that for his niece. Either that, or I expose his selfishness to every person of truly high standing—even to the pope!"

"God's eyes! The pope!"

"Yes! And by coming up here, I've secured the final arrangements. Scarpian leaders are lurking nearby in the wilderness even as we speak, and four nights ago...."

Count Bogardu was pacing away now from the window, with Count Remba in his wake. It was no longer easy to hear what he was saying. "I made Julian take me out there.... Spoke to their chief....

Desperado if ever there was one....Bearded devil.... Just what we need...." Count Bogardu's voice faded away into the night. A final "grrrk!" came from Count Remba. Then there was silence.

Brother Arcadius snapped his fingers in unmonklike vexation. Making sure that the counts were no longer anywhere near, he went off to give Brother Ormun his book. He tried to puzzle out what he'd just heard. Scarpian mercenaries were the best, the wickedest, the most expensive fighters that ever there were, that was for sure. Did Father Julian really keep some of them on retainer? When he traveled with merchants, were those merchants not merchants at all? Did he keep this great secret close, in the Julian way? And had he really been faced down and shamed by Count Bogardu?

Try to stop being utterly stupid, Bogardu. When Lady Aurelia had been telling her long, sad story, weren't those the words that she'd said her mother had said? If you were Count Bogardu, and you were trying to get the better of Father Julian, of all people, wasn't it...well...stupid to be so sure you'd succeeded? Didn't it make more sense to be in doubt?

But if Father Julian had tricks of his own to play, what sort of tricks would they be? In this business of high-level marriage, nothing an assistant librarian could think of really added up.

Over the next few days, the plans for transporting Lady Aurelia to Count Remba's castle took their final shape. Count Bogardu took complete charge of things now. He drilled and re-drilled his ten men in the courtyard, and Count Remba's too. He bawled their instructions over and over again. They were to pull up their mules in formation, thus, around the bride on her jennet. They were to wheel them to the left, and circle to the right. They were to understand that there'd be reinforcements—*Scarpian* reinforcements. A band of Scarpian mercenaries and their commander would soon be arriving. The commander would be a war leader of the highest rank. He had emergency orders in case of trouble. If trouble came, they should all follow his lead. The counts' men nodded eagerly. They were glad to know that they'd have this formidable help.

Brother Arcadius learned about all this at second hand, in bits and pieces of comments from monks whose duties took them near all the drilling. He doubted that he was always getting the right information. Even Brother Marcus couldn't always be there at the kitchen door, listening in, and making sure that he caught every word, or got the words right that he did catch. The day watchmen were always on hand, but their attention was supposed to be trained outside the courtyard, not in it.

What he knew for sure was that only nineteen men were being drilled at a time. The counts' men were still taking turns standing guard outside Lady Aurelia's window. Pangur Ban continued to be mightily interested in Lady Aurelia, and the men continued to be determined to shoo him off. One of Count Remba's men took a more lenient view, and let Pangur sit there awhile before taking action. Then Lady Aurelia's slim fingers would often be seen wistfully waving, and the chaperone's shout would ring forth: "Chase him away!" It was sad and worse than sad. It was cruel and wrong!

The commander arrived.

Yes, he was wildly bearded, and where his face wasn't covered by a tangled, bristling beard and mustache, it was covered by his helmet, and a wickeder-looking person had never peered through rust-rimmed eye holes, not even among the savage Viking Danes. He might well have been a Dane and no mistake. Violence radiated from him like heat from an oven. To the stable master's confusion and chagrin, this counterpart of the long-dead Attila the Hun, on Father Julian's own command, would be the one who'd ride the new mule to the wedding. He was already riding it every day. He trotted it this way and that about the courtyard, explaining battle plans and ways and means to the counts' men in a tight-lipped snarl. They'd be the ones who rode closest to the bride, he told them. But he himself would take charge of her at the first sign of trouble.

His band of followers arrived, riding up out of the scrublands on their mules. They didn't quite match their commander for fearsomeness, but they were fully helmeted and wildly bearded too. They were to be waiting outside the courtyard on the day of departure, and their commander would then deploy them as he saw fit.

Brother Arcadius tried not to think of Lady Aurelia in the midst of a melee involving clubs and swords and battle-axes. If anyone did try to carry her away, they'd want to take her alive, wouldn't they? But what about Father Julian? How would he fare? Thoughts like these served only to drag a person down, and had to be banished. Father Julian didn't look worried, anyway. Or maybe...maybe he actually looked very worried. With Father Julian, you simply could never tell.

Count Bogardu looked gloriously pleased with himself and with all the arrangements, which after all were his own.

Count Remba kept to himself, and stayed out of the way.

The final hours came for the departure. The cavalcade aimed to set off before sunrise. The monks had not been invited to be present at the leave-taking: the courtyard would be crowded enough without them. But they hadn't been told to stay away, either. Although obedience was Brother Arcadius's first nature, his second nature, which was somewhat different, was in the fore. He wanted to be there to wave an encouraging goodbye to Lady Aurelia. Pulling his robe on over his tunic and breeches, he made his way as inconspicuously as possible toward the courtyard. He slowed down when he recognized the little shape trudging ahead of him. Count Remba was on his way to the courtyard too. With him was one of his guardsmen, talking to him urgently and swinging an empty sack. It was the fellow who'd always been nice to Pangur Ban.

Low to the ground, a white shape came forward through the darkness. Pangur Ban had finished his night's mousing in the kitchen, and was prudently heading away from the noisy courtyard and its thronging mules. In spite of the sadness of Lady Aurelia's leave-taking, Brother Arcadius couldn't help smiling at his cat's common sense. Pangur came closer, the guard spoke on, and Count Remba yelped... What was it he'd yelped?

"God's eyes! If she likes the cat, get her the cat!"

Brother Arcadius stopped dead in his tracks. For half a heartbeat he stood frozen, stupefied by what was taking place before him. Pangur snatched up! Pangur in the sack slung over the guard's shoulder! Pangur being carried off to the courtyard at a run! Brother Arcadius's wits returned to him and he ran too, past Count Remba, through the refectory door and down the long corridor. Gasping, he reached the farther door and hurtled into the courtyard. A strange sight met his eyes.

Outlined against a shadowy, shifting audience of transfixed mules and equally transfixed riders, the guard he'd followed appeared to be frantically dancing now with the sack—the twisting, lunging sack—that held Pangur Ban. The guard's mule was there, being held in place with difficulty by a comrade. The dancing, capering guard was trying to climb into the saddle and hang on to the lunging sack too. His mule was not giving way to horse-like panic, but it was rolling its eyes in gravest doubt and beginning to back away. And the other mules in the courtyard, they too were now backing away. And the, the, the *cat-snatcher*, the *brazen cat-snatcher*, now had one foot in the stirrup, and was juggling the sack instead of dancing with it—

And the sack burst open despite his clutching hands, and out of it

137

stormed an enraged and desperate cat that leaped across the saddle to the neck of the next mule over, and leaped from that neck onto another, and leaped from that second neck to a nearby rump, and then to a rider's shoulder—

Sensible or not, every mule in the courtyard went out of control. A demonic cat was upon them, slashing, clawing, biting, yowling, hurting them, striking extreme agitation into their hearts. Ignoring the urgent whacks from their riders' clubs, they surged this way and that, kicking and rearing. Blows that their riders meant for them landed on other riders instead. Shouts and curses mingled with thuds and groans.

"Pangur Ban!" Brother Arcadius threw himself into the wild melee. Pangur Ban couldn't find a way down, that was the trouble. Wherever he leaped, there was a mule, or a mule's rider, and the way to the ground that might have seemed open for a moment closed again. Brother Arcadius struggled forward. A mule's sweaty rump swung into him, another mule's yellow teeth closed hard on his arm, a third mule's knee slammed into his stomach and doubled him over.... He had to reach Pangur Ban, he had to.... That vile thievery couldn't have been on Lady Aurelia's orders, it couldn't....

A big hand reached down from somewhere above and seized him by the nape of his hood. One rider, at least, was still in control of his mount and had come to the rescue. Whoever it was had a wild beard and a helmet like the mercenary commander, but the eyes peering grimly down at him were... *Father Julian's?* The next thing Brother Arcadius knew, the rider had tapped his mule on the flank, and the mule moved forward, and he, Arcadius, was being half lifted, half walked over to the nearest wall, with his feet barely touching the pavement. "Stay out of this," the rider told him in a low, tense growl. He turned his mule back toward the fray. At the same moment Pangur Ban found the ground, spied Brother Arcadius, and sped into his arms.

Brother Arcadius stood panting against the wall and clutched his cat for dear life. He tried to collect himself and understand the chaotic scene before him. Lady Aurelia was over there by the refectory door. Her father had her by one arm, her chaperone by the other. She was shouting at them and trying to pull away. The bearded rider with the surprising eyes wasn't back in the fray after all. Instead, he was riding out through the courtyard gate. His eyes may have seemed like Father Julian's, but Father Julian himself, strangely enough, was up there on the walls. He seemed to be watching for something. And the mob of outraged mules was calming down again, after a fashion, but that wicked fellow who'd tried to steal Pangur Ban was over there on the ground, being tended to already by Brother Salix. And there was Count Remba, peering out from behind Count Bogardu and looking bewildered, but from outside the courtyard....

From outside the courtyard, where the Scarpian guards were still waiting in formation, there came the sound of a mule briskly trotting steadily nearer. Another moment and through the gate it came, Father Julian's noble mule, the king of all mules, with the ferocious Scarpian commander in the saddle. Making a wide circle around its agitated brethren and their shaken riders, it drew even with the refectory door. There it paused, and Count Bogardu and the chaperone together pushed a struggling Lady Aurelia upward into the commander's arms. Holding her firmly with one arm, and bending his bewhiskered head close to hers— poor Lady Aurelia!—he clucked to the mule and it broke into a canter. Commander, captive, and mule flashed by Brother Arcadius in the blink of an eye, and the captive was weeping, but was she also...*laughing*?

Why would she be laughing?

Count Bogardu was laughing too, there was no doubt about that. Looking ready to burst his tunic in triumph, he was clapping a bewildered-looking Count Remba on the shoulder and calling out to the guardsmen on their mules. And all of those men, in spite of their disarray, were laughing and cheering too, and getting their mules back into some sort of order. "We're on our way, men!" shouted Count Bogardu. "Now go with him! Assist him! Follow his every command! Forward! For—"

The rest of his cry was never completed, for at the gate the bearded commander halted his wonderful mule and wheeled it round again, facing into the courtyard. Left arm supporting Lady Aurelia, left hand holding the reins, he reached beneath his cloak with his right hand and drew out a hunting horn. He raised it to his lips. A bright and piercing sound broke through the dawn. *Suddenly Suddenly Suddenly Oh!* cried the horn, *Suddenly Suddenly Suddenly Oh!* The men waiting outside the walls raised a great cheer. "Hurrah for Bold-Heart!" they shouted. "Hurrah! Hurrah!" And then the mule was wheeled round again, and it bore the commander and Lady Aurelia away at full speed into the morning, into the beautiful dawn, and the men outside the courtyard followed, still cheering. The drumming of hooves, the joyous shouts, and the repeated bright calls of the horn receded into the distance.

"It's...*him*," whispered Count Bogardu. He sounded as if he were being strangled. He'd turned pasty white. "It's *him*," he repeated, his voice rising. Eyes bulging, he stared down at Count Remba, and turned from pasty white to a throbbing red. "It's your *son!*" he screamed. "He's stolen my daughter! Don't just stand there! *Do* something!" But Count Remba did just stand there. He seemed unable to move or speak, and his eyes were bulging too.

Count Bogardu turned to the dumbstruck guards on their mules. "Do something!" he shouted, and the men made a shaky effort to follow orders. The mules, though, were having none of it. They'd been clubbed. They'd been yowled at and clawed by a maddened cat. But in no way had they lost their powers of reason. They knew perfectly well that the magnificent dark brown creature with the splotch on its hip was many times faster than they were. They were in no condition and of no mind to set off on a useless chase. It was madness to think they could ever catch up with it. Enough was enough. They braced themselves against all demands and tantrums and refused to move.

Father Julian smiled down at his kinsman. "It seems that we had no Scarpians after all," he said. From far in the distance came a faint, final *Suddenly Oh!*

Count Remba, goggling about this way and that, found his voice at last. "God's eyes!" he said.

* * *

Supper that night was marked by the joy of Count Remba. His delight at not being a bridegroom was a wonder to see. He sat beaming about him and never once cleared his throat. His old peevish suspicions were eclipsed by sheer relief. Count Bogardu and Lady Aurelia's chaperone were in their rooms, being attended to by Brother Salix. He trusted they'd be feeling better in a matter of days. Father Julian addressed the assembled monks in quiet tones. Due to a sudden indisposition of the bride's father, the wedding had been called off, he said. His niece was being escorted to her brother's home. She'd borrowed a mule that belonged to Spiritus Sanctus, but it would soon be returned. He opened a book that was lying ready to hand, a book of saints' lives. He read a selection from it. Whatever he'd meant to say about the wedding had now been said.

* * *

"He'd better come back safe and sound!" cried Brother Bruno. His thoughts were all for the mule, the pride of his life.

* * *

"Called off?" said Brother Marcus in a hoarse whisper. "*Carried off* is the way I'd put it, if you ask me." He looked this way and that, making sure that Keti was asleep in his kitchen bed, and that nobody else was nearby. Keeping his ear to the ground, he'd finally pieced together what must have happened, or at least a good part of it. That Bold-Heart person had never been married at all. He and young Julian had plotted to save Lady Aurelia. Knowing the two young hotheads would act with or without him, Father Julian had done his best to reduce the risks. He'd bought a mule that none of the counts' mules were likely to match in speed and stamina. He'd let Count Bogardu think that his strategies were working, to catch him off guard. "But I can't understand why all those mules went berserk," he said. "The stew kettle needed my attention just at that moment, so it all beats me."

"It beats me, too," said Brother Arcadius. When all was said and done, the whole thing was Julian business. If Brother Marcus had missed a certain small detail of the great rescue, it was best for assistant librarians to just keep mum.

* * *

One month later, Brother Arcadius received the second and third letters he'd ever gotten in his life. The first one filled him with relief, joy, and great pride—pride for the writer, his own Mam, who'd learned her letters so late in life. She wrote that his family was well and standing in high esteem with the new king, Edward the Elder, who seemed likely to be as good a king as his father Alfred, who had sadly just died.

He tucked the letter into the willow basket that held the first one she'd sent him. Then he turned to the other letter he'd received that day. It was from Lady Aurelia and it was very long. It was written, by and large, in excellent Latin that seemed to be the writer's own. Here and there he could see where a word had been scraped off the parchment and replaced with a better choice. He nodded approvingly. The corrections showed a proper concern for high standards in writing. He read the letter avidly. It told him a good many things that he already knew from Brother Marcus, or had figured out. It also told him things that he didn't know.

Dearest, Kindest, Best Brother Arcadius! Even though I am now the happiest person in the world, my happiness could never continue if you thought for one moment that I ever tried to steal our hero, Pangur Ban. No, the misguided idea was Count Remba's. He and my father are very different now. Count Remba is overjoyed that he doesn't have to get married, especially to me. And my father is chastened, and recognizes his presumption in thinking he could outwit my uncle, and his foolishness in thinking that the two best sons in the world would ever plot against their fathers!

I attribute his failings, and the failings of Count Remba, to their age. Being in their fifties, and never too bright to begin with, they are prone to all sorts of frailties of the mind. I pity them, and have freely forgiven them for their attempted cruelty. You can be sure that their sons will always give them respect, and shelter too—should it be needed.

So, dear Brother Arcadius! The whole idea was to abduct me with no serious harm to anyone or anything, man or mule. So my dear Bold-Heart pretended to be married, and my brother pretended that he'd been called into service, and they laid their plans. But it was feared all along that success could not be assured. That is why everything was kept strictly secret from me, lest false hopes be raised. Our three conspirators often were racked with the gravest misgivings. Yet the alternative was to throw me into a life of abject misery, and none of them had the heart for that! If I had known what they intended, though, I believe I would have found the courage to sacrifice myself, for so much could have gone fatally wrong!

It was our wonderful Pangur Ban who made it certain that all would be well. All by himself, and without doing serious harm to a single man or a single mule, he made it impossible for my father's men, or Count Remba's men, to come after me in any timely way. I am sure that if he'd given things an instant's thought, he could have found a way to simply jump down and run off. Instead, he put those mules into such a state that they could barely move, so I'm told, let alone come chasing after me. I believe, and I will always believe, that he was inspired by Heaven. (It was my dear brother, by the way, who took you to safety in the courtyard. He says you are brave, and sends you his regards.)

So all is well now, dearest and best Brother Arcadius. My chaperone has been sent flying, my tutors are back, and I will stay with my brother until I decide to marry. My beloved Bold-Heart agrees that I can wait as long as three years. (He is properly clean-shaven again, by the way, and so is my brother.) Then we will marry and raise our family—and we shall be as happy as Judith and her Iron-Arm, I know. I am determined to call one of our sons Tammis. And I have been promised the gift, very soon, of a white kitten, whom I shall call Pangur Ban II.

So seeing that I have used a great deal of parchment in expressing these my thoughts, and wanting very much to be a thrifty and provident wife for my Bold-Heart, I shall end by saying that in me, Brother Arcadius, you have a true friend for life.

With the *utmost* affection and sincerity, I am Aurelia *Judith* de Juliani et Bogardu, the Countess-to-be Aurelia de Rodhrighu-Rembarian.

Shaking his head in wonder, Brother Arcadius read Lady Aurelia's letter through a second time. He would always be glad that he'd met her, and that things had worked out so well for her. But when all was said and done, now that he'd seen life among the higher-ups at almost first hand, he was very glad to be a monk, with a cat, in a monastery.

He reached into the wallet that hung at his side and took out his writing tools. He supposed he should send a reply, although he was not sure of what it should say. It would have to be something short and vague, it went without saying. Father Julian's secrets were Father Julian's secrets. It was not for an assistant librarian to give them away. To give them away, or to keep accounts of them lying around. He would have liked to keep Lady Aurelia's letter just for the friendship of it, not because—*never* because—her warrior brother had paid him a compliment and said he was brave. But he couldn't. He picked up the knife that was made for the purpose and began to scrape the words away from the parchment, one by one.

Soft fur brushed affectionately across his ankles, and he looked down and smiled. "I'm sorry I have to destroy this letter, Pangur Ban," Brother Arcadius said, "but you and I don't need it to remember what happened." He scraped a bit faster. *Brother* and *Arcadius, Tammis, Pangur,* and *brave* fell into fragments, which he brushed away.

"Mrrrrrrr," said Pangur Ban.

THE VANISHING HEAD

In which realism in art makes a premature
appearance, and much comes of it

AD 899

Vespers was over. The monks of Spiritus Sanctus, Brother
Arcadius among them, were waiting in their cells for the call to
supper. When it came, they would emerge from one or another
of the eight buildings that housed them, and pace in silent procession
to the dining hall.

During this peaceful, meditative time of day, Brother Arcadius
usually recited psalms to himself—the peaceful, meditative ones—
savoring their beauty, and feeling in harmony with himself and the
world around him. He was doing so now when a sudden scrabbling
noise from the hall outside his door stopped him in mid-word. Sighing,
he hurried to open the door and peer out. It was just as he thought. A
big white cat was wildly batting a pine cone this way and that over the
stone floor. "Pangur!" he whispered urgently. "Get in here!"

Pangur Ban, the monastery's peerless mouser, looked at him for a
moment, up and down. Then, in obedience to whatever whim of his
own, he swatted the pine cone through the door and into the cell, and
came in himself to be petted.

"I shouldn't pet you," Brother Arcadius told him, but he was
doing so as he spoke. It was puzzling, though. Pangur Ban, a very
sensible cat, had never shown any great interest in playing games. And
even though he was very socially minded as well, he'd mostly stayed
out of the buildings where the monks had their cells. It was only in the
last week that he'd suddenly begun to chase pine cones around the hall
floor in this particular building only, at this particular time of day.

Something about the noise the pine cones made as they rattled against the floor here in the evening seemed to attract him. It had also called forth a few querulous protests from nearby cells—"Arcadius, will you attend to that cat?"

Brother Arcadius never liked to annoy his brethren, and never liked to be singled out for any reason. By rights Pangur belonged to the whole monastery, not to himself alone. Except for the few things that could fit into a small willow basket—rare letters from home, or a holy relic or two—property was held in common at Spiritus Sanctus. But he was the one who'd brought Pangur here in the first place, so if Pangur made any disturbance, of course he should stop it. He suppressed the unmonklike thought that the pine cone's rattling hadn't been all that loud. "Play your game outside, Pangur," he admonished the purring cat.

"Mrrrwrrr," said Pangur. He leaped lightly up to the cell's one narrow window and sat on the sill a moment, preening. Then he leaped down to the ground outside and went on his way. The bell in the courtyard watchtower near the main gate sounded its call. Brother Arcadius gathered up his mealtime gear, his bowl, mug, knife and spoon—not his property either, really, but Brother Salix, the medicus, insisted that such things should not be shared. He located Pangur's pine cone off in a corner and picked it up to throw it away outside. His brethren were already filing into the hall and heading off to the refectory. Head bowed, thoughts mostly at peace despite things like pine cones and over-sharp hearing, he joined the procession.

The autumn air was refreshing and mild, and the bell's pure repeated sound was its counterpart. Monks from the other buildings converged upon the path in orderly fashion. Up the slight rise they went to the refectory, and through its wide door, and soon they were quietly entering the dining hall. Father Julian, head of the monastery, was already seated at his table above the others, up on a dais. With his dark gaze upon them, the monks sat down too at the first available places they came to, as was the rule.

Brother Marcus's kitchen workers moved here and there, with little Keti, the kitchen boy, intent among them. They were setting bowls of gruel and baskets of breads and cheeses and fruits and greens down on the tables, and flagons of well-watered wine. Mornings, with a day's urgent work ahead of them, the monks of Spiritus Sanctus had their simple breakfasts dished out to them as they stood in line, and ate on the run without ever sitting down. But suppers were more ample and leisurely.

"Brother Arcadius...." The sudden, startling whisper came from behind. Turning, Brother Arcadius found himself looking down, just slightly, at Brother Zossimus, the monastery's elderly woodcarver. Wrinkled and wispy, with a tonsure of fluffy white hair, Brother Zossimus always had the air of an exceptionally timid mouse peeking fearfully from its hole in the wall—wanting not to scurry out to snatch a crumb of something, but to apologetically put a crumb back. Apart from two or three truly ancient and shrunken old fellows who spent their days and nights lying speechless on their cots in the care of others, Zossimus was the one monk at Spiritus Sanctus who was actually shorter and slighter than Brother Arcadius. It was pleasant to be taller and heftier, not to mention bolder and possibly more worldly, than somebody else. All the same, this was not the time or the place to stand around talking. A quick and inquiring nod from Brother Arcadius elicited the carver's next whisper. "Brother Arcadius, do you still go on your walks?"

"I do." As the monastery's assistant librarian, Brother Arcadius was under strict orders to take a good hour's walk every day, lest he injure his health and his keen young eyesight by poring too assiduously over manuscripts. There was no point in having an assistant librarian who could no longer assist.

"Then if you do...tomorrow...could you stop by my workshop just for a moment? I...I have something beautiful to show you.... I mean, I...."

Belatedly, Brother Zossimus seemed to realize that he was in the way of a good many people behind him. Brother Arcadius nodded a hurried yes, and the wispy little fellow moved quickly on. Soon after, with everyone seated, Father Julian said grace and then supper got under way. Nobody seemed to have noticed the moment's exchange, but a rule had been bent all the same, by the timidest monk of them all. What could it be, this beautiful thing that called forth such, well, daring?

"Eating or just looking tonight, Arcadius?" muttered the monk sitting across from him. It was one of the courtyard watchmen, Brother Kongro, off duty now until dawn.

"Oh, eating," said Brother Arcadius in a half whisper, and filled his bowl.

Now and then throughout the next day, Brother Arcadius looked up briefly from his reading and writing in the library to wonder again what Zossimus had to show him, and why the old fellow had singled him out. He hardly knew Brother Zossimus, after all. Maybe nobody did. The monks at Spiritus Sanctus didn't gossip about each other, for Father Julian never would have allowed it. But in spite of that there seemed to be a sort of understood feeling throughout the monastery that Brother Zossimus was easily flustered, or easily tired, or something. That woodcarving in a small and limited way was maybe as much as he could manage. All of this seemed to set him somewhat apart

His place of work set him apart also. Brother Zossimus spent his working days in a shed outside the monastery walls, around the corner from the main gate. Here he slowly carved the pegs and knife handles and other small objects made of wood that were sometimes called for. Here he also slowly and lovingly carved saints. Carved them, and now and then sold them to travelers passing by.

A large party of merchants had once bought seventeen of them, but such sales were rare. When a number of saints had accumulated unsold, Father Julian had them bundled up and sent off to some market fair or other, where they found takers, almost always, at a quarter of a quarter of a quarter penny for ten, or half that, or less. These profits were added to the monastery's fund of petty cash. So no one could say that Brother Zossimus wasn't contributing, but it might be said that he wasn't contributing much.

If monks had been in the way of buying things, Brother Arcadius might have bought one of these saints himself. He'd seen them quite often when passing by on his walks. They were all carved and painted with the greatest care. Their faces were all alike and looked very saint-like, and all their robes were brown or blue. Some of the saints were taller, others shorter. Some had beards, some didn't. Most were men, but some were women. Some had black or brown hair, others were blond. And if you looked closely and thought about it, you could tell who they were meant to be. Saint Peter, for instance, stood upon an unmistakable rock. Saint Paul held a scroll—surely it was a scroll—that was neatly labeled "Epistles" in carefully painted tiny letters. Saint Jerome had a lion crouching at his feet. You could tell it was a lion and not a dog or a goat by the mane.

A while back, a saint that Brother Zossimus was especially proud of had been contemptuously rejected as a gift by an overbearing visitor who had turned out to be—but there was no point in picking at old wounds. The saints were excellent saints and that was a fact. If Brother

Zossimus wanted to show him a new one, then Brother Arcadius wanted to see it. When the afternoon sun dipped lower in its daily perfect circle around the earth, and the shadows attained the length that meant it was time for his walk, he headed off for the carver's workshop to do just that.

"Oh, you did come, Brother Arcadius! How kind of you! Thank you! You won't be sorry." Eyes shining, Brother Zossimus beckoned his visitor into the shed that served as his shop. Wood shavings and sawdust littered the floor, and an assortment of awls, adzes, planes, and gouges hung from the walls. The place was fragrant with the smell of wood. "Now, stay right there and I'll—" Zossimus ducked behind the set of battered shelves that held his array of saints and came back in view with something in his hand. "Brother Arcadius, if you will just shut your eyes—I want to surprise you—and hold out your hand, I'll —"

Brother Arcadius did so. Something cool and hard was pressed into his hand. He opened his eyes and looked to see what was there. A man's face in darkest wood peered up at him with narrowed, measuring eyes that fairly seemed alive. The lips, tightly pressed together and drawn a bit to the side, seemed to smile as if at some private joke. Gaunt cheeks, raised eyebrows, and a wrinkled forehead contributed to the whole living, thinking expression. Brother Arcadius had never seen anything like it. It was so real that it made him uneasy, as if he held someone's actual head in his hands, shrunken but sharply aware. Part of him thought it was wonderful. Part of him didn't like it at all.

"Do you see?" Brother Zossimus whispered delightedly. "Do you see how different it is?"

"That I do!" Brother Arcadius said sincerely. The little head was about the size of a squirrel's head, but felt much heavier in his hand than its size would indicate. Skill, or time, had polished it to an overall soft gleam: it was not nicked or scratched in any way. Surely Brother Zossimus had not made this extraordinary thing. Or had he? Better to ask some other sort of question, something that couldn't be taken as an insult. "What sort of wood is this?"

"I don't know," said Brother Zossimus, wide-eyed. "It has to be from somewhere far, far away. But the head itself—Brother Arcadius, if you think a moment, maybe you'll recognize it. It's something that you have seen every single day! Or maybe I should say, you see it but you don't!" The woodcarver pointed to the doorway. "Let's go out in the sun, so you can have a better look."

151

See it and don't see it, every day? Well, *don't* seemed to have the upper hand. Outside the shed now, Brother Arcadius turned the carving over in the sunlight. The back of the head was as beautifully finished and real-looking as the front, except for one thing. A square opening had been cut deeply into it. Within that square, Brother Arcadius's gently probing finger could feel what seemed like tiny walls set against each other at right angles—a maze for fleas, was it? Or what?

"You can't guess?" asked Brother Zossimus. He was practically on tip-toe with delight. "You really can't guess?" He studied Brother Arcadius's baffled face for some sign of comprehension, then cried, "It's from the screen behind the altar! The master builder of our monastery, it's his own face! He carved it! He carved the whole screen too, in the beginning, all those years ago!" Brother Zossimus gave the head another adoring glance and continued, "I wanted you to see it close up, Brother Arcadius—you in particular—because you are so helpful and kind to me when I come into the library, and so careful with the books, and I can tell you love beautiful things...."

The kind, helpful, and so-on assistant librarian frowned in confusion. "If it's from the altar screen, how did you get it here?"

"It's because Father Julian asked me." said Brother Zossimus. "I mean, he asked me two months ago if I had time to be caretaker of the altar screen, and keep it in repair, and give it a good, thorough cleaning once a week, and I said I did, and that's what I've been doing ever since, and when you're so close to it and really see it—oh, it is such a wonder! Such a joy! You can't imagine how fine it really is!"

Brother Arcadius supposed he could imagine it. The pictures in the library's beautiful copy of Genesis were wonders and joys for sure, and maybe this screen was too, seen at close hand. From where he stood in church, with the candlelight flickering, and the candle smoke drifting about, and the shadows shifting, all he could tell was that the screen was as wide as the altar and maybe twice its height, and covered with all sorts of intertwined designs and figures that he couldn't make out. He'd never been able to see exactly what the screen depicted, and indeed had never given much thought to it, either. But this head? Brother Zossimus still hadn't explained how he'd come to have it. If it had broken off in his care, he wouldn't be looking so happy, would he? "Um, do all the carvings come off the screen? So you can clean them?"

"Oh, no," said Brother Zossimus. "It's just this one, and even Father Julian didn't know about it. The whole screen is made of pinewood, and nothing comes off except this head. I found that out when I was cleaning it. I saw that the head was made of this different kind of wood, whatever it is, and when I touched it, I felt it move under my hand, just slightly. So I went to Father Julian to tell him that it seemed loose, and ask him what he thought we should do about it, and he said he'd never taken much notice of the screen at all, except to see that it needed a cleaning...."

He paused for a long breath and then went on. "And he said that if there was just one wobble in something so old, we shouldn't worry about it, and that we'd just peg it back on if it came off. So I asked him why the head was made of different wood, and whose head was it. He said he guessed it would be the master builder's head, but anything else about it he didn't know. But he got his great book down from the shelf —you know the one I mean...."

Brother Arcadius did know. The book had been brought out and consulted any number of times since he'd come to the monastery. It set forth the history and the rules of Spiritus Sanctus, along with other matters of importance. "So—did the book tell you all about it?"

Brother Zossimus came closer and spoke lower. "It said—these are the exact words—'The master builder of Spiritus Sanctus was Nardo of Cremona, who also carved the screen behind the altar, with his likeness in dark wood upon it.' Then it went on to something completely different, something to do with the lake, I think it was. But there were letters in the margin, very faint: U, UE, UW, UN, US, U. And U, US, UN, UW, UE, D. I asked Father Julian what they meant, and he said he had no idea."

"I certainly don't," said Brother Arcadius. He turned Master Nardo's likeness over in his hand so that the square opening was uppermost. "Does it have something to do with this?"

"That is exactly right, Brother Arcadius," the carver said. "But at the time, with the head attached to the screen, the opening didn't show. Father Julian knew nothing of it, and I didn't either. But hour after hour those strange letters nagged at my mind, if you understand me, and I kept thinking, *They mean something. They mean something about this screen.* And slowly it came to me that E, W, N, and S often stand for—"

"Oh!" said Brother Arcadius. He'd become so taken up in the tale that he didn't even realize that he was interrupting. "Oh yes! They stand for the four directions—the four corners of the earth—the four winds—"

"For East, West, North, and South, yes," said Brother Zossimus, his eyes gleaming. "And U and D often indicate Up and Down. So I went back to Father Julian and told him what I was thinking, and he came with me to watch and see how it went. I pulled on the head with great care, holding my breath. It lifted up from the screen a good quarter-inch. Keeping it up, I was able to move it east—not where east really is, but where they'd show it on a map. Then I did the same for west, and north, and south, and it came off in my hand. Even though that's what I thought might happen, and even though Father Julian had said not to worry, my heart almost stopped! But then I saw the square on the back of the head, and I saw that carved into the screen where the head had been there was another square with grooves in it that fit the walls within the opening on the head. It's all a very, very clever lock and key, Brother Arcadius. To put the head back, you just go the other way and then press down, to lock it. It's not hard to do, really," said the carver with modest pride. "You just have to see those few letters and figure out what they mean."

"But why would the builder do all that in the first place?" asked Brother Arcadius.

"I wondered that too," said Brother Zossimus. "But then the answer came to me, I think from above. The rest of the screen is just as wonderful as this is, but it's all saints and angels and the Heavenly Spirit...all higher things, you see. So I believe that this Master Nardo wanted his likeness to be there on his beautiful work, but he also wanted to show that although he had carved such glorious images of these higher things, he was not higher himself, you know? He was proud of his wonderful skill, but humble too, do you see? So he carved his likeness from this very different kind of wood, and made it so that it could be removed. I think that's what he thought, if I dare to say so." The carver shook his head in wonder. "I asked Father Julian how Master Nardo could have seen himself so clearly, and Father Julian said he would have had a very good mirror. Somebody rich might have had one, and lent it to him."

Brother Arcadius had never spent time with rich people, and had never seen a good mirror. Any mirror he'd ever seen gave you the general idea, very blurrily, that you had two eyes, a nose, a mouth, and so on, but never let you see details like the ones that stood out so remarkably on the wooden head. "Or maybe he had someone else carve the head for him?"

"Oh, I don't think...I mean, I suppose it could be," said the carver doubtfully. "But there's a 'Nar' carved just below the jaw, if you look for it.... I don't think he'd sign it that way if it wasn't his.... I think he was truthful, just like the whole carving is truthful...."

Brother Arcadius gave a token glance at the letters below the jaw, then carefully returned the head to Brother Zossimus's waiting hand. No word against Master Nardo would sit well with the little carver, that was for sure. "So Father Julian is happy about the secret lock?"

"Oh, he is!" cried Brother Zossimus. "He even tried it himself, several times. And then he did something very wonderful, and I think you've already guessed it."

"I'm no good at guessing," said Brother Arcadius. "You'd better just tell me."

Brother Zossimus drew a tremulous breath. "He's letting me keep it with me, Brother Arcadius. Not forever, of course, but for a fortnight. For fourteen days I can keep it here in my workshop, and bring it out into the sun where I can really see it, and turn it this way and that, and measure every part of it, carefully, carefully.... And if I do all that, Brother Arcadius, I think I'll be able to carve a head exactly like it, except for the type of wood. I'll have to copy it in pine, I imagine. But if I...if I could make just one perfect thing like this.... If I just could...." Brother Zossimus held the head up to the sun, then pressed it to his heart. "I would be so happy, Brother Arcadius. And if I learned that skill, my saints would turn out better too, don't you imagine? And that would help the monastery, wouldn't you say so?"

"I think your saints are excellent as they are," Brother Arcadius assured him firmly. Who'd want a saint's face that showed all the wrinkles, and peered at you with a peculiar smile? That was most definitely not the purpose of a saint. "I wouldn't change them."

"You're kind, Brother Arcadius. You're just very, very kind," the carver said. His voice had dropped to nearly a whisper again. "I'm so glad you're my friend. But my saints.... I used to think quite a lot of them, you know. But that's before I ever worked on the screen and saw what Master Nardo could do. So I have to make use of this wonderful chance, if I can, but...." Brother Zossimus held up a warning finger. "But Father Julian doesn't want anybody to know about it, though— not the lock, and not the chance he's giving me. I asked him if I could tell you, and he said I could. But he told me to tell you not to tell anyone else."

"You can be sure I won't," said Brother Arcadius with great feeling. Who'd ever dare to go against Father Julian's command? It was good, though, to know that Father Julian thought he was trustworthy, at least. For the past year he'd had weekly lessons with Father Julian in the arts of reasoning—lessons which included the torments of that game called chess. The lessons and games had never gone all that well, and he was sure that by now he'd been written off as stupid, at least in that area. True, you never could tell what Father Julian might be thinking. But "stupid" seemed likely. Stupid or not, more time had gone by than he'd realized, and he had work to do at the library. "Well, I should be going along now," he said.

"Oh...oh yes...of course you should," said Brother Zossimus. He cradled the precious carving in loving hands. "But if you can..... If you have time now and then.... If you'd like to stop by now and then and see how I'm coming along.... I mean, with the copy I want to make..."

"I will," Brother Arcadius assured him, and took his leave.

Over the next two weeks, Brother Arcadius stopped by twice at the carver's workshop, and found dejection there. Measure each feature though he might, stare every which way at the head in the sun though he might, sharpen his knives though he might, think and try and toil though he might, Brother Zossimus's copy did not match up to the original. So he made more, with an air of desperation. Three heads, five heads, six.... He was working much faster than usual, knowing that he had to put Master Nardo's masterpiece back on the screen before long, but that was only part of the trouble, he claimed. His copies had gone all wrong from the very first strokes. He'd studied them and studied them and studied them, but couldn't think why.

Not being a carver himself, Brother Arcadius had no idea why, either. The noses, the mouths, the eyes did look true to those on the head Master Nardo had carved, yet somehow they missed the mark. Apparently there were mistakes that were too small for the eye to take in, but that added up to failure. The original features were alive. You might not like them, but they inspired wonder. They compelled you to gaze in fascination at them from every angle. The copies didn't.

"They're good carvings anyway," he told Brother Zossimus. "I couldn't have done them."

"They're not good," whispered Brother Zossimus. His shoulders drooped.

But Brother Zossimus's fortnight was nearly at an end. All in all, Brother Arcadius was glad of it. It wasn't his place to pass judgment on Brother Zossimus, his elder by so many years. All the same, he felt that the carver was making too much of things. The sooner the head got put back on the screen, the better. In church though, off and on, out of friendship, Brother Arcadius reminded himself to at least glance at the screen and see if he could make out the figures on it, but he never could, not with the candles flickering and the shadows dancing, and candle smoke drifting here and there. And hulking Brother Atalf always somehow managed to stand right in front of him, and if it wasn't him it was somebody else.

The screen could have been covered with images of marauding Danes, for all that Brother Arcadius could see.

The fortnight ended, and the wonderful head was restored to the screen. "I hoped that Father Julian could give me another week, but he couldn't," Brother Zossimus said mournfully. "He said he'd do it if it belonged to him, but it's the monastery's, so it has to be kept where it belongs. And he said...he said he hoped I wouldn't keep on worrying about it. But I've been thinking that maybe...." With a visible effort, Brother Zossimus tried to force brightness into his voice. "Those heads I've carved.... If I stained them with walnut juice and then I oiled them, maybe they'll look more like the real thing."

"Well, maybe you should," said Brother Arcadius uncomfortably. He'd hoped that this whole business would just come to an end, but here it was, going on.

"I will try it," whispered Brother Zossimus, drooping again. "I will let you know if it helps...."

The days passed.

Brother Arcadius tended to his work in the library.

He interrupted more of Pangur Ban's pine cone games.

He went down to ignominious defeat in his chess games with Father Julian.

He went for his walks.

Off and on, Brother Arcadius tried to see if he could at least make out Master Nardo's wonder-work in its place on the screen. That place would be on the lower left, just above the altar, so Brother Zossimus had told him early on. And sure enough, a dark patch was there in that very spot, the first time he looked. But then the shadows shifted, and he wasn't sure. And the next day, no dark spot was there, but the day after there seemed to be one, or maybe not.... The patch appeared and vanished, appeared and vanished...

Like the shadow it was, he concluded. Or it could be the head, he supposed, taking on a new appearance with every shift in the light.

And there was library work, and meals, and walks, and lessons, and chess games and church, and library work—and meals, and walks, and lessons and chess games and church—and on a Friday, in church, during vespers, with the candles flickering and the shadows dancing and the candle smoke faintly coiling here and there, and Brother Atalf scratching his nose and chanting in his thunderous way, and Brother Silvanus shifting from foot to foot because the floor was quite cold, and Brother Marcus thinking all too clearly that he needed to get back to the kitchen and stir the stew, and Father Julian gravely intoning the solemn words of the ancient service—it was on that Friday that Brother Zossimus let out a terrible shriek and fell to the floor.

Vespers came to a jarring halt. Father Julian strode forward, and Brother Salix the medicus helped the fallen carver to his feet. Brother Zossimus stood there trembling. "What is it?" Father Julian demanded. "What's wrong?"

Brother Zossimus wrung his hands. "It's gone," he whispered. "Master Nardo's—it's *gone*."

Father Julian looked down at the stricken carver. "Brother Zossimus," he said, "we will deal with this matter shortly. Meanwhile, you are in no condition to stay here. Brother Salix will take you to the infirmary. I will come as soon as mass is over." Supported by Salix, Brother Zossimus stumbled toward the door. Father Julian turned back to the bewildered assembly of monks. "We will finish the service," he said. "Then we will congregate in the dining hall. Do not return to your cells for your eating things. You will have your suppers, but they will be delayed. And sit, please, with the others of your house, and look to see if anyone is missing." He looked from one questioning face to another. "You will get a full explanation of all this in good time, but that time is not now."

He raised his voice again in the words of the mass, but who at the moment could think of mass? Everyone's mind was fixed on what had just happened. Chanting was ragged. Puzzled eyes glanced here and there. Brother Arcadius, though, thought he knew what had happened, and thought that everything would soon be resolved. Master Nardo's clever device could not have locked securely when the head was so reluctantly replaced. It had locked only part way or not at all, or perhaps the lock had even broken. That would be a misfortune, but it was not the end of the world. The head had simply fallen down behind the altar, that was it. Father Julian would not want to get down and scrabble around for it in front of ranks of monks who were not supposed to know about it, and who were assembled for holy mass. He'd find it when everyone was out of the way in the dining hall, and then he'd come and give some sort of explanation, and the trouble would be over.

But that didn't happen. Mass ended, the monks went off to the dining hall, sat down at the tables, waited, quietly traded words of concern and bewilderment, waited....

Hardly anyone had been able to make out the few words Brother Zossimus had choked out to Father Julian. "What did he say? Did he say 'It's *dawn*'? Did he say 'It's *gone*'? What's the matter with him?"

After half an hour of this Brother Marcus stood up. "Send for me if I'm needed," he said. He summoned his kitchen help with a jerk of the chin—Brother Alvas, Brother Homelius, Brother Sandro, and little Keti the kitchen boy. With his crew trailing behind him, he strode toward the kitchen.

"You're supposed to stay with your house," shouted Bruno, the stable master.

"Do you want any supper tonight?" Marcus demanded. "Or breakfast tomorrow?" He didn't wait for an answer. "Come on," he said to his helpers. Keti was clearly in doubt as to what he should do. "Keti, it will be all right," Brother Marcus told him. "You're not in any house, anyway. You sleep in the kitchen, remember? So let's go, let's go." He beckoned again to his workers, and they filed through the kitchen door.

Marcus and his band of helpers had not been gone long when Brother Arcadius saw a white shape appear at the hallway door, low down. Pangur Ban, as perplexed as anybody, was clearly wondering why supper wasn't out of the kitchen and on the tables yet, and what difference this might make to his night's mousing. He withdrew, and shortly after a faint clatter arose outside in the corridor. The pine cone game had come to the refectory. A chorus of many voices rose in protest. "Arcadius, would you tend to that cat?" Growing steadily hungrier and unhappier with the whole odd situation, people were very much on edge.

"Here, Pangur." In the corridor, Brother Arcadius confiscated the pine cone from unwilling paws, and slipped it into his wallet. Then he lifted the big cat off the floor and held him, just for a moment. "Be patient, Pangur Ban!" he said. Ears flattened, eyes narrowed, Pangur turned his face away and yawned widely—an obvious insult—then leaped to the floor and prowled away. Brother Arcadius sighed. He wondered what was keeping Father Julian so long. It couldn't have been hard to find the fallen head, but maybe it had been hard to put it back. Or impossible, if the clever lock was broken. Or maybe—a chill and unwelcome thought—the shock of everything had been too much for Brother Zossimus. Maybe he was lying in the infirmary gravely ill.

Another half hour passed, or maybe more. It certainly seemed like more. People had been told to sit, so they sat, but they shifted uncomfortably in place. Those sitting near windows craned their necks to try to tell time by the rising moon, but it was not in view from anywhere in the hall. Pangur Ban prowled by the doorway a few times, but played no more games. Monks counted and recounted their tablemates, always concluding that except for Brother Zossimus and the kitchen crew, nobody was missing.

They were concluding something else as well. The words that Zossimus had choked out must have been, "It's gone." What it boiled down to was that something was missing, and that everybody was under a cloud. And hungry and thirsty too, and with a great need, among some, for the nearest latrine. Brother Arcadius listened to the rising litany of conjectures and complaints, and kept silent.

But then at long, long last, Father Julian appeared in the doorway. Brother Marcus must have been listening for him, because he and his helpers simultaneously came back from the kitchen. Father Julian walked past the assembled monks and Keti in silence and went to his usual dining place above the rest. He stood beside the table there. He looked around for attention. The monks sat in dead silence, waiting. "Is everybody here?" he said at last.

"They're not at their table, Marcus and them, Father," called Brother Bruno.

"I see that. Thank you."

"They didn't sit down at their tables at all, Father."

"Thank you, Brother Bruno." Father Julian's dark gaze fell on Keti, solemn and worried at Brother Marcus's side. "Keti, would you say there's enough bread to feed everybody tonight, and tomorrow at breakfast as well?"

Keti pulled himself manfully together and nodded firmly.

"Then, Brother Marcus, with Keti's help, will you see to it that everyone gets bread at least, tonight? What about wine?"

"There's plenty of wine, but not enough cups to go around," Marcus said. "Salix, can we share cups this one time?" From the back of the room, the medicus nodded his assent. "And I can serve cheese and onions too. And grapes."

"Then do so," said Father Julian. "Now, everyone, I want you all to know that Brother Zossimus is resting quietly in the infirmary, and Brother Salix says that his life is in no present danger."

Brother Arcadius sighed with relief, then fastened on the words *no present danger*. Why *present*? Why not just *in no danger*? Frowning, he leaned forward to hear the next words, whatever they might be.

"I don't want to make a great mystery of this," Father Julian said. "In brief, it seems that an object belonging to this monastery has gone missing. This object is simply part of the screen that stands behind the altar—a part that, ah, can be taken off or put back on at will." Pausing, he looked for a moment from one table to another, studying the monks who were studying him in turn.

"Everyone should understand," he continued, "that this object has no value whatsoever, except as a keepsake that is part of this monastery's history, and that belongs to each of us, one and all. At a market fair it will fetch nothing. Slipped into the hands of some trader it will fetch nothing. If it has been taken by some misguided person here, it will bring no gain to that person, only loss. How, then, should we proceed? It is possible that a foolish theft has been committed, and possible that it has not."

There was a general stirring of people and voices, but Father Julian shook his head. "We won't discuss this matter further until you've had a chance to eat and refresh yourselves. You may get up now and move freely around the room while food gets put on the table. Those who wish to use the latrine should line up by the kitchen door, but don't get in the way of the food coming in." Father Julian smiled faintly, or possibly didn't. "You are free to discuss this matter among yourselves, and I will hear your thoughts over supper."

There was silence for a moment, and then another general stir. Some monks hurried to form a line for the latrine. Others moved about, or gathered in groups, quietly talking. Still others simply waited with longing for the meal. Keti, looking much revived, hurried about, setting a few cups down at each table. Then he sped back to the kitchen and returned with a basket of coarse bread. He set it down on the nearest table and hurried off for another. Brother Marcus appeared with Father Julian's rock crystal goblet and silver service, which was always kept stored away in a kitchen cupboard. Brother Arcadius paced this way and that until a hand fell on his shoulder and a voice said, "Arcadius, you're on good terms with Zossimus. What's going on here?" It was Brother Silvanus, the head librarian. For once Silvanus was not attempting to make any jokes. His sparrowhawk's visage registered nothing but concern. "I don't know," said Brother Arcadius. Bracing himself to fend off probing questions, he was immensely relieved to hear Father Julian calling everyone back to their tables.

For a short while everyone simply ate in silence. Each table's shared cups were eagerly passed from mouth to mouth, because the wine tonight, for whatever reason, was as unwatered as it was on important feast days. All around the room, people's moods were visibly lifting. Only Father Julian made no move to eat or drink. At last he called for the discussion to begin.

Brother Mishel, the stonecutter, raised his hand. "Is this why Zoss —I mean, Brother Zossimus—was upset? In the service?"

"At my request, Brother Zossimus has been taking care of the screen," Father Julian said. "It needed a thorough cleaning, and he has done that. He knows it in every particular. During vespers tonight, he saw that the object in question was missing. Rightly or wrongly, he feels that the screen is his responsibility. He did become very upset."

Brother Sifari, one of the courtyard watchmen, spoke up. "Father, this missing object—what does it look like?"

"It's a carving of the face—the whole head, really—of the man who oversaw the building of our monastery, and who carved the screen. It's done in dark wood and could fit into your hand."

"It's old, then," said Brother Sifari.

"As old as the monastery, yes," said Father Julian.

"Well then," said the watchman, "couldn't Brother Zossimus carve us a nice new one? Then the screen will be fixed and he won't have to worry."

"We fix broken things all the time," put in the monk who served as wagon master. "Our wagon wheels—"

"My concern is not for the screen at this moment," Father Julian said. His eyes were intensely dark, but his voice was even. "We don't yet know whether or not a theft has been committed, but if it has been...then, even though the missing object is of no value in worldly terms, we are dealing with a serious issue. I ask now for your thoughts on how to proceed."

Brother Lukas, a farm worker, spoke up gravely. "Father, did you talk to Brother Zossimus in the infirmary? Did he say anything?"

"Only what I've told you."

Brother Murta, the vineyard master, raised his hand. "Father, does he get to go into the church any time he wants to? Brother Zossimus, I mean? To clean the screen?"

"Nobody's barred from the church at any time," Father Julian said. "Whoever has time may go there. I believe we all know that."

"Well, that's what I'm driving at, Father," said Brother Murta. "He's got lots more time than anybody else."

Brother Malachi stood up. He kept inventories for the kitchen, the dairy, and the vineyard. "I think we should search for this thing," he said.

Father Julian looked at him steadily. "Where?" he asked.

"In Brother Zossimus's workshop," Malachi said. "Now, while he's not here. He's the only one of us who had anything to do with this thing. I'm not accusing anybody of anything, but—well, I just think we should make a search."

Father Julian looked about the room. "Stand if you agree." Table by table, people stood. It was clear that well over half of the people at each table wanted the search to happen. Father Julian nodded. "Be seated," he said. "I appoint Brother Malachi head of this search, then. He will select three people to help him. I, of course, will go along too." Once more he looked from place to place. "And if the missing object is not found in the workshop, then what?"

The room became very silent. Feet shuffled, heads were down. Brother Arcadius felt sure that he could tell what people were thinking. The missing head was small, the monastery by comparison was huge. The head could be in anybody's willow basket, put there by some malicious prankster, maybe. It could be down any latrine. It could be up a tree. It could be way out there by the bee hives. It could be in the pine woods, or in the scrublands. It could be in a quarry. It could be in the library, Brother Arcadius thought miserably. He could just imagine Brother Malachi, or Brother Atalf, or Brother Ziegmunt, for that matter, roughly shoving precious manuscripts this way and that in their zeal to search everywhere. He caught Brother Silvanus's eye and saw that Silvanus also looked very concerned. Well, if Malachi wanted to search the library, Malachi would have to just stand by while the librarians themselves did the actual work.

Brother Silvanus stood up. "Father," he said, "if the head isn't found in Brother Zossimus's workshop, then I think we should search no farther." A chorus of yeses came from every table. There was not a no to be heard, not even from those who'd said yes to searching the workshop. "I also think that this matter will simply be settled in confession," Silvanus went on. "Whoever took this thing will confess to you, Father, and put it back in your hands if it still exists. At least, I would hope so."

"I would hope so too, for that person's sake as well as everyone's," said Father Julian. "We realize, of course, that only a public confession will settle the matter for good and all—will prevent us from falsely suspecting each other." With that, he ordered Brother Malachi to choose his fellow searchers. Malachi did so, and the group set off to Brother Zossimus's workshop. But the mood in the room had changed. Slumped at their tables, sick of the whole business, vexed with Zossimus, vexed with Malachi, uncheered even by the wine cups still going around, people muttered to each other edgedly. Nobody wanted thievery to go unpunished. But nobody wanted to just keep sitting there, either. All this fuss, and over what? A stupid old head! Brother Arcadius glumly mulled over everything that might pertain to the matter. His thoughts grew darker and darker.

Although he did not excel in the lessons in reasoning that he took with Father Julian every week, one dictum made good sense to him, and had stood him a few times in good stead. It was the dictum that the simplest explanation for something was likely to be right.

The simplest explanation for the missing head was that Brother Zossimus had taken it. Except for Father Julian, who surely didn't count, nobody except Brother Zossimus had seen the faded letters in the book of rules. Only Brother Zossimus was in and out of the space behind the altar several times a week. He knew how to take the head from the screen. He loved the head. He wanted to study it until he could make a head like it.

Brother Arcadius buried his face in his hands and tried to block out the murmurs of everyone around him. He felt that he could actually see, with his mind's eye, a balance with one pan labeled *guilty*, and the other, *innocent*. Into the pan marked *guilty* dismal facts were dropping like cold stones, one by one, weighing it down, down, down. Simple had it. Simple won.

The great book of rules.... What did it have to say about monks who were thieves? Wispy little Brother Zossimus, shamed and locked up in prison....

Brother Arcadius shut his eyes tight at the very thought.

On the other hand, there was a different sort of fact that ought to be considered too. Maybe Simple was not as simple as all that. Brother Zossimus was tremendously afraid of breaking rules. Brother Zossimus revered Father Julian and asked his opinion in everything. If Brother Zossimus had been so foolish as to steal the accursed head (Brother

Arcadius was vexed to the point of using chancy language), he would find it very hard to study it and measure it out in the open air, in sunlight, which would be the whole point of taking it, after all. And then there was that time when a real thief—an outsider, fortunately—had been apprehended right out there in the courtyard. Brother Zossimus's outrage had not been feigned. Did such things amount to nothing? Did they or didn't they outweigh the arguments for guilt?

Time crawled horridly by. Brother Arcadius was almost at the point of thinking that maybe he'd stolen the head himself, in a fit of sleepwalking or something—he did know the directions for unlocking the lock, after all—when Father Julian returned to the refectory with Malachi and Malachi's fellow searchers. They came back with nothing, except for stains of walnut on Brother Malachi's hands. He'd thrown himself too eagerly into the search.

But that, for now, was the end of the matter. Father Julian adjured everyone to speak privately to him if they knew anything more, or to reveal their great lapse of good judgment to him in confession if they had taken the head. Then he said that now they could all go back to their cells. "In your groups, please, as you always do." Everyone complied, wearily, wearily.

Everyone got up the next day feeling that nothing had been settled, and that everything was amiss. That feeling continued throughout the week. Told that he must by Father Julian and the medicus, Brother Zossimus stayed on in the infirmary. Brother Arcadius hurried to pay him a visit and found him sitting in bed, a huddled heap. "It's just gone," he whispered. "I don't know where it is. It's gone, I don't know where it is. It's gone, just gone...."

The whisper went on and on, over and over, both then and—so people said—for the next six days. Word went round, very quietly, that the carver's mind and spirit were broken, and that he'd be dead in a matter of days. But when Friday came round again and the monks convened at Father Julian's orders for a final word regarding the missing head, in came Brother Zossimus on Brother Salix's arm. Looking neither to left nor right, he let the medicus guide him to a table. Head bowed, he sat down. The monks around him nodded their greetings to him, but there was no warmth in those greetings. They were curt, polite, and reserved—very reserved. He didn't look up.

It would have been a very good thing to go over there and sit by him, thought Brother Arcadius, but there was no chance of that. Father Julian, standing beside his table on the dais, had raised his hand for

165

attention and was starting to speak. "It is time to bring this matter to a close," he said. "No one has come forward with any further information, no one has confessed. Perhaps no thievery was involved, but that seems unlikely. Yet there are times when earthly judgments are of no avail. If there is anyone here who sits in actual guilt, that guilt is between him and his maker." He looked around. "Between him and his maker," he repeated with emphasis. "For our part, unless anyone cares to make a serious argument the other way, bringing up things that perhaps we haven't yet considered, or perhaps haven't given enough weight to, I say that we must cease now to spend any further time on the matter. Gone is gone. I—yes, Brother Zossimus?"

The little carver had risen to his feet. All eyes were on him.

"Yes, Brother Zossimus?" repeated Father Julian, "Do you wish to speak?"

"I wish to speak," said Brother Zossimus. His face was ghastly white, but a mask of determination all the same. Brother Salix had stood up too, but the carver ignored him. Fists clenched, he marched past the tables where his brethren sat intent and staring. "I wish to say...." He reached the dais and stepped up onto it without asking if he might. Breathing hard, he looked from face to face. Salix was now at his side, but he seemed not to notice. Nor did he seem to notice that Father Julian was regarding him with something like astonishment—or maybe it wasn't astonishment.

"I wish to say," said Brother Zossimus, "that I hate a thief." His voice was shaking, but it rang throughout the great hall as he spoke on. "I wish to say that we should all hate thieves. I wish to say that on all this earth there is nothing lower than a crawling, sneaking, greedy, wicked thief. I wish to say that a thief like that, a thief who would steal from a beautiful screen, behind an altar, in a church, in a monastery— and sneak off with something that belongs to everybody, to his own brothers—of all the wicked thieves on earth, that thief is worst! I wish to say that no, we should not forget that crime—never, never, never! I wish to say he should be punished and no mercy shown to him, that wicked thief! That he should be taken and thrown into prison! That he should rot there for the rest of his miserable life! That his dead body should be flung on the ash heap for dogs to chew! I wish to say...I wish to say...."

The carver shuddered and drew a great breath. Brother Salix and Father Julian were reaching for him, but he waved them away. His voice rose higher. "I wish to say that the wicked thief...that the wicked,

wicked thief...that the wicked, wicked, *wicked* thief is me!"

His voice died away into silence, but his anguish permeated the room. People squeezed their eyes shut, or stared hard at the floor or the ceiling. Taut fingers pressed against chins and foreheads. The assembly might have been turned to unhappy stone. Even Brother Malachi looked anything but triumphant. But Father Julian had risen from his chair. "Will you sit down, please, Brother Zossimus," he said. It was a command. Trembling, Brother Zossimus complied. Father Julian stood looking at him. He seemed to be weighing what to say. The whole hall waited in silence for his response. But when he spoke, all he said was, "Will you tell us more?"

"I put the head back like you said, Father, and I left it there. But then.... But then I wanted to see it in the sun, just one more time. So I went into the church after dark," said Brother Zossimus. He was speaking quietly now. The throng of monks had come back to life. Those at the farthest tables were standing up and straining to hear him. "Nobody was there. I took the head from the screen. I went back out, to take it to my shop. I wasn't going to keep it. I just wanted to take a close look at it again, then put it back. But just outside the door, I tripped. I fell face down and the breath was knocked out of me. The head fell from my hand. For a while I couldn't think, I couldn't see, I couldn't move. But when I did move...when I got up and searched for Master Nardo's head, I couldn't find it."

"Did you look all around? When it fell, it could have rolled."

"I searched everywhere I could. I combed the ground inch by inch, I looked in the bushes, in the tall grass, but it was dark, and it was gone, and I couldn't find it...." Brother Zossimus's voice was rising again. He clasped his trembling hands together. "Then every day I tried to look for it in daylight, without anybody noticing, but there was always someone around. And every night I tried to find it, but I couldn't. And then, during mass, I thought, I will just pretend that suddenly it's gone. And I got the words out, this dreadful lie, in church, during mass, and I became a wicked, lying, evil thief." Brother Zossimus looked toward the ceiling and shut his eyes. Once more his listeners sat as if turned to stone.

Father Julian spoke into the silence. "And if you'd been caught in the act of taking the head, then what?"

"I would have told you it had just fallen off and that I was going to put it back," said Brother Zossimus. "I would have lied to you, Father. I should be put to death."

The silence continued.

"It seems to me," said Father Julian at last, "that your biggest sin is the sin of pride, Zossimus. You rank yourself too high, perhaps as a craftsman, but certainly as a criminal. I don't condone your very misguided action—far from it—but a moment's rational thought should tell you that you don't measure up to the great evil-doers of the world. Attila the Hun, Nero, Pontius Pilate, Judas, *Zossimus*? I don't think so."

Brows wrinkled slightly, Father Julian glanced about the room, but didn't appear to be seeing anybody. "As for being able to copy Master Nardo's head, there are some craftsmen, Brother Zossimus, whose gifts come from above so lavishly that it defies understanding. Aping those gifts is also theft, I would say—not least, theft from oneself. We should learn from others, yes, and we should strive to become more able in what we do. But above all, we need to define what our own gifts are. A Zossimus should strive to be a Zossimus, not a Nardo. Does what I say have any meaning?"

"Yes," whispered Brother Zossimus. "But I didn't want...I didn't want to be a Zossimus."

"Unreasonably, since you are Zossimus," said Father Julian. "And in carrying out your unreasonable desire, you caused a great unnecessary upheaval in this monastery, deprived your brethren of their hard-earned suppers, brought them all under suspicion, and lost the thing you think so highly of."

"We should search for it, Father," called out Brother Kongro. "It's got to be near the churchyard door."

"Unless someone picked it up and kept it," interrupted Brother Carolus. "Whoever did it should confess—"

"So are we back where we started, suspecting each other again?" asked Father Julian. For once the Julian mask slid aside, and his lips tightened in obvious distaste. "We've heard one confession today. Shall we talk ourselves into believing that there should be more?" He paused, then half turned toward the door, listening. From out in the corridor a faint clatter was coming nearer and growing louder. "Arcadius...." he said. The sound continued. "Arcadius, if that is the cat, would you tend to it, please?"

Brother Arcadius rose, mortified. Did Pangur have to start up that game of his right here, right now? Feeling that many disapproving eyes were boring into him from all sides, he went out into the corridor. Yes, there was Pangur, frisking and leaping and swatting something back and forth, down by the stone figure of the mighty Charles Martel, the monastery's founder in the long ago. Charles Martel might well have known Master Nardo...might have hired him, in fact...might have been, maybe, the one with the excellent mirror....

What was Pangur playing with? It was too large to be a pine cone, and too dark. Pine cones were not the size of a squirrel's head. Pine cones were never that dark. Pine cones did not make such a weighty clatter against a stone floor. Heart pounding in sudden realization of what he might be seeing, Brother Arcadius walked down the corridor toward Pangur Ban, and Pangur Ban...his own cat Pangur Ban...swatted Master Nardo's head straight at him.

He scooped it up from the floor. He turned it around and around in his hands. There was mud and a strandlet of moss in its square opening. There was a faint scuff mark along the right cheek. Otherwise, it was whole and undamaged. Even the tip of the nose was undamaged. Pangur's wild play had done it no real harm at all, nor did Pangur seem at all unwilling to give it up. Brother Arcadius started to polish it on the sleeve of his robe, then stopped. Let everybody see the mud and the strand of moss. Let everybody realize that it must have been in the churchyard all this while, and not tucked away, say, in anybody's willow basket, including his own.

Brother Arcadius, assistant librarian and virtual owner of the great cat Pangur Ban, went back into the dining hall. With all eyes upon him, he strode toward the dais and held up the head for all to see. Brother Zossimus staggered to his feet and let out a cry of joy. Father Julian's eyes grew darker than any eyes had a right to be. He held out his hand demandingly. Brother Arcadius gave him the head. He turned it round and round. Throughout the hall, from every table, a great murmur rose. Father Julian's right hand, the hand that was firmly grasping Master Nardo's masterwork, motioned for silence. "The lost is found," he said.

He turned to Brother Zossimus. "Brother Zossimus, on this count you can rest easy. The carving is undamaged, and in a short while you and I together will put it back where it belongs. On another count you can rest easy too. Your full and very public confession absolves all of your brethren of any guilt in this matter. You yourself, of course, have done wrong and must pay for it. I rule that you will not remove this carving from the altar screen again, unless you are rescuing it from a clear and present danger—fire, say, or a plague of wood-boring ants, or any other such thing. And I rule that henceforth you will use your talents to carve, in your own way, saints for any of your brethren who would like to have them. I think that would be a greater contribution to the monastery than any copy of this head." In ringing tones, he addressed the whole assembly. "Who among you would like to have one of Brother Zossimus's saints?"

Brother Kongro frowned uncertainly. "I always did want one," he said, "but I thought they were only for sale."

"These would be free, of course."

Brother Kongro turned to Brother Zossimus. "Then I would like a Saint Paul," he said.

"I've always wanted your Saint Peter," said Brother Mishel, the head stonecutter. "With the rock."

"I'd appreciate a Saint Luke," said Brother Silvanus, smiling. "When you have time."

Brother Atalf, the hulking man of heavy work, looked at his hulking counterpart, Brother Ziegmunt, and then at Brother Zossimus. "We'd like—" he began.

"I...I don't think I can remember all this. I might forget," Brother Zossimus quavered.

"Brother Zossimus will take everybody's orders tomorrow when he has a chance to write them down," said Father Julian. "This meeting is now over and we will adjourn." Then, stepping down from the dais with Master Nardo's carved image still firmly in his hand, he walked toward the door.

Brother Zossimus fell in behind him, with the medicus at his side. Already there was a different look in the woodcarver's eyes. Already he looked...maybe...just slightly...restored, and maybe even *included*. His fellow monks followed him. Pangur Ban took in the advancing crowd and scampered out of the doorway and down the corridor. Brother Arcadius looked after his retreating figure with love in his heart. If there was a saint for cats, he wanted one.

* * *

"It's clear to me," said Brother Marcus, "that Whitey was right there that night, under the bushes, see? So when Zossimus tripped and fell down and dropped the head, and was lying there in a daze, Whitey just came out and scooped it away. Thought it was something to play with." Marcus chuckled. "Where did he keep it, though, for all those days? It might have been under your bed, Arcadius. Might have been under your bed all the while."

* * *

"The cat took it away by magic," said Brother Atalf. "Turned it into a pine cone. That's why they didn't find it. Then he magicked it back again. You want to stay on his good side, you know? That cat."

* * *

"Zossimus is a brave, honest fellow, confessing in public that way," said Brother Silvanus. "I wouldn't have thought he'd had it in him. An honest craftsman, too, knowing quality when he sees it, even if he can't measure up to it himself. I hope he gets my saint finished before I'm too old to know what it is. I'll be proud to have it, and what's more, I'm telling him so."

* * *

Brother Arcadius paused for a moment in his library work, pleased with the idea that had come to him out of nowhere. He didn't want to make himself look foolish, going around asking if there was a saint for cats. But what he could do was ask Brother Zossimus to carve him a Saint Jerome and the lion, but with a lion somewhat on the small side, with no mane, and painted white. For lions were just very big cats, wasn't that so? Very big, but no bigger in spirit than a certain cat who'd settled a terrible problem, whether he knew it or not. A cat, furthermore, who now seemed to have given up pine cones once and for all.

That head...that vanishing head.... It still kept vanishing, not from the screen these days, but simply from sight. No, it wasn't that he was looking for it in the wrong place. He absolutely knew the exact location. But even so, with the candles flickering, and the candle smoke curling about, and the shadows shifting, sometimes you saw it and sometimes it just seemed gone. But still it was there.

A white shape materialized on the library windowsill, and Brother Arcadius turned to say hello. "You're going to be part of a carving someday, Pangur Ban," he said. "At least that's the plan. What do you think of that?"

"Mrrrwrrrrw," said Pangur Ban.

THE BEAUTIFUL POEM

In which the pursuit of poetry calls for a real burst of speed

AD 899

Tammis, the seventh son of Dublin's only brickmaker, was tagged as unusual from the beginning. During mass, as a red-headed, wide-eyed, scrawny infant in his Mam's arms, he listened dumbstruck—anyone could see it—to the sonorous sounds of the ancient Latin service, so different from the slurred, broken-down, everyday Latin that was spoken outside the church. By age three, should some unfortunate priest drop a syllable or mispronounce a word, little Tammis would point a finger in protest and have to be carried out sobbing and given a good talking-to. Also by age three he was unaccountably deciphering the words and figures on the brickyard's tally sheets.

So the priests, intrigued, wrote up a few Latin sentences for him —"Tammis is a boy...Tammis is a child of God...Tammis has six older brothers...Tammis has two younger sisters." He deciphered them, too. The good monks at the monastery heard about him and grew intrigued also. They took him under their wing and gave him lessons in reading and writing every day. These kind and caring teachers kept a pot of honey on the table to reward the child for work well done. Plenty of honey passed his way at every lesson and he smacked his lips over it, but absentmindedly: honey was good, all right, but it was clear to everyone that all he really wanted was to see, say, read, and write Latin and more Latin. His first attempts at Greek and Hebrew soon followed.

In these times the Dubliners were under the dangerous rule of the marauding Viking Danes. Ingmar the Heartless and Halbdan the Mad and the rest of that vicious crew swaggered about with their villainous bands, took what they wanted to take, wrecked whatever they wanted to wreck, killed anybody they felt like killing. On a whim, years before Tammis was born, they'd burned down half the monastery and hurled most of its precious books into the River Liffey—would have hurled all of them, but they got bored.

They needed bricks and people who knew how to make and lay bricks to build up a new Danish Dublin on the ruins of the Dublin they'd destroyed, so they left the brickyard and Tammis's family alone. They also lost interest in the monastery after they'd wrecked so much of it. So Tammis was able to have his lessons there, and looked upon its remains as his second home. People started calling him Tammis Scholar instead of Tammis Brickmans, or Tammis Bricker, or Tammis Brick. He was three, he was four, he was five, and one day, when he was five....

His Da—his strong, laughing Da who gave him horseback rides on his shoulders around the brickyard—rushed to the rescue of some neighbors who were being tormented by a wandering gang of Halbdan the Mad's ruffians, and was brought home dead. That was a sad day indeed. But the two eldest of Tammis's keen-eyed and stalwart older brothers were grown up by then, and more than ready to take over the brickyard. Everyone agreed that young Tammis was cut out to be a monk and a scholar, no ifs, ands, or buts about it. So the years went by and that is what he became. Tammis Scholar was Brother Arcadius now—Brother Arcadius, almost eighteen, and far, far away from Dublin across two seas.... Brother Arcadius, assistant librarian at Spiritus Sanctus monastery, in the mountain country between the Frankish lands and Italy.

He was still an undersized fellow, so much so that the constant joke at Spiritus Sanctus was that it wouldn't take much of a wind to blow him away. But day in, day out, he was happy. His family was out of reach of the Danes, at least for now. They'd safely relocated to the late King Alfred's lands across the water from Ireland, lands that King Alfred's son Edward the Elder was staunchly keeping Dane-free. So there was his one big worry out of the way, at least as much as it could be in this chancy world. He was free to enjoy his daily work in a grand —a remarkable!—library that had accumulated the amazing total of five hundred bound manuscripts in prime condition, and a good number of others that were halfway ruined, and a trunkful of fragments that had yet to be carefully gone over. Today, though, he was somewhat distracted from the tasks before him.

For one thing, there was the cricket to think about. It was a black, glossy, speedy creature, of mammoth size for a cricket, and it had moved into the library some days ago with its piercing chirp. Brother Arcadius urgently wanted to catch it and keep it, at least for a while. It would be a splendid addition to the reading and writing lessons that he was giving to Keti, the little kitchen boy. He and Keti could discuss it and write about it, in good Latin, of course, and doing so would add all sorts of words to Keti's reading vocabulary and his written vocabulary too: *scuttle*, *shiny*, *hiding*, *chirping*, words like that. It would also give practice in the correct use of prepositions and some of the more difficult verb forms and the subjunctive: "The cricket *would like* to be free again."

Looking forward to all this, he'd had Brother Zossimus, the monastery woodcarver, fashion a cage for the cricket—a roomy cage about two hand's breadths long by one wide. Working very quickly for once, for Keti's sake, Brother Zossimus had created a thing of beauty. It was stoutly built, too, and pegged to a heavy base that not even a big white cat could overturn. One had to assume that the monastery's champion mouser, Pangur Ban, would be looking in on the lessons too. "Pangur *would like* to eat the cricket.... Pangur's paws do not fit *through the bars*...." Keti loved Pangur Ban, as did Brother Arcadius, but it would not be good to have the teaching aid consumed before the pupil's very eyes.

Or caught and eaten before the lessons even began. That's what would happen for sure if the cricket came out from hiding while Pangur Ban happened to be visiting the library...as Pangur Ban did almost every day...as Pangur Ban was doing now. The big fellow had leaped onto the windowsill from out of nowhere and sat there purring and kneading his paws against the stone. There was nothing for it but to give him his usual welcome. "Good afternoon, Pangur Ban," said Brother Arcadius, keeping an eye out for the cricket all the while. If need be, he'd scoop up the cat, drop him back out the window, close the shutters, and make it up to him later. "Come in, come in. Good to see you!"

Pangur carefully licked one forepaw, then the other, taking his time with it. After a good few moments—no cricket as yet—he leaped down to the floor and then up onto Brother Arcadius's lap. Brother Arcadius gave in to the charm of him and administered a hearty petting. Pangur was more, much more, than just a very excellent cat and a champion mouser. He was more than just a cat who had solved more than one problem in the monastery simply by being himself. He was the broad-chested, big-pawed creature who not two years before had been a wretched rag of a half-grown kitten, struggling in the hands of a cruel sailor—as cruel as Halbdan the Mad, that sailor!—in a lurching boat on the cold, gray Irish Sea.

Brother Arcadius had also had been in that boat, on the first stage of his journey from Dublin to Spiritus Sanctus. He'd been barely sixteen, already missing home, already missing the monastery in Dublin, already seasick—very, very seasick. But he'd stood up to that sailor, and he'd rescued that kitten, and he'd named that kitten Pangur Ban, a good Irish name signifying whiteness—not out of any particular regard for whiteness, but simply because Pangur happened to be white.

And suddenly, in the here and now, a robin swooped down onto the windowsill, cocking an insolent eye at Pangur Ban, and there went Pangur, up and after it. The robin flew into a nearby tree. Pangur, outside now, settled himself onto a patch of moss to keep an eye on the bird. He looked likely to stay there for a long while. This was a good time for the cricket to come out from wherever it was, if only it would.

The cricket didn't.

Pangur remained on his patch of moss for a moment more. Then he got up and prowled away.

Well, there was no help for it. Squaring his shoulders, Brother Arcadius turned again to the other thing that he had to attend to this morning: the book lying open before him. He re-read the Latin words on the parchment page, and sighed. They still said what they'd said when he'd read them before. And yes, they were written in church Latin, all right—but church Latin that fell wide of the mark. *Crabbed* was the word for it. *Grating* described it, too.

"Brethren, why should we honor and cherish and obey the rules laid down by our Fathers of the Church? The answer, Brethren, is that we should do so because we are supposed to honor and cherish and obey the rules laid down by the Fathers of the Church. And why did the Fathers of the Church lay down those rules so that our souls might not perish? The answer, Brethren, is that they laid down those rules so that our souls might not perish. And why...."

Brother Arcadius frowned down at these words and read them over, unwillingly, yet again. They'd been written two hundred or so years before by a certain Father Vituperatius, otherwise unknown.

Being unknown was nothing to hold against anyone. Outside of Spiritus Sanctus and his family and the dear monks and priests back in Dublin, Brother Arcadius himself was, after all, pretty much unknown. But why couldn't this person Vituperatius set up a proper argument that advanced his cause in a sensible way, instead of just going around and around in circles?

"Why are the heathen all sunken in error, Brethren? The answer is because all the heathen are sunken in error."

In Brother Arcadius's view, it was an abuse of a beautiful language and a terrible waste of precious ink and parchment, not to mention time, to write like that. Ever since his first days, almost, at Spiritus Sanctus he'd been not only studying advanced Greek and slightly less-advanced Hebrew with the head of the monastery, Father Julian, but taking very basic lessons in reasoning with him as well, lessons that included the reasoner's game of chess. He didn't shine in his lessons in reasoning. In fact, he had to struggle to wrap his mind around them most of the time. They never seemed to accord all that well with the unreasonable world as he knew it.

All the same, by now he'd somehow absorbed enough of such studies to recognize that Father Vituperatius's arguments were a prime example of *circulus in demonstrando*, as Father Julian would say. You weren't supposed to answer a question by just repeating the words of the question and let it go at that.

"Why should we loathe evildoers, Brethren? We should loathe evildoers because it is right to loathe them."

Brother Arcadius sighed. There were pages and pages more of this to get through. One of his jobs was to prepare an index for each book in the library—a handy list of the topics it dealt with, along with their page numbers. It was work with a great and important purpose. Most of the monks at Spiritus Sanctus, like most people in the wider world from kings to serfs, did not know how to read and saw no reason to learn. There wasn't much to read in the first place. There had been many books in the long ago, and many schools and teachers too, but Rome had fallen and these things had gone by the wayside.

Spiritus Sanctus had been founded partly to protect learning and help bring it back. Indexes were meant to help achieve this aim. If books were easier to use—if people didn't have to wade through every page to find matters of interest—then the monks who could read at Spiritus Sanctus might want to read more. And if they read more, then their brethren might want to read too. And each person who learned to read could help teach another. With more readers, more books might be made. And so, little by little, learning could grow.

"And why, Brethren, should we block our ears to the wiles of the heathen enticers?"

No cricket as yet.

"We should block our ears to the wiles of the heathen enticers because we—"

That chirp—might that be the cricket? No, it was just that same cheeky robin, tuning up. Well, patience was in order. And if it turned out that there couldn't be a cricket, then there wouldn't be a cricket. So back to the book.

"And why, Brethren, should we—" Brother Arcadius sat bolt upright and looked closer at the words he'd just read.

No, it was not a trick of the light. Beneath the circular rantings of Father Vituperatius there were other words, almost invisible, but there. Brother Arcadius nodded to himself. It was clear what had happened. When Father Vituperatius had decided to put his circular thoughts into writing, he'd taken into account the high cost and most likely the scarcity of new parchment. Somehow he'd acquired some old stuff, already written on. He'd scraped off the old words, but here and there he hadn't scraped them off enough.

There was nothing unusual about that. Anyone dealing with old manuscripts—new ones too, for that matter—came across overwritten pages all the time. In his experience, the underlying writing always turned out to be an old farm list or something of the sort: X cows, XII sheep, or whatever. But the words beneath Father Vituperatius's words looked like something different.

The words beneath Father Vituperatius's words looked like a poem.

Brother Arcadius carried the manuscript over to the window and looked at it in the better light. *In...e..dun....* Was that first word, buried under Vituperatius's "Why, Brethren"...was it *Incedunt*? The next word, beneath "Should we"—could it be *arbusta*? The third...was the third actually just *er*? No, surely it would have to be *per*.... Laboriously, wishing all the while that Father Vituperatius had not used such dark ink, or had never written at all, he made out all the letters that he could, one by one. Then, with his stylus on his waxed tablet, he set down what he had, and looked at the result.

> Incedunt arbusta per a ta, s c rib s ca un
> Pe ce lu n ma n s q erc s, e cid t r i ex

And in much smaller letters, at the bottom margin, "nnius rica."
His scholar's mind filled in what the missing letters had to be.

Incedunt arbusta per alta, securibus caedunt
Percellunt magnas quercus, exciditur ilex....

With such things as crickets and lessons utterly forgotten, Brother
Arcadius savored the words on his tongue. This was old, old Latin,
rich, powerful, magnificent Latin. Honey was nothing to it. And it
painted a picture that set the mind ablaze with...yes, with wonder.
People...Who? Why?...were felling tall trees in a forest grove. Great
oaks crashed down. Brother Arcadius saw them fall with his mind's
eye. *Magnas quercus...exciditur ilex....* Brother Arcadius prayed there'd be
more of this. He turned to the next page of the manuscript, and the
next, but saw only the words of Vituperatius and more words of
Vituperatius. Well, he would have to go over each page of the entire
thing, carefully, carefully, in the best light available, not allowing
himself to miss the faintest word.

It was not a task that he could go on with right now. He would
have to ask Brother Silvanus for permission to spend time on it. He
was sure he'd get that permission. The head librarian would see the
value of it, certainly. So would Father Julian. It wasn't every day that
people discovered great poetry hiding behind—behind nonsense,
might as well say it. Both men would be pleased, no question, with this
amazing find. They wouldn't say so straight out, most likely, but still!
The demon of pride would have to be firmly banished, but even so it
would be a moment a person could cherish.

But whose great poetry was it? Not much poetry of any kind had
survived the crash of the ancient world, at least in the west. But the
little he'd seen did not resemble these lines here. The bits he'd seen of
Virgil were smooth and polished. The bits he'd seen of Juvenal were
raw and angry. But these words had a power and a majesty all their
own. Those small letters along the bottom...*nnius...rica....* Hadn't there
been...hadn't he heard of a poet called Ennius? And hadn't that poet
been good friends with Africanus, the general who'd conquered
Hannibal in the long, long ago?

Well, if the words were that old, they were heathen enticements
for sure. Brother Arcadius smiled to think of Father Vituperatius, all
unknowing, setting his circular thoughts down over verses that he
would have detested if he'd ever bothered to read them. He couldn't

have read them, or he would have scraped harder. Ennius himself, though, would have written on a scroll, not on a parchment page. So if this poem was his, it was surely just a copy of the original, or a copy of a copy, or a copy of a copy of a copy...not done in the time of Ennius, but pricelessly valuable still.

Sternly telling himself that he'd better spend no more time in conjecture—that he'd better not conclude that the poet was Ennius, either—Brother Arcadius reverently closed the manuscript and set it aside in a clean, fresh willow basket, with one last lingering glance. Its cover was in bad condition, that was for sure. It was pitted and gouged, and the pits and gouges were grimy with ground-in dirt, and some gnawing creature had chewed one of the corners away. There'd been plenty of misadventures before it had ever come to Spiritus Sanctus. Well, now that the treasure within had been discovered, the binding would have to be given a good cleaning, or even replaced.

But now it was truly time to stop this unmonklike gloating. Reminding himself that he hadn't given a thought to catching the cricket for at least the past half hour, he atoned for that by opening the top of the cage. Now if he did catch the creature, he could drop it right in. He checked that the moss in the bottom of the cage was still damp, and that the two acorn cups down in there still had water in them. Then, despite his best intentions, he looked lovingly once again at the willow basket with its precious contents. Brother Silvanus was having an afternoon meeting with Father Julian. It would be so good if he came back soon, or better yet now, so that he could see the poem. Hearing a noise at the door, Brother Arcadius stood up in happy anticipation.

But it wasn't Brother Silvanus. It was Brother Atalf, who'd never been known to come within shouting distance of the library. Brother Arcadius put on his best librarian's smile and raised his hand in welcome. "Come in, come in, Brother Atalf," he said. "May I help you with something? And where is Brother Ziegmunt?"

Brother Atalf mulled over these questions with a knotted brow. He and his true blood brother Ziegmunt were the monastery's indispensable heavy workers, big hulking fellows who were hardly ever seen apart. Brother Marcus, the head cook, was constantly saying that they were as strong as twenty oxen. Then, in a very low mutter, he always added something that sounded like, "and almost as smart." But that would have been an insult, and insults were not permitted at Spiritus Sanctus, so maybe that wasn't what he was saying, at all. Maybe what he was saying was, "And also, they're smart."

At any rate, Brother Atalf had now come up with an answer. He pointed in the general direction of the refectory. "He didn't want to come in," he rumbled. "Told him to go on ahead." He squinted warily across the table at the rows of manuscripts on their shelves. "Those're the books?"

"They're the books," said Brother Arcadius. "But how can I help you? What brings you here?"

"Brother Silvanus. Says he'll be a while yet. Said I should tell you." Brother Arcadius swallowed his disappointment. His duty right now was to put Brother Atalf at ease. To show him around, maybe? Or would that be too much? But now the big fellow was frowning down at the gnawed, battered, precious, miraculous, Heaven-sent manuscript in its willow basket. "That one's old?" he asked.

"Very old," said Brother Arcadius. It was always good to give a bit of instruction to people like Brother Atalf, as long as one kept it brief and didn't try to lord it over anybody. "It's probably two hundred, three hundred years—" He broke off. A small black shape out of nowhere had just shot from under a cabinet and sped across the floor. Keti's cricket had made an appearance at long last. Brother Arcadius dropped to his knees to see where the creature might be. Had it retreated back into some dark corner? No, there it was, over there just beyond the table. Quietly, carefully, so as not to startle it, he crawled closer to it, one hand poised ready to catch it. Up above him, Brother Atalf was saying something that he only half heard. It was something to do with coats—no, with *goats*, and going to feed them.

"All right," Brother Arcadius called up to him. He crept closer to the cricket. He heard the door close. Brother Atalf would be wanting to catch up with his brother Ziegmunt and get on with feeding the goats, or whatever it was that he had to do. Ah, the cricket still hadn't moved. Brother Arcadius slid his cupped hand slowly through the air over it...he'd never been aware that Atalf had anything to do with feeding goats...over it...over it...now!

He had it, he had the cricket! It struggled scratchily in his cupped hands. He stood up. He dropped it into the cage that stood waiting for it. He closed the lid and brushed his hands together in triumph. Two triumphs in one day. He looked over at the willow basket that held the manuscript.

The willow basket was empty.

He looked again and again. How could it be empty? He looked again and again at the long bare table. He looked again and again at the long bare floor. He looked behind and on all sides of the cricket cage on the long bare table. He stopped himself from looking inside the cage. He forced himself to understand that the manuscript was gone. Propelled by horror, he raced out the door.

There was Atalf, way up ahead. He'd caught up with Ziegmunt. The two big brothers were just going into the refectory, most likely cutting through it on their way to somewhere else. He raced after them. Racing, he shouted, "Atalf! Ziegmunt! Atalf!" Racing faster, he used all the breath he could spare to shout at them again. "Atalf! Ziegmunt! Atalf! Atalf!"

They didn't hear him. The heavy refectory door closed behind them, and nowhere could he see anybody to help him. People were all at their work, and nobody's work had brought anybody out here where anybody could hear him. He tripped on the hem of his robe, but managed to right himself and keep on running. He gained the refectory door. He tugged it open. Atalf and Ziegmunt were nowhere in sight. He ran down the corridor, past the long row of niches for candles or lamps, past the stone image of the mighty Charles Martel, founder of the monastery and grandfather of the mighty Charlemagne. He emerged through the farther door into the courtyard. Brother Sifari and Brother Kongro, the day watchmen, were on duty there, a blessed sight. They looked askance at him, but he gave them no time for comment. "Atalf!" he gasped at them. "Which way did he go?"

Brother Kongro, up on the walls, pointed toward the path that led to the monastery farm. "That way," he said.

"Did he have something in his hand? Something like a book?"

"Didn't notice," said Brother Kongro, with due concern. Kongro was very much a reader, and Kongro knew Atalf, and Kongro was starting to put two and two together that something was wrong. So was his companion, the always earnest Brother Sifari. "All I noticed was that Ziegmunt was with him. Guess you'd better get running," Kongro said.

Brother Arcadius nodded and stumbled on. He hadn't dared to ask Kongro and Sifari to ring the watchtower bell and sound an alert. That would call Atalf back, all right, but it would summon everybody else as well. Quarrymen, plowers, tree fellers, carpenters, ditch diggers, everyone would have to drop what they were doing and come hurrying in—for two lines of a poem. And there'd be Father Julian, too. The watchmen would never have agreed to do it, and rightly so.

But that thing that Atalf had said....

That thing he'd said about feeding the goats....

184

Parchment was made out of hides, and goats ate hides....

Goats ate anything.

He went on past the long western wall of the kitchen garden. Maybe Atalf and Ziegmunt were in there, on a bench, resting? That didn't seem likely. But maybe they'd dropped into the kitchen itself for some soup, or a bit of bread, or a quick swig of watered wine. As heavy workers, they were not begrudged extra rations. But if that's what they'd done, then the manuscript was not yet in danger. The best thing to do was to get to the goat pen, get there ahead of Atalf, stave off disaster.... But maybe Atalf didn't even have the manuscript? Or maybe he aimed to use it for kindling, or who knew what?

At the fastest pace he could manage, Brother Arcadius headed for the goat pen. The rutted path to the farmlands seemed to go on forever. But Atalf and Ziegmunt, as a rule, were not fast movers. They couldn't have that much of a lead over him, could they? Unless the devil or some such unholy being had put it into their minds to break into a run. One sandal caught on a rough spot on the path and came off. He kicked the other one off too for the sake of an even stride, although his strides by now were hardly strides at all. His eyes stung and blurred, and he barely had enough breath left to think where he was at. He'd been chasing after Atalf and Ziegmunt since he'd been born, that's what it felt like. And he'd be chasing after them until he became an old man. Everything in the world had withered away except for chasing. When he died, there would be no Heaven, only chasing.

He rounded a bend and then at last he saw them in the distance: the two big brothers leaning against a fence. A fence with goats on the other side of it, but Brother Hyssop, the goat-tender, seemed to be nowhere in sight. He sucked in all the air he was still capable of sucking and screamed, "Atalf! Atalf! Ziegmunt!" They didn't hear him. He stumbled on. He waved at them wildly. "Atalf! Ziegmunt!" They didn't see him. "Atalf...."

Ziegmunt looked up, looked around, and then looked down the path and saw him. He nudged Atalf. Atalf looked up, looked around, and then looked where Ziegmunt was pointing. Together they watched the assistant librarian stagger up the path. There was no book in Atalf's hands, no book in Ziegmunt's.

Bent almost double, barefoot, gasping, Brother Arcadius gained his quarry at last and collapsed against the fence. Goats were milling about on the other side, nosing at fragments of something scattered on the ground. He trained imploring eyes upon Brother Atalf.

"Did...you...take...the book?"

Brother Atalf's broad face beamed down upon him. "I did. Thank you, Brother."

"What did...where is...what did you do with it?"

Brother Atalf's brow knotted in puzzlement. He pointed over the fence. "Fed it to 'em," he said.

"You fed...the book...to the goats." Brother Arcadius felt as if he were slowly freezing.

Brother Atalf frowned. Belatedly, so did Ziegmunt. "I ast you," said Atalf. The two brothers stared at the weird little assistant librarian, who was climbing, headlong and barefoot, over the fence.

Let it be here, let the poem at least be here! Incedunt *arbusta per alta...securibus caedunt....* Brother Arcadius fell to his knees and searched the ground in a shifting forest of prancing hooves. Goat lips nibbled at his robe, but he smacked them aside. He gathered up everything that he could gather, then let it all drop again. There was nothing left, not even a single whole letter. The mangled remains were beyond all scholarship.

Percellunt magnas quercus.... Brother Arcadius ran in desperation to the goat shed. He grubbed around in vain in the darkness there. How long he did so he couldn't say, but he emerged at last, filthy, defeated, and beside himself with hopelessness, shock, and rage. Atalf and Ziegmunt were still standing there, baffled. "You took that book and fed it to the goats," he said to Atalf again. "*You took that book! You fed it to the goats!*"

"I ast you," Atalf repeated. "You said, 'All right.'"

"I..." Brother Arcadius stepped back, wholly beaten. Yes, he had said that. Thinking back, he could hear his own voice, clear as a bell, stupidly, stupidly, stupidly saying those fatal words. *Feed...goats* was all that he'd really heard Atalf say, but his scholar's mind—hah! on it!—had smugly filled in what he thought was the rest of it. Have to go now and feed the goats. And he'd answered, All right.

By now it had sunk in to Atalf that some sort of puzzling thing had gone amiss, but what was it? He looked at Ziegmunt for help, but Ziegmunt just shrugged. So he gave his explanation once more, hoping that this time that little Arcaperus fellow would catch on. "I ast you," he said. He added, for good measure, "I ast you if it was old and you said yes. And I ast you if I could feed it to—"

Brother Arcadius held up a hand to stop him. He couldn't bear to hear it even one more time. "I know you did, Brother," he said. "It wasn't your fault. I didn't hear what you were asking. I'm sorry."

"You were crawling around—" Brother Atalf started to say.

"I know I was. It's not your fault. I'm sorry."

"The goats liked it a lot," Brother Atalf said. He was starting to beam again, although with caution. So Brother Ziegmunt was starting to beam again too. "They ate it all up in a flash."

"So I saw," said Brother Arcadius tonelessly. He managed a sort of wave and turned away. All he could do now was go back to the library. Go back to the library and explain what had happened.

Running was out of the question. If dragons had been swooping down on him, he would not have been able to run. If gangs of Danes had come swarming out of the fields to catch him and kill him, he would not have been able to run. He plodded. He had enough wit left to retrieve his sandals from where they were lying, but he didn't bother to put them back on. He just walked along in a daze. Now that he no longer needed them and wished not to see them, there were plenty of monks around, coming and going. But none of them were among the people he really knew. Most of them walked with their heads down, intent on their business. Thank goodness for that. A few of them gave him quick sidelong glances, but nobody stopped him and said, "What happened to you?" Brother Marcus and his whole crew were working non-stop in the kitchen, as he could tell by the clamor. The two watchmen weren't looking his way. He managed to get by them without attracting their attention.

He entered the refectory and went down the broad corridor that separated the reception room from the dining hall. He passed the stone image of Charles Martel receiving light from the Holy Spirit. He tugged the farther door open and went on out. Pangur Ban emerged from some nearby bushes and ran to join him. For a heartbeat, Brother Arcadius entertained the hope that Pangur was somehow coming to the rescue, as he'd done twice before when precious things were feared to be lost and gone forever. The wish gave way quickly to reality. Pangur just wanted to greet him and nothing more.

Brother Arcadius did his best to look pleased to see him. No matter how many great poems were lost, he loved Pangur and always would love him. But now was no time to stop and give him a petting. Father Julian might happen by, or Brother Dietrich, Father Julian's secretary. The dark gaze of the one, the uncanny uncreased neatness of the other—there were times when such things were more than a person could bear.

And Pangur, right now, didn't even want to be petted. He was clearly put off by his friend's bare, filthy feet and equally filthy robe. He gave Brother Arcadius's shins a mere token rub, then darted away. It was then that Brother Arcadius realized one more thing: in pursuit of his poem, his beautiful lost poem, he had left the library both untended and unlocked. Not that the monks of Spiritus Sanctus were library abusers—they were hardly library users. But still! A hundred Brother Atalfs could have blundered in and done who knew what. The monastery had put in much time and effort over many years, and paid out who knew how many pieces of money, to collect those books on its shelves, and there were things like the wonderful Genesis, with those pictures.... Lock It Up When You Leave was the rule, and Brother Arcadius hadn't.

I'm no librarian, he told himself over and over, in new agony. *I'm no librarian.* But librarian or not, he was now at the library door. He was at it, but he didn't go through it. He could see through the nearest window that Brother Silvanus was in there by now, and working. He swallowed a prickle of tears and pressed his lips together to keep them from trembling. He stamped his bare feet into the grass to clean them, realizing with additional horror that those same filthy feet had just tracked who knew what all down the refectory corridor. He was no librarian and also he was no monk. He brushed and scraped the filth from his robe as best he could. Then he opened the door and let himself be seen.

"Hail Caesar—" began Brother Silvanus. It was the same old joke he trotted out every day, comparing his assistant Arcadius with a feckless young emperor of the same name who'd lived long ago. In spite of that, the librarian's tone was highly irritated. He was about to give his assistant a dressing down. But that intention was swept aside when he saw the assistant's blotched face and highly unkempt appearance. "Arcadius, what happened?"

Brother Arcadius told him in a rush of words. Brother Silvanus listened without comment. "Well, go and get cleaned up," he said, when the short and sorry tale had ended. "Then come back and give me the details." He glanced at the cricket cage. A loud chirping was coming from it. "You didn't lose the cricket, at least."

Brother Arcadius fled to his building. He washed up outdoors, using a rag and a dipperful of water from the cistern. His breeches and tunic were wearable. His sandals were too, because they'd never come anywhere near the goat pen. He went to his cell and put on his other robe. He'd have to wash the rag and the dirty robe out in the lake. He would do that in the first spare moment he had after Brother Silvanus agreed—he'd have to agree—that Assistant Librarian Arcadius was no librarian, and that he, Arcadius, had been and was and always would be an utter disgrace to the monastery and the library, a good-for-nothing...a fool.

But when he returned to the library to face up to the storm that was bound to break upon him, no storm did. "Sit down," said Brother Silvanus. "And cheer up, Mighty Caesar. It wasn't you who told Atalf to stop by the library. I should have known better. Now this poem you found—do you remember any of it?"

There needed to be a storm. A storm was deserved. At the very least, there should be a good talking-to. But did he remember the poem? Now that he'd begun to calm down, he found that he did. Those two wondrous lines had been inscribed in his mind and heart from the first moment. What he had forgotten, completely, was the fact that he'd copied those scattered letters onto his waxed tablet. There it still lay on the table, an aid to remembrance. An aid to remembrance that at this moment wasn't needed. In an unsteady voice that gained strength as he went on, Brother Arcadius recited the all-too-few glorious words.

> Incedunt arbusta per alta, securibus caedunt
> Percellunt magnas quercus, exciditur ilex....

"That's all there was of it, on that page anyway," he told Brother Silvanus. "Maybe there was more of it on another page. And maybe there were other poems." The thought of what might have been lost filled him anew with anguish. Even so, he saw again in his mind those men striding mysteriously through the high forest, and the great oaks toppling. "But those letters at the end, the n-n-i-u-s, and r-i-c-a.... I thought of the poet Ennius, and his friend Africanus."

"And so would I think of them too, Tammis Scholar," said Brother Silvanus intently. "And what you need to do now, if you can still hold a pen after the shocks of the day, is to set it all down on parchment. Wax can melt, and if it's your wax it probably will. Copy the single letters arranged as you saw them, and your reconstruction of the words. I think your reconstruction is right, but Father Julian will want to decide that for himself." He held up a warning forefinger in mock solemnity. "But I forbid you to overlay the words of Vituperatius upon those lines, Arcadius, for the sake of making an exact copy. I read one page of him, and handed the book over to you without delay. Too bad for me. If I'd had more patience with him, I would have discovered our poem, and not you."

And he laughed, and Brother Arcadius grinned feebly and did as he was bidden. By the time he'd gotten to "rica," he was feeling that he might be something of a librarian again—something of one, not much of a one. The next day, when Father Julian actually went so far as to say that the reconstruction was probably right, and that the two lines were a good find, and shrugged off the loss of the manuscript, Brother Arcadius felt full librarianship returning to him.

The copy he'd made of the overlaid letters and reconstructed lines was put securely away, to be looked at again now and then, and wondered about always. Was the reconstruction really right? Was the poet really Ennius? Or was all this just a great error? Errors could happen!

And now and then, and for a long time after, Brother Arcadius found himself foolishly hoping that Pangur Ban might turn up with the missing page in his jaws. Or might lead the way to the lost manuscript lying somewhere in a clump of bushes, or some such thing. Or stare intently at a library shelf, and there the lost book would be, because Brother Atalf had taken a book, but not the book. But none of that happened. The two lines that had been rescued would have to do, the lines and the fact that Keti's lessons with the cricket went extremely well—the cricket being transferred for each lesson to the bottom of a very deep pail where it could race freely around and not be eaten. *The cricket is very safe, so the cricket is happy.*

And little by little, so was the assistant librarian quite happy again, except for a very small corner of his heart—the corner where the loss of what might have been chafed like rough cloth against skin, or a speck of grit in the sandal. And goat's meat, or goat's milk, or goat's cheese could not be enjoyed, but had to be swallowed down with grim determination for a good long time, and a time after that as well. And for a good long time and a time after that as well, Brother Hyssop the goat-tender complained that his goats kept going around and around in circles, and making him dizzy.

THE LILY-WHITE CHEEK

In which tables are turned, and some are turned upside down

AD 900

At first they were just moving dots on the horizon, but they came on fast, riding toward the monastery of Spiritus Sanctus: Duke Ulrich and his five men. They were expected. They'd sent word ahead by means of a barefooted landsman from a village where they were resting, thirty miles to the west. They'd be at the monastery in four or five days, the landsman had said. They wanted him to be paid for bringing the message. Half a groat, maybe, they'd said. They'd said they would pay it back once they'd arrived.

So Spiritus Sanctus gave the messenger his half a groat, and gave him supper and a bed for the night as well. He went off again in the morning, fortified with provisions for his journey home—a large round of bread, a skinful of watered wine—and the monastery prepared to receive its notable guests.

Like most members of the high nobility and the high clergy, Duke Ulrich was kin to Father Julian, the head of the monastery. They were fourth half cousins or triple full cousins or something of that sort. The duke and his men had been fighting the Lombards in Spain, on behalf of the Saracens and the pope. But that alliance was over, so now they were heading back to the duke's lands in the northeast. A kinsman of Father Julian's, a true fighting man, an actual duke—visitors like that didn't come often to Spiritus Sanctus. In the kitchen, the dining hall, the reception room, the guests' quarters (not the ones for common travelers in the courtyard, but those adjoining Father Julian's residence), the bustle of preparation was intense.

Brother Arcadius, assistant librarian of Spiritus Sanctus, had no part to play in welcoming the duke, but he was aware of all the commotion just the same. Pen in hand, bending over the book and the piece of parchment before him, mind on his work—mostly on his work!—he couldn't help being sorry, a little, that the duke hadn't arrived an hour earlier. Then he might have seen him ride in. Under orders from the medicus to take a daily walk to keep up his health and strength, he'd hoped that part of his walk today would coincide with the party's arrival. He'd hung back in the courtyard for a good many extra moments when the oncoming dots had first been sighted. But although they'd been approaching fast, he'd run out of time.

He consulted the page he'd been reading and added more words to the parchment, in his neat, careful hand: *Saint Onorius, born, page XXV, shipwrecked and rescued by dolphins, page XXVI.* As so often, he was making a so-called index for yet another book in the library—a list of the topics, with page numbers, that the book dealt with. It was an important task. If the hard-working monks of Spiritus Sanctus had lists like these to consult, they could find things they wanted to read about more easily, and then maybe they'd read. So should he let his mind keep straying away to things like dukes? No, he shouldn't.

Saint Electrus, born, tried to convert emperor, thrown to lions.... Brother Arcadius paused again, pen uplifted. He wondered if Pangur Ban was up on the high roof over the dining hall, keeping out of the way. The big white cat, the monastery's prize mouser, was none too happy with the bustle and commotion over the duke. So he'd taken to spending hours in his rooftop refuge, coming down now and then to see if things were taking a calmer turn, and to do his nightly work of mousing in the kitchen. A sociable cat, but also a sensible cat, he could be counted on, usually, to go about things in a sensible way.

Saint Fermatus, born, page XXX.... Brother Arcadius thought back to the time, two years before, when Pangur Ban had been a mere half-grown kitten, and he himself had been barely sixteen, setting off on the long, hard journey to Spiritus Sanctus. They'd both been on that boat coming out of Dublin. He'd been seasick, and Pangur, a stowaway, had come up out of the cargo and been snatched up by a wicked sailor who was going to kill him—the sort of person who'd throw a saint to the lions. Well, the sailor had been paid off with a piece of money, and Pangur had come on to Spiritus Sanctus too, and people were glad of it, generally. Brother Marcus, the head cook, was especially glad, for never had the kitchen been kept so free of mice. And Keti the kitchen boy was also especially glad. For Keti, Pangur was the sun, moon, and stars.

...Preached in Antioch and exiled to desert island, page XXXII.... The bell in the courtyard watchtower began to ring. The duke and his men had arrived. Brother Arcadius was not all that interested in dukes as such, or at least he didn't think so. But a warrior duke, a brave man, a survivor of battles, a sort of Father Julian with armor and sword....

"Arcadius."

Brother Arcadius came to with a guilty start. He met the stern gaze of the person across the table: Brother Silvanus, the head librarian. He'd be in for a dressing down now, and serve him right. He'd been daydreaming more than working, that was for sure.

"Arcadius," Brother Silvanus said again.

"Yes," murmured Brother Arcadius, with lowered eyes.

"Arcadius, go look at the duke," said Brother Silvanus.

"I..."

"Go look at the duke, Arcadius," said Brother Silvanus. "Go look at him now!" He flapped his hands in the air, in a pushing gesture. "Out, *out*!" he cried.

"But I—"

"Out, I say, or we're sending you back to Dublin," Brother Silvanus said. "You and the cat."

It sank in that Brother Silvanus, as more often than not, was hiding kindness in a great show of exasperation. "Thank you," said Brother Arcadius. He hurried to the door.

"You're done for the day," said Brother Silvanus. "If anybody asks, I sent you. You're there on library business. I've found the book that Father Julian wanted to see. So *Vale*, O Mighty Caesar! Farewell! But the wind's picking up out there. Don't let it blow you away."

"All right," said Brother Arcadius. He would have liked to say more words of thanks—quite a few of them!—but words of thanks never sat well with Brother Silvanus. Best to just do as he was told and leave it at that. Suiting action to thought, Brother Arcadius went out into the bracing cold of the March afternoon. It was amazing, though, how the head librarian managed to slip those two jokes in, day after day. The joke about the long-ago Emperor Arcadius, who'd been very young and very inept and no "Mighty Caesar" at all. And the joke about the wind. Well, Brother Arcadius was used to all that. He was the youngest monk on the premises by a good ten years, and the shortest and slightest except for tiny little Brother Zossimus, and he couldn't deny it. Even so, he was in no danger of having the wind blow him away! Lowering his head against the occasional sharp-edged snowflake that came whirling at him, he hurried on to the refectory, tugged open the heavy door, and went on in.

There was much more light in the corridor than usual. The small lamps in the wall niches were aglow all down the long expanse that led to the dining hall and the reception room. There were lots of people there too, going or coming, or engaged in last-minute tasks like polishing door handles. Delicious aromas from the kitchen told of food being cooked that would really be fit for a duke. The monks' suppers were tasty and filling, but no more than that, and Father Julian always ate whatever the monks did, but Duke Ulrich might well be expecting much finer fare. And if he wanted it, he would get it. Brother Marcus's cooking skills were of the highest, and he welcomed every chance to show them off. Reminding himself that he was here to see the duke and not think of food, Brother Arcadius went on to the reception room.

The clopping of hooves and the occasional snort or nickering bray from out in the courtyard told him that the travelers' mules were already being led away to the stables. So the duke and his men would be coming in very soon. Father Julian would be with them, giving his kinsman a proper welcome.

The reception room was ready for them. It was a very long room, and usually very bare, for Spiritus Sanctus never had to do much receiving. But now it shone in the unaccustomed light from its hanging lamps, and a number of stools from the storage area there at the back had been brought forth and set about: footstools and taller stools both, for the comfort and convenience of the travelers in the first moments of their arrival. They'd be wanting to divest themselves of their armor and weapons, and wash the dirt from their faces, their hands, and their feet. Two of the taller stools, and two footstools, held basins of water. Brothers Nikolas, Baudwin, and Ambroz hovered nearby, ready to attend to the needs of this servantless party.

A scattering of other monks were in the room, too. Brother Salix the medicus, for one, in case he was needed. And Father Julian's secretary, for another—Brother Dietrich, a spotless figure in a robe always free of wrinkles. Waxed tablet in hand, stylus poised, he was ready to take any note, run any errand. Brother Arcadius slipped past him and stood by the medicus, hoping it wasn't presumptuous to stand so far up front. Then he reminded himself that no, it wasn't presumptuous. He'd been sent here on library business. He had to stand somewhere.

And now, were they coming?

A gust of chill air and a whirling of snow from the corridor, as the front door was opened...a sound of voices in conversation...the tread of soldierly feet...a clatter of metal, a smell of hay and mules....

Yes, it was them.

Here came Father Julian. And right alongside him there came a shortish, wiry, travel-worn figure who was talking—no, *chattering*—to him, clasping his arm and punctuating his words with gestures and laughs. Was this the duke, or was it some sort of, well, jester? But no jester would hang on to Father Julian's arm. It was a bit of a let-down to decide that this had to be the duke. Behind him came his five men. With barely a pause they started removing their gloves, unlacing their armored leggings, sliding out of their armored vests. Gear fell to the floor and was gathered up by the attendant monks. Sword belts with short swords in their sheathes were carefully unbuckled and handed over for safekeeping. Hands and feet were gratefully dipped into basins of water, and water was eagerly splashed onto wind-burned faces.

"Oh yes, it was quite a campaign," Duke Ulrich was saying. Standing there in his crumpled tunic and worsted hose, he looked even less like a duke than he had before. "Quite a campaign. The fur flew, Julian! Good of you to give us this welcome and—Gauli, what's wrong?" He'd turned and was speaking to the tallest of the men who'd come with him.

Brother Arcadius's eyes had been drawn to this man from the very first moment. He was a strange and impressive figure, that was for sure, far more like a duke in stature than the actual duke. He looked to be taller, in fact, than anyone in the monastery, including the immense brothers Atalf and Ziegmunt. His shoulders were as broad as theirs, too. But his arms and legs, though well muscled, were lean and slender, and his hips were narrow. What stood out about him otherwise was that after removing his gloves, he'd done nothing else except stand there, with his sword still slung discourteously at his side. And although his companions were all bare faced, his face was hidden. It was entirely covered by some sort of very odd, very soft-knit, very *fleecy* mask.

"Gauli, you need to take off your sword, you know," said Duke Ulrich anxiously. "And you'll need to—what's that?" The tall man had muttered something. "Your mask? Who's going to wash your mask? Why, one of these kind monks will wash your mask—won't they?" he demanded of Father Julian.

"Brother Ambroz will wash it excellently," said Father Julian in his usual even tones. If he was puzzled, he showed no sign of it. His family had been negotiators and arrangers for royalty and other such people from way back. Being unreadable was in his blood, if not in his kinsman's. "He will care for it exactly as he's told." He raised an eyebrow at Brother Ambroz, who visibly fought back a shrug and nodded instead.

"There, Gauli," said Duke Ulrich winningly. "You can take your mask off now with no need to worry." He turned to Father Julian. "Has to have his mask when he's outdoors," he said indulgently. "He has a wonderful complexion, you know, and he's very protective of it. He has five of those masks, in fact. His mother used to knit them for him when she was alive, and now I've found a woman who can knit them like she did." He turned back to Gauli, who had not yet moved. "Go ahead, now. I'll make sure that everything's taken care of."

Slowly, slowly the tall Gauli reached up and removed his helmet. He set it down on a stool. His fine-spun pale hair was matted from the journey. With his fingers he brushed it into place, carefully smoothing it and arranging it over his ears. Then, reaching behind, he untied the mask and lifted it...slowly, slowly...away from his face.

Brother Arcadius had been brought up never to stare, but he regretted that right at this moment. The man's face was as odd as his mask. Odder. Cupped by the fine pale hair, it was a long oval that narrowed down as if it were going to come to a point, but squared off instead. His nose was long, with flaring nostrils. His lips, close under the nose, were pouchy, and as red as ripe cherries. His very wide-set eyes were tiny and round, like little icy blue beads, with pupils like specks. And his skin—the skin of his face, the skin of his hands—was flawless, creamy white, unwrinkled, unmarred by any sign that it had ever actually been out in the world at all. Brother Arcadius had never imagined anything like it.

"Now, Gauli," said Duke Ulrich soothingly, "if you will hand me the mask, I will give it to the good monk here, or you can give it to him yourself. And then you can slide out of those uncomfortable things, and take off your sword because that is the rule here, and no one here aims to harm us—and then we can all go to our rooms, where we'll find everything needed for our comfort."

Gauli considered these words for a moment. Duke Ulrich and his four companions watched him intently, as if waiting for some sort of storm to break. Then Gauli handed the mask to Brother Ambroz.

"You need to get all the dust out of it," he said. "There's a lot of it. You should rinse it until it all goes away." His voice was low and had a muffled tone, as if it too were somehow masked. "And don't let it stay wet. Make sure it gets really dry."

With the mask clasped in his hands like a live thing that might escape, Brother Ambroz looked uneasily at Father Julian. "You can get started on that now," Father Julian said. Ambroz left, with Gauli's fixed gaze following him to the door. Once Ambroz was out of sight with the precious mask, Gauli unbuckled his sword belt at last, and removed his armored vest and leggings.

Brother Arcadius abruptly decided that he'd looked his fill. He'd seen the duke, and he'd seen this odd fellow Gauli. He wasn't supposed to go back to the library, and in just a short while it would be time for vespers. He might as well just go to the church and wait for the others. He caught Brother Dietrich's eye and murmured his library message. Then he went on his way.

After vespers came supper. By then the gusty afternoon had resolved itself into a fine clear evening, with an orange-rose glow of sunset fading slowly in the west. Walking back to the refectory with his brethren for the day's final meal, Brother Arcadius spied Pangur Ban by the infirmary, prowling along on some errand of his own. Now that the commotion attending the duke's arrival was over, Pangur was cautiously returning to his life on the ground.

Brother Arcadius went on to the dining hall. There, as luck would have it, although he no longer cared about it one way or the other, he got to look at the duke again. Sitting down, by rule, at the first available place that he came to, he found himself next to the dais where Father Julian's table was laid. Father Julian was seated up there already. Duke Ulrich was right beside him, talking, talking. But tall Gauli and his four companions were seated at regular tables, some distance away. The kitchen crew moved this way and that about the hall, setting out food and drink with practiced dispatch. Then Father Julian said grace, and the meal began. The monks, as always, ate in restful silence. The chatter of Father Julian's kinsman went on and on.

Eavesdropping was just as bad as staring, but overhearing couldn't be helped. Brother Arcadius did his best to ignore the stream of words from above, but his best wasn't up to the task. They were spoken in penetrating tones, those words, and they kept on coming. "You asked about the name 'Gauli,'" Duke Ulrich was saying to Father Julian. "I call him that because he's old Gaul to the core, Julian, with one of those Gaulish names that go on forever in the most ridiculous way—*Athafulthagofferix*, or something like that. Even you couldn't pronounce it. And yes, I discovered him in one of my own villages, growing up there, his talents wasted—although they would have singled him out sooner rather than later. He's a prodigy, Julian. A prodigy!" The duke broke off to spoon up some of the stew that had just been served him. "Delicious, Julian! I must steal away your cook—Is it Marcus? Do I have the name right?"

"Marcus, yes. I keep him chained to the wall," Father Julian said amiably. As always, his dark gaze scanned the hall. It lingered a moment on the duke's men at their distant table.

"But Gauli," Duke Ulrich went on. "But Gauli—it's his *speed* that does it for him, Julian, and his...well, his *magical* sense of where his enemies are at every moment." The duke's chatter became a rhapsody. "In Spain, you know, this one time, the Lombards had Scarpians with them—*Scarpians*! The worst of the worst, Julian! Invincible fighters! They were all around him, fifty of them, hewing and hacking at him, their swords flashing up and down, and in the center of all that there was a fountain of blood—a *fountain*, Julian! It spurted and spurted into the air, in the midst of this whirling commotion, and I knew I'd lost him. I knew he had to be dead. Damned fine fish paste."

The duke took another judicious bite of fish paste on bread, and then returned to his tale. "But then came the call to retreat, not ours, but theirs, and it turned out, Julian, that every drop of blood was Lombards'—Lombards', and Scarpians'. My man stood victorious in the midst of the carnage, soaked with gore—his mask and everything soaked—but none of it was his, Julian. He should have been dead ten times over, but he was completely unscathed."

"He doesn't appear to be eating."

"Oh, pay no attention. He never eats much. He lives on heroism, you might say—sheer heroism. He cleaned that nest of Scarpians and Lombards out in two days, and there were many of them—many, Julian. The rest of us helped him, of course, but in fact, we were barely needed. Our allies were offering me kings' ransoms for him, but—" The duke gave a brief, derisive laugh. "They offered in vain. He is the one and only reason why I'm able to travel without a cumbersome mob of expensive guards and baggage handlers. Brigands dare not come near. And peasants and villagers...why, they take one look at him, and run to bring us the best of everything they have."

"He keeps looking our way. Does he want something?"

"Oh yes. He wants you to allow him to show off his speed and skill. I told him you'd certainly do so. It's something to see."

"No weapons are to be used anywhere on these premises, Ulrich."

"He doesn't need weapons, Julian. I think he could get by, in a pinch, with no weapons at all, at any time, under any circumstances. The speed and the force of his hands are his real weapons." The duke paused to eat more of his stew. "The speed and force of his hands," he repeated. "I've seen him shatter oak planks with them – shatter brick walls! And in the pass of Roncesvalles, Julian, where those bastards destroyed Charlemagne's rear guard that time—"

"As in the songs," said Father Julian.

"Yes, as in the songs! Exactly as in the songs!! We took that route because we had to, coming home, and I was on edge every moment, I freely admit it, Julian. But those devilish Basques never showed their faces. They knew that *he* was with us, and they stayed away. Excellent, excellent fish paste. Amazing fish paste. And the stew! That subtle flavor of...I don't know what. What is that flavor, Julian?"

"I don't know either, Ulrich. I promised to free Marcus from his chains, and he still wouldn't tell me."

"Ah, you're jesting, Julian. But you will give Gauli his chance now, won't you? Otherwise he will find it *so* hard to sleep. He's all anticipation, Julian. Can't you see it?" The tall, odd fellow's companions were stolidly eating, but Gauli himself was sitting intent and unmoving beside them, like someone about to reach a bursting point.

Father Julian gazed at his kinsman under lowered brows for a moment. Then he rapped on the table and called for attention. The clinking of spoons and knives completely ceased. His voice rang through the sudden silence. "Immediately after supper there will be a demonstration of military skill—unarmed military skill—in the reception room," he said. "Those who wish to see it should go straight there when you've finished eating. You can come back for your eating gear later." He turned to Duke Ulrich. "Will a quarter hour of this allow for a restful sleep, Ulrich?"

"Oh, I would say so," said the duke. He went back to his stew and fish paste.

Brother Arcadius was of two minds about watching Gauli's demonstration of force and speed, and came close to deciding not to. Chatter and masks and icy blue eyes with pinpoint pupils—he'd had enough of all that. As for one man fighting off fifty, all by himself....

No, he didn't believe it. But then curiosity got the better of him. He'd seen a duke, so he might as well see this. Like the rest of the brethren heading off for the great display, he left his eating things behind as directed. He'd wiped everything spotlessly clean, as always, with his last crust of bread. It wasn't the week when he had to wash them, by rule, with that stuff called "soap" that Brother Salix the medicus made for them to use, and then boil them into the bargain, back at his building, but they certainly looked as clean as if they'd been washed and boiled.

He crossed the corridor to the reception room. A good many monks were there ahead of him, and more were coming behind. There was going to be quite a crowd. Brother Salix the medicus was there, and Brother Marcus with wide-eyed little Keti. Brothers Alvas, Homelius, and Sandro, the kitchen crew, were standing nearby. Brother Kongro, the day watchman, now off duty, was right behind them. The two hulking brothers, Atalf and Ziegmunt, stood alongside.

As Brother Arcadius edged into a spot where he'd have a clear view, he hit his shin against something hard and almost tripped. One of the footstools brought out for the travelers hadn't been put away yet, that's what it was. It lay upside down at his feet, short-legged, squat, and very much in the way. He picked it up so it wouldn't trip anybody else. He saw that Keti was watching him and gave him a quick smile. Keti waved solemnly back.

Now Gauli entered the room, with a smiling duke and an unsmiling Father Julian on either side, and his four companions coming along behind. He stepped into the center of the room. For just a moment he stood there motionless. Then his arms began to whirl, faster and faster. In an instant they looked like a thousand arms, whirling in a blur so fast that it stunned the mind. And now his whole body began to whirl round and round, as fast as the blur of his arms, while his hands, like a thousand hands, flashed in every direction. It could now be believed that he'd conquered those fifty men...those fifty *Scarpians*, the best of the very best....

Or the worst of the very worst, depending on which side you were on....

"Step in!" he shouted. "Try to get past my guard! Step in!" Nobody moved. "You won't be touched," he shouted again. "I'll know where you are! Step in! Try and get past my g—"

His words broke off, and suddenly he was whirling toward the door. Before Brother Arcadius could sort things out, before he could see that Pangur Ban had come to the doorway and was peering doubtfully in at all the commotion, Gauli was crying, "A cat! Yes! A cat!" And suddenly, suddenly, whirling all the while, he'd seized the astonished Pangur and was holding him, struggling and snarling, one-handed by the nape of his poor neck, while the other hand whirled on in its ceaseless blur. "I hold it close!" Gauli shouted. "Close to my face! It tries to get me! Tries, but can't! Can't get past my hand! Can't get past my guard!"

Then everything happened at once and blended together—Brother Marcus's roar of protest, Keti's shrill cry of dismay, Brother Arcadius in blind fury trying to go to the rescue, people telling him not to and pushing him back—and wild Gauli's flawless cheeks glowed pink with joy, and his free hand moved this way and that in its ceaseless blur—

—And Pangur Ban reached through that blur in a faster blur in the next instant, and laid his tormentor's cheek open from eye socket to chin.

Blood welled. Gauli's hands went slack in shock. Pangur Ban fell to the floor, righted himself, and backed slowly away, spitting and hissing. Every hair on his body stood straight up and his eyes stared. Reaching the door, he turned and fled. Brother Arcadius, coming back into himself with a mighty effort, saw that there was no point in chasing after him. Pangur had gotten away before he'd been harmed. He'd be wanting only to hide for a while, most likely up there on the roof. Once he'd had time to calm down, he could be lured back into the world with soothing words and a favorite treat. Brother Marcus across the room was clearly explaining as much to Keti, who was staring after the cat with awe...with pride...and with round-eyed deep concern.

Brother Arcadius caught the little boy's eye and nodded affirmingly—*He'll be all right*. He forced himself to keep on calming down, but it wasn't easy. Pangur could have died from being whirled about like that. Gauli had his nerve, treating a cat that way. It served him right that Pangur had struck back, served him right that his dear precious cheek was all bloody, served him right that he was now huddled up on the floor....

Huddled up on the floor? Because of a scratched *cheek?*

His duke and his four comrades had sped to his side, but Gauli seemed not to see them. His legs had folded beneath him and he wasn't just huddled up but moaning too. The moans became wails that chilled the heart and did not cease.

Duke Ulrich and the others were kneeling all around him, talking urgently to him, trying to get him to look at them and listen to them, but it seemed that for him they were not there—that for him, nobody was there. The feeling of "Serves him right!" had been widespread around the room, expressed in quick nods and quirks of the lips and even the barest hint of a chuckle or two. Now all of that gave way to consternation. Taken aback by that unearthly wailing, everyone—even Father Julian—seemed at a loss.

No, not everyone. Brother Salix the medicus had gone over to his old army comrade, Marcus the cook. Fiercely intent as always on his task of healing, he was already unfastening the keys from his belt and handing them over. "You know what to bring," he told Marcus. "And I'll want a pail of hot water too, of course, and clean rags, all you can spare, and a mug and a spoon...."

Marcus was already turning to go on his mission. "Keti, you stay here with Brother Arcadius," he said. "I won't be long. And Alvas, you come with me." Brother Alvas hurried to join him and they strode away. Brother Arcadius, heart still hammering, hurried over to take charge of Keti. The little boy, as always, was doing his best to wear a brave face. "Pangur Ban beat him, didn't he?" he whispered.

"He certainly did."

"Should we go find him pretty soon?" It was a sign of Keti's great love for Pangur that he was saying all this. Keti was a child of few words, and preferred it that way.

"Cats really do like to go off by themselves when they're upset," Brother Arcadius told him. "Then they come out of hiding when they're good and ready."

"But where do you think he is?"

"He's been up on the roof a lot, these past few days."

"Oh!" said Keti. His anxious face lit up, just for a moment. "He'll be safe up there!"

He fell silent again. The horrible wailing was dwindling into sobs. Brother Salix knelt down beside the stricken man. "You're in no danger," he said. "We want face cuts to bleed a lot. It helps them heal." His quiet words were easy to hear in the hushed room. "I will clean and seal your wounds, taking every care. You should stay very calm now, and know that you'll be given good help. After a while, I'll give you something to help you rest."

"Listen to the good medicus, Gauli," urged Duke Ulrich. "Listen to him."

204

Gauli's head sank lower, but he didn't resume his wails. "My cheek," he whispered. "My skin." He pressed his hand to his bloody cheek and sobbed again.

Serves you right, thought Brother Arcadius for the twentieth time. *Now maybe you know how it feels, eh?* He had no qualms about thinking this unmonklike thought, none at all. But his heart had stopped hammering, and he was starting to know once more what he was about. His left hand clasped Keti's shoulder, yes, and his right hand held.... What did it hold? Oh, the footstool. Still the footstool. He couldn't sit down on it, not when everybody was standing. And he didn't feel like walking the long length of the room right now to put it back where it belonged. For all he knew, it was supposed to stay up front here. It seemed best for now to just hold it, and so he did.

But now Father Julian was taking charge of things again. Monks who wanted to leave were free to do so, he said, but they should collect their eating gear from the dining hall before they went back to their cells. Those who wanted to stay and give the injured man their silent support could do so. Out of his line of sight in a shadowed spot, Brother Mishel the chief stonecutter pantomimed the swipe of a cat's paw and grinned the briefest of grins. Brother Arcadius grinned briefly back. Yes, the injured man would be getting silent wishes, all right.

A handful of monks left to return to their cells. The rest stayed, glued in place by the novelty of this unexpected diversion. The room was still full when Brother Marcus and Brother Alvas came hurrying back. Marcus carried a huge basket loaded with things from the infirmary and the kitchen, and Alvas was toting two steaming buckets of water. Basins, mugs, spoons, ladles, clean rags, pouches of medicines, a tin of Salix's soap—these things and more were unpacked and set down within Salix's reach. "Take your keys before I mislay 'em," Marcus told him. Salix refastened the keys to his belt without a word. His attention was all on Gauli and nothing else.

Duke Ulrich, his four men, Father Julian, and everyone now watched intently as Brother Salix got to work. He started by washing his hands with soap and water for what seemed a very long time, a ritual that he always claimed was extremely important. After that, things went more quickly. He filled a new basin with fresh water, dipped a rag into it, and cleaned the blood, both dry and flowing, from Gauli's face, revealing the ravaged cheek. Gauli flinched and trembled. "There's only one very deep claw track here," Salix said. "The rest are on the surface."

Holding the main wound open with widespread forefinger and thumb, he poured a mugful of hot water over it. Gauli shouted with pain. Bloody water soaked into his already bloody clothes. Some of it pooled on the floor. Brother Alvas threw down a rag to soak it up. Brother Salix now washed the entire cheek, and the long main wound, with soap and water. Gauli trembled and wept. Duke Ulrich moved in close to his prodigy and held his hand. "It will be all right, Gauli," he kept whispering. "It will be all right."

Brother Salix rinsed away the soap and turned to his own set of special spoons, very tiny brass ones that he kept in their own leather case. Choosing the tiniest one—its bowl was the size of a hollowed-out cherry pit—he measured powders of different colors from various pouches into a beechwood cup and blended them well. Spreading the deepest claw track well apart again, he packed it with this mixture. Then he covered the entire wound with a folded rag and told Gauli to hold it in place. Gauli could not bring himself to do that, so Duke Ulrich held it instead. Everyone watched spellbound as the bleeding slowed and stopped. Brother Salix waited a moment. Then he sealed the main wound with a very familiar concoction, the one that he always used for sealable wounds, a sticky mixture of cobwebs, pine gum, and various powdered herbs. The monks standing round about nodded approval. Gauli might be strange and uncanny, but Salix was doing just what they figured he'd do. "That should heal well," he said.

However, he wasn't through yet. Sitting back on his heels, he considered his powders again. He chose seven, and measured them into the cup with that tiny spoon. Five spoonfuls of this, three of that, half a spoonful of this other, just a pinch of something else...he blended this mixture together, he filled the cup with hot water, he stirred and stirred.... The room filled with a healing fragrance that did the heart good. "If you'll lift up your head...." he said softly to the shivering Gauli, "If you'll drink this...."

Eyes tightly shut, Gauli lifted his head, and sip by shuddering sip he drank the potion down. "That will help you rest well," Brother Salix assured him. "Soon we'll help you walk over to the infirmary. You will sleep there tonight, and I will stay with you." He looked over at Duke Ulrich, who was hanging on every word. "In a moment he will feel much calmer, and things should go well." With quick movements the medicus emptied the basins of bloody, soapy water back into a bucket, put the tiny brass spoon back in its case, and tucked the pouches of powders back into the basket that Brother Marcus had brought. He stood up. Brother Alvas collected the kitchen things and moved them aside. The diversion was over.

"Did you hear that, Gauli?" whispered the duke. "Things should go well."

Gauli made no answer. His head was down again, drooping lower and lower. Now and then he shuddered. Now and then he sobbed. Duke Ulrich put an arm around his shoulder and whispered words of encouragement in his ear. His comrades got to their feet and stretched their legs, frowning down at him now and then to show their concern.

"When is he going to start feeling better?" whispered Keti. His expression was guarded. He could see that everyone was supposed to be wishing this cat-tormentor well, but he was quite sure that he didn't want to do that. No matter how many others shared those feelings, endorsing them out loud would never do. "Brother Salix says soon, Keti," said Brother Arcadius. He trained his eyes on the medicus as the moments passed by...several moments...a good many moments...more moments, maybe, than Brother Salix had expected? Brother Salix suddenly looked as if something might be going amiss.

And Gauli, all of a sudden, stopped crouching in place. He sprang to his feet. His little ice-blue eyes with the pinpoint pupils glared this way and that. People drew back in alarm. His chest swelled. He clenched his fists. He bared his teeth. His marred face twisted into a demon's mask. "Where is the cat?" he screamed. "Where did he go? I'll kill him! I'll kill him!" And knocking the clutching hands of Duke Ulrich aside, he ran headlong from the room, long legs pumping, pale hair flying. He came to a stop in the corridor just for a moment, a fearsome shadow in the flickering light of the lamps. Then he turned to the dining hall door and went on inside. Crash! came the sound of long tables toppling over. Crash! came the sound of hurled benches hitting the floor. If he came back....

Brother Marcus was already trying to close the door to the reception room. It was rarely shut and dragged against the stone floor. "Atalf, Ziegmunt, help him," Father Julian said in his tone of quiet command. Trembling, the monastery's two behemoths forced themselves forward. Before they could reach Marcus's side and lend him the power of their mighty arms, Gauli came screaming out of the dining hall again, bringing sheer blank terror with him—but he raced on by. The infirmary, the library, Father Julian's residence, the church, the monks' quarters—assuming he didn't turn back, he'd be heading that way. The farther door slammed and cut off the sound of his screams.

"He's outside," Brother Marcus said grimly. "Hope nobody else is." Those standing by exchanged glances of deep distress. By now, so long after supper, most likely the monks out there would all be in their cells, but it was not yet the hour when they had to be in them by rule. Brother Silvanus, thought Brother Arcadius. Frail little Brother Zossimus. Brother Dietrich. They were among the many who hadn't stayed for Gauli's demonstration. They couldn't begin to know how dangerous he was.

"We need to call in the night watch," said Father Julian. His voice was calm, but his words came rapidly. "That is, they should come inside if he's not in the courtyard, or go over the roofs and find shelter if he is. Stay away from him at all costs, at any rate."

Everyone nodded in quick agreement. Keeping watch in the regular way would be of no help. The refectory blocked too much of the view of places where Gauli was likely to be. Ringing the bell would draw people out of their cells when they'd better stay in them. And challenging him, or trying to give him orders—

Brother Kongro of the day watch stepped forward. His comrade, Brother Sifari, hadn't stayed for the demonstration either and might be outside somewhere, unawares. "I'll warn them," he said. "I'll go to the kitchen and call to them through a window. But, Father, if the courtyard's clear they can help me warn everybody else. We'll go along behind the infirmary and the library and then cut over to our buildings. That way we won't be so exposed."

"Do so," said Father Julian. Kongro went off to the kitchen at a half run. Father Julian turned to the others. "Wherever the Gaul may be, some of us will need to distract him from doing harm. Marcus, Salix, you were soldiers. I want you to join me in this. You also, Mishel and Henriz. Not you, Arcadius. Now then, the rest of you—"

"They'd better go to the kitchen cellars, Father," said Brother Marcus. "Two ways out, and the outside door's the same gray as the walls. In the dark he won't spot it. The door to the kitchen is iron-bound on the kitchen side. That ought to slow him down."

Father Julian nodded briskly. "Quickly and in good order, all of you," he said. "Alvas, you know the cellars best. You'll be in charge. Lead the way. Take Salix's medicines with you. We mustn't lose them. Brother Atalf, Brother Ziegmunt, remember that the cellar door's reinforced with iron. He'll find it hard to break through. With your great strength, you'll be able to keep it shut from within until my group arrives to draw him away. That will be your task. I know you'll do it well."

"We'll keep the door shut, Father," whispered Atalf, but he and his brother Ziegmunt looked sick with fear.

"He could damage his hands hitting iron," muttered Duke Ulrich. "He mustn't!" He hurried over to his four soldiers. "Go out there and reason with him. Bring him in."

They shook their heads in unison. "Can't do it, Duke. Not when he's like this."

"But he'll hurt himself!" wailed the duke. "Bring him in, I say!"

"Can't," said the soldier who appeared to be the leader. "Can't," said the others.

"Move forward to the cellars, please," said Father Julian. "You also, Ulrich. Now, Marcus, Salix, Mishel, Henriz, the first thing we'd better do is put out the lights. If the Gaul comes back, the darkness will help shield us, and we don't want him to be able to start a fire." Even as he spoke, he was lowering the first of the hanging lamps on its heavy chain, and capping each burning candle with its brass snuffer.

"All right, the rest of you," said Brother Alvas. "Follow me. Everyone stay with a partner." He looked uncertainly at Duke Ulrich, who'd stopped pleading with his soldiers and was pushing his way forward past them and everybody else. But scolding a duke was nothing he knew how to do, and it was time to get the whole line moving ahead. "Everybody, we have to go two by two down the cellar stairs," he said. "They're narrow, remember that. Just keep to your place in line, all right? And just stay calm."

Brother Arcadius clutched Keti's ice-cold hand and moved forward with the rest. *Not you, Arcadius* rang in his mind. To be like his strong, brave Da who'd faced up to the Danes, to be chosen by Father Julian to go out there and deal with Gauli, to dodge and dart and distract him from hurting people.... He could do that, he thought. He was sure of it. Still, he knew it was right that he should stay with Keti.

Stay calm, stay calm.... The line moved in orderly fashion toward the dining hall door. There were thirty pairs of people in that line, more or less, Brother Arcadius thought, and he and Keti were more or less in the middle. Brother Vincus and elderly Brother Philippi were directly ahead, and Brother Hyssop and Brother Bruno, directly behind. The rest of the line was in shadow. The reception room was dark now and Father Julian and his daring band were moving down the corridor, extinguishing the oil lamps in their niches as they went. Despite the darkness, the line to the cellars kept moving along at a good speed.

Then it came to a sudden stop. Word was coming down the line that the dining hall was already in darkness, too. The kitchen crew had extinguished some of the lights after supper, and Gauli, it seemed, had wrecked the rest, miraculously without setting the room ablaze. And darkness was wanted, darkness was needed. Darkness was a shield against attracting Gauli's attention. But the great room was a shambles. It would not be easy to get to the cellars. The line was going to have to pick its way in darkness around shattered benches, overturned tables, and piles of all sorts of debris.

Brother Arcadius berated himself inwardly. Just as with chess, he never managed to think far enough ahead. He should have foreseen that there'd be delays. He should have sent Keti off with the kitchen workers who were leading the line. Alvas, Sandro, Homelius—they loved the little boy as he loved them. He would have been safe with them now at the head of the line, just a quick dash away from the cellars. Instead....

Instead here he stood with his blockhead of a teacher, a person who couldn't even figure out where to put down a footstool. He couldn't just drop the thing, here in the dark. Somebody would fall over it and get hurt, even badly hurt, as sure as could be. That could be added to the list of the fabled accomplishments of Brother Arcadius, all right: he'd set down a footstool and caused an accident. Well, in all the excitement he'd forgotten again that he had it. Maybe they could all take turns sitting on it down there in the cellars, if they ever got there. What a help that would be. Or maybe, if Gauli turned up, they could ask him very politely to stay very still, and then hit him on the head with it. Thanks to Arcadius and his undroppable footstool, everyone would be safe.

The line crept on through curls of acrid smoke from the extinguished lamps. People's eyes glittered in the starlight that came through the windows above. Father Julian and his band, a group of shadows, were halfway down the corridor, close by the stone image of Charles Martel. They'd removed their encumbering robes and stood ready to take action if Gauli came back, or go find him if he didn't. In every heart was the hope that Gauli by now had collapsed from his exertions, or from the shock of his wounded cheek, or that the calming draught had finally taken effect. Maybe he was just lying senseless out there in the dark. Let it be so. Oh, let it be so!

The line picked up speed, then came to a halt again, picked up speed, then came to a halt again. People groaned in dashed expectations, glanced at each other in unspoken terror, prayed for themselves and for Kongro and his companions somewhere out there on the grounds, with not a hint, so far, of how they were faring. Had they managed to warn the others? Had they come face to face with Gauli? Might they be dead?

Stay calm, stay calm.... Up ahead in the dining hall, somebody abruptly shouted, and then another person shouted, and the line stopped short again. Father Julian strode up to see what was going on. A confusion of frantic voices told the terrible news. Gauli was not lying senseless out there in the dark. He had come into the cellars. Yes, the cellars! He'd found the back door after all and let himself in. Brother Alvas had heard a barrel tip over, and he'd heard Gauli's footsteps coming up the cellar stairs, and then they'd gone back down. And nothing more had been heard. Was he still down there, or where? Brother Atalf and Brother Ziegmunt were piling broken benches against the kitchen side of the cellar door, but its bands of iron were on their side, not his. They were hurrying, doing their best. But if Gauli was down there and aimed to break into the kitchen, their best might not be good enough.

Duke Ulrich came rushing back from the dining hall. He cowered into the shadows against the wall, his mouth working. The line, which had been so orderly so far, started to break. People grasped that they could have been down in the cellars when Gauli found the way in, grasped that now there was no plan of escape and nowhere they could go. Father Julian raised a calming hand. "Panic won't help," he said, low-voiced. "I'm sure you know that. If he's in the cellars and tries to break through the door, you'll know from the noise where he is and you'll have time to escape. Go to the pine woods if that's the case, and hide there. For now I'll go outside and—"

Down the corridor, the farther door opened. Someone came rushing in. It was Brother Kongro. "We heard him! He's out there! He's coming!" he shouted. With Mishel, Salix, and Marcus, he took up his stance by the stone image of Charles Martel. Father Julian joined them.

The great door to outside crashed open again. Gauli stood there, framed in the starlight. Then he came straight on. Father Julian's brave group rushed to deter him. He burst through them as if they weren't there and still came on. There was no time even to scatter. Furious, demented, roaring, in full power and in full stride, murderous hands whirling, he bore down on the people who stood frozen there outside the dining hall door—bore down on Keti. And Brother Arcadius, not aiming, not thinking, in the terror of the moment almost not existing, took a better grip on the stool he'd been holding all this while, and bowled it fast and true at the pumping shins, and the stool connected.

Gauli ran up and over the wobbling top of it. It launched him into midair. His whirling arms scrabbled for purchase and found nothing. Face forward, he hit the stone floor with a sickening, squelching thud. Then he lay silent. A trickle of blood ran sidelong past his chin.

"Arcadius!" cried someone—Brother Mishel, was it? It was a cry of wild approbation, and others took it up. "Arcadius! Arcadius!"

Father Julian picked himself up from the floor and came forward. One side of his face was puffing up and turning purple, but his eyes were warm. "Excellent work, Arcadius," he said. "Thank you."

Brother Arcadius couldn't speak. The footstool had ended up over there by the dining hall door, upside down and minus a leg. He wished it were whole again, so that he could sink down on it. He looked at the silent, stricken form of Gauli and looked away. He looked down at Keti, and the sheer love in the little boy's eyes, undeserved as it was, made him want to weep. He'd thrown a footstool, that was all. He hadn't even thought to rush Keti to the head of that slow, inching line, although as it turned out it was just as well that he hadn't. Everything he'd done right had been a mere accident. If luck hadn't been with him...*Keti, you would have been killed*. But he found his voice. "Thank you, Father," he said.

Duke Ulrich, his face contorted, was bending now over his fallen prodigy. He'd crowded ahead in panic on the way to the cellars, and he'd rushed back in panic when they were no longer safe, but now the duke in him had come back full force. "This is a dreadful thing, Julian," he said. "I would say that it's murder." But Brother Salix had limped painfully over and knelt down at Gauli's side. "He's not dead," he said.

Monks stepped back in alarm on every side. Brother Atalf crossed himself in abject fear. "But I can't guarantee he'll survive," Salix continued. "His skull may well be broken. The brain inside the skull was surely dashed against the bone with tremendous force. The calming draught I gave him may be taking its true effect now, too, which can't help. His loss of blood can't help either."

"What can you do for him?" demanded Duke Ulrich.

"Keep him warm, first and foremost," said Brother Salix. "We can put robes around him for now. I'll give him mine if someone will go and find it. I don't remember where I took it off."

"I do!" cried Brother Henriz. I'll bring it over, and yours too, Father."

"And bring mine," said Brother Mishel.

Brother Kongro shook his head as if bringing himself back to the regular world. "I'll go tell the others it's all right now," he said. He frowned down at Gauli. "He must have stayed close to the refectory all the time. Nobody got hurt out there, and we never saw him."

Brother Salix looked up. "I want more robes. Five or six of them. You can have them back when we get him to the infirmary." Six robes were reluctantly handed over, Brother Arcadius's among them. Salix made another request. "Atalf, Ziegmunt, could you bring a spare shutter from somewhere? Where's the one we carried Miklas in on, last year?"

"I know where it is, and I'll bring it, Brother, but I don't want you to make him better," rumbled Atalf.

"I'll warn you in plenty of time if he shows signs of waking up," said Brother Salix. "Now get the shutter, please."

Atalf went off on his errand. Ziegmunt followed him. The medicus continued tucking robes around Gauli. Father Julian looked down at him. "You want to take him to the infirmary," he said. "But I want him in prison, in chains. You can make a bed up for him there. I have no objection to that. But I don't want him loose on these grounds again."

"He goes to the infirmary, Father," Salix said calmly.

"To the prison, Salix."

"The infirmary, Father. If you want, I'll tether his ankles, to slow him down. But I assure you there's no need for it."

"You were sure about your calming draught too," Father Julian said.

The medicus hesitated for a moment, then shook his head. "That had to do with forces no eye can see, Father," he said. "All I can tell you is that out of hundreds of times, no one else has ever been affected that way by that draught. Well, he's an unusual man, but his injuries now are readable to the eye and say just one thing. He's injured to the point of death. He's also in my care. If he lives, it will be weeks or more than weeks before he can so much as sit up, let alone be dangerous. I'll tie his wrists as well as his ankles if you insist. But I'll leave enough slack so that he can move a little, and I will allow no chains."

These words of disobedience caused a stir, but Father Julian, after a heartbeat of silence, just said, "So be it." He turned to Duke Ulrich. "You plan to leave tomorrow, I know. But when this man is able to travel, you will send transport up here for him, please, and get him out of here."

"But—" The duke glanced over to where his soldiers were standing, all in a huddle. He lowered his voice. "If he regains his abilities, that's a different story. But he's no earthly use to me like this, Julian. And think of the costs and difficulty of sending transport up here for him. You can send him back to me if he recovers, and that should be enough. I'll give you some pence for his expenses right now, if you wish. Or we can settle the bill later. There was that half groat for that messenger too, or was it a quarter.... A quarter groat, I think it was...."

"He's your liege man, Ulrich," Father Julian said. "Do you mean that your concern for him, all this time, has simply been for a...a utensil, a weapon? You'll take him back properly the moment he can travel. If you don't, I assure you that you will figure in many, many songs, just like the heroes of Charlemagne's rear guard—but the songs won't be to your credit. And regarding payment for my damaged dining hall...."

"We shouldn't discuss that here," said Duke Ulrich. He drew his cousin out of earshot down the corridor, still talking on and on in urgent whispers. Father Julian gazed levelly at him and listened unmoved. Atalf and Ziegmunt came back with the shutter. They helped the medicus lift Gauli onto it. Then, with some trepidation, they carried him away. Except for Brother Arcadius, the monks who'd lent their robes followed behind to get them back. "Get mine too," he called. "Arcadius!" they shouted in tribute. "Arcadius!"

They were already turning it into a joke, and that felt better. Brother Arcadius found he could muster a laugh. Being a hero was something like seeing a duke. It didn't live up to what you thought it might be. With Keti, he went into the wrecked dining hall and groped his way past overturned tables and broken benches to the place where he was quite sure he'd been sitting. There, despite the darkness, close by the shattered remains of Father Julian's rock crystal goblet, he managed to find his battered bowl and mug, his flattened spoon and his bent knife, and bore them off to the kitchen to see Keti into bed and bid him a good night. Brother Marcus was waiting there already. "You'll want a nice bowl of something good, the two of you," he said, and they didn't argue. "And you'll want to greet our other hero," he added. Eyes aglow, ears forward, tail aloft, a sleek shape materialized from the shadows.

"Pangur Ban!" Keti cried. "Pangur *Ban!*"

* * *

March turned into April, April into May, and Gauli lay motionless in the infirmary, barely breathing. He lay on straw, so that in the many times each day that he soiled his bedding, it could be easily changed. His face and upper body were shielded from the roughness of the straw by clean rags. He sucked unknowingly on other rags that had been moistened with water, or with fortifying tinctures and potions, or with broth. His flaccid arms and legs lost their muscled strength and became mere sticks, even though Salix flexed them many times a day. But sticks or no, when the flexing was over, they were hobbled again in obedience to Father Julian's stern command, despite—so Salix thought to himself—the pointlessness of it. But one fine May morning the patient opened his eyes and spoke.

Brother Salix looked round in surprise.

"So..." Gauli gingerly moved his hobbled arms and his hobbled legs. "So...I was captured, was I?" His voice was weak and almost could not be heard.

"Yes," said Salix. "You were captured."

"That's very good," murmured Gauli. "Because I think I was a very bad man."

"A very active man, certainly," said Brother Salix. He smiled to himself at the understatement.

"I don't want to be...an active man," murmured Gauli. "I like this room. It's nice."

"Yes, it's nice," said Brother Salix. "In a while, I'll help you sit up and give you some broth from a spoon. Do you know who you are?"

Gauli stared at the ceiling. "I'm...I'm..."

"Yes?"

"I'm a...I'm a pilgrim," Gauli said.

"Well, so you are," smiled Brother Salix. "And your name is...?"

"Placidus," murmured Gauli.

He closed his eyes and went back to sleep. When he woke up, he was still Placidus. The days went by and he grew stronger—and remained Placidus. Talk of Lombards, Scarpians, and Duke Ulrich left him politely puzzled. He had never heard of such things and wanted no part of them. He stared with no recognition, and indeed no interest, at the mask that Brother Ambroz had washed for him all those weeks ago. It gave him great pleasure to feel, again and again, the ridged scar that ran down his face from eye to chin—a token of his capture. And finally, the first week in June, there was nothing for it but to fit him out with pilgrim's gear and send him on his way.

There were many who doubted that he should be given his freedom, but they needn't have worried. He gave that nice white cat who'd become so friendly a final pat and went off down the trail, heading south, turning now and then to wave goodbye. And for years and years thereafter, travelers up and down the roads often spoke fondly of that lean, weather-beaten, scarred, gentle, odd-looking wanderer called Placidus.

* * *

Looking back at it all, Brother Atalf knew he would never forget it as long as he lived. The way he'd howled and screamed, that fellow, and broken up the dining hall! And then he'd gone off so gentle and nice and quiet. Well, if he ever came back and got upset again, the cat would take care of him. He should never have messed with the cat. Never should have riled him. It wasn't the library fellow who'd sent that stool to the target, so straight and true. The cat had been casting a spell, that's what it was....

* * *

In time, one of the carpentry monks got around to fixing the footstool. "It stays in the reception room, though, Arcadius," said Brother Silvanus. "Anybody tries to give it to the library, I'll say no. No telling what you might do with it."

"No telling," said Brother Arcadius. "No telling at all."

* * *

Keti burrowed deeper into his warm bed in the kitchen, thinking things over. Brother Arcadius had been brave! And that was the truth.

Yet Pangur Ban had been braver—wasn't that so? Right there in the bad man's hands, right there next to his face, he'd kept his courage up, and he'd won. Pangur Ban!

* * *

"A letter's come from Duke Ulrich," Brother Dietrich said. "He says he'll need time to make the arrangements, but he'll send for the Gaul, he hopes, in three or four months."

"Tell him the bird has flown," Father Julian said.

* * *

Curled up in a warm patch of sunlight on a library windowsill, Pangur Ban dreamed. He dreamed of invincible claws ripping through shocked flesh. He dreamed of streams of blood pouring down a ravaged cheek. He dreamed of that strange, whirling person, wild as a barn cat but nowhere near as dangerous, who'd been taught a lesson and taught it well....

Brother Arcadius, bent over his work nearby, looked up and smiled. "Dreaming of mice again, Pangur?" he asked.

"Rrrowrrr," said Pangur Ban.

THE WHEREABOUTS OF SAINT GEORGE

In which Spiritus Sanctus becomes sorely troubled,
and the distant past provides a remedy

1,000 BC — AD 900

In the sun-warmed glade, midway between the forest and the lake, on the broad shoulder of this sheltering mountain where Others have never yet come, he crouches to make the pattern for his people. Pattern of the moon, pattern of thriving and safety. Fingers of this hand, fingers of that hand, and finger, finger, finger besides, that is the number of the stones he's gathered, the number of the moon. He's chosen only the good stones that are pale and unmarred and as round as the moon in her fullness. With his keen-edged flint knife he's sharpened his drawing stick. With his stick he's traced on the ground the shape of the moon. Now, on the moon-shaped line he's drawn, he lays the moon-round stones down, one by one, and for each, as he does so, he speaks the words of the moon.

And this he will do many, many times over, day by day, for his people.... The People...so that they'll be safe from sickness and want and Others forever and ever....

...Proud Gaul of the White Horse Clan, at last you've found a mountainside so remote that Julius Caesar's hellions will never find it. Here you'll strike back, you and your warrior band. Or your children, or your children's children. Yes, Gauls will strike back. And here stands the Horse that Gauls have brought to this mountain—not the Gauls who went down to defeat, but the Gauls of the White Horse Clan, who will rise again. The fierceness and fineness of it, the flowing curves of mane, tail, eyes, lips, nostrils, neck, and haunches, the strength and goodness of the stone from which it's made—this is what it means to be a Gaul. This is the spirit, Romans, that will bring you down.

So on the broad shoulder of this sheltering mountain, the Gauls of the White Horse Clan will bide their time. Sustained by lake and forest, they'll lay their plans. They'll build their shelters. They'll forge their weapons. These devilish round stones that are everywhere underfoot, causing even the sure-footed to slip and fall—they too can be put to good use. Shot forth from slings, they'll smash through breastplates and helmets, through chest bones, through skulls, through brains! And that will be just the least of it, just the beginning! So tremble, Romans! The White Horse will prevail....

...A tough campaign, but it's over. Worst part of it was getting up here. The battle itself was nothing. As always with these Gauls, there was a lot of whooping and yelling, and then they fled. Fled, and got captured. The ones that didn't get killed. There'll be plenty of prime new flesh in the slave markets now.

Gaius Marius Ursus of Trajan's XXII Legion, called Primigenia, bows his head and thanks Mithras for the victory, that this nest of White Horse Gauls has been cleaned out. Eight or nine emperors back was when they'd first come here to stir up trouble for Rome whenever they could, but it had taken only two hours to send them flying, them and their White Horse too. Not that he, Gaius Marius Ursus, had laid eyes up here on any sort of horse. But "White Horse" was the name these Gauls went by, before they came face to face with the Primigenia. Woe to the vanquished, eh?

Ursus knows that it's always Mithras who makes the difference. Some of his comrades are putting their trust, these days, in those crosses they've hung around their necks. Well, they're wrong, but that doesn't matter. They're good fighters anyway, and worthy fellows. And one of them's a real artist with stone. Last year, before this campaign, he'd made stone figures of some of the other legionaries, and put their names on them, and the name of the legion too....

Ursus would like to have one made of himself, and set it up somewhere with a victory wreath behind it, and dedicate it to Mithras, and to the power and might of a Rome that would last forever....

...Brother Arcadius, assistant librarian of Spiritus Sanctus monastery, walked uphill past the vineyards. He was vaguely aware that it was a beautiful afternoon of peaceful, golden sunshine, and that the mountain view was a splendid thing to see, and that the keen air smelled deliciously of ripened grapes. All the same, he knew this path like the back of his hand, almost, and his mind was elsewhere. *Though I speak with the tongues of men and of angels and have not charity, I am become as sounding brass, or a tinkling cymbal....*

Brother Arcadius knew these words as well as he knew the path. Better than he knew the path, actually. He'd known them and loved them for most of his eighteen years. At age five, already, he'd been able to say them by heart. But tomorrow Brother Arcadius would be having his weekly lesson in Greek with Father Julian, head of the monastery. He'd already been proficient in Greek when he'd first arrived at Spiritus Sanctus, two years before. So the lessons were getting to be...you might say...advanced.

And though I have the gift of prophecy, and understand all mysteries, and all knowledge, and though I have all faith, so that I could move mountains, and I have not charity, I am nothing.... Tomorrow, the beautiful words of Saint Paul, which he'd known forever in Latin, would have to be recited to Father Julian in Greek. And then Father Julian would question him endlessly about them—grammar, syntax, meaning, everything...in Greek. And he would be expected to answer every probing question promptly and intelligently...in Greek.

It was a challenge that Brother Arcadius was eager to meet. He did indeed want to bring his Greek—and after that, his Hebrew—up to the good level that his Latin had long ago reached. So for the past week, on the daily walks he'd been ordered to take to keep up his health and his strength, he'd been murmuring his careful and hopeful translation of 1 Corinthians 13 over and over and over again, revising it, polishing it, replacing a carefully chosen word with one that seemed even better, wondering all the while how Saint Paul would have phrased things, for Saint Paul had written in Greek—Greek that was lost. *And now abideth faith, hope, charity, these three, but the greatest of these is—*

Ouch! A sudden slap of something against his chest, and a sharp and painful poke of something against his right shin, brought him back into the world. It was that fallen tree limb again, the one that lay alongside the path and sent its side branches annoyingly into the way— the one that had taken him by surprise last week, at this very spot. Or was it a new one? No, it was the same. There was the side branch that had somehow curled itself into the exact shape of the Greek letter theta. And there was the empty bird's nest, wedged upside down between two other branches.

Rubbing his shin, Brother Arcadius considered the fallen limb in mild surprise. It was unusual at Spiritus Sanctus to have things like fallen limbs just lie there for an entire week. Ordinarily, the monastery grounds were vigilantly and energetically cared for by the two hulking monks called Brother Atalf and Brother Ziegmunt, with help, if need be, from monks of similar though lesser build.

But Brother Atalf and Brother Ziegmunt—blood brothers to each other, they actually were—were usually well able to handle their work alone, and did so with gusto and zeal. Brother Marcus, the cook, often said that each of the brothers was as strong as twenty oxen. Then, after that, he frequently added something else, in a mumble, under his breath. Whatever he mumbled, it sounded like, "and almost as smart." Then again, he might be just mumbling, "and also, they're smart." Insults were strictly forbidden at Spiritus Sanctus, so maybe "and also, they're smart" was most likely what he was saying. On the other hand....

Brother Arcadius would never say so, not even in a mumble under his breath, and tried his best not to think so, but Brother Atalf and Brother Ziegmunt weren't people who gladdened his heart. He didn't hold it against them that they couldn't read or write and didn't want to. There were plenty of unlettered monks at Spiritus Sanctus, and plenty who had an aversion to letters as well. But Atalf and Ziegmunt, after two years, still looked at him as if he were some sort of weird insect, still seemed to feel that his work in the library was no work at all, and still continued to think that his name was "Arcaperus." These things got tiresome after a while.

Worse yet—oh, much worse yet!—was the fact that not many months before, in a horrible misjudgment that was his fault more than theirs, they'd taken a manuscript that was very important to him, important beyond all telling, and they'd....

They'd fed it to the goats, that's what they'd done!

To the goats!

But to dwell on such things was unmonklike behavior indeed. It ran counter to 1 Corinthians 13 in any language. Scholars weren't supposed to just study great thoughts and let it go at that. They were supposed to try to live by them. The best thing to do when certain baser notions came intruding was to lift one's mind to a higher plane at once, and not be a sounding brass or a tinkling cymbal.

So looking at things from a higher point of view, why weren't Brother Atalf and Brother Ziegmunt on the job with this limb? They'd been around for meals, hadn't they? So they couldn't be just gone. They weren't on the job because...because.... A buried memory came slowly back of Father Julian making an announcement last week at supper, an announcement that Brothers Atalf and Ziegmunt were going to...well, they were going to do something, but Saint Paul had gotten in the way of just what. Brother Silvanus, head of the library, would know.

Pretty much back in the world once more, Brother Arcadius resumed his walk, then stopped again and smiled in sudden good cheer. Up ahead there, from behind that clump of thistles beside the path, there'd been a sudden flash of white. The whiteness now materialized into the monastery's champion mouser, Pangur Ban, coming up to say hello and be petted. Two years before, Pangur had been a derelict nameless stray, a stowaway in a boat on the Irish Sea. Brother Arcadius, then barely sixteen, had been on that same boat, on his way from his native Dublin to Spiritus Sanctus, a long, hard journey away. He'd rescued the cat—just a half-grown kitten, really—and named him Pangur Ban, a good Irish name signifying whiteness, and brought him here to the monastery, and knew as surely as he knew his Latin that in all the world and through all time, there was no cat that could hold a candle to him.

"Hello there, Pangur Ban!" Brother Arcadius leaned down to give the cat of his heart a proper welcome. Wretched and scrawny no longer, Pangur was now sleek, broad-chested, weighty and muscular, a cat to reckon with, a cat who cleared the monastery kitchen of mice as efficiently as Brothers Atalf and Ziegmunt usually cleared away debris. There now, that was charitable thinking. Saint Paul and probably all other saints would approve.

Tail waving regally, Pangur brushed confidingly against his friend's sore shin with feather strokes, twice, then leaped ahead toward the monastery. Brother Arcadius followed, thinking hard. Yes, Brother Silvanus would know about Atalf and Ziegmunt, but wouldn't it be better not to have to ask him? Silvanus was a kindhearted man and a fine librarian, but also, maybe, a bit too prone to tease. A *lot* too prone to tease, in fact. He would have quite a bit to say about assistant librarians who couldn't remember their own names. So think, Arcadius! Brother Atalf and Brother Ziegmunt were going to....

They were going to....

They were going to do some exploring, that was it! How could he have forgotten something like that, even for a moment?

Words he'd heard through a haze of Saint Paul came back to him now. A stretch of the monastery's holdings had never been properly looked at, that was it. It was difficult terrain, and nobody had ever thought it worth bothering with. But Father Julian had decided that it was time to see what was there, and that the best people to take a first look would be Atalf and Ziegmunt. If anybody could force their way through an overgrown wilderness, it would be them. Well now, that was another charitable thought. Two in a row!

Pleased with himself for capturing the memory, and for thinking well of his fellows, Brother Arcadius went on to the library. Now that he had some command of the basic facts, he felt he could safely ask Brother Silvanus to tell him more. "Oh," said Silvanus, "I don't have much more to tell you. It's that stretch just north of the vineyards, and a bit west. Ten square miles or so, I'd say. Not all that large. Not completely unexplored, for that matter. Some charcoal burners go through there now and then, I believe, but as far as I know they've never said much about it. Even that busybody Marcus doesn't know much about it." The librarian's smile belied the criticism. He always saved his sharpest comments for people he really liked. He wasn't being uncharitable. He was just being himself.

"So...what do you think they'll find there?"

"Oh, lots and lots of those little twisted trees, mostly. The same ones you see taking hold just past the vineyards, and out in the scrublands. Big rocks and gullies, too. A couple of springs. And a lot of snakes. Ah, there's the bell for vespers. Let's go."

* * *

After vespers came supper. Over his bowl of gruel (mashed turnips seemed to be in it, tonight) Brother Arcadius took charitable notice of Brothers Atalf and Ziegmunt, a couple of tables away. The two hulking fellows looked pleased with themselves and the world, no mistake about it. They were beaming down at their gruel and around at their neighbors. Obviously, their new task agreed with them.

As heavy workers, they were entitled to more than one helping of everything—nobody begrudged them the extra food. So along with the quarrymen and latrine shovelers and various others, they were still spooning up gruel and munching bread when Father Julian rose and quietly asked for attention, which was given to him immediately, as a matter of course. Indeed, he'd hardly needed to ask. His mere standing was signal enough. All faces turned expectantly his way. His dark eyes scanned the room, and he nodded.

"Tonight," he said, "let us give thought to the life of Saint George." The monks settled themselves to listen. Father Julian often added interest to the evening meal—and encouraged interest in the library, it was to be hoped—by reading aloud at supper. He usually chose to read about great deeds of long ago—deeds of valorous faith sometimes, or sometimes just deeds of valor. He'd said more than once that every monk should know something of the vanished past—indeed, the shattered past, although he never called it that: the past that had turned the Roman Empire, for instance, inside out and upside down, and transformed it into now. Tonight, though, as he sometimes did, he was talking instead of reading.

"Saint George's life was sadly short and is quickly told," he said. "He lived some seven centuries ago, when emperors still ruled in Rome. He was born to a family of rank and wealth, it seems, who made their home not far from the famous city of Constantinople, which as you know is many hundreds of miles from here. The emperor at that time was named Diocletian. George served as one of the emperor's special guard, the Praetorian Guard, as it was known. That means that he must have been an outstanding soldier. But he was also a Christian, and the emperor had taken to persecuting Christians. When George bravely stood up for his faith and asked the emperor to stop the persecutions, his service as a fine guardsman made no difference. He was done away with on the spot."

There were murmurs of dismay around the room. Brother Homelius, one of the kitchen crew, raised his hand. "How did the emperor kill him?"

"He had him tortured and then beheaded, so it's said."

Brother Mishel stood up and was acknowledged. "Why did the emperor want to persecute Christians anyway?" he asked.

"Diocletian was a soldier himself. Perhaps he was afraid that too much talk of mercy and forgiveness would have a bad effect on the fighting spirit of the legions."

Brother Mishel sat down, satisfied with the explanation and with Diocletian too. It would be bad for legions to lose their fighting spirit. The emperor had just been thinking of the good of all. "Oh, I see," he said. Mutters of dissent came from the monks sitting near him.

Father Julian raised a calming hand. "It goes without saying that Diocletian had a huge responsibility to protect the empire, but he could have dealt with the matter much more reasonably. And perhaps he thought so, too. Not long afterwards, partly perhaps because of

George, the persecutions ceased. I would tell you more, but this is all that's come down to us in the histories—at least, in any history known to me. If there are further questions, I may not be able to answer them properly. But we can take a short while longer for any discussion."

At the start of all this, Brother Atalf and Brother Ziegmunt had stopped eating to pay full attention, all aglow. They'd looked expansively happy before, but the words "Saint George" had seemed to add to that happiness. Then, moment by moment, a change had come upon them. Their beaming smiles had been replaced by looks of perplexity. Now Brother Atalf set down his spoon and raised his hand. "Father?"

Father Julian's dark brows rose in inquiry. "Yes, Brother Atalf?"

The big monk got to his feet, swallowed several times, then said in his rumbling voice, "Father, he had a horse."

"I beg your pardon?"

"Saint George had a *horse*, Father. And he killed a dragon. You left out the horse and the dragon."

"I didn't know about them," said Father Julian equably. "How does it happen that you do?"

"From our church back home," said Brother Atalf. Brother Ziegmunt nodded in firm agreement. "On the back end of it. There's picture. It's Saint George and he's on a horse and he's killing a dragon."

"With a spear," put in Brother Ziegmunt.

"An allegory, perhaps...." began Father Julian.

"No, Father, a dragon!" said Brother Atalf. His deep voice trembled, just slightly. "The priest said so. Saint George killed the dragon. He rode a horse and he killed the dragon. He was the best saint." Brother Atalf sat down. In a low, low voice he added, "That's why I became a monk."

"And that's why I became a monk, too," said Brother Ziegmunt. "For Saint George, and for my brother Atalf."

"I see," said Father Julian. He looked affably about the hall, from face to face. "Let us all remember that when new information comes to us, it's best to think about it carefully. It may very well be that Saint George did ride a horse upon occasion, and did kill a dragon. Let us thank Brothers Atalf and Ziegmunt for bringing us these new ideas for our consideration.... Yes, Brother Atalf?"

Atalf had risen to his feet again. "Was he ever here, Father? Do you think he was ever here?"

"Up on this mountain, do you mean? Saint George?"

"Yes," rumbled Brother Atalf. "It's rough going for horses. But his horse could've done it. It's a good, strong horse. In the picture."

"Or Saint George could have left his horse behind and come up on foot," said Father Julian. "But riding or walking, as a guardsman he had to stay with the emperor, and I don't know that Diocletian was ever here. But there again, many of the old records have been lost. It could have happened, Brother Atalf. That's all I can say."

"If he got up here, would he put up a statue, Father? To show he was up here? You said they liked to do that in the old days." Brother Atalf sat down again, waiting for the answer with knotted forehead.

"A statue is possible," Father Julian said.

"I think he did come here," said Atalf again in that low, low voice. Frowning, he picked up his spoon and slowly finished his fourth serving of turnip gruel.

* * *

"Your king is dead, Arcadius," said Father Julian. The week's highly successful Greek lesson and very satisfactory Hebrew lesson had been followed by the usual disaster in chess. "You see, when I moved my castle here, you should have considered that—" There was a muted knock at the door. Brother Dietrich, Father Julian's secretary, peered in, perfect as always in manner and grooming alike. "I hate to disturb you, Father," he said, "but Brother Atalf and Brother Ziegmunt are out there in the courtyard. They've found something they want you to see. They are being very stubborn about it."

Father Julian set his castle back down on the chessboard. "Arcadius, let's go see." Pleased to be included, and pleased that the torments of chess were suddenly over, Brother Arcadius followed him.

They went through the refectory to the courtyard. Brother Atalf and Brother Ziegmunt were waiting there, muddy and sweaty and happy. There was an angry-looking red lump the size of a small turnip on Ziegmunt's brow, but still the two brothers were swinging their arms and shifting from foot to foot with delighted anticipation. Something bulky stood at their feet, covered up in a pile of old sacks that were muddy too. Whatever it was reached about to their knees. "He was here, Father!" cried Brother Atalf. "We found it! A statue of his horse! Saint George's horse!" Reaching down, he swept the sacks aside and revealed what stood within.

Yes, they'd found a horse, all right, no doubt about it: a grimy, moss-covered horse made of some kind of dingy whitish stone that wasn't marble. On second look, though, was it a horse, actually? That head seemed more like a lizard's, to be truthful. No, no...the hooves, the mane, the tail, the ears, the neck...it was a horse, a very peculiar, curvy, rampaging horse, with long lizard-like eyes the shape of willow leaves, and a lizard-like snout. It appeared to be very old, and also very heavy. But Atalf and Ziegmunt had carried it here in the arms of love.

Father Julian bent down for a closer look. "Where'd you find it?" he asked.

"We're making a path down there, Father," said Brother Atalf. "Like you told us to. A bigger one, because there's a path there already. It's, like, just a thread. Those charcoal burners made it, maybe. And somebody put a big pile of stones there, round ones, under the weeds. We stepped on 'em and we went sliding, didn't we, Brother?" said Atalf to Ziegmunt in glee. "And Father, my brother fell right over forward and knocked his head on something, there in the weeds, and it was Saint George's horse, and that's how we found it. My brother and me, we found Saint George's horse."

"Well," said Father Julian slowly, "Brother Salix will need to treat that head of yours, Ziegmunt, but the horse is a wonderful find, and I thank both of you for it. Still, we need to consider, don't we, that a great many people have ridden about on horses over the years. In any case, it puts us in mind of Saint George, does it not. At this time, it would not be reasonable to insist upon anything further."

Some of the light went out of the finders' faces. "Do you mean it's not Saint George's horse, Father?" asked Brother Atalf.

"I mean that it may or may not be Saint George's horse," said Father Julian. "But even if it isn't, it is a fine addition to our monastery, and we should place it...." Rather too swiftly, perhaps, he pointed to the darkest corner of the courtyard, where the refectory wall made a sort of zig-zag that was shadowed even at noon. "We should place it there, where people who wish to do so can seek it out, and yet it will not be in harm's way. Thank you again, very much, for bringing it here. It's good that you're here in time for the midday meal. You'll want to get ready for that."

"I guess so, Father." And Brother Atalf, now very much less radiant, picked up the horse as if it weighed nothing and carried it with trudging steps over to where he'd been told to put it.

"It will be Gaulish work, Arcadius," said Brother Silvanus in the library that afternoon. He'd listened with keen interest to his assistant's brief account of what had gone on. "You can be sure that it's as pagan as pagan can be. Not the sort of thing that a monastery should have in its courtyard. They would have made sacrifices to it. Blood sacrifices and so forth. Father Julian knows that perfectly well. We've both seen horse shapes like that before, in the form of brooches and belt buckles and so on. Fellow in Cologne collects things like that and knows about them."

"But could it be the work of a Gaul who cared about Saint George?" asked Brother Arcadius, charitably. "They weren't all pagans back then, were they?" The monastery had had quite a run-in with a Gaul not so long before, and that Gaul had turned out to be rather saint-like at heart.

"A Gaul who cared about Saint George would depict Saint George," said Brother Silvanus.

It was logic that could not be denied.

It was also the sort of logic that seeped, little by little, into the minds of Brother Atalf and Brother Ziegmunt. Already, in the courtyard, their first joy had started to dim. The horse had been placed in a dark corner, and that was the start. After that, Father Julian had made no mention of it, didn't even announce at supper that they'd found it. A horse, but no saint.... If he didn't mention it, they didn't want to either. For a few days they hurried back to the wildlands each morning at dawn, and put in many long hours of desperate searching, but nothing more came to light. Then they asked if, instead of exploring, they could just stay close to the monastery again for a while, and take care of whatever was there that might need attention.

They received the permission they asked for, but it soon became clear that their old duties were not a joy to them any more. Now they had time to attend to the grounds again, but their efforts were feeble and fumbling and painful to see. Chores they'd have done in a moment now took days. Small mishaps occurred that wouldn't have happened before. Their heads drooped, and their shoulders slumped, and at mealtimes, fourth helpings dwindled to two, and then barely one. Going into the third week, it could clearly be seen that the two brothers looked thinner, grayer, seedier. Their brows were painfully knotted, always, and they never smiled. A silent misery emanated from them and pervaded the entire monastery—a monastery that was starting to look rather seedy itself.

"They're *thinking*," Brother Marcus the cook confided to Brother Arcadius. "They really shouldn't." But he said this in tones of concern, and no words at all were muttered under his breath.

Everyone else also worried about the brothers, for their own sakes and for the monastery's as well. "No, it's not malingering," said Brother Salix the medicus to Father Julian, who had suggested no such thing. "Call it heartsickness or sickness of the spirit or what you will, it's a genuine malady, and it's dangerous. You see it in the army quite often. A soldier will be tried to the limit. He'll receive not a single wound. Then, suddenly, his heart or his spirit breaks from the things he's done and seen, and after that, it's just a matter of time before he simply wastes away. Or else he does some fatal, foolish thing that kills him on the spot."

"Atalf and Ziegmunt have never served in an army," said Father Julian, but he was listening carefully.

"True enough," said Brother Salix. "But something's bothering them that they can't explain. It appears to have something to do with the horse they found."

"It coincides with finding the horse, but it can't be the horse," Father Julian said. "I thanked them for finding it, and I let them put it in the courtyard. It has to be something else that's on their minds."

"Whatever it is, they can't tell me," the medicus said. "Either that, or they don't want to tell me. I'm at a loss. I will continue to try to cure them with herbs and infusions. And of course we'll all pray for them, that goes without saying. But if none of that works, one way or another we're going to lose them. They'll fall prey to fevers that would not have harmed them before. Or a fatal accident will happen that wouldn't have happened before. We have a job ahead of us, Father, if we're to bring them back to what they were."

"I'll talk to Atalf again," said Father Julian. "If he pulls out of whatever this is, his brother will too." He walked out to the path where the big man, with the morose and silent help of his brother, was slowly and wearily dragging away a mere section of the fallen limb that had obstructed the path for nearly a month now. "Brother Atalf!" he said. "Anyone can see that the days go by and you remain in distress."

"I don't, Father," said Brother Atalf in a husky whisper. "I don't do that."

"Then what is wrong? Can you tell me?"

"It's my eyes, Father," whispered Brother Atalf. He glanced over at Brother Ziegmunt. "And it's his eyes, too. Everything looks gray.

Trees, flowers, food, him.... Everything looks gray."

"And do I look gray too?" asked Father Julian.

Brother Atalf hung his head and did not answer.

"You believe...that you are not believed about Saint George's horse?"

Brother Atalf looked up, then quickly down again. "Nobody does believe it, Father. People laugh at it."

"I've heard no laughing. I will tolerate no laughing."

"You don't have to hear it, Father. You just feel it."

"Do you feel laughter coming from me, Brother Atalf?" asked Father Julian. "I would hope not, because—" He paused, and took a deep breath. "No laughter comes from me, Brother Atalf, because it would be very unreasonable to conclude, on the basis of what little evidence we have, that the horse you have found is not Saint George's horse."

"But that's the thing," said Brother Atalf. His head hung lower. "It's just a horse. It doesn't say 'George' on it, or anything. I thought it was his horse, and then I thought some more, and now...." Brother Atalf turned away, not in discourtesy, but in utter sadness. "Everything's just gray, that's all. Just gray."

He returned to his work in the same weary way as before. Monks didn't out-and-out gossip about each other, and Father Julian offered no explanations, but word began going round that it all had something to do with that funny-looking horse, the one that was now standing there in that dark corner. The brothers had found it, or something. It hadn't been praised enough, or something. So people, some of them, started praising it. A word here, a word there—monks didn't make speeches. But the words did no good. And Brother Marcus said that he'd overheard Father Julian offering to move the horse into the sunlight, but if that offer indeed had been made, it did no good either. "They're thinking, that's all I can say," Brother Marcus kept saying. "Thinking hard, but I can't guess what they're thinking about."

It was sad, all right, thought Brother Arcadius. And it would be very uncharitable and unmonklike to think, even for a moment, that the brothers were being paid back for feeding that book to the goats. So he didn't. Instead, he felt drawn to go see the place where the horse had been found. Not that he thought he'd find anything to help out in the matter. No, he just felt that he ought to go there and look around. Impelled by that urge, when it was time for his daily walk he put on his thick winter stockings, because he knew how scratchy and stabby things could get in the wild. Then he set out.

Before he had gone far, Pangur Ban sprang out from a tall stand of tufted grasses and came along with him. Heading downhill and north past the last vineyard, they went on until the wildlands began, unmistakably the wildlands, a jumble of rocks and free-growing vegetation and stunted trees like twisted willows, just as Brother Silvanus had supposed there'd be. Up ahead, hewn branches and withered chopped-off grasses and weed stalks marked where Brother Atalf and Brother Ziegmunt had begun clearing the way. Pangur, all curiosity, leaped lightly toward the various heaps of debris. Brother Arcadius followed more slowly.

To his left the ground was very rocky and still fairly open, but the willow trees grew very thickly on his right. Barely taller than he was, they covered much of the slope he and Pangur had just descended. Their leaves, narrow and pointed, fluttered in the slightest breeze. Their twisted branches formed barriers that not even Atalf or Ziegmunt, in their full strength and the best of spirits, could just walk through. Past those barriers, up on the rise, back where he'd just come from stood Spiritus Sanctus. No one trying to see it from here would catch even a glimpse of it. There was the rising wall of fluttering leaves and twisted branches, and there was the sky. Except for those two things, in that direction there was nothing else.

The way forward was quite a different story. There was the long stretch of ground that Atalf and Ziegmunt had cleared. Alongside that, reaching as far as Brother Arcadius could see in two directions, straight ahead to the north and downhill, but also off to the east, a rampart of fissured rock reached up to a height of perhaps fifteen feet. It marked the beginning of a widespread area of higher ground. Craning to see what might be up there on those heights, Brother Arcadius could only make out that more willows were growing there. Willows, and some sort of creeping shrub that hung long gray-green tendrils down the rock face.

Brother Arcadius paused to lay out his plan. Straight ahead, where Atalf and Ziegmunt had been working, the ground was muddy indeed. The brothers' huge sunken footprints were everywhere, half filled with brackish-looking water that reflected the sky. The weed patch where those round stones lay hidden was visible too, and that place that looked so, well, squashed, must be where Ziegmunt had fallen and hit his head on the horse. But the way along the east-running part of the rock wall looked dusty instead of muddy, and there were no footprints there that he could see. Maybe that was the more promising way to go.

Pangur Ban decided the matter by coming to a halt where the mud began, raising a paw in distaste, and then darting eastward. There was enough room between the rock and the willows for a person to follow, just barely, and Brother Arcadius did so. He didn't much want to get muddy either, and why look around where the brothers had already searched and found the horse, but nothing else? Maybe this other way would lead to something, well, different.

Pressed between the rampart of rock and the willows, he followed the retreating form of Pangur Ban. There were thorns in those shrubby tendrils that veiled the rock, and willow branches caught at his robe and his hood. But there was a path underfoot, he realized, a path like a thread for sure, barely the width of his foot, but still a path. Worn down that way, it couldn't be anything else. So people had come this way, but they hadn't been Atalf and Ziegmunt, that much he could tell. Maybe it was those charcoal burners. Or the Gauls who'd made the horse. Or Diocletian's guards...

Guards like Saint George, maybe.

Because who knew?

The willows pressed closer. Brother Arcadius was sometimes hard put to it to keep away from those tendrils with their thorns. He smelled the dry sweet smell of sun-warmed grasses and leaves. He heard the chirring of insects, and the occasional note of a bird, and then the faint music of water trickling down the face of the rock. Pangur Ban, up ahead, had leaped lightly over the little pool it made, and now Brother Arcadius, following him, stepped over it, glad that there was just this bit of wet going and not any more.

Once past the wet stretch he decided to step off the path as much as the willows would let him, just for the fun of it. If he left the path in this remote place, then maybe, just maybe, he, Tammis Scholar of Dublin, assistant librarian of Spiritus Sanctus, would be standing where no other person had stood before. Or not. Most certainly not. There was a curious thing on the ground here, among the willows. He forced their branches aside for a better look. Somebody'd been in here before him, right enough, and made a pattern of stones down there on the ground, the same round kind of stones that had led to Brother Ziegmunt's finding the horse. Six of the stones were scattered all about, but the seven that remained in place formed a perfect half circle, coated with mud and lichens though they were. Cleaned up they'd be white, he could tell, and the whole pattern, restored, would be a white circle. Who could say what it was all about, and who had made it? The charcoal burners maybe had made it. All of a sudden he felt like just going on.

He wormed his way back to the path. It could take a good while to find a spot where maybe no other person had walked before. He supposed he ought to head back to the monastery, get out of his thick winter stockings, and get on with everyday life. The stone pattern had given him sort of a solemn feeling, he couldn't say why. Whoever'd made it, he certainly wished them well. He leaned against a narrow stretch of bare wall where no thorny creepers hung down. He looked idly around for Pangur Ban, but didn't see him. That was nothing to worry about. It was likely that Pangur knew these wildlands quite well. He prowled around by himself all over the place every day, Pangur did. Stayed away from the farm, because that's where the tough barn cats reigned. But otherwise—

"Meow!"

Brother Arcadius, startled, looked about him. Pangur's cry had seemed to come from right behind him, but right behind him was the rock. There was a crack in the rock, but no cat could have gotten through it. No snake, even, could have gotten through it. Brother Arcadius tried to peer into it anyway, to see if Pangur, somehow, had gotten in there. Maybe he'd gotten up to that higher ground and fallen into some kind of a pit and couldn't get out.

"Meow!"

The cry came again from the rock, but no longer from right where he stood. If Pangur had fallen into a pit, it was quite a long one.

"Pangur, I'm here!" cried Brother Arcadius. He went sideways along the path as fast as he could, facing the rock, searching it for crevices wide enough to admit a cat, standing on tiptoe now and then to see if Pangur might be up on that higher ground.

"Meow!" This time the cry was even farther down the path, but low to the ground. "Pangur Ban!" Brother Arcadius called to him. "Pangur Ban!" His voice echoed back at him. He reached the place from where the last cry had come. The rock there was thickly overgrown with those hanging creepers. Unmindful of thorns, he started to brush them aside. His hands plunged into a chill hollowness. He swept aside the creepers with hurried strokes, and saw what lay behind them, and his jaw dropped. He'd found a *cave*.

Or rather, Pangur Ban had found it. Brother Arcadius, as his eyes adjusted to the darkness, saw Pangur's ghostly-looking form moving this way and that about the interior, exploring it. Being careful to watch out for sudden drop-offs, Brother Arcadius followed Pangur inside. It was a true cave, all right. From where he stood it ran back for a good eighteen feet before it disappeared into the general darkness, and there was no telling how much more of it was out of sight. Maybe it reached back as far as where he'd first heard Pangur's cry, or maybe by then it was not a true cave, but a tunnel.

Well, that was for other people to find out. He had no wish to grope into the chilly dark. The view that was closer at hand held more than just darkness. Over there at the very edge of the enclosing shadows, the rock above was broken through to the world outside, admitting a thin shaft of daylight—and also water, that dripped slowly, slowly, down onto....

With a gasp of utter astonishment, Brother Arcadius saw that Pangur Ban had discovered more than a cave.

* * *

"Thank you, Arcadius, for coming straight to me and not spreading this all about," said Father Julian. The thanks were brisk and brief, but they warmed the heart. "We'll go down now, with lamps, on the pretext of admiring the path that Brothers Atalf and Ziegmunt have begun," he said. "Collect Brother Silvanus for me, will you, and you can show us the way."

It was a fine feeling and no two ways about it, leading his superiors to a discovery that he himself—no, *his* cat Pangur—had made. The monastery's cat, he should say, but even so! He fought an unequal battle with the demon of pride, then told himself he'd resume the struggle later. Neither of his elders saw any need to put on thicker stockings for the expedition. Arcadius, after all, had made the trip with no trouble. So the three of them, headed by a cavorting Pangur, strolled toward their destination as if they were merely taking the air. Lamps and tinder and flint were concealed in their wide sleeves.

Once past the farthest vineyard, they went down to the wildlands and took the eastern path, and sidled along single file between the wall of rock and the willows. Brother Arcadius didn't point out the pattern of stones. It didn't seem like anything that ought to be stared at, that pattern, not even by Father Julian or Brother Silvanus. Instead, he took them directly to the cave, and they lit their lamps, and they gathered around the form that stood under the dripping water.

"It's a legionary's dedicatory statue," murmured Brother Silvanus. Father Julian nodded. "It's dedicated...I believe...to Mithras." The librarian's questing fingers gently explored the letters that were carved into the stone, and gently explored the figure itself. It was a full four feet high, twice as high as the horse, not counting the horse's head and neck, and was clearly made from a different kind of stone. "It's too bad that it's stood under this dripping water all these years," Brother Silvanus went on. "Most of the letters are filled in with deposits from dissolved stone, but I can make out....

"I can make out the M, I, T, H of 'Mithras.' We're not dealing here with any Christian at all, let alone a saint. Also, here is a nice bold G, but it goes along with a very dim A and I: the first three letters of 'Gaius,' I would say. The fellow's name was Gaius, not George. And he served with the XXII legion called...P, R, I, M, and that's all I can make out of that. Sunlight, maybe, will show us more. Oh, and here it clearly says 'AD TRAIA,' so it's dedicated to the Emperor Trajan as well as to Mithras. So, Father, this is beyond all doubt the figure of a legionary— see the sword—and it was made about two hundred years before Saint George was ever born."

"I think it can serve a good purpose anyway," said Father Julian. "But what's this?" He moved his lamp so that it cast light on something lying on the ground. It was a length of stone in the form of a long, very shallow S, with a spiky design of laurel leaves incised upon it. Its counterpart lay in pieces nearby. Whatever these were, they appeared to have fallen from a brick wall that stood between this part of the cave and the further darkness behind. "This would have been a triumphal wreath behind the figure, I would think," said Father Julian. "It could serve a good purpose too."

Brother Silvanus glanced at him keenly. "Any port in a storm, eh, Father?" he asked.

Father Julian made no reply. Instead, he did something completely unprecedented: he reached down and gave a quick pat to the head of Pangur Ban.

* * *

"So is it Saint George, Father?" asked Brother Atalf reverently. The big fellow was bursting again with joy and pride, and so was his brother Ziegmunt. They knew that Brother Arcaperus was mixed up in their happiness somehow, but he never would have been down there if they hadn't cleared a path—and besides, the cat would have been leading the way. Apprised of the great discovery by Father Julian, they'd hurried down to the cave to fetch it back. Now the stone soldier that had to be Saint George gazed resolutely forward, sword held point up. At his feet lay the long stone S with its spiky design.

"The horse alone is one piece of evidence," said Father Julian carefully. "Now we have the warrior, and we also have—" He pointed decisively at the stone S, and drew a long breath. "We also have what may well be part of a dragon."

"The tail, Father!" chortled Brother Atalf. "After Saint George killed the dragon, he cut off the tail!" He pointed at the bold letter G that began the name Gaius. "And this sign here is the sign of George, is that what you said, Father?" He clearly wanted those words to be said again.

"'G' is the first letter of 'George,' certainly."

Brother Atalf sighed with satisfaction, but cautiously. His forefinger scanned the XXII, the AD TRAIA, the MITHRA, and the PRIM, and the mostly unreadable array of letters that nine centuries of dripping dissolved rock dust had filled in. "That there's a number, but these other marks, what about them?"

Father Julian's whole posture was one of firm resolution. "Over the years, others must have found the cave. You know how it is. People carve their initials and their comments where they don't belong. These marks have nothing to do with Saint George."

Brother Ziegmunt nodded wisely. "There's initials carved on our church, too, back home. Count Orko's men carved 'em. They were drunk."

"Those things happen," said Father Julian. "Now, it's a fact that statues of this sort were often painted, back in Saint George's time. I would like to see this statue get a nice coat of whitewash, obscuring the letters and numerals that don't belong. After that, it ought to be painted with a tannish tone for the face and hands; dark blue, I would say, for the garments; dark brown for the hair, a fine bright red for the 'G'...."

"And the sword should be silver, Father," Brother Atalf urged. "Swords are silver." Silver paint was very dear, but Father Julian nodded in quick agreement. "And the dragon's tail! It ought to be green!" Atalf went on. He pointed to the curving section of stone wreath. "And the horse has got to be white, like in the picture." His brow knotted with worry again. "And they ought to go there by the gate, shouldn't they, Father? So everybody can see them, there by the gate?"

Father Julian looked thoughtfully up at the sky and down. "As for the site, we should consider the wishes of the saint," he said. "First and foremost, he went to court—the emperor's court—to protest against the persecutions. And it was from that court that orders came to kill him so cruelly. For that reason alone, he should not stand here in a *court*yard. Secondly, the name George signifies 'farmer,' as you may know. It denotes an affinity with the land. I would like to see this statue set up, along with the horse and the, ah, dragon's tail, on the knoll that overlooks our farmlands, our pastures, and the lake, from which we draw the abundance that keeps us alive. I would like to see Saint George as a guardian figure there. That would accord far more with him than any courtyard. And I would like Brother Mishel to construct a fine grotto there, as a protection from the elements, and there we will have a location worthy of Saint George."

Brother Atalf stepped back to think it over, and Brother Ziegmunt stepped back too. Then, like the high sun of summer, their smiles reappeared. "That would be good, wouldn't it, Ziegmunt?" said Atalf. "Yes, that would be good, Atalf," said Ziegmunt.

"And now," said Father Julian, "let us go in and make ourselves ready for our evening prayers."

Brother Atalf and Brother Ziegmunt ate, that night, with their old hearty appetites, and every monk in the refectory was glad to see it. The big fellows were at their fifth helping when Father Julian rose and cleared his throat to speak. The hall fell silent. "As many of you have noticed by now," he said, "new and important findings have come our way. First, Brother Atalf and Brother Ziegmunt discovered a stone horse in the wildlands, and postulated that this might be an image of Saint George's horse."

The two brothers nodded gravely. The long, important-sounding word was what they had done. "Second, because they labored mightily to begin a path into a region of our grounds where none of us ever walked before, a cave was discovered today." His eyes flicked toward Brother Arcadius, then flicked away. Brother Arcadius was more than happy to remain unacknowledged in this matter. Best to have no weird insect librarians intruding on the brothers' glory. It was good to see joy in Atalf's and Ziegmunt's faces, it truly was. Saint Paul had it right.

Charity was the greatest thing, for sure.

"Within that cave," Father Julian went on, "was found a statue of a soldier, a Roman soldier, bearing a sword. On that soldier is inscribed the letter 'G,' the first letter of the name 'George.' Beside the statue was found a piece of stonework that strongly resembles part of a dragon's tail. We are fortunate to have three pieces of evidence, instead of merely one, to indicate that once, many years ago, this mountain upon which our monastery stands was visited by true greatness."

His dark eyes swept the hall from face to face to face. Without exception, every face was bright with relief, every face was resolutely happy. Everyone, Brother Arcadius too, gazed with gladness upon the revived and delighted Brother Atalf and Brother Ziegmunt. And upon them all, and the dining hall, and the monastery, and upon the broad mountain where so many others over the years had hoped their hopes and dreamed their dreams and planned their plans, the golden light of charity descended.

* * *

"They just wanted more evidence, then," said Brother Marcus. "I said all along they were thinking, but that really *is* thinking. Goes to show you just never know."

* * *

"Well, it was the cat that found it," said Brother Atalf. "The cat always knows. And then it lets Arcaperus know. But sometimes it doesn't. How much Arcaperus knows is up to the cat."

* * *

"I don't feel right about the deception," said Father Julian. "I've led two simple minds down an absolute path of unreason. That's wrong."

"Not in terms of what's best for the monastery," said Brother Salix. "And you pulled them out of their misery." He added a pinch of something to a steaming cup of herbs and spring water. "Here, drink this."

* * *

"So you've found a cave now, Pangur Ban," said Brother Arcadius. "You're an explorer, that's what you are. And you've found a Roman soldier, and a broken wreath or whatever it was, and you've put the whole monastery to rights, that's what you've done." He petted the lithe form that was purring in his arms. "But I wonder who he really was, that Roman soldier? And what he was doing up here? And who made the horse? And I wonder who made that pattern there in the willows? If it wasn't the charcoal burners, then who would it be? The world's a big mystery, isn't it, Pangur Ban? Or maybe you have all the answers, but just won't tell me? Is that how it is?"

Pangur's purring grew louder and louder, as if in agreement. Brother Arcadius smiled at the notion of Pangur explaining the world in his own kind of language. "Cattish" might be the name of it, thought Brother Arcadius. Well, Latin, Greek, Hebrew, and Irish he knew, but Cattish, he feared, was beyond him. He set the cat down. "Time for you to go mousing, Pangur," he said.

"Mrrrwr," said Pangur Ban.

THE MISSING MAGICAL INGREDIENT

In which truth and justice find a staunch defender,
and Brother Sifari receives a great shock

AD 900

Keti, the kitchen boy of Spiritus Sanctus monastery, had never known the day or year of his birth, but was thought to be six years old or thereabouts. He had spent much of his young life in the clutches of two villainous step-parents, Oghrin and Ulka by name, never speaking to them and never appearing to hear them, because he feared and hated them so much. They'd assumed he was deaf and dumb, a burden on them, and hated him back. Finally he'd overheard them planning to kill him, but he'd found refuge at the monastery instead. Now he'd been safe and sound at Spiritus Sanctus for over a year, with no need at all to maintain his old frozen and terrified silence. Even so, he still found it hard to speak.

Sometimes, in fact, it was almost impossible. Kitchen talk, as a rule, didn't pose any problems. Feeding well over a hundred monks three meals a day didn't leave much time for long-winded conversations. Everything had to be done on time, to the moment, and questions were urgent and simple and easy to answer. "Keti, did you pick the basil yet? Where'd you set the sour milk? Give that bowl a stir for me, will you? Quick!" With a yes, a no, a nod of the head, a pointing finger, or at most a few words, he could give his response and not think twice about it. His lessons in reading and writing proper Latin with his friend Brother Arcadius didn't pose any problems either. Although he didn't find Latin quite as thrilling as his teacher did, Keti truly loved pleasing him, and did so by learning his lessons and learning them well. But in the kitchen or in his lessons, if he had to explain what he thought about something...if anybody wanted him to go on and on about something, or start talking in terms of *maybe*, or *perhaps*, or *because*, or *I'd rather*, or any other such complicated and tricky thing where you really couldn't tell if you were right or wrong....

Something in him froze up, once again, and he felt numb all over, and his ears rang, and his jaws locked, and he just couldn't do it—with one exception. It happened every night, that exception, after the day's work was done and it was time for bed. Keti slept on top of an enormous cupboard, high, deep, and wide. The capacious old thing—it had doors at the lower level, and open shelves above—had been part of the kitchen ever since the beginning, or so it was said. Its age matched the number of monks in the monastery!

It was grand to be up there, a good eight feet above the kitchen floor. High up though it was, it was safe in every direction. For one thing, the cupboard stood flush against the stone wall of the kitchen, so nothing could fall off that way except maybe crumbs. And because the huge old thing was so battered and gouged and even scorched down one side already, from mishaps over its years of hard use, the monastery had given permission to damage it still further, for Keti's sake. A carpenter monk had firmly pegged in and braced a nice strong wall around the other three sides—not around the whole cupboard, of course, but just around the top, where Keti slept. This wall was low enough for him to peer over, but high enough to prevent him from rolling off. Then a springy ladder had been fashioned from saplings and lashed into place, so that he could climb up and down.

It was like being a king in a castle or the captain of a ship, thought Keti. At the foot of his mattress there was room for him to store things —his few spare clothes, and a leather bottle he could fill with water to sip at in the night when he felt thirsty, and a small roll or hunk of cheese to eat then too, a bit at a time, when he felt hungry, and a wooden saint that Brother Zossimus, the monastery woodcarver, had made for him. Sometimes in the night he pretended that the saint was a soldier, and marched it up and down over his knees, and gave it quiet commands. But always, every night, sooner or later, there came a tremendous rushing and rustling and squeaking and general commotion from the floor below: the great mouser Pangur Ban was hard at work, keeping the kitchen free of marauding mice.

After Pangur had slaughtered or scared away the first wave of marauders, there was always a lull while the next wave gathered its wits and its courage to try again. During that lull, Keti could count on a visit. From the floor to a cool ledge of the nearby oven to Keti's domain, Pangur always came leaping up in two mighty bounds. He'd settle warmly on Keti's chest for a moment. He'd walk daringly up and down the narrow ledge of the little wall for a moment. He'd brush himself against Keti from head to foot for a moment. He'd purr. He'd peer at Keti with his gleaming eyes. He'd knead Keti's straw-sack mattress with his big forepaws. Then he'd settle down again close by and listen. And in the night, with Pangur Ban listening, Keti could talk.

The talk, in fact, poured freely out of him. During the day his mind, moment by moment, grew brimful of ideas. Pangur Ban might send mice flying, but with ideas he did the opposite, so Keti felt. With gleaming eyes, pricked ears, quivering whiskers, and soft comments, he drew ideas forth.

"Do you know what, Pangur?" Here was a thing that had stayed in Keti's mind all day, nagging at him now and then. "Do you know what?"

Pangur Ban didn't know what. His "mrrrowr" was a question. He gazed at Keti with alert and expectant eyes.

"Brother Arcadius was in the kitchen this morning when you weren't there. He didn't stay very long, but everybody started talking about—guess what?"

"Mrrwr?"

"The shape of the world!" said Keti. It had been so different and so interesting. From his corner where he'd been scrubbing out pots, he'd listened with all his might. "And Brother Homelius said he didn't know what shape it was and he didn't care. And Brother Sandro made a joke, and said it's like a big pricker bush, and everyone laughed. And Brother Marcus said—" Keti paused and thought about it again. That had been the really interesting part. "Brother Marcus said that long ago, a wise man saw the shadow of the earth! On the moon! And the shadow was round! So Brother Marcus thinks the earth has to be round. But Pangur, how would the wise man know it was earth's shadow? Couldn't it be some other shadow? Or maybe it wasn't a shadow, it was something else?"

He'd wanted to ask those questions when his elders were talking, but the words wouldn't come. So he'd just kept on scrubbing his pots and listening.

"And Pangur," Keti went on, "Brother Arcadius said...." It made Keti feel good to think of his kind, funny teacher. Brother Arcadius was eighteen, the youngest monk in the monastery by a good ten years.

But all the same he was twelve years older than Keti, just about. So you couldn't say that Brother Arcadius was really all that young. But he was a great scholar in Latin, Greek, and Hebrew, so Brother Marcus the head cook said. And sometimes he would recite some poem or other, and stand up and pace the floor while he said the words, and his eyes would glow like Pangur Ban's, and he would almost seem to tremble, he loved the words so much that he was saying. But in the kitchen this morning....

First, he'd very much wanted to know where Brother Marcus had heard about the shadow, and which wise man said it, and Brother Marcus said he couldn't remember. So Brother Arcadius felt bad about that, a little. But then he said that he didn't know about shadows, and that guessing the shape of the world was outside of his realm, but whatever shape it was, it had to be flat. Flat, with a wall around it. Because otherwise people would keep falling off.

"Mrrow."

"So that's one thing he said, Pangur Ban." Keti paused reflectively and murmured the words "Pangur Ban" again. To him they were poetry. They were the first words he'd said—the first words he'd been able to say—when he escaped from his oppressors and broke his long silence. They were Irish words, because Pangur most likely was Irish, and an Irish person had named him—Brother Arcadius himself, who'd started out life in a place called Dublin, far over the seas. If the name "Pangur Ban" signified whiteness, as Brother Arcadius said it did, then it was a very good name for Pangur Ban, who would have been just as perfect in any other color, but happened to be white. "And he said it didn't feel flat, but it had to be flat so it could have a wall around it, because if it didn't, and people got around to the other side, they'd either fall off or they'd be hanging on upside down like ants on a branch. And Brother Marcus said he'd heard about people like that."

"Mrrow!" Pangur Ban rolled over on his back and waved his paws in the air.

Keti rolled over on his back, too, and waved his hands and feet in the air, thinking. "It's outside of my realm," is what his teacher had said. And Keti had figured out that Brother Arcadius had meant to say, "I don't know anything about it." And neither did Keti know anything about it. But with just Pangur listening, it didn't matter. "The sun and the moon and the stars are round," he told Pangur, "so I think the earth is round too. I think they'd all match. But are they round like balls, or just round like dishes? I don't think it's like dishes, because...."

And on he went, thinking and talking, until the lull below was broken by new squeaks and scrabblings, and it was time for Pangur to resume his mousing. If his elders had heard Keti's flow of ideas, they would have been truly amazed. But now the time for talking was over again. Pangur leaped down to the floor and got back to work. Keti went to sleep. Morning came, and the kitchen boy was silent again.

At his lesson that afternoon, at the long table in the library, Keti got everything right, as almost always, and received his customary reward of bits of bread dipped in honey. But Brother Arcadius seemed unusually grave. "Keti," he said, "I know you were listening to our talk about the earth being round or flat and all of that, yesterday. And I could tell you had ideas of your own. So what I'd like you to do for me today is to take a moment to put your thoughts together, and then tell me what they are. Could you take a stab at it, please?"

Keti froze. He could feel his legs and arms going numb. He could hear the ringing start in his ears. His jaws had locked tight, and it was impossible to speak. Impossible, almost, to move.

Brother Arcadius raised his eyebrows high, leaned forward, and smiled his most encouraging smile. "Would it help if Brother Silvanus stepped out for a while?" The head librarian was intently looking through books in one of the cabinets. It was doubtful that he'd heard a word of what had been said.

Keti managed to shake his head. No, it wouldn't help.

"Well," sighed Brother Arcadius, "I know you'd tell me your thoughts a word at a time, if I asked the right questions. But that's not how people converse as a general rule. It's fun to converse now and then, and I'd like you to try it. You wouldn't expect to be good at it, right at the start. It's a thing with a knack to it, like swimming."

Keti had no idea how to swim. He stared at his teacher in silence.

"Or like...or like scrubbing a pot good and clean," Brother Arcadius continued. "Which is something I happen to know you do very well."

Keti's ears rang louder. He stopped looking at his teacher and stared at the table instead.

"Or Pangur Ban could listen in too, and meow now and then," said Brother Arcadius, very gently. "Or to begin with, you could talk to Pangur and not to me."

Keti stopped staring at the table and stared at the floor. At night on his cupboard was when he talked to Pangur. And beneath the ringing of his ears the warning thought came that conversing was a perilous thing, that conversing was nothing you could actually ever get right. He shrank farther down in his chair.

"Well, Keti," said Brother Arcadius with another sigh, "can you tell me the indicative perfect, third person singular, of the verb *scire*? In the active voice?"

Oh, that was much too easy. That was beginner's work. "Scivit!" said Keti, and straightened up in his chair.

After that, in his dreams sometimes, Keti saw himself conversing. He looked very small, as if he might be three. He was half starved, and covered with welts and bruises. He was high in the air, balanced barefoot on a rope stretched over a fearful pit with monsters in it, picking his way along step by terrified step. His wicked stepfather Oghrin held one end of the rope, his wicked stepmother Ulka held the other. They signaled each other wickedly with their eyes. One more step and they were going to shake him off.

He woke up from those dreams with his head buried deep in his straw sack, and his quilt wadded into a ball. No, not even for Brother Arcadius was he ever going to converse.

One night, in one of those dreams, one of the monsters in the pit turned out to be Father Julian, head of the monastery. The part of Keti's mind that got right answers knew that this made no sense. It was Father Julian who had welcomed him into Spiritus Sanctus, Father Julian who'd explained that Oghrin and Ulka had been sent away and would never be allowed to come back. So Father Julian was on his side, wasn't he. So said the part of his mind that got right answers. But the other part of his mind said something else.

He's on your side for now, is what it said. He has the say over everybody here, is what it said. He's some kind of a duke, or his uncle is a duke, or something. If he gets mad at you, he can put you out. Or send you back to Oghrin and Ulka again. And he sits by himself up on that big box at mealtimes, and he used to have a cup made out of a big hunk of crystal, but it got broken, so he has a silver cup now, and his plate is made out of silver, and so are his knife and spoon. And everybody does what he says as soon as he says it. And his smile is nice when he smiles, but mostly he doesn't. And his eyes are very dark, and they don't always match with the words he's saying. And if he's starting to hate you, how would you know? How would you ever know?

Don't give him a chance to hate you, the scared mind said. *Don't give anybody a chance to hate you*, it said.

Those dreams and thoughts were terrible. The everyday life of tasks and lessons—the ones you could get right with a bit of thought and effort—helped block them out.

Fortunately, the threat of conversing soon passed. Brother Arcadius gave up on it, and lessons went back to their old comfortable form, with plenty of things to get exactly right, beyond all doubt. And most of the time the work in the kitchen went on at a happily breathless pace, and Keti loved it, and loved the four monks he worked with. Brother Marcus, Brother Sandro, Brother Homelius, Brother Alvas, he loved them almost as much as he did his teacher.

Each of these men had his specialty. Brother Alvas carried things up and down from the cellars, and tended the fires, and plucked or skinned and dismembered fowl and game. Brother Homelius mixed and kneaded dough, and scrubbed out the great kettles that were too heavy for Keti to deal with, and brought in big pails of water from the spring beyond the kitchen garden. Brother Sandro, a dexterous man, was first chopper, getting things ready for the final judicious chopping, slicing, dicing, or mincing of Brother Marcus.

Brother Marcus was the head cook. Along with working hard on his own special tasks, and helping out with everyone else's, he directed what all of the others had to do. He allowed Brother Salix the medicus to give him healthful suggestions as to what should go into the gruel that the monks always had for supper and breakfast, and he went along with Salix's insistence that there had to be greens and fruit of some kind at every meal, whether fresh or dried.

Otherwise, his word was law and everyone's command. He ran his kitchen with an iron hand, and nobody minded. For one thing, he was good-natured most of the time. For another, the midday meals he served were always magnificent, even in Lent—and midday meals were the ones that counted. The hard-working monks of Spiritus Sanctus looked forward to them, you might say, prayerfully.

From Monday through Saturday, the main midday dish was ordinary stew. Brother Marcus's ordinary stew was not ordinary. It was the equal of any stew served anywhere, even to popes and kings. So said all the high-placed visitors—Father Julian's relatives, mainly—who'd happened to dine with mighty people like that. But on Fridays Marcus also served his marvelous fish paste, and on Sundays he served his even more marvelous herbed game stew. Then you might think you were truly dining in Heaven. The fish paste recipe was complicated, and he worked on it all week long. The herbed game stew was even harder to prepare. Watching the master bring it to its weekly perfection was like watching a sorcerer casting magic spells.

Each ingredient in it, and there were many, had to be prepared ahead of time in its own particular way—browned in lard, or coarsely chopped, or finely chopped, or ripped instead of chopped, or minced, or marinated, or dipped in beaten egg and rolled in meal, just so and not too much, or shredded, or seared, or pounded, or rolled up and tied around a packet of herbs, or crushed, or pressed through a horse-hair sieve, or poached, or steamed for three fast counts, or ten slow ones, or whatever else Brother Marcus thought it was best to do. Since you couldn't depend on having the same ingredients week after week, it wasn't a recipe that could be learned by heart.

But one thing never changed. Along with the game and the fowl and the things from the garden and so forth, three other ingredients always went into that stew. Only Brother Marcus—and Father Julian, of course, and probably Brother Salix—knew their names. They were powders from the East, that was all that anyone knew. And they were fabulously expensive, so it was whispered, even though no one really knew how much they had cost. At any rate, they were so important, and so rare, and so costly that Brother Marcus kept them locked up, each in its own iron box, on the long chopping table that he shared with Brother Sandro, and kept the boxes chained to the wall that was right behind it, as well.

On Mondays, when the special kettle of herbed game stew first began to simmer, he stared into it intently for a while, sniffed the fragrances starting to rise from it, then unlocked the first box and brought out a small cloth pouch. He undid its drawstring and took a pinch of the pale yellowish-brownish powder that was inside. Sometimes the pinch was smaller, sometimes larger. Sometimes he heated it up, very gently, with a bit of fat. Sometimes he stirred it into a cup of wine. One way or another, it ended up in the kettle. The pouch was quickly locked up in its iron box again. A fragrance arose that made the mouth water and the heart beat faster. On Thursday he unlocked the second box and in the same way added the second powder, a darker yellowish-brown than the one before, but the results were the same: the mouth watered, the heart beat faster. The second pouch was swiftly locked back up like the first. On Saturday....

This time the powder was a deep, rich red, and there were purple flecks in it, and the fragrances it brought into being dazzled the mind, and caused everyone who came near to stop in their tracks and breathe deeply, and feel almost like poets, whether they were simply leading a mule down the path to pasture, or shoveling out a latrine, or washing rags for Brother Salix with soap and water in a wooden tub, or standing watch on the courtyard walls. Then the pouch was locked up, and there was a final night of slow simmering, and then it was Sunday. The herbed game stew was served at the midday meal and everyone thanked Heaven for it—and thanked Brother Marcus too, and all his help. Flushed with the kitchen heat, red, almost, as his third and rarest powder, pleased that yet again he'd made everyone so happy, Brother Marcus stood at the kitchen doorway and beamed upon the diners, one and all.

Keti felt that none of this could be improved. The steady sameness of every week, the expected excitement of the moments when Brother Marcus added the powders, and the way he then wiped any remaining powder from his fingers with a tiny bit of some leaf that figured in the recipe, and then threw the powdered leaf into the pot, so as not to waste even a grain of costly rareness, and the way that he and Brother Sandro worked at the long table together—

The way they worked together was a marvel, too. Brother Sandro always started at one end of the table, and Brother Marcus at the other. But as the day went on and chores piled up around them, they often got closer together, working away at top speed all the time, until at last they were almost elbow to elbow. Brother Sandro always had to do a great deal of peeling, shucking, or discarding outer leaves and tougher stalks. He tossed anything that could be used again for cooking off to one side, into a wooden tub. Everything else went over his shoulder onto the floor, to be carried away to the farm for fodder and compost.

Then came the important thing for Keti. When the tub got too full, it was his job to dart in and move the contents into smaller pails that he could haul out of the way. When the piles on the floor got too high, he had to dart in again and clear them away too, by hand or with his broom. Also—and this was *very* important—he had to quickly search through all of the discarded things to make sure that there were no mix-ups—that "use-agains" didn't get caught up in "don't-use-agains," or vice versa, or that no spoons or knives or any of Brother Marcus's precious gougers and graters hadn't dropped down where they might be accidentally thrown away. And all the while, above him, the knife-work went on in a drumming, driving rhythm, sometimes faster, sometimes slower, but always urgent, as another fine meal moved toward its completion.

Making sure that nothing good was wasted or lost—Keti loved all his kitchen tasks and loved doing them well, but this was the one that was closest to his heart. Just as Pangur Ban was the best mouser, so Keti hoped to be the swiftest and the most careful searcher, finder, and saver.

"Do you like your work in the kitchen, Keti?" asked Brother Arcadius, in extremely correct Latin. Brother Arcadius knew very well that Keti liked it, but this was a lesson.

"Yes, I like my work in the kitchen, Brother Arcadius," Keti answered, with equal correctness.

"What do you do there?"

"I sweep, I carry things, I scrub pots."

"Whom do you help in the kitchen, Keti?"

"I help Brother Marcus, Brother Sandro, Brother Homelius, and Brother Alvas."

"And do they thank you for your help?"

"Yes, they thank me for my help." Except that Brother Marcus talked so much and added so many words to his thanks that sometimes it almost seemed like conversing. And Brother Sandro, very much like Keti, hardly ever talked at all. So he never actually said "Thank you." Instead—and Keti liked this very much better—every once in a while, when nobody else was looking, and Keti wasn't expecting it, Brother Sandro would make a very funny face right at him. He would cross his eyes, or wiggle his nose, or stick out his tongue, or do all three things at once, and then smile at Keti as if to say, "Don't laugh. It's a secret."

This was even funnier because Brother Sandro, the rest of the time, just worked away with a long, drooping face like a tired old mule's, never changing expression, hardly ever moving any part of him except his busy arms and hands. And no matter how hot it was in the kitchen, even when the others had removed their encumbering robes and were working just in their tunics and breeches, Brother Sandro always stayed fully dressed. His wide sleeves flapped this way and that as he worked away at full speed, and often even slid down over his flying hands. Then he'd shake them back up his arms without even a heartbeat's pause in what he was doing. There'd been a visitor to Spiritus Sanctus who'd fought off fifty enemies at once with the speed and force of his hands alone, in Spain. Brother Sandro was probably not as fast as that, but he was certainly more than fast enough for the kitchen.

"And why do you like working in the kitchen, Keti?" ventured Brother Arcadius. He leaned back in his chair and gazed peacefully out the window, as if this question was just one more regular question. But under the peacefulness, there was a waiting look.

"I like working in the kitchen because...I don't know." The answer started off boldly and ended in a whisper. Being useful, helping out, Brother Marcus's magic powders, Brother Sandro's funny faces, the robe with its flapping sleeves, the cupboard and the long chopping table that fit so flush to the wall, the ovens, the fireplaces, the importance of making sure nothing good got thrown away.... How many words it would take to answer that question! How easy it would be to get all sorts of things wrong! How impossible, to ever get it all right!

"I don't know," whispered Keti again.

Brother Arcadius smiled. "A very good lesson anyway, Keti," he said. He moved the bread and honey invitingly closer. "Now, just to yourself, not out loud, see if you can think of one reason why you like to work in the kitchen. Then maybe next week you can write me one sentence about it."

Having just one "because" and being able to write it down made things easier. Over the next several days, Keti worked out a sentence and practiced writing it on his waxed tablet. *I like working in the kitchen because I can help.* Saturday was the day he was supposed to write it out for Brother Arcadius, but in the hours before his lesson, two things happened that broke the kitchen routine. Brother Sandro and Brother Marcus had been working away almost elbow to elbow, but now it was time to give the herbed game stew its final touch. Brother Marcus unlocked the box that held the third powder. He took out the pouch and frowned at it for a moment, thinking things over. Should he mix the red powder with wine, or with cream, or heat it in butter?

He shook his head no. He spooned a tiny bit of it into his hand, carefully, carefully. He went over to where the stew was gently bubbling. With a magician's sweeping gesture he added the wonderful powder to the stew and stirred it round, releasing the fragrance that made angels lean down from Heaven. He brushed his hands free of any remaining powder, making sure that every grain fell into the stew. He wiped them clean for good measure with a sprig of basil, and added that to the pot.

He took up his stance once more beside Brother Sandro. He reached for the pouch to lock it up again. He lifted it high to keep it out of the way of Brother Sandro's furiously chopping knives and flapping sleeves, and the discarded cabbage leaves that were flying into the air in a storm of green. Then he paused, for there was a commotion at the door that opened onto the courtyard.

"Marcus, are you in there?" Brother Ferruccius, one of the farm managers, was on the threshold, looking very angry.

Brother Marcus immediately looked very angry too. "You see me, don't you?" he bellowed.

"Marcus, how come you've been mouthing off against my turnips?"

"Last load was half rotten," roared Brother Marcus. It was easy to see that he'd once been a soldier. He looked ready to charge straight at Brother Ferruccius and throw him out of the doorway. Keti watched open-mouthed, half appalled, half fascinated.

Brother Ferruccius did not look frightened. "Was not half rotten," he shouted.

"Five rotten ones right on top," thundered Brother Marcus. "And that was just the first look! So get the hell off my doorway! I've got food to get ready! Go and—"

He stopped thundering and looked around, puzzled. The other kitchen workers did too. A strange sound had just come from behind the cellar doorway. It came again, a dismal, imploring yowl.

"Pangur Ban!" cried Keti. He rushed to the heavy, iron-bound door to open it. It would not move for him.

"Whitey!" exclaimed Brother Marcus." How'd he get down there?" He stomped over to give Keti a hand with the door.

It stayed shut, and Brother Alvas hurried to join them. Being the one who so often worked in the cellars, he knew the door's ways. "Didn't he leave this morning after you fed him?" he asked Brother Marcus.

"Thought he did," said Brother Marcus. "But that's him yelling, all right."

He stepped back and let Brother Alvas pull the door open. Fur bristling, a sooty Pangur came stalking out. He stared at Keti and everyone with accusing eyes and then circled the room with skulking, offended dignity, staying as close to the walls as he possibly could. The door to the courtyard was still open. When Pangur got to it, he darted outside. Keti's heart lurched in dismay. Pangur Ban with his feelings hurt, Pangur Ban unhappy! Brother Ferruccius was also taking his very offended leave. Hands clenched, head down, he was striding back toward the path that led to the farm.

Brother Marcus cast a disdainful glance after him. "I'll have it out with him later," he snarled, but it was easy to see that his temper was already cooling. He closed the third spice box with a firm clang, and locked it. "Keti, don't look so worried. Whitey's fine. He's a little annoyed, that's all."

"Never guessed he was down there," said Brother Alvas. "He never went down there before."

"Must have heard a mouse down there after I fed him," said Brother Marcus. "Now let's go, everybody. We've got the big meal to serve!"

So they served the meal, and Keti had his lesson, and Brother Arcadius liked the sentence, and Pangur Ban appeared, looking white and happy again—Brother Salix had given him a good cleaning, it turned out. And the day after that was Sunday, and the herbed game stew was received with silent hosannas, as always. Even Brother Ferruccius could be seen smacking his lips, while pretending he was wiping them. And Monday came, and the next batch of herbed game stew was started, and the first iron box was unlocked, and the powder added. And Tuesday came, and Brother Marcus and Brother Ferruccius made up. And Thursday came, and the second iron box was unlocked, and the second powder added, and then came Saturday, and it was time to add the red powder....

With Brother Sandro furiously chopping turnip greens beside him, Brother Marcus unlocked the third iron box. He opened the lid and reached in to take out the pouch. But he didn't take out the pouch. His fingers scrabbled this way and that as if feeling about for something. He stepped back and then forward again. He peered down into the box. He closed it, then opened it again and peered into it again, and peered all around the long table and then under the table, while pieces of turnip greens kept raining down all around. Then he banged his fist on the table and shouted, "Stop!"

Brother Sandro and everyone stopped working and looked at him, startled. "It's gone," he said. "The pouch. The third pouch, with the third powder. It's not there."

"Not there!" said Brother Homelius. "It's always there."

"It isn't now," said Brother Marcus. "All right, everybody, start thinking. Last time I used it was Saturday. I took it out...there was the thing with Ferruccius...the thing with Whitey...I put in the powder...I locked it back up...."

Keti shrank into himself, thinking hard. His ears were ringing, his arms and legs felt numb. This was even worse than being asked to converse. He remembered seeing the pouch dangling from Brother Marcus's hand. He remembered the commotion and the upsets with Brother Ferruccius and Pangur Ban. He remembered rushing to help serve the big midday meal. He remembered thinking about the sentence for his lesson. He did not remember sifting through the tub of discarded leaves and the sweepings on the floor, the way he was always supposed to. He must have done that, because he always did. But usually he could think back and see himself doing that. This time he couldn't. Rotten turnips and Pangur Ban being trapped in the cellar —these things had taken his mind from his proper work.

"Are you sure you locked the box when you put it back?" asked Brother Alvas.

"It was locked just now when I went to open it," Brother Marcus said. He groaned. "If it's gone—Father Julian isn't going to like this. There was probably two years' worth of powder left in that pouch. The monastery pays an arm and a leg for it—a fortune for it! He won't let me order any more before it's time to. Two years with my herbed game stew not measuring up! And maybe he won't let me order it ever again. And that will be that. Think back, everybody! Come on, think back!" He scowled at Brother Sandro. "You were chopping cabbage, I remember that."

Brother Sandro looked back at him with his old mule's face. "Ferruccius started yelling."

"Your hands never stopped, I remember that too," said Brother Marcus. "If your knife caught the pouch broadside and knocked it out of my hand.... If it went flying...."

Brother Homelius rubbed his forehead, thinking hard. "I was looking that way, Marcus, watching Ferruccius. I saw those cabbage leaves flying, but I never saw any pouch."

Brother Marcus chewed his lips, a man in anguish. "If it did end up on the floor.... You looked around for things, didn't you, Keti, when you took the leaves out of the tub? And when you swept up?"

It is frightening in the kitchen if you've made a big mistake. "I don't remem..." whispered Keti. The rest of "remember" caught in his throat.

"Never mind," said Brother Marcus hurriedly. "I think you did." Brother Alvas and Brother Homelius quickly joined him. "We saw you looking, Keti," said Brother Alvas. "Both of us did."

"You're sure the latch caught?" asked Brother Homelius. "The latch on the box?"

"I heard it catch," Brother Marcus said.

"You dropped the pouch into the box, not off to the side?"

Brother Marcus stared at the ceiling, racking his brains. "I *think* I did. Oh God, I can't recall."

Brother Alvas spoke up. "The cat came out and went around the whole room – remember?"

"Circled the whole thing, right up against the wall," agreed Brother Homelius. "He was slinking around like maybe he had a mouse."

Pangur Ban doesn't mouse in the kitchen except at night, thought Keti. He tried to say the words out loud, but his throat wouldn't let him. *He doesn't even want to be in the kitchen except at night. There's too much noise, and he hates to be underfoot. And besides—*

"After he got over there right under your table, I thought he looked like he might be carrying something," Brother Homelius went on. "I've seen him do that in the courtyard a couple of times. He slinks around the walls with a mouse in his jaws. Or a bird. Or whatever he's caught."

"Those pouches look a lot like mice, come to think of it," said Brother Alvas. "Right shape when they're full of powder, string hanging down like a tail. I seem to remember—it's coming back to me now—I'm pretty sure I remember that he left this room with something in his mouth, and something like a tail was hanging down. Except that—now I remember—it looked more like a string and not so much like a tail. I would have said something, but I never gave it a thought." He looked at Brother Marcus and cleared his throat.

Brother Marcus scowled up at the ceiling, then scowled down at the floor. "He's always been attracted to those powders, and the pouches do look like mice," he said, very slowly and unwillingly. "And he does take things sometimes, like pine cones and...." His voice was trembling slightly. "It'll be ruined by now, lying out there in the wet and the mud. I'll have to tell Father Julian, but I need time to think...time to figure out what I'm going to say." He groaned again. "I guess we can all search the kitchen tonight after supper. Maybe we'll find it. Who knows? And if we don't find it, maybe nobody will notice that the stew tastes different." He tried to muster a hopeful smile, and failed.

"All right," said Brother Alvas. "We'll give it a try."

And they did give it a try. The five of them searched for an hour after supper, but found no pouch. Keti felt miserably sure that he knew why.

He hadn't kept his mind on his job. He'd let the pouch get mixed up with the cabbage leaves, the ones that were not to be used for cooking again. Mixed up with the cooking pile, it would have been noticed. By now it had been carted off to the farm, fed along with all the day's food scraps to poultry and animals, or chopped into the earth. Pangur most certainly had never carried it off.

Brother Marcus brushed aside Keti's hopeless attempts to explain that Pangur could not be the culprit—that the only possible culprit was Keti himself. "Don't worry about it, Keti," he kept saying. "If it's gone, we'll just have to deal with that. Whitey's a sensible cat, but still, he's a cat. Nobody's mad at him, you don't have to protect him. It was all my fault. And maybe tomorrow they won't notice that anything's different."

But from Brother Ambroz to Brother Ziegmunt, everyone did notice. The fragrance of the stew that got served was not the fragrance that everyone expected. People looked questioningly at their bowls and then at each other, spoons uplifted. Then, spoonful by spoonful, they ate the stew in their bowls, every mouthful, and nodded and said it was delicious, and so it was. But the wonder and glory weren't there. This was not Brother Marcus's magnificent herbed game stew as they'd always known it. Something was missing. Even Father Julian frowned briefly down at his first spoonful, before going on to polish his plate clean.

And the next Sunday was yet to come.

"Keti, you're not attending to your lesson today," said Brother Arcadius. "What's wrong?"

Keti shook his head. He could not speak.

"That was a very good sentence you wrote for me last time," said Brother Arcadius. He read it again, out loud, from Keti's waxed tablet. "'I like working in the kitchen because I can help.' I know you're a good help, too, Keti, because I see how—Keti?"

Tears were streaming down Keti's face. He couldn't stop them. He felt Brother Arcadius's arm around him, and wept into his sleeve. If it tore him apart, he was going to have to say something. "They're blaming him," he wept. "They keep blaming him."

"Who's blaming whom?" said Brother Arcadius, taking good care to keep speaking very correctly. By rights this was still a lesson.

"In the kitchen," Keti wept. "They keep blaming Pangur Ban."

"Because...?"

"They think he took something. He couldn't have."

258

"Can you say what they think he took?"

Keti shook his head again. "They're wrong!" he said. "They're *wrong!*"

"But, Keti—"

Keti sat up and looked his teacher in the eye. "Tell Father Julian," he said.

Brother Arcadius took his pupil's hand. "You want me to talk to Father Julian about this."

"Yes! Tell him!"

"Keti," said Brother Arcadius slowly, "that's impossible on two counts. First, you're not giving me enough information. I'd feel very foolish going to Father Julian and saying, 'The kitchen says that Pangur Ban took something, but they're wrong.' Think of the questions Father Julian would start asking. Think of what *you'd* start asking, if you were Father Julian. And then, for the second count, this appears to be kitchen business. You are part of the kitchen, Keti, and I'm not. It's in your hands."

"He'll make me leave," said Keti in the faintest whisper. It hurt to say every word.

"Make you leave!" exclaimed Brother Arcadius. "He wouldn't make you leave."

"He made *them* leave."

"Made whom?"

"Oghrin. And Ulka."

"Oh, well," said Brother Arcadius, with a shadow of a laugh. "Of course he made Oghrin and Ulka leave. They're killers. We don't let killers stay at Spiritus Sanctus. But you haven't killed anyone lately, have you, Keti?"

Keti recognized that this was a joke, but he did not think it was at all funny. He did not answer.

"I'll tell you what, though," said Brother Arcadius. "If Father Julian ever did make you leave—and I'm sure he never would—Pangur Ban and I would leave with you, and we'd all go to live in Wessex over the sea, and make bricks for the king. That's my solemn promise to you, Keti."

"All right," whispered Keti. He was pretty sure he knew the way to the sea. It was way back over the grasslands, toward the setting sun. He'd come here from that direction to begin with, along with Oghrin and Ulka and Oghrin's two mean-hearted sons.

"The other thing I can do for you, and I can do it right now," said

Brother Arcadius, "is help you decide what you'll want to tell Father Julian." He frowned. "This missing thing—would it have anything to do with the herbed game stew? The way it didn't taste like itself, yesterday? Brother Marcus's special powders are no secret. He's talked about them himself often enough. We all know he uses them. We just don't know where they're from, really, or what they're called or what they really are."

Keti didn't know that, either. But knowing that Brother Arcadius knew part of the story made the rest of it easier to tell. Not that easier was easy—no, not at all. Haltingly, with every word a torment, wanting to get everything right and nothing wrong, he explained about Brother Ferruccius, and the cabbage leaves flying through the air, and the chopping table, and the wall, and Pangur Ban coming up out of the cellar, and the cabbage leaves in the tub, and the cabbage leaves on the floor, and his duty of making sure that nothing important ever got thrown away. "And I wasn't careful," he finished in a whisper.

"So you think the pouch got carried out in a pile of leaves."

Keti nodded.

"And got eaten by goats, or something...."

Keti nodded again.

"And you feel certain that Pangur Ban couldn't be to blame."

"Yes!" said Keti in a fierce whisper.

"Well, go to Father Julian now, and tell him what you've just told me. You know where he lives. You'll knock at the door that you see there out the window—that one right there—and Brother Dietrich will open it. He's Father Julian's helper, you know that. He'll ask you what you want, and you'll say you want to talk to Father Julian. He'll ask if it's important, and you'll say yes. You may have to wait awhile, but you can practice your words in your head while you're waiting. After you're done, if you're by yourself, come over to me and tell me about it. But if you're with somebody else—"

"With *whom?*" whispered Keti.

"Well, maybe Father Julian will want to go over to the kitchen to see for himself, and ask you to go with him. Or he'll send you over there with Brother Dietrich. Just do what he tells you. It's kitchen business, Keti. It's in your hands. Go take care of it!"

So step by halting step, knowing that Brother Arcadius was watching from the window, Keti crossed the space between the library and the building where Father Julian worked and lived. It was taller and wider than the long, low buildings where the monks had their cells, although just as plain. Knees shaking, he walked up three steps and knocked at the heavy door. It opened, and Brother Dietrich peered out.

"Keti?" said Brother Dietrich, in mild surprise. Keti hadn't thought that Brother Dietrich would know his name. "Come in, come in."

Trembling, Keti obeyed. The door shut behind him.

"What can I do for you?" asked Brother Dietrich.

"I...Father Julian...." whispered Keti.

"Father Julian wants to see you?"

"No...." Keti managed to shake his head and point to himself. "I...." He struggled to bring his thoughts back into his mind. *Brother Ferruccius. The table. The wall. Pangur Ban. The cabbage leaves in the tub. The leaves on the floor. The table, the table.* His hands were like lumps of ice. His tongue didn't want to move. His arms and legs had gone numb again. His ears were ringing.

"You wish to see Father Julian?"

Keti forced his head to nod.

"Is it important?"

Keti nodded again.

Brother Dietrich went to another door across the room. It had a very fancy latch, with lots of iron leaves and a crown in the middle and things. He opened it and murmured a few, a very few words. He turned back to Keti. "He'll see you now."

Keti, frozen and burning, made the long, long walk to the door with the latch. At the threshold his legs stopped moving and his eyes, almost, stopped seeing. But his ears faintly heard Father Julian's voice in the distance, and the voice was saying, "Come in."

He managed to do so, just barely, and the voice said, "Sit down."

All the chairs were tall. Before he could sit down, he had to boost himself up. He managed to do that and sat there terrified. His feet dangled off the ground. He made sure they stayed very still. He waited.

After that, nothing happened. Slowly his eyesight cleared and his tongue began to thaw. Father Julian was sitting across the room at a table, writing on a piece of parchment. His eyes were on his work, his pen moved swiftly.

Keti didn't want to see anything more of him. He stared down at his own knees and shivered inside. He tried not to look up, but sometimes his eyes disobeyed him. So he saw that the room was very plain. The walls were white. The floor was stone. The table was dark. Keti's chair was one of three, all in a row. A single shelf on the wall behind the table held some books. One was very large and had a lot of gold on the cover, the rest were smaller and plain.

There was a piece of thick cloth on the floor. It was as red as the missing powder. It had lots of designs on it in black, white, and brown, and white ends like somebody's haircut. It was a rug, he guessed. Oghrin and Ulka had talked about stealing rugs. And over in the corner, on a spindly-looking table with a chair on either side, there was a board marked off in squares, with strange little stone figures standing on it, some black, some white. Or whitish, anyway. Was that the game that Brother Arcadius moaned about now and then? He made his eyes look down at his knees again.

"All right, what's this about?" Father Julian's voice came at him without warning. He felt as if an arrow had shot him, but he managed to stay on his chair. And he managed to arrange his tongue in his mouth so that it might speak. And he thought of going away to Wessex over the sea, with his teacher and Pangur Ban. And he forced his jaws to open, and he forced his breath to breathe, and he croaked out his words, one by one.

The kitchen. The pouch. Brother Ferruccius at the door, talking with Brother Marcus. He didn't say yelling, he didn't say quarreling, he didn't say rotten turnips. He left all that out.

Pangur Ban's cry from the cellar. Pangur Ban slinking around the walls. The cabbage leaves and all of that. The *table*. The *wall*.

"I wasn't paying attention," he said, in a voice that seemed to come from far away. "Pangur Ban didn't take it. I wasn't careful. So it got thrown out."

But Father Julian had gone over to the spindly table in the corner. He tapped the board that had those stone figures standing on it. "Do you know what this is?" he asked.

Staring, Keti shook his head no.

"Well, come over here and sit down, and I'll show you," said Father Julian. He waited while Keti did as he was told. Then he sat down too. "This is chess," he said. "It's a game of pure reasoning." He began picking stone figures up from the board and naming them. Pawns, castles, bishops, horsemen, king, queen. He demonstrated the ways that the different figures could move, and how they could be captured. "If your pieces box in my king so that no matter what he tries to do he'll be caught on the next move, then you've won the game," he said. He demonstrated everything again. Then he put the figures back on the board in their proper places.

"Now, suppose you move that piece to this square," he said, pointing.

"The pawn?" said Keti. He moved the piece as he was told. His voice no longer seemed to be coming from so far away. It was easier now to breathe. This little world marked off in squares was like the verb *scire*. It made sense.

"I'll move my pawn to here," said Father Julian. "Now, perhaps your horseman can go here?" Keti moved the horseman. "And I'll move my pawn to there." Father Julian tapped the square. "Now, why not bring out your queen to here?"

"I can't do that," Keti said. He'd forgotten that he was sitting across from Father Julian. He'd forgotten about the lost pouch, and even about the injustice to Pangur Ban. All he saw was the wonderland before him, the wonderland where things could be very complicated, and yet if you got them wrong, you could see why.

"And why not?" asked Father Julian.

"Because if I do, then that one"—he pointed—"can catch this one, and then that one"—he pointed again—"gets my king."

"Oh? Why not move your king?"

"Can't," said Keti, absorbed. "He's blocked in. Except, wait! I could move—"

Father Julian stood up. "All right," he said. "Now, here's what you're going to do. I want you to keep on studying Latin with your teacher, but I also want you to study chess with me. And reasoning. I know they keep you busy in the kitchen, but we'll work out times when they can spare you. You'll want to learn number work and the abacus with somebody, too—Salix, most likely, or Dietrich. And now, let's go see about the pouch."

And so they did. There was consternation in the kitchen, and also in Keti's heart, when they arrived. Brother Marcus, Brother Homelius, Brother Alvas—it was hard to stand there while they stared at him dumbfounded, but how could he let them go on blaming Pangur Ban for something he never could have done? Brother Sandro, anyway, wasn't staring. And Father Julian wasn't scolding or anything. He was simply talking.

"I thought I might be hearing from you sooner or later, Marcus," he said. "I gathered when I tasted Sunday's stew that something had been lost, somehow, or destroyed, perhaps. But I'm here because it seems there's been talk of blaming the cat. Keti's concerned about that. He wants to show us that the cat couldn't have done it. Keti?" He held his hand, palm up, to Keti, to invite him to give his reasons. Somehow, somewhere, between the library and here, giving reasons had become not just terrifying, but also possible.

"It's the table," Keti said haltingly, word by slow word. "Nothing falls in back of the table. Because it's always touching the wall. Everything goes into the tub, or down on the floor in front. Brother Marcus doesn't throw anything. He just chops things that are all peeled and ready. Brother Sandro throws things, but just into the tub and down around his feet."

"So if the pouch were caught up in all the chopping," said Father Julian agreeably, "it wouldn't end up by the wall, where the cat was walking. Do I have this right?"

Throat-clearings and coughs came from Brother Marcus, Brother Homelius, and Brother Alvas. It was hard to tell what those sounds were meant to convey. Brother Sandro just stood there gazing at nothing, with his arms crossed over his chest. His wide sleeves drooped down.

"Brother Sandro or Brother Marcus could have kicked the pouch over to the wall by accident, though," observed Father Julian.

Keti shook his head yet again. He pointed under the table. The front legs were braced with cross bars. It would take a tremendous kick to get anything past them. Anybody kicking like that would have been noticed. While he was trying to decide how to say all this, Father Julian spoke once more.

"Keti wants to clear the cat from blame," he said. "If it's true that the cat stayed close to the walls, I think he has done so. He also believes that he himself must have overlooked the pouch when he was cleaning up. In other words, he believes that he's to blame. But I think that's far from proven. If the powder weren't so expensive and hard to get, and if it didn't give this monastery so much enjoyment, I'd be inclined to dismiss the whole matter. As it is—I think there's something I'm not being told."

He looked from face to face. Brother Homelius and Brother Alvas turned very pale. Brother Marcus turned the same shade of red as Father Julian's rug or the missing powder. He started to say something, but choked on his words. Brother Sandro's tired mule's face did not change at all.

There was a long silence. Father Julian broke it at last. "I could convene the monastery, and take this matter up in a public forum," he said.

Three pairs of eyes flicked toward Keti, then away. Brother Marcus tried again to choke out some words. Tried, and failed. Brother Sandro stared straight ahead.

"There's no way that I shall leave this unresolved," said Father Julian.

"I—" stammered Brother Marcus. "I mean, we...he...." Beads of sweat had formed on his brow. He looked imploringly at Father Julian.

Keti stepped back, stricken. He'd thought only of removing false blame from Pangur Ban. He'd never meant to cause trouble for his friends in the kitchen—his elders. Chess was like a clear, bright path leading to rightness. This was no bright path to anything. It was a *mess*.

And then Brother Sandro stepped forward. "All right, I'm sick of this," he said.

Everyone stared at him, but he did not stare back. He snapped his fingers instead and waved his left hand, with his wide sleeve flapping around it, in dizzying arcs. With his right hand he pulled the pouch...*the* pouch....

From Brother Marcus's left ear.

Brother Marcus let out a bellow of disbelief. He lunged for the pouch, but it was gone again. Brother Sandro snapped his fingers and brought it back....

From Brother Alvas's armpit.

Then from Brother Homelius's sandal.

Then from thin air.

Brother Sandro cupped it in his two hands, just for a moment. Then he tossed it over to Brother Marcus, who caught it and staggered over with it to the box it belonged in. He opened the box, dropped the pouch in, and locked it up. His eyes were staring halfway out of his head. So were Brother Alvas's and Brother Homelius's.

"It was just too damned tempting," said Brother Sandro. He looked from one stunned person to another. "And I suppose you'll say *damned* is the word, but I say—whatever. I've wanted out for a good long while now. I traveled with a show, and I fooled myself into thinking I wanted the quiet life, like you've got here. I'm a magician, and a good one, and being shut up in this kitchen is wearing me down. You were dangling that pouch from your fingers, Marcus, and yelling at Ferruccius—"

Father Julian's eyebrows went up, just slightly, and lowered again as quickly as they'd risen. He hadn't heard about that yelling business.

"So," continued Brother Sandro, "I waved my sleeves around a bit, and threw a few more cabbage leaves into the air, and whisked that pouch out of your hand with the point of my knife and hid it in my robe, and you forgot you hadn't dropped it in yet, and locked the box —"

"Are you working with an accomplice?" Father Julian asked.

"No, that's too complicated, Father. I figured I could sell this powder myself, and start a good new show with some of what I'd make, and save for my old age with the rest. But, Keti, I never wanted to throw any blame on you, or on anybody. And no harm's been done to the cat. People don't like to be blamed, but cats don't know the difference. So when Alvas said the cat might have done it, that was fine with me. Nobody would be in trouble, and the whole thing would work itself out. I aimed to wait a few days, and then just disappear. You shouldn't have let it bother you, Keti, see?"

"But Pangur didn't do it," said Keti urgently. "So blaming him is *wrong*." Part of him realized with astonishment that saying all these words had been quite easy—sort of. Another part felt crushed about Brother Sandro. Crushed that he'd stolen the pouch and felt so good about it, evidently. Crushed that he'd said a bad word in front of Father Julian and didn't seem to care about that either. And crushed that Brother Sandro was now in trouble.

But Brother Sandro was catching his eye and making a last secret face—so quickly that he might not be crossing his eyes and wiggling his ears at all. "So I'll be off then," he said. "Up and over the walls."

And before anyone could move or gather their wits, he'd thrown off his robe and raced out the courtyard door in his tunic and breeches. A farm cart happened to be halted over there by the western wall, loaded with barrels. He leaped from the ground to the highest barrel in one bound, giving Brother Rugarius the driver a terrible scare. With another bound, he reached the top of the wall. Then he was swinging from the branch of a close-growing pine tree. Then he was gone.

Brother Sifari came rushing in from the courtyard, wild-eyed. "Someone just—"

"Brother Sandro was taking his leave of us," Father Julian said.

Brother Sifari gaped from one face to another, waiting for explanations that were not coming. Brother Marcus went and unlocked the third box again. He pulled out the pouch and held it up by its string. It dangled like a mouse held upside down. It was not as plump as the kitchen workers remembered. Brother Marcus nodded. "He took a good quarter of it with him, I'd say," he said.

And before Brother Sifari's baffled eyes—and Keti's—the three kitchen men broke into snorts of laughter, and even Father Julian smiled a very brief smile. A magician-thief in the Spiritus Sanctus kitchen! Who would have thought it? No, it wasn't really funny, but it was...funny.

But Keti couldn't say what he himself was thinking. There was a storm inside him of grief, relief, triumph, misery, confusion, and who could say what. It was out of his realm why the men were laughing like that. He did know, though, that he was going to miss Brother Sandro and fear for him, thief or no—and hope he'd be happy now with his magic show. He was going to have to figure out why Brother Marcus, Brother Homelius, and Brother Alvas had looked at him and each other so strangely, and what Brother Marcus had been trying and failing to say. He was going to relish his lessons in chess. He was going to have to figure out why his dear teacher, Brother Arcadius, didn't like that wonderful game. He was going to have to give up all thoughts of moving to Wessex. Oh, there was just so much he was going to have to do! And there'd be so much to tell Pangur Ban tonight, up on the cupboard!

* * *

"Father, all of us knew that Whitey hadn't taken the pouch," Brother Marcus said. "But we all thought that Keti had just overlooked it, and let it go out with the leavings. We didn't want him to feel bad about it. We know how much he wants to do things right. Felt he'd suffered enough, you know? So we didn't want to just come out and blame him. Alvas thought up a good story and we just went along with it. We searched just to make things look good, but we knew we'd never find it. Then when you came in with Keti, we got all tongue-tied. We knew he cared about Whitey, but not to...you know...that degree."

"He was standing up for something else as well, Marcus," said Father Julian. "He cares about truth also—to that same degree."

* * *

"The stew today is better than it's ever been," murmured Brother Kongro to Brother Malachi. "Last Sunday there was something missing, but today—!" He stopped talking and gave the stew the ultimate tribute of eating it reverently.

"Amen, Brother!" Brother Malachi murmured back, and joined him in doing the same.

* * *

"So if I castle now, I think you'll get me in three moves," said Keti. There'd been three lessons in chess now, and each one was even more interesting and thrilling than the one before.

"I'd say four," said Father Julian, with hidden joy. To have a student like this, instead of that very dear but unteachable (when it came to chess) Arcadius!

Keti fell asleep that night up on his high cupboard, and dreamed that he was knocking on Father Julian's door. But the man who opened the door was somebody else in Father Julian's robe. Not old, not young, not fat, not thin, but thinner rather than fatter, he smiled down at Keti and Keti liked him at once. Liked him a lot. "Aha, my younger self!" the person said. "I'm glad you're stopping by. Come on in, and let's have a game. Ten-move limit, all right?" And Keti went in, and they played, and it was a draw.

It was a puzzling dream, and yet very agreeable. And Keti thought he might tell Brother Arcadius about it, and see what he thought. But when he woke up in the morning and tried to recall it, he couldn't. Not a bit of it could he remember, try as he might. Nor did it ever come back to him again. Only the good feeling of it remained, to be added to all the good feelings he already had.

* * *

"Pangur Ban," said Brother Arcadius, "I know that Keti likes people to get things right. But if they hadn't been blaming you, I don't think he would have found it in himself to speak up. I'd say that you are the magical ingredient where he's concerned." The big cat looked up at him with gleaming eyes.

"Mrrrowwr," said Pangur Ban.

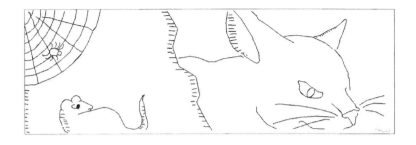

THE MEN FROM METZ

In which it's one thing after another,
and Brother Arcadius is not amused

AD 900

Earth and sky had taken on the faded colors of early November. The day itself felt faded and listless, but Brother Arcadius, assistant librarian at Spiritus Sanctus monastery, resolved to ignore it all. He went along the downward path with firmer strides.

What he planned to do—what he'd made up his mind to do that afternoon—was to go look about in the scrublands, the wildlands to the east of the monastery. Brother Salix the medicus had found a useful sort of healing mushroom there now and then. It would be a good thing to bring back more. The scrublands were a jumble of high ground and low ground, thickly overgrown with low twisted willows and spreading junipers, along with brambles and briars and inconvenient plants of every description. But paths led through it here and there, and he aimed to find one and venture along it for a while, and see what he could see.

The path he was on was a much-used path that skirted the scrublands, but did not lead through them. It sloped downhill at a steeper angle now. Brother Arcadius had to lean back on his heels to keep from going faster than was wise, considering the slick dampness of the ground just here. He did not wish to take an undignified tumble. Even a year ago he might have enjoyed the risk, but he was eighteen and a half now, a responsible person, a librarian, a scholar, a teacher, and he felt the weight of his years. He had an example to set, and wished to set it. He—

"Mrrrwrrrwow!"

An unexpected shape darted out from the undergrowth. Brother Arcadius bent down to say hello. "Good afternoon, Pangur Ban! Are you coming with me?"

"Mrrow!" Pangur Ban, the great white mouser of Spiritus Sanctus monastery, usually a sociable and a sensible cat, was not all that white today and not all that sociable either. His coat was streaked with grass stains. Burrs were stuck to his broad chest like badges of honor. The big swift-moving paws that terrified all mousedom were muddy. His tail lashed ceaselessly and ferociously from side to side, and his gleaming eyes, usually so amiable in expression, were sharp and intent upon something that couldn't be seen, at the moment at least, by any mere human. Brother Arcadius recognized that here was a preoccupied cat in full hunting mode. He managed to get a few pats in all the same. When he resumed his walk, Pangur went with him, slinking along close to the ground, an arrow on legs.

Ah, here was a narrow path leading into the scrublands. Brother Arcadius hesitated, wondering if he should follow it, or continue on until he found another. He might as well just follow this one, he supposed. The paths would surely all be much alike, narrow and twisting and tricky to walk on. A charcoal burner and his sons used them now and then, so he'd been told, to get to wherever it was they wanted to go. They weren't often seen at the monastery, which made its own charcoal, but once in a while they came by.

Well, a few fragments of charcoal would be a useful discovery too, if he came upon any lying along the way. Much less useful than charcoal or mushrooms, but much more interesting, maybe, would be a cave. Wide stretches of land hereabouts had turned out to be riddled with caves. Some of them were only a few feet deep. Others extended far back into utter darkness and might well be connected.

He'd stumbled across one of the latter kind himself, a mile and a half or so to the west from where he was standing. It had contained a stone figure of a legionary, made in Roman times in the long ago. Outside the cave, but not far from it, another stone figure had been discovered, a prancing horse. It too had been made in Roman times, although by Gauls, not by Romans. Legionary and horse were now essential adornments to the monastery grounds. Brother Arcadius doubted that he'd find anything like that today. The dreary sky and dreary landscape seemed to foretell that mushrooms and charcoal were the most that would come to light.

At any rate, thought Brother Arcadius, he'd go down this path and turn back in just a while. By rights, he supposed, he should have told somebody that he planned to go into the labyrinth of the scrublands, but he'd decided not to. He wasn't breaking a rule, and he didn't intend to run any risks. He'd be walking safely along a path and looking for mushrooms, that was all he'd be doing. He was the only monk at Spiritus Sanctus who'd been firmly ordered, both by Brother Salix the medicus and Father Julian, the head of the monastery, to take a daily walk for health and strength. He didn't like to remind people about that.

He knew very well that his walks were meant to serve a good purpose. They were supposed to prevent him from being too much of a scholar and poring too much over the closely written parchment pages of the many, many books in the Spiritus Sanctus library—five hundred manuscripts in prime condition, along with others that were damaged in one way or another, and a trunkful of assorted bits and pieces of pages. He'd been accepted into the monastery not just because of his outstanding scholarship (a scholarship he modestly and sincerely deprecated), but also because of his youth. A youth's keen eyesight, the possibility that a youth might have many good working years ahead of him—these advantages had to be safeguarded. There'd be no point in having an assistant librarian who needed assistance himself.

Good purpose or not, in his view the walks made him seem privileged, and he didn't like that. True enough, most of the other monks at Spiritus Sanctus didn't really need or want further exercise. They got enough of it in the course of their daily work. But he got to walk, and they didn't. That was one thing that made him uncomfortable. The other was that too many people viewed him as some sort of weakling. He had the misfortune to be the youngest monk in the monastery by a full ten years, and the shortest and slightest except for one. The constant joke was that someday the wind was going to blow him away. A while back, he'd singlehandedly brought down a dangerous killer, mainly by luck alone, or something like it. Help from above must have played a great part in it. Since then the jokes had been fewer, but still they went on.

So he hadn't reported to anyone today that he was going off into the scrublands. He'd just set off. Truth to tell, he very much enjoyed his walks, even though he didn't enjoy being ordered to take them. Interesting things had happened during them, time and again. Even when they were just routine, Pangur Ban was often with him for company. And if Pangur Ban happened not to be with him, then there were his thoughts, thoughts of Latin, of Greek, of Hebrew, of poetry. And there was also the beauty of nature round about, at least usually. On this charcoal-and-mushroom day, the beauty was very muted, to say the least. Even the magnificent high mountains in the far distance were hidden from view, veiled by low-lying clouds.

Anyway, onward! Brother Arcadius left the main path behind and struck off toward the east. The charcoal burners' path, if that's whose it was, was as narrow, twisted, and bumpy as the westerly paths that he already knew. Like many of them, it was downright wet in places besides, because here and there little streams rose up from underground, just as they did to the west, and trickled across it, glinting under the dull sky. Pangur Ban had left it entirely and was slinking through the undergrowth, belly down, faster and faster. He had a victim in sight, no doubt about it. Brother Arcadius hoped it wouldn't turn out to be some hapless, grounded songbird.

But Pangur hesitated, slowed, and then came to a complete stop in a tense crouch. Brother Arcadius came to a stop also, to catch his breath and decide whether or not to go on. Up ahead, the path leveled out and looked drier, too. On the monastery side, it was hemmed in by stand after stand of those thick-growing, twisted willows. On the downhill side it was walled in by mighty rocks that rose higher than his head all along the way. Except that the rocks here were free-standing, separate boulders instead of a solid rampart, this was the same landscape as where they'd found the cave. But aside from all that, didn't he see mushrooms growing just up the way?

Whoosh! A small, roundish, dark brown, hurtling form shot out of the rumpled grasses to his left and vanished at breakneck speed into the maze of rocks. Whoosh! Pangur Ban hurtled after it in furious pursuit. Brother Arcadius, who had almost lost his balance in surprise, steadied himself and shook his head, marveling that creatures with legs so much shorter than his could move so fast. Pursued and pursuer were both out of sight already, with only the trembling of the undergrowth to mark where they had gone.

He wondered for a moment what sort of creature Pangur was chasing—a vole, perhaps? It had seemed too large for an ordinary mouse, but too small for a field rat. So yes, it was probably a vole. And yes, Pangur Ban, a very sensible cat—usually—would probably give up the chase if it proved to be too difficult, and not go too far afield. But he'd certainly have to be given a good cleaning and grooming when he returned to the monastery, with his catch or without it.

Brother Arcadius walked on. Willows pressed against him on his right, blocking off even a glimpse of Spiritus Sanctus, up there on the higher ground. Giant rocks walled him in on the left. But the path did grow easier to walk on. When he reached the patch of mushrooms, he found that they did not in the least resemble the ones he hoped to find. But since he no longer had to struggle to make his way forward, he set off again.

He rounded a bend and then another bend. Then came a good long stretch of fairly level straightness, although the willows and rocks still pressed close on either side. Peering ahead to the farther end of that straightness, Brother Arcadius saw that up there, the path seemed to come to a sudden end, disappearing into thick growths of briars and brambles. When he drew closer to this blockage, though, he saw that the briars and brambles weren't growing there at all. They were cut-off stalks, and they'd been piled there, it seemed, in a very purposeful way.

Human hands had put this barrier in place, that was for sure. Could it be the charcoal burners? Brother Arcadius asked himself. Who'd done it if it wasn't them? Brother Atalf and Brother Ziegmunt, the two hulking heavy workers of Spiritus Sanctus, hadn't been coming out here as far as he knew. And if they had been, why would they want to block the way? Was there danger up ahead?

There didn't seem to be. The path just seemed to go along as it had before. Brother Arcadius edged carefully around the piled-up briars and brambles. For a moment he stood quite still, looking around him and listening for he knew not what. All he saw was the path before him. All he heard was the occasional sigh of wind riffling through willow leaves, and a distant harsh cawing of crows. Of Pangur Ban and the fleeing vole there was no sign. Of the mushrooms that Brother Salix would welcome, there was likewise no sign.

Pulled on by curiosity now as much as by mushrooms, Brother Arcadius moved forward, step by step. There was no reason, really, to go that slowly, except that he wanted to hear Pangur coming back through the bushes, if that was what the cat was going to do. "Pangur," he called, low voiced and listening. He clicked his tongue, too, but no cat materialized at his feet, or anywhere. "Pangur...." Could Pangur have gone back to the monastery already? Was he enjoying a snack of vole in the kitchen garden? Was he up on the walls, being petted by the watchman? "Pangur.... Here, Pangur...."

I ought to go back too, thought Brother Arcadius. Still he went on, with the willows crowding him on his right, and fissured rocks rising on his left—closely joined now, and thickly covered with mats of shrubby tendrils hanging down from above. Those tendrils hid thorns, as he knew well. That same sort of plant had veiled the rampart of rock where the stone legionary had been found. Thinking of pierced fingers and caves and mushrooms and cats and legionaries, he walked on.

He took a long step over another wet patch. He bent to take a closer look at what might be a tiny mushroom poking up from a clump of old leaves beside the way. It was no mushroom at all but a bit of bone, left over, no doubt, from an owl's or a fox's feast. Or Pangur's. And then he went on. He came to a place where the willows thinned out a bit and receded somewhat from the path. Something large and solid was in there among them that was not a willow—

And before Brother Arcadius, walking by, had time to tell himself that he'd better turn and see what this thing might be, it had burst out onto the path behind him, and a hand came down on the back of his neck like a sledgehammer, knocking him to his knees, then pulling him up again.

Stunned, and with racing heart and throbbing knees, Brother Arcadius tried to look back to see who was there, but the hand wouldn't let him. It pushed him forward instead. "Just keep walking, you," said a voice. It was a thick, meaty-sounding voice, as if whoever was back there had a tongue that filled his whole mouth. Brother Arcadius had no choice except to obey. He tried to make sense of what was going on. If this was some bandit....

"I don't have any money," he said. His voice sounded strange in his ears, distant and reedy. The hand at the back of his neck gripped him harder. He stumbled onward, twenty paces...then forty, maybe...then maybe twenty again...then more.... From the long stretch of rock-wall beside him there came a breath of cold air and a sense of emptiness. Here was a cave. He was pushed through thorny hanging tendrils into its darkness.

"Move and you're dead," said the thick voice. It echoed against the surrounding walls of the cave. Brother Arcadius did not move. He wanted to rub his hurt knees, but didn't dare. Over there by the mouth of the cave, his captor—a large, shadowed shape in the patch of gray daylight there—blocked the way out and was making very strange movements. Oh, he was lighting a lamp, that's what he was doing. Brother Arcadius recognized the sharp scratch of flint striking iron. A wick flared and commenced to burn with an unsteady light. The floor and walls of the cave came fitfully into view, and other things too—a nearby rock, big enough to sit on...a low bench that looked as if it had been knocked together by impatient hands...an axe and a cudgel leaning upright against it...another lamp, unlit...some sacks...some pails.

In the flare of the lamp, the shadow by the door was a shadow no longer, but a man as largely built as Brother Atalf or Brother Ziegmunt, although not quite as tall. He pointed to the rock. "Sit down," he said, and Brother Arcadius sat. The rock was bumpy and cold beneath him, and he was quite sure that plenty of blood had congealed on one knee. But his heart had stopped its wild hammering. He was able to think again, at least a little. Able to talk a little, too. "Are you the charcoal burner?" he asked politely. He doubted very much that the answer would be yes, but it wouldn't hurt to ask...probably. He waited a moment for a response that didn't come. Then he said, "I didn't mean to trespass on your path." His voice sounded piping and thin, a weakling's voice for sure.

He got no answer. The man set the oil lamp down on the cave floor. The smoke from it drifted up slowly to narrow crevices in the cave's ceiling, and through, and out. The man sat heavily down on the rough-hewn bench. He didn't seem at all concerned that somebody might see the smoke, not to mention the light, and come to investigate —somebody large and strong like Atalf or Ziegmunt or better yet, both of them together. The notable things about him were his huge hands and the head that seemed too small for his big body. He picked up the cudgel and laid it across his knees. His eyes were small, with dark bristly lashes. They were pale blue, maybe, or gray—it was hard to tell which. Brother Arcadius gave them a single quick glance, then looked away.

"You're from up there," the man said in his thick voice. "From that monastery."

"I am," said Brother Arcadius. His own voice—thank Heaven— was starting to be his voice again, or nearly so. After all, hadn't he grown up among the savage Danes? Hadn't he seen just about the worst that people could do? Being pushed down a path and pushed into a cave—if that's all that was going to happen, then where was the harm? *I'll show you where*, whispered an inner self deep inside him, but he ignored that frightening whisper, and sat up straight.

"You're a monk," the man said. His big hands fondled the cudgel. A mean-looking thing it was, hefty, long, knobby, and fashioned—you could just tell—from some sort of wood that would be as unyielding as iron. "A monk," he repeated.

Well, with this robe and this hood, and if I come from the monastery besides, what else would I be? thought Brother Arcadius, but it would not do to say those words out loud. "I am," he said.

"I hate a monk," the man said. There was a dreamy tone to his words. He was talking more to himself than to his captive. Brother Arcadius understood that he didn't mean *a* monk, literally, but monks in general—himself included. "I hate a monk," the man said again.

Brother Arcadius decided it would be best to make no answer. In quick glances, he studied the cave around him instead. It was larger than the one he'd discovered just months before, with much help from Pangur Ban. But the crevices in the floor and ceiling, and the sound of water dripping in the farther shadows, and the smell of chill dank earth and stone – these were the same. And the Romans had been here too. Beyond the big fellow and that cudgel of his over there, a brick wall about two arms' lengths wide rose from floor to ceiling, just as a brick wall did in the other cave.

To that other wall, long ago, the Romans had attached a stone garland incised with a design of laurel leaves. Also they'd left behind that stone figure, a good four feet high, of a Roman legionary, with his legion's name and number carved across his chest. There was no stone figure and no garland here, but the brickwork told the story. The Romanness of the place was unmistakable.

"Took our statues," said the man on the bench. He rapped the cudgel against the floor, twice, softly. He looked directly at Brother Arcadius with his little eyes. It was clear that now he wanted a response.

"Your statues?" Two words were all that it seemed wise to say.

"We had a soldier, back in our other cave," the thick voice said. "And we had a white horse, pretty close to it in the weeds."

"Um..." said Brother Arcadius. Yes, those were the things that the monastery had taken. They hadn't been stolen, though, by any means. Had they been given by their long-ago makers to this fellow? Of course they hadn't. And was he one of the charcoal burners, or wasn't he? And just who was this "we" that he was talking about? The other charcoal burners, or somebody else? Some him, some her, some them? Where were they, then?

The feeling of cold stone in the stomach, the chill in fingers and toes, the dance of fear in the back of the mind—Brother Arcadius told himself to ignore all that. It was time to be more than just a lump on a rock. He sat up straighter, squared his shoulders, and cleared his throat. "Have you lived here long, then?" he asked.

"Sometimes we live here," the big man said. "And sometimes we don't." There was some education in that thick voice. Whoever he was, he must have had some schooling. It wasn't likely that he was a charcoal burner. And he'd set down the cudgel again. That was an encouraging sign. Conversation, maybe, was all he craved.

"So...where do you come from, originally?" asked Brother Arcadius.

"Where do I come from, originally?" There was a disquieting hint of mimicry in the question. "I come from—*originally*—Metz."

"A good long way from here," said Brother Arcadius. He did his best to speak heartily, with judicious touches of respect and admiration thrown in. "Did you walk all the way here, then? Or did you go by river part of the way?" *And what are you doing here in the first place, with your cudgel and your barricades and all?*

No answer came to his question, but the big man was talking. "I like Metz," he said, half to himself again. "Always like to go back there, when we get the chance."

"Beautiful place, is it?"

An unpleasant smile formed on the man's face. "It's beautiful," he said. He leaned forward and reached into the shadows under the bench, behind the axe. He brought up a cruel-looking knife with a whetstone tied to the handle. He undid the stone and began to sharpen the blade. He worked slowly, paying great attention to each stroke. "Don't try to run out of this cave," he said in his thick voice. "It would be a mistake."

"I wasn't going to," said Brother Arcadius. He congratulated himself, a bit, that he felt quite calm. There was absolutely no reason at all not to be calm. If he jumped to his feet and tried to run out of the cave, then yes, he might be in trouble. He understood that. But if he just kept sitting here, calmly, so calmly....he'd be able to look around him and notice things.

He'd be able to notice, for instance, that behind the wall of Roman brickwork the cave went on with no apparent end, just like the cave he'd found. That cave had gone back and back, and the ceilings had become lower, and the sides had closed in, but still Atalf and Ziegmunt had been able to keep crawling along in it. Then it had gotten too cold, and they'd run out of interest—no more stone soldiers in it, no sign of a horse. So this cave and that one really might run on through rocks and darkness until they joined. A person could hide in their depths if he got the chance, and even find his way out to safety....

The big man was talking again. Holding up that knife and sighting along the edge of it, and talking. "We got eighteen of them," he was saying "Eighteen of them in one night, in Metz."

"Eighteen of what?" Brother Arcadius asked politely. He'd managed to suppress a startled laugh. "Eighteen in one night...." It might have been Brother Marcus, the head cook of Spiritus Sanctus, reporting on how many mice Pangur Ban had killed the previous night. Every morning, standing in the breakfast line, Brother Arcadius was given the latest tally: *seventeen last night...twenty.... You won't believe this, Arcadius, but last night he got twenty-nine....*

By now Pangur Ban was probably back up at the monastery, prowling around with the vole or whatever it was in his mouth, assuming he'd caught it. And by now, Brother Silvanus, the head librarian, would surely be wondering where his assistant librarian might be. Except that today was the day the assistant librarian studied Hebrew with Father Julian, after which came a lesson in reasoning and then a chess game, which Father Julian would win in fifteen or so rapid moves. So Father Julian and not Brother Silvanus would miss him. Except that today was the day that Father Julian had postponed those lessons...postponed them until tomorrow.

"People," said the man on the bench.

People? What people? Brother Arcadius collected his straying thoughts with difficulty.

"Eighteen in one night," said the man on the bench again. "You know how you do it?"

"I...."

"You have to find the poor," said the man. "It won't work with anybody else. You find the poor where they cluster, under the bridges or down in the drains, or in a poorhouse if there is one. There's one in Metz. You go among them, and you talk with them, and you listen to them, and you always agree with what they say, see? If they like the king, or they like the pope, or they don't like them, or they think next year will be better, or it will be worse, or if they think they'd be better off in Aachen, or Cologne, you just nod and smile and say, 'Amen, my friend.'"

The man reached into the dark beside him and came up with a different whetstone. He studied it a moment, then pulled the blade against it with easy strokes. "And maybe you share a few bits of food with the young ones among them, say from seven on down," he said. "And then, when they all lie down to go to sleep, you lie down too. And then you get up, and you drift among them like a shadow, and—" He held up the knife, and grinned, and drew a finger across his throat. "If you do it right, there's never a sound out of them, except maybe a gurgle, now and then, or a sigh. And in the morning, where are you? You've washed the blood off yourself in the river, and you're gone."

"But...." Brother Arcadius struggled to find words. "Why?"

"Why?" The big man grinned again, immensely pleased with himself. "Because you've got the knife, see? And they're nothing."

"What do you mean, they're nothing?" This was just some made-up story. It had to be. It was perfectly true, of course, that people killed other people. They did it all the time. But not even the Danes went sneaking around in poorhouses, cutting people's throats because they were poor.

"They're just the poor," said the man. "So what good are they? Nobody thinks twice about them."

"But it's wrong!" cried Brother Arcadius. "And if that's what you do, you'll.... Don't you want to go to Heaven?"

The man's cheeks puffed out in a snorting laugh. "There isn't any Heaven."

"But of course there is!" cried Brother Arcadius. He was finally, genuinely, definitively shocked.

"Isn't," said the man calmly. He held up his knife and studied the blade again. Then he lowered it, and swiped it twice more against the whetstone.

"There *is*," said Brother Arcadius. Pulling himself together as best as he could, he tried to frame his words with the utmost care. "And we all get to go there," he said. He didn't believe those people who said otherwise. "It might take a while if we have to work off lots of sins, but we don't get shut out. If we stop doing wrong, and if we are truly sorry for—"

He broke off, for the hanging tendrils over the mouth of the cave were swept to one side again and a man, a blessed man, stepped in. Rescue, rescue at last!

Except it wasn't.

The newcomer looked from Brother Arcadius to the man on the bench, and then back to Brother Arcadius. "Where'd you get him?" he asked.

"He was on the path," said Brother Arcadius's captor. "Where've you been, Kem?"

"Looks like the wind could blow him away," said the man called Kem. "Where on the path, Hruk? Past the barrier?"

"Yes, he was past it," said—Hruk? Could anyone, even a remorseless slitter of throats, actually be named "Hruk"? The answer to that was obviously yes. Here sat the man with that name, and the name suited him. Kem, though, was an ordinary-looking man of moderately stocky build and medium height, with alert gray eyes. Maybe he was more reasonably-minded, too. Maybe he didn't know about the silent throat-slitting. Maybe he'd just let a person go. Maybe— "Anyway, I was just telling him about Metz. But I didn't tell him about Cologne or Aachen or Paris yet. Or London or—"

"What do you want to tell him all that for?" asked Kem mildly.

"Because I get a laugh out of it, watching his face go red and then white and then back to red again."

Brother Arcadius hadn't realized that his face had been doing that. Maybe it was doing that now. At any rate, he had better start thinking, hadn't he? Before Hruk and Kem here decided to turn on him. If they did. With that knife. Or that cudgel. Or that axe. It would be so frightening if that happened. And it would hurt so much. And it was so cold and hard and uncomfortable sitting on this rock. He forced himself speak up. "I imagine that some of those places are harder to work in than Metz," he said. He tried to maintain a conversational tone.

"'Bout the same," said Hruk.

"Do they all have poorhouses to stay in?" asked Brother Arcadius. He shifted about on his rock as much as he dared, trying to find a spot that wasn't so hard. He slid his feet sideways, too, because a crevice in the floor nearby, wider than most, was breathing dank air on his ankles.

"Not all of them, no," said Hruk. He swiped the knife against the whetstone three more times, and eyed the axe.

"Of course, I imagine that they all have very nice bridges to stay under," said Brother Arcadius. "My guess is that maybe you might be cramped in the drains."

"What he's doing," said Hruk to Kem, unexcitedly, "is he's trying to get us talking. Trying to string us along. Like What's-Her-Name. In the tale."

"Well, he's yours, anyway," said Kem. "Make up your mind how you want to deal with him."

"I'm thinking," said Hruk. "You could guard the way out, and I could get him scampering all around. That would be enjoyable."

"If there's time for that," said Kem. "But there may not be, because—"

"I'd better tell you," said Brother Arcadius—he swallowed hard and started over again. "I'd better tell you that up at the monastery, they have...they have a...." Hruk might know a tale or two, but so did he. His Mam had told him plenty of them, back in the days when he'd barely come up to her knees. "Up in the monastery, which is right up there beyond those willows, they have a stone. A big stone, made out of crystal. A seeing stone it is, a very magical thing. They look into it ten times an hour, all day and all night, and it shows them everything that's happening on the mountain. Right now they'll be looking in it, and they'll be seeing me sitting here, and they'll be seeing you, and hearing you too, because it's not just a seeing stone but a hearing stone, and—"

Hruk looked at Kem, and Kem looked back at Hruk. "Not likely," Hruk said.

"And if you just let me go, they'll see that you mean well, and I'm sure they'll return your horse and your soldier too," said Brother Arcadius.

Kem shrugged. "The legionary, you mean, and the Gaulish horse. Lived most of my life without 'em. I can live the rest of my life without them, too."

"And if they have you, then we don't have a thing to bargain with," put in Hruk. "A child could see it. But anyway, you're not getting out of here alive. Nobody sees us and lives. Nobody ever."

"Well, it must be hard for you to go to markets, then," cried Brother Arcadius. His best tries had come to nothing, and now what on earth was he supposed to do? "Killing all the merchants and all the shoppers besides, the moment they lay eyes on you."

"Don't be ridiculous," said Kem. "We don't do that."

"It's just people who ever see us doing our work," said Hruk. "Those are the ones we don't allow to live."

"Which brings me back to what I was saying before," Kem said to him. "They don't have any seeing stone up there, but they do have their routines. I think they'll be missing this one before too long. So—" He broke off. The courtyard bell was ringing up at Spiritus Sanctus. The clear tones floated over the land, calling the monks to prayer.

Brother Arcadius listened to it with inexpressible yearning, and also with new hope. It was more than a call to prayer. It was a chance for rescue, if he used the chance wisely. "It's the alarm bell," he said. "They've noticed I'm not where I should be, just like you said, and they've started the search."

"Hardly," said Kem "It's the call to vespers. Same thing every night. Monasteries are monasteries. The one up there's no different from the rest. You really need to stop lying, you know. Make up your mind that it will do you no good." He turned to Hruk. "So as I was saying—"

"Searching for me," insisted Brother Arcadius, "with huge, ferocious dogs. We keep hundreds of them."

"Oh yes," smiled Kem. "We hear them barking all the time."

"I hear them now," Hruk chuckled. "Rowf, rowf, rowf."

Kem's alert eyes crinkled briefly in amusement, but he shook his head. "We've wasted too much time here," he said to Hruk. "Remember those men we saw yesterday? Off to the west there, and we thought they were just moving on?"

Hruk nodded. "The three of them, right."

"Well, that's another thing I came in to tell you. I came across signs that they're probably still around. So we've got them to think about, and then there's the monks, if they do start searching for your little friend here. It's not a good situation."

"I guess not," said Hruk.

"I want to clear out of here now and just move on," Kem said. He was serious now, and full of quiet purpose.

I want you to clear out too, cried Brother Arcadius in silence from his rock. *I really do*. The dank air breathing up from the nearby crevice was getting colder and colder, but that was not the main reason why he felt as if he were freezing. Freezing all over his body, except for his head. That was burning. Frightened from head to foot, that's what he was. Frightened to think what this pair might decide to do next. They were so nastily calm about everything, so viciously matter-of-fact. If they'd shouted and roared like Danes, it would have been better.

He imagined leaping up, seizing Hruk's knife, and then what? Why, he'd drop it down the crevice there, that's what he'd do. It would just fit. That would leave the cudgel and the axe, but at least Hruk would have to get a new knife later on, and serve him right. But although the mind might come up with these fine ideas, a person would have to move to carry them out. The body of Brother Arcadius did not wish to move. Or rather, it wished to move, but it couldn't. All it could do was huddle in fear on its rock.

It could still see and hear, though. "Tie him up, legs and arms, so he can't move and waste time," Kem was saying.

"I wanted to watch him scamper," Hruk said with regret. "Once in a while it's so great, if they know what you're doing."

"Another time," said Kem. He watched from the mouth of the cave as Hruk reached under the bench once more and pulled out two lengths of rope. "Get him secured, and then I'll go out and watch to make sure we're alone. If I don't see anybody, you can have some time with him. If I do see anybody, I'll give my—"

"Your hawk cry," nodded Hruk. He was advancing on Brother Arcadius with his ropes. He was binding one trembling wrist to the other. He was bending to do the same to two frozen ankles, binding one to the other.

"My hawk cry," Kem said. He turned toward the back of the cave for a moment, listening. Then he relaxed. "Dripping water, back there. It almost sounded like—never mind. All right, you've got him. He's ready, that's good enough. Get to work on him, but if you hear the regular hawk cry, just cut his throat then and there. Don't lose any time. Drag him back there—"

Kem waved a hand toward the back of the cave, the part that lay in darkness behind the Roman wall. "Dump him into the drop-off. Don't fall in yourself. Escape through the caves. If you don't see me there at the other end, we'll meet up in the usual place. Now, I grant you it's unlikely, but if I give the cry without stopping, on and on, then don't waste time killing him, even. Just get out. Don't worry that he's seen us. First things first. We'll just lie low for a while. We've never killed anybody important. When it isn't anybody important, people forget. Listen for the hawk, all right? Three cries, a pause, then three cries again means kill him fast. Or cry, cry, cry, cry and so on without any pauses means just get out—do you hear?"

"I hear," said Hruk. "Hawk cry. Caves. Other end. Usual place." He picked up his knife from the bench and gave it a final swipe against the whetstone.

"Then enjoy," said Kem. "If there's time." He vanished into the evening darkness. Faint sounds came of upward motion on the fissured wall of rock outside.

Hruk grunted approvingly. "Like a monkey," he said. "He goes up those walls like you wouldn't believe. Brains too. A good partner."

Once again he advanced on Brother Arcadius. Knife in hand, he made a few slow cuts in the air, muttering to himself, thinking things through. "Eyes first.... No, I want him to see what's going on.... Nose first, then. Ears next. Then eyes...." He took a step back to think things through again. "There's no fun in fast, really," he mused. "The real fun's in slow. I'd like to do slow...."

Help me! wailed Brother Arcadius in silence, there on his rock. His nose! His ears! His eyes! It mustn't be! He didn't want to live even a heartbeat without them! *Father Julian! Brother Silvanus! Brother Salix, Brother Marcus, Brother Atalf, Brother Ziegmunt, help me! Brother Kongro, Brother Sifari, Brother Anybody—help me!* A big hand had his chin in an iron grip, tipping it back, clamping his jaws together. He could not so much as scream. His Mam, his brothers, his sisters, back there in Wessex.... Keti too.... Oh, they were going to miss him so much. And wonder what had become of him, if he never got found. And if he was found, they would all be so sad. And Pangur Ban would be sad too, wouldn't he? Terribly sad he would be, terribly, terribly sad. *Mam, Father Julian, somebody! Help me! Heaven help me!*

Bound though he was, he struggled to get away. He scraped himself sideways over the rock. His eyes squeezed shut for fear of seeing the knife. Then they flew open for fear that he wouldn't see it. Above him, his cruel tormentor gave a laugh of delight and bent closer. Struggling was almost as good as scampering. Eyes shut, eyes open, the gloating face above him, the rock, the floor, and then again the gloating face, the floor—he was being pulled this way and that in Hruk's search for the best position—*Heaven help me!* he begged. The face, the floor, the rock, and the floor again.... *Mam! Father Julian! Somebody! Help me!*

It shot from behind the Roman wall then, the small dark shape hurtling across the floor, a tilted stream of motion in his frantic sight. A larger and whiter stream of motion came just behind it. Hruk was a thing in their way and nothing more. Straight up his back and down his front those two streams went, pursued and pursuer, as if he were merely a road made just for them. They vanished again into darkness. Hruk flung out his arms in shock. The knife went flying. It clattered to the floor somewhere behind the rock.

Hruk stared open-mouthed from one empty hand to the other. Beyond him in the darkness a wild commotion of snarls and pounces was going on. From somewhere outside came the hawk cry, again and again. Over and over it came with never a pause, its urgency mounting. Wild-eyed, Hruk turned and fled past the Roman wall into the depths of the cave. Kem's hawk cry sounded from farther and farther away, until there was silence.

Brother Arcadius rolled off the rock and landed behind it. Righting himself with difficulty, he groped on elbows and knees for the knife he'd heard fall. The hurtling shapes that he'd seen, the scuffling and pouncing going on in the far corner, everything that had happened—none of it had any meaning. His one idea was to find the knife and drop it into that crevice—the one that had breathed cold air at him for so long. And now he had it, the knife, but his bound hands wouldn't grasp it. So he nudged it along instead. And here was the crevice, and here was its dank clammy chill, but the knife caught on the edge and wouldn't go in. And then it did go in, but only part way. So the crevice was not as deep as a person might think. And over there in the darkness, the white shape had again misjudged a lunge. The dark shape flashed past the knife and slipped down into safety at last.

Brother Arcadius collected some of his terrified wits. He gave thanks to the powers above who had saved his life, and his eyes and his ears and his nose and who knew what all. Reason slowly came back to him, and recognition. "Pangur Ban," he said. "Oh, Pangur Ban!"

Pangur came out from the darkness, breathing hard. With a single disgruntled glance at the crevice—he was a sensible cat and could accept final defeat—he padded up to Brother Arcadius and snuggled close. It had been an epic hunt, a hunt to end all hunts, a hunt of long, creeping approaches and tense, crouching silences, a hunt of sudden wild bursts of speed and tremendous pounces, a hunt for poets to sing about forever, and the signs were all over him—from the grass stains and burrs and smears of mud that he'd started out with, to the berry-juice stains and cave-soot and sticktights and brambles that he'd accumulated along the way. He was a terrible mess, and he had never looked so beautiful. "Thank you, Pangur Ban," murmured Brother Arcadius. "Oh thank you, thank you." But he owed his rescue to another creature also. "And thank you too," he croaked down to the vole. "Thank you, vole, and long life." It was wondrous how somehow the canny, fast-flying little creature had held out so long against a mighty hunter like Pangur Ban.

But what was he doing, just sitting here like a fool? What if Hruk and Kem came back for their belongings? Or to finish him off after all? Reluctantly, Brother Arcadius went about the difficult business of getting to his feet. He wasn't just tied with ropes, he was tied with the aftermath of a long, long fear. Tied with ropes...it occurred to him that knives cut ropes, and that a knife, in fact, was sticking up from the crevice right beside him. "You've got to think faster than that, Tammis

Scholar," he muttered to himself. With many awkward movements, he managed to lift up the knife between his hands and aim it at the ropes that tied his ankles together.

But aiming was not enough. The knife wobbled in his tethered grip and refused to bite down as it should. And now it occurred to him that he really should try to get rid of the axe and the cudgel too. So he let the knife fall and tried to stand up again, but then gave that up and reached for the knife again, because he had to get rid of that too, didn't he? Except that he'd better cut himself free with it first.... Only this time he couldn't grab onto it. It slid away from his scrabbling fingers time after time. But then....

But then!

There came a sudden sound of footsteps on the path outside, and the curtain of shrubbery was swept aside again, and his heart stopped....

But it was not Hruk or Kem who stood there peering in, but a stranger. A rather sooty stranger, with two other sooty strangers behind him. The worn-out mind of Brother Arcadius managed to draw a reasonable conclusion. "Would you be the charcoal burners then?" he asked.

The stranger in front, much older than the others, didn't bother to confirm the obvious. "Why are you tied up?" he asked.

Upon which, Brother Arcadius poured out the whole story. Before he was halfway done, the eldest charcoal burner had picked up the knife and knelt down beside him and cut through his bonds. And just as the last rope fell away, more footsteps were heard stomping down the path. It was Brother Atalf and Brother Ziegmunt, looking for him.

"How did you find me?" Brother Arcadius asked.

"Missed you at prayers," Brother Atalf said. Brother Ziegmunt nodded. "Brother Zossimus did. Not my brother and me."

"Well, how did you know where to look?"

"Brother Kongro. He said you took the path east of the pine woods. When you went on your walk. There's lots of people looking for you." The big man—a blessed sight to the eye he was, right now—looked down upon Brother Arcadius with disapproval. "You caused a lot of trouble."

"I know," said Brother Arcadius. "I really know." There were times when Brother Atalf was simply right. Then he and Atalf and Ziegmunt and the three charcoal burners set off for Spiritus Sanctus to tell the whole story. They carried the axe and the cudgel and the ropes and the bench and the knife back with them. Pangur Ban followed behind. When the path grew quiet again, the vole crept back to her nest through the tangle of willows, a long, long way, and received a great welcome from her broodlings there.

And up at the monastery, without delay, word was sent out to cities all through the lands, telling of Hruk and Kem, and their foul deeds, and what they looked like. And they were soon apprehended in the city of Lyon, those scoundrels, and hanged in the public square, and serve them right! And Pangur Ban received high praise for his wonderful deed, and was given two or three extra servings of fish paste and herbed game stew, but it took a good month, and the full art of Brother Salix the medicus, to get him all white again.

* * *

"And never mind about the mushrooms," said Brother Salix. He trained his fierce gaze on the repentant assistant librarian. "Just let us know where you're going, next time. That's the new rule."

* * *

"Those villains of yours," said Brother Silvanus, "turns out they attended the monastery school in Metz for quite a few years. Apparently they didn't take to the training." He frowned across the library table at Brother Arcadius. "From now on, Mighty Caesar, you're to tell people where you are going before you go. I'm too old to come to terms with a new regime."

* * *

Brow knotted, Brother Atalf picked up the big tub of rocks as if it held feathers and thought about the strangeness of assistant librarians. It was a good thing Arcaperus had that cat to help him, he grumbled to himself. Otherwise he'd be turning up missing every day. With these thoughts lodged firmly in mind, Atalf strode off toward his brother Ziegmunt, who was waiting for him to help patch up a barn wall.

* * *

Days had gone by, but Brother Arcadius still couldn't get over how once he'd saved Pangur Ban's life, and now Pangur Ban had saved his—accidentally, true, but still! He cast a loving glance at the cat of his heart, reclining there on the library windowsill. "Well, you didn't come back with a vole, Pangur Ban," he said, "but at least you came back with me."

"Meow," said Pangur Ban.

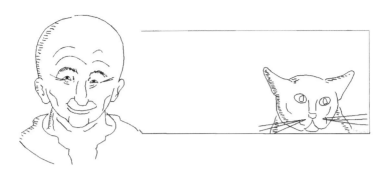

THE ROUNDNESS OF THE WORLD

In which many wonders are revealed, and secrets
are told, and nothing goes along in the usual way

AD 901

"**Y**ou should have noticed, Arcadius, that taking my bishop would expose your queen and make it impossible to protect your king." Father Julian, head of Spiritus Sanctus monastery, aimed his intense dark gaze across the chessboard at Brother Arcadius, assistant librarian.

Many such gazes had been sent across that board over the past three years, and always at the same recipient. It wasn't that Brother Arcadius was unwilling to learn. Obedience was his first nature and always had been, at least most of the time. And it wasn't that he was stupid. He also took lessons in extremely advanced Greek and Hebrew from Father Julian, and excelled in them. He hoped to excel in the arts of reasoning as well someday—or at least Father Julian hoped that someday he'd do so. In Father Julian's view, chess games were one means to that end. In Brother Arcadius's view—

He'd vowed from the beginning to improve his game for Father Julian's sake, if not for his own. But the doings of pawns and queens and castles and all of that always evoked in him a feeling of....nothing. He found it hard to keep his mind on them.

Today seemed to be worse than usual. Outside it was serene high summer, with blue skies above, golden peacefulness below, and stately processions of clouds along the horizon. There was no accounting for the feeling of oddness within him, the feeling that something *different* was going to happen. It was the sort of feeling a person might fall prey to now and then in spring or in fall, on the days when soft winds whispered disturbingly of great changes to come, and hearts stirred in response.

Brother Arcadius wondered if growing older might have something to do with it. On the day after the day when spring came round again he'd be twenty. Twenty was a considerable age. When he turned twenty, he'd still be the youngest monk in the monastery by a full ten years, but no one could say that he wasn't grown up.

"A far better move would have been to...."

Thoughts of the library kept distracting him also. After all, he was a librarian first and foremost, with five hundred books in his care, and one of those books, with a wonderful piece of poetry in it, had not that long ago been bitterly lost—fed by a horrible mischance to the monastery goats!

To the *goats*!

"Whereupon your bishop, thus....."

Oh, if only he had that lost book back again! If only he could leaf through it and see if, by chance, more poetry might be hidden within its pages!

"...Had you taken my pawn before I brought out my bishop...."

Another cause for distraction was that the bell in the courtyard watchtower had rung some time ago, signifying that Brother Kongro and Brother Sifari, the day watchmen, were offering the monastery's hospitality to somebody. Some traveler, or maybe travelers. Nobody of much importance in the worldly scheme of things, because the bell had only rung once. But it was always interesting when travelers stopped by. Interesting to see them, and to hear their tales of where they'd been and what they'd done. Spiritus Sanctus being off the regular track for most purposes, wayfarers didn't happen by all that often.

"Your move then, Arcadius. Remember what I just told you, and think carefully."

Brother Arcadius poised his hand over the pawn he was tempted to advance, and thought carefully. Of chess, only of chess, not of strange stirrings in the heart, or turning twenty, or lost books with pieces of poems in them, or travelers, or....

"Make your move, Arcadius." Father Julian spoke calmly, as he always did, no matter what the situation. He never let himself be distracted, that was for sure. He never let his feelings get the upper hand, either. He hadn't even looked up at the sound of the courtyard bell. All right, move that pawn to *there*, thought Brother Arcadius. No, no, this other one then, but maybe not? Consider the horseman—no, it had been taken. Consider the....

Move the castle, then. Move it to that square right there.

"Check."

Brother Arcadius suppressed a deep, deep sigh.

"Concentrate."

He concentrated, fruitlessly. Time passed, and then more time passed, and then still more. He felt Father Julian's steady dark gaze upon him, he felt the force of what Father Julian wasn't saying. Some of it could be guessed at, but the rest?

The rest was like chess. You could guess, but you wouldn't know. In Brother Arcadius's first year at the monastery, Father Julian had once appeared to lose his temper, but his apparent rage had been deliberate, to make an effect. Otherwise, day in, day out, he rarely ever either smiled or frowned. For the most part, his dark eyes sometimes grew darker, maybe, or sometimes seemed less dark...maybe. But different degrees of darkness, if such there were, never gave any clear signal of anything. If and when he showed his feelings, it was never by much.

Time crawled. The heart-stirrings, the sense of oddness and longing increased. The chess disaster continued.

There came a sudden sound of voices from the adjoining room. Father Julian's secretary, Brother Dietrich, was talking to...Brother Kongro, the watchman? What was Kongro doing away from the courtyard? Well, he must be heading back there, for his voice was receding. And now there came a quiet but rapid knocking at the door —the secretary's. Brother Dietrich was a forthcoming, sleek, trim, capable monk whose robe always mysteriously remained free of all wrinkles, no matter how small. In a conscious effort to emulate Father Julian's calm manner and reasoned responses, he always knocked quietly. Brother Arcadius had never known him to knock rapidly.

"Yes?" called Father Julian.

Brother Dietrich opened the door just slightly, as if he were trying to block it. He looked flustered. He'd never looked flustered before. "Excuse me, Father," he said, "but there's a person here who insists you'll want to see him. They couldn't persuade him to wait, out there in the courtyard, so Brother Kongro brought him to me."

"No such person is expected," said Father Julian. He moved his queen ahead one square for their customary end, and began placing the chessmen back on the board, one by one, in their proper places. Some other monk, or Keti, the kitchen boy, would lose to him more interestingly some other time.

"He says you'll want to see him now," said Brother Dietrich. Then he gasped, "Wait—you can't—you need permiss—" The door swung back. An old man stood on the threshold. He was short—shorter than Brother Arcadius, and barely taller than tiny little Brother Zossimus, the woodcarver. But his chest and shoulders were broad and his limbs, for his size, were rugged. He was barefoot and bare legged, and the short robe he wore was stained with the sweat and grime of long travel. His head was very round and entirely bald. His ears and nose were large, his smile was wide, and his eyes were shining.

Father Julian stood up so fast that his chair tipped over. He paid no attention to it. He rushed across the room, dropped to his knees, and seized the old man's gnarled hands and kissed them again and again. "You came yourself," he said in a hoarse whisper. "You came yourself!" Brother Dietrich and Brother Arcadius stared at each other in bewilderment. The scene before them defied all understanding. It was nothing that either of them ever could have imagined.

"Well, I wanted to see you again, Julian," the old man said. "But since I've only gotten as far as your doorstep, I'm not quite here yet, am I?"

Father Julian collected himself, somewhat. He got to his feet. "Come in," he said, still in that strange hoarse voice. He drew the old man into the room and dismissed Brother Dietrich was a flick of the hand. Brother Dietrich withdrew in haste, closing the door behind him. Brother Arcadius retreated into a corner and stood there. He didn't think he should stay, but he hadn't been dismissed, either. He couldn't just leave without being told to do so.

"I never meant that you should come yourself," Father Julian said to the old man. "It's too far, too much to ask."

"Everything went very well," the old man replied. "You needn't think twice about it. And in a moment you won't, because see what I've brought you." He reached into the threadbare bag that was slung over his shoulder. He pulled out a lump of something. It looked like a small, grimy rock. "It's wax," he said, as if he were answering a spoken question. He broke it open with one smart rap against Father Julian's writing table and extracted a wad of brownish cloth that was wrapped around something. He unwrapped the something. It looked like some kind of whitish material, folded again and again into a thick square. He unfolded it and smoothed it out on the table.

Brother Arcadius had never seen anything like it. It was like cloth, in a way, but different. It was covered with strange designs, and also with writing. "It's called 'paper,'" the old man said. With his eyes shining more brightly than ever, he handed whatever it was to Father Julian. Father Julian scanned the words and the designs in obvious disbelief. He scanned everything again, much more slowly. He muttered something to himself. Then he turned to the old man again.

"Whose is it?" he asked.

"The one you were hoping for. He never travels, but he sends you his regards."

"He's proficient in Greek."

"Oh, very much so. He would have preferred to write in his native tongue—"

"Which, of course, I wouldn't be able to understand," said Father Julian. "And he gives a solution?"

"Yes, in that very small printing, there on the back, arranged to resemble a flower. That's to help hide it from you until you're ready to see it."

"I—" Father Julian didn't finish whatever he meant to say. He strode over to the chess board instead and began setting the pieces down in a new pattern, glancing from them to the words and designs on the page of paper and then back again, and muttering distractedly to himself, as if the rest of the room had ceased to exist. Brother Arcadius felt as if the foundations of his world had toppled. Father Julian did not behave in this way. He shouldn't behave in this way. He *couldn't* behave in this way. Yet there he was, staring and muttering and biting his lips and looking as if he'd gone mad.

"He'll be all right," said the old man, smiling. "I brought him a thing he's long set his heart on—a chess problem devised by the world's greatest master, who lives a long way from here. It shows the layout of the pieces toward the end of a game, and says that Black can checkmate in three moves. Or maybe four. I don't play at that level myself, so I don't really remember. Anyway, I believe it will keep our dear fellow busy for quite a while." He held out his hand. "And you'll be Brother Arcadius. Come along with me while I apologize to the nice secretary."

"But who—" Brother Arcadius tried to frame a sensible question, and tripped over his tongue and over his churning thoughts. The old man knowing his name—well, that was no mystery. Brother Dietrich would have mentioned it to him, when he was trying to keep this stranger from intruding on the game. *He's busy now, he's giving a lesson to Brother Arcadius, our assistant librarian.*

But was this person a Julian too? Some sort of kinsman? A duke or a king? A former pope? Looking like some wretched beggar, as in some tale? As when some god or someone like that appeared in a shabby disguise, to test people? He'd come from far away? *How* far? As far away, maybe, as even Constantinople? And was he going to introduce himself, or what?

Brother Arcadius followed the old man out to the other room. Brother Dietrich sat there in stupefied misery, biting his nails. He jumped up as they entered. In silence his trembling lips formed the word *bewitched*.

The old man looked at him kindly. "I promise you he's not bewitched," he said. "Call in to him if you want to."

Brother Dietrich rushed to the door. "Father…. Are you bewitched?"

"No!" snapped Father Julian, without looking up. "Go away."

Brother Dietrich slunk back to his chair. He sat down, but he looked like a horse getting ready to bolt.

"He's perfectly fine, you see, but he's concentrating," the old man told him. "He's used to figuring things out in a flash, as I'm sure you know, but I've brought him a challenge—a chess challenge—that he's finding difficult. As he wanted me to. It's my present to him." He looked from one stunned face to the other. "He was my dearly-loved student, you see, back when he was fifteen."

"You were his *teacher*?" asked Brother Arcadius, dumbfounded. The question burst forth before he could stop it. He hadn't meant to be rude, but weren't teachers supposed to look…well, more dignified? Not that there was anything wrong, really, with this person's odd barefootedness and his odd short robe and his general griminess. Maybe he'd met with some sort of disaster on the way here. If he had, why wasn't he saying something about it? The differentness that the day had promised—yes, it was here.

"It follows that I was his teacher, yes," said the old man, with a smile. "I was also—I suppose I should apologize for it—the culprit who introduced him to chess."

"I—we—" Brother Arcadius stammered. By rights it was Brother Dietrich who ought to be talking, but the secretary seemed to have lost the power of speech. "I don't know who you are."

"Sometimes I don't know, either," the old man said. "But if you

298

mean that you'd just like a name to call me by, 'Nikko' will do as well as any." He turned to Brother Dietrich. "Be of good cheer! Father Julian will give his mind its long-deferred workout, and then he'll be himself again. You'll see. Meanwhile, Brother Arcadius is going to escort me to that beautiful lake I spied on the way here, so that I can get cleaned up. If you want to talk to me, that's where I'll be. Or I'll be up on that knoll across the path from the lake, drying off. My need for a bath is urgent, I think you'll agree. Teachers should look like teachers, no question about it. At least when they can." With that, he turned to the door. "Shall we go?" He held out his hand so invitingly that Brother Arcadius fell in behind him and followed him over the threshold without hesitation.

He felt that he had to, but did he want to? Toppled foundations or no, he decided that yes, he did. He wanted Father Julian to be himself again, that was for sure, but he also wanted to walk to the lake with Father Julian's teacher, this Nikko. Except that he wasn't going to call any teacher just "Nikko." It was going to be "*Master* Nikko" or nothing at all. And a more dignified name than "Nikko" would be very welcome, but "Master Nikko" would have to do for now. It felt good, very good, to be walking along beside him, no matter how odd he looked. Ordinarily Brother Arcadius preferred to just blend in with everyone else around him, and liked to think that lately, he'd been doing that much more successfully. He wasn't blending in now, but he didn't care.

Did people feel like that when they'd been bewitched? Had Master Nikko bewitched him, if not Father Julian? He considered the question briefly and then gave it up. The blue sky,...the fine fresh air,...those slow processions of beautiful clouds along the horizon...the golden day...the undreamed of but very welcome escape from that chess game.... It was like poetry, walking along with Master Nikko side by side, heedless of perplexed sidelong glances from those passing by, heedless of things like *blending in* and *not standing out*.

Behind them, Father Julian's door slammed shut and a distraught figure hurried toward the infirmary—Brother Dietrich, cutting across the paths with headlong strides, his robe flying out behind him. "There he goes, fetching your medicus," Master Nikko said. "I thought he would, didn't you? I was sorry to leave him in such an unhappy state, but I want to get on. The refectory that I came through on the way here with that diligent watchman of yours—is that the quickest way to the lake?"

"It's almost the quickest," said Brother Arcadius. He supposed it was good that Brother Dietrich was running for help. He himself just wanted to keep on walking. But how did Master Nikko know that it was the medicus who was being fetched? There was no sign on the infirmary saying "infirmary." "If we go through the kitchen garden, that's quicker still."

"Then let's go through the kitchen garden," Master Nikko said. "Although I enjoyed my walk through the refectory. It was hurried, but I got a good glimpse of the image of Charles Martel."

"He was our founder," Brother Arcadius said. On behalf of all Spiritus Sanctus, it seemed right to try to put in an intelligent word. "It shows him receiving light from the Holy Spirit."

"It does indeed," said Master Nikko. "Although he mostly preferred to receive it in smaller amounts." Here was another puzzle, for Charles Martel had been dead for a hundred and fifty years, and all the books said that he was very pious. So why would Master Nikko think otherwise?

But here was the old green door to the walled garden. Brother Arcadius tugged it open, still puzzling things out, and they went through. Master Nikko gazed about with delight, and rightly so. The garden was in its full glory at this time of year, a shimmering tapestry of greens and golds and purples, with touches of scarlet and white, all intermingled with glancing sunlight and violet shade. The air was rich with the song of birds and the droning of bees, and with the scent of fertile soil, dark, soft, and warmed by the gentle sun.

Cinder paths divided the garden into sections. On one of these paths Keti the kitchen boy was filling a bark basket with pea pods. He was all but done with the task. The basket was close to being full.

"Master Nikko, this is Keti," said Brother Arcadius. Keti scrambled to his feet and ducked his head. "He works in the kitchen, and he also studies Latin with me, and reasoning and, um, chess with Father Julian, and ciphering and the abacus with Brother Dietrich back there, and with our medicus."

The old man looked at Keti with assessing eyes. "A sharp mind and a keen learner," he said gravely.

"That's very true," said Brother Arcadius. He caught Keti's eye. *Keti, you need to say thank you.* Shy Keti managed a hesitant "Thank you, Master." That was a proper and courteous reply, and about as many words as Keti could be expected to say to a stranger who was, well, so very strange.

"But who's this?" Master Nikko asked. His eyebrows went up. He was suddenly very intent. A white cat had come into view from behind a patch of fennel and was approaching slowly, step by delicate step, as if in a ceremony. When he came to the big crocks of catmint farther on, he broke step and made a quick, wide detour around them. Then he came on again, step by ceremonious step. "Who is this...personage?" Master Nikko asked again.

"Oh, it's our cat, Pangur Ban!" Keti said in a joyous rush. Brother Arcadius stared at him. Not only had Keti spoken without hesitation, but now he was going on. "He works in the kitchen, like me. He's our mouser. He caught fifteen mice last night, and that's all that came out."

"What sort of name is 'Pangur Ban'?" Master Nikko asked. His eyes remained fixed on Pangur, as Pangur's were fixed on him. There was no feeling at all here of a cat approaching a person. It was rather as if two...well, all right...*personages* were taking the measure of each other.

"It—" Keti started to answer the question, but then stopped short. He looked over to Brother Arcadius for guidance. Had he been rude, saying so much to this stranger? Was it right for him to answer? Brother Arcadius smiled at him reassuringly. *Keti, that's good. Go on.* Not in a joyous rush now, but with dignity, feeling the responsibility of speaking for his teacher, Keti drew a breath and went on. "It's an Irish name, and it means that he is white. My teacher named him, and my teacher is Irish. Also, my teacher saved his life. On a boat, when a sailor was going to kill him. My teacher took him away from the sailor, and brought him here."

"But it seems you have several teachers," Master Nikko said.

"I mean my first teacher, Brother Arcadius," Keti told him.

"So one hunter reached out to help another, then," Master Nikko said. "That's as it should be." Factually-minded Keti studied the ground. His teacher was a teacher, not a hunter. But Brother Arcadius took the meaning and nodded to himself. He'd never thought of himself that way before, but yes, he was a hunter—a hunter of words and books and poetry and learning, just as Pangur was a hunter of mice, not to mention other things too. Like birds. And voles. It was a thought that accorded with the odd and different feeling of the day— with the *poetic* feeling of the day. He tucked it away in his mind to think about later.

Meanwhile, that hunter Pangur Ban had settled into a pose of quiet alertness nearby, sitting up straight, forepaws close together, tail tucked neatly around him, eyes never once leaving Master Nikko, this curious stranger. The old man made no attempt to call him closer, but his whole attention was on him all the same. "Does he always dodge away from catmint like that?"

Keti showed clear signs of being all talked out, so Brother Arcadius stepped in to answer the question. "Always. He detests it."

"It's more as if he respects some great power in it," Master Nikko said haltingly. He frowned. "But power in catmint? It's good for the common afflictions of daily life – toothache, upset stomach, and such. And of course it makes most cats delirious. But otherwise—" He shrugged. "But time's going on," he said. "I should get to the lake." As if in response to these words, Pangur Ban rose and stretched himself once, then went on his way, ears forward, belly close to the ground. A suspicious rustling near the garden wall had claimed one hunter's rapt attention.

With a start, Brother Arcadius remembered the library. He was due to be back there soon. He turned to Keti. "Keti, if it's all right with the kitchen, will you run and tell Brother Silvanus not to expect me? Or ask Brother Kongro to tell him? I'm with a, a friend of Father Julian's, and I'll make up all the work I missed tomorrow. Oh, and if anyone needs to find me, I'll be at the lake, or up on the knoll. Better hurry."

Keti dashed off.

"He'll remember all that," Master Nikko said. He spoke with certainty.

"Oh, absolutely," Brother Arcadius said. He couldn't imagine what it would be like to be Father Julian's teacher, but teaching Keti was an absolute pleasure, that was for sure. "He could remember ten times that, word for word."

They walked on, leaving the garden by the farther gate. Master Nikko was silent. He still seemed to be pondering the question of catmint. Brother Arcadius therefore was silent too. They walked past the goat pen where the poem had been destroyed. The goats were walking around and around in circles, but when Master Nikko approached, they stood still and looked at him intently. Brother Arcadius took careful note of it, but Master Nikko just nodded and walked on by. They came to the pasture. Off in the distance Father Julian's splendid mule, the one with the coat of deep rich brown and the showy white splotch on its hip, abruptly looked up from its gazing and stared their way. "A fine creature, and the right choice for that journey," murmured Master Nikko.

The goats, the mule, and now this talk of "that journey"— Brother

Arcadius added these things to a mental list that was growing long. But maybe some of it could be explained. The mule had played a great part indeed in a crucial rescue, and maybe Father Julian, in one of his letters....

"No," said Master Nikko. "Julian never writes to me about monastery business," he said. "Indeed, he rarely writes to me at all. He wouldn't know where to reach me, most of the time. Earnest wishes for my good health, respectful inquiries about the chess problem I promised to send him—that's what his letters consist of and nothing more."

I didn't ask him about it, I didn't, thought Brother Arcadius. *I'm sure I didn't, and I won't ask him now.* They walked on in silence until, rounding a bend, they saw the lake before them.

"Ah, here we are!" cried Master Nikko. Hurrying forward, he reached the stony shore before Brother Arcadius and went straight into the water. Robe, shoulder bag, tunic, breeches, and all, he waded out to a rock a good twenty long paces or more away from the land. The water out there was already up to his shoulders, and it was cold water too, as Brother Arcadius knew well. But Master Nikko did not so much as flinch. With just his head and shoulders showing above the water, he stripped down to his bare skin and placed his dripping clothes and shoulder bag upon the rock. From his bag he took out a hunk of white stuff. He rubbed it between his hands and over his head.

Was it some sort of soap, then? Brother Arcadius wondered. Spiritus Sanctus had soap, made by Brother Salix, but it was soft, runny stuff, not any hard lump. Master Nikko bent this way and that, cleaning himself from head to foot. Cleaning his garments, too, rubbing them well with the soap or whatever it was, plunging them up and down in the water, then laying them back on the rock when he judged them done.

Brother Arcadius watched him closely. Master Nikko was safe enough, he supposed, as long as he stayed by the rock, but if he tried to go farther out, or if he accidentally stepped into a deep spot.... Brother Arcadius did not know how to swim. Splashing around near the shore was one thing, but going as far as the unknown terrain around the rock was quite another. If he had to go rescue the strange old man...the very strange old man...the man Father Julian had knelt down to....

Well, there was that long fallen branch not far from the water. He picked his way rapidly toward it over the stones. If he got it in the water, he could hang on to it and paddle over to Master Nikko in advance of need, and Master Nikko could grab it, and they'd paddle back safely to shore. He reached it and dragged it toward the water as fast as he could—it was very much heavier than it looked, and didn't slide all that quickly over the stones.

His mind was churning. Father Julian, Keti...people didn't act like themselves around Master Nikko. Cats didn't act like themselves. Goats and mules, even, didn't act like themselves. And Master Nikko answered questions before they'd even been asked, and knew things he couldn't have known, and he had come from far away...how far away? And would he be offended if a person politely tried to get a few straight answers? Reaching the water's edge, Brother Arcadius looked up from the branch he was dragging and froze in alarm. No old man was in sight anywhere! Master Nikko was gone!

Yes, gone—but beyond the rock, a wavering track on the water indicated that something large was swimming beneath the surface. Then the old man bobbed into view, smiling and waving. With swift strokes he swam back to the rock. Pulled his breeches back on in the concealing depths of the water. Picked up his robe, tunic, and bag from the rock. Waded dripping back to shore. Took in the branch and the agitated and now somewhat damp assistant librarian in one quick glance.

"A very kind thought," he said, "and I do thank you. It could well have made the difference between life and death. But there's a long spur of land out there that I could have walked back on. My head would have been above water all the way." His smile darkened and his expression became almost somber. "I don't take risks with myself, I assure you," he said. "Or at least I try not to. Come, let's dry off on the knoll."

They climbed the long slope to the broad top of the knoll. There were no trees up there, only low-lying juniper bushes that did not block the sun. A warmish breeze stirred ceaselessly through them. Master Nikko spread out his wet robe and tunic on one of them. Then he reached into his wet bag and brought out a new thing, not soap, but a small wooden figure. "I stopped to talk with your woodcarver when I was passing by," he said. "Brother Zossimus, a good man. He wanted to give me one of his saints. I disappointed him greatly by choosing this." He handed the figure over to Brother Arcadius.

"But it's not finished," Brother Arcadius said. The little figure, darkened and damp from its soaking, was more like a simple oblong than any saint. The features were mere markings, hardly like features at all, and the robe merged roughly into the base. "Um...which saint is it supposed to be?"

"That's not been decided yet," said Master Nikko. "But I'd like it to dry out awhile in the sunlight. I'll set it down over there by your Saint George."

"There's a long drop there," Brother Arcadius warned him. "Watch out for it." Master Nikko had said that he didn't take risks, but not far from where he was heading, the knoll fell sharply away fifty or sixty feet to lower ground. There was something else to think about, too. Once again Master Nikko appeared to know something he couldn't know. There really was a grotto dedicated to Saint George over there, but from here it looked like an ordinary big rock and nothing more.

"I'll be careful, I assure you," Master Nikko said. He went over to the grotto. Brother Arcadius framed and reframed his growing list of questions. He felt as if he were back by the lake again, getting ready to plunge in, but without the branch. Soon he could be in deep waters indeed, if he wasn't careful. If he offended Master Nikko...made him angry...ruined the bright day....

The old man set his saint down in the sunlight, then came back and sat down in a patch of soft-fronded yarrow. He leaned back for a moment and studied the clouds that were slowly moving along the horizon. He cocked an ear toward distant noises that came from the world down below. From the foot of the knoll's sheer drop, but at some distance away, faint thuds could be heard as of some sort of heavy work being done.

That would be Brother Atalf and Brother Ziegmunt, most likely, thought Brother Arcadius. He frowned inwardly at the thought of them, just for a moment. Not that he held unmonklike grudges against them—he didn't!—but through his own fault, they'd caused his book, with that wonderful piece of poetry in it, and maybe more poems in it too, to be destroyed. Destroyed, and they'd never seemed to feel that it mattered at all.

"To be oblivious is to be human, I suppose," Master Nikko said. He stopped watching the clouds and turned to look at Brother Arcadius instead. His keen gaze was steady and kind. "Ask what you want to," he said.

Brother Arcadius's heart began to beat faster. The question he most wanted to ask, should he ask it first? *Master Nikko, are you a...?* He decided he shouldn't. Best to start with something more ordinary. He squared his shoulders and managed to get the words out. "Master Nikko, you've traveled so far.... Have you ever been as far as Constantinople?"

"I've been there often," said Master Nikko. "And you want to know what it's like there, and so I'll try to tell you." He spoke as if choosing each word with the greatest care. "Much of it is crowded, noisy, and dirty, like any city. The rich part of it is like a treasure trove. The buildings are plated with gold and studded with gems. The dome of the great basilica with its splendid colors weighs half the earth, almost, yet when you stand beneath it and gaze up at it, it seems to float in the air. The man who constructed your monastery—a Master Nardo, wasn't it? Of Cremona?—he would have been spellbound by it. And there are pictures made of tiny chips of colored glass that show the emperors and empresses in their finery." Master Nikko smiled to himself. "Justinian, Theodora...they gleam and shine in the pictures and look truly alive, and their dark eyes are the very image of the eyes that discomfort you across that chess board, although as far as I know there isn't any connection...."

Brother Arcadius barely heard these last words. "Dark eyes" and "chess board," even, passed him by. Caught up in what he wanted to ask next, he almost forgot about being polite. "And the libraries?" he urged. "Did they let you into the libraries?"

Master Nikko came back into the world with a "huh!" of amusement. "Never did," he said. "Just as I think you've heard, libraries are for the very privileged few in Constantinople. But learned theologians are everywhere, arguing with each other and splitting hairs. Living books, you could call them, if you care for that kind of book."

Brother Arcadius didn't want to hear more about any argumentative theologians. He'd met one when he was seventeen. He fervently hoped he wouldn't meet another. And he was sorry, very sorry, about the libraries, but there were more questions to ask, and time was fleeting. There went the bell, ringing for mid-afternoon prayers. He bowed his head and prayed briefly. He'd have to make it up another time. For right now.... "And have you gone beyond Constantinople, Master Nikko?"

"Oh, time and again I have," the old man said. "Too many times I have. But don't be misled if I don't seem excited about it. Constantinople is a wonder, and there are plenty of wonders beyond it. You can go by ship to some of those places, but I generally walk. Or ride a mule or a horse or a camel, sometimes, but not very often—"

A camel, mused Brother Arcadius. How strange it would be to ride on a camel. There was a picture of one in one of the library's travel books, looking quite a lot like a very short-eared mule, with short, stumpy legs like a badger's, and three humps on its back, and a very long curving neck.

"Their necks are long, but their legs are actually longer," smiled Master Nikko. "And some have one hump, some have two, but none of them have three. If there were a bare patch of dirt here to draw on, I'd draw you a picture myself. They're fine, useful animals, much regarded in those parts. At any rate, one way or another, from Constantinople I cross over to the land of the beautiful horses, and go east a long way through the land of the gentle sages, and then head on to the land of the next farthest song."

"And what song would that be?" asked Brother Arcadius, enthralled. It seemed to him that even the sunlight was listening, that even the clouds had slowed in their stately progression. The sounds of Atalf's and Ziegmunt's labors seemed to come from another world.

"I'm not sure that it is a song," Master Nikko said. "The language is very complicated in those parts, and I've never mastered all of its ins and outs. But 'next-farthest song' is what it sounds like to me. 'China,' some people there call it. It's where paper comes from, and where Father Julian's chess master lives."

"And it's very far from here," said Brother Arcadius. It would have to be, but he wanted to make sure. "Very, very far."

"Very far from here, yes," agreed Master Nikko. Leaning forward, he rubbed his gnarled feet.

"So..." said Brother Arcadius. "So...when you were that far away, did you see the great wall?"

"The great wall." Master Nikko raised his eyebrows reflectively. "Do you mean the one that was built by the Qin emperors? You've heard of that wall?"

"I mean the really great wall," said Brother Arcadius. "Not built by people. The one that keeps people from falling off the earth. I thought it would have to be there, all that distance away." Or could there be even more land still farther along? He'd given the size of the earth much thought, off and on, over the years. He'd given the shape of it even more thought. He'd listened to people who claimed that the world had to be round, and he had to admit that there was a curving look and feel to it sometimes.

But how could people keep their balance on it, if it was round?

And how could you wall people in so they wouldn't fall off? If the world were round, where would you place a wall, so that it would work? If you placed it around the middle, like a belt, it would be sticking out sideways, wouldn't it, instead of standing straight up? The people above it would slide down and pile up on it in big heaps, like cherries rolling down the sides of a basket. All the people below it would fall straight off into thin air. There'd be nothing to stop them.

If Brother Arcadius had picked up any one thing from his lessons in reasoning with Father Julian, it was that the simplest answer was probably right. The simplest answer here was flatness. Flatness, and a wall. A magnificent wall, standing straight up, with angels floating by on the other side. Surely Master Nikko would have to know something about it.

For many long moments the old man made no answer. All he did was stand up and stretch again, and rub his arms as if he were trying to warm them. Might he be feeling the lack of his tunic and robe now? Should a person offer him the robe from the person's own back? It wouldn't fit over his broad shoulders, but he could drape it around him. And a person would be extremely glad to do this. No, Master Nikko was smiling and shaking his head. No robe was needed. Instead.... "You've traveled a long way yourself, Brother Arcadius," he said. "And I dare say that wherever you went, the sky was above you."

"Oh yes, it was always above me," said Brother Arcadius. He hoped this was somehow leading back to the wall.

"And assuming you were standing up, the ground was underfoot."

"Underfoot, surely," said Brother Arcadius.

"Would you say that the sky is up, and the ground is down?"

"I would," said Brother Arcadius. "If you're on the water, the water is down, but...there's ground under that."

"That's very true," said Master Nikko. "And did you ever fall up, Brother Arcadius?" he asked.

Fall up? What a notion! How could anyone do such a thing—fall up? "No," said Brother Arcadius.

"Well...." said Master Nikko. His hands made delicate rounded motions, as if he were shaping something into a ball. "You might imagine something round, wrapped up in sky. Something so large that the smallest part of its curve stretched from here to, well, Padua. It would stretch out so far, so far, before and behind you, this curve, that it would never look to you like a curve at all. And no matter how far you went, the sky would always be up there over your head, all things considered, and the ground would always be down there under your feet, and you could be sure that you'd never fall into the sky...."

Brother Arcadius closed his eyes for a moment, imagining himself as a tiny figure on that long, long curve, with the sky overhead always, and his feet on the ground. The sky itself would be the wall then, wouldn't it, and a very beautiful and grand wall, too. He could see how that could be, but the thought made him dizzy.

"It's just something to think about," said Master Nikko. "And here's another thing. If you were to tell the people who live beyond Constantinople about...let's say...Dublin, they'd wonder how anything could be so far away. The regular people, I mean, not chess masters and such. They might even think that it's where the earth comes to an end."

"Would they now!" exclaimed Brother Arcadius. Dublin at the end of the earth! He closed his eyes again to rest his mind. Far-distant people thinking that he was far distant.... Of course that would have to be so, if you thought about it. But thinking too much about it just at this time, or of long curves and up and down and the rest of all that! He didn't want to do that. He needed to ask the rest of his questions while he still had the chance. "So...is it dangerous going there, that long, long way?" he asked after a moment. He didn't like to think of Master Nikko being in danger. The question he most wanted to ask was boiling up inside him, but he wanted an answer to this other question too.

"Oh, often it's safe enough," Master Nikko said. He was looking down and speaking almost to the ground. "Even very safe, some of the time. And interesting and pleasant too—some of the time. And when it isn't, why then you just hope to blend in with the earth around you. To have nothing, ask for nothing, be nothing." He nodded toward the juniper bush where his robe and tunic were drying, and toward his shoulder bag lying there in the grasses. "I acquired those things within just a few hundred miles of Spiritus Sanctus. Owning them could have been quite dangerous, before. I was hard put even to bring along that lump of wax with the chess problem in it. I've learned to keep things very simple when I'm on the road."

"Master Nikko." Brother Arcadius swallowed hard. His most important question could be put off no longer.

"Yes, Brother Arcadius." Master Nikko stood very straight and folded his arms. The curve to his lips did not look at all like a smile.

"Master Nikko...." Brother Arcadius drew a deep breath and then spoke on. "Are you a, a higher being? Like a king? Or an angel, maybe? Or some sort of god? Sent here to test us, like in tales?"

"I'm none of those things," Master Nikko said quietly. "But if I were, you'd have no need to worry, Brother Arcadius. You were ready to brave the water to come after me, and you were ready to lend me your robe to keep me warm. You've given comfort to me—comfort and courtesy. And because of all that and more, I owe you answers and I will give you answers...."

Again the old man's voice trailed into silence. He went over to the juniper bush and spread his robe out again in a different position. He moved his tunic to a different bush and smoothed out its wrinkles. Then he began to walk toward the place where the ground fell steeply away. Brother Arcadius quickly rose and joined him. They came to a stop near the edge, but not dangerously so. Way down there, dwarfed by distance, the little figures of huge Atalf and Ziegmunt could be seen. They were preparing to fell an enormous pine tree, is what it looked like. They'd made the first cut but had stopped to trim away some low-hanging branches. Master Nikko stood looking at them, and looking beyond them. Then he turned abruptly away.

"I was a prince of sorts," he said at last, "but so long ago that it's ceased to matter. No king, no hero, no poet you've ever heard of had yet been born. The most ancient cities you've heard of did not yet exist. Do you believe all this, Brother Arcadius?"

"I—" Brother Arcadius didn't want to be asked for his opinions. He only wanted the story to go on.

"I lived in the land between the two seas—the Black Sea, the Caspian. My family was very rich, and I was very handsome. My hair was thick and black, and I had, I believe, the beauty that young people can have when they're as yet unmarred by time. I had just turned fifteen. To celebrate the occasion my family had given me a gold nose clip that I liked very much, and a fine bay horse that I liked even more. Wearing the one and riding the other, I set off down the road to put my new horse through its paces. And coming toward me on that road, Brother Arcadius, there was a beggar. I anticipate questions."

"Not from me!" cried Brother Arcadius. The pause in the story was almost too much to bear, like the loss of the book with its piece of that beautiful poem, and maybe its poems. He saw with surprise that they were walking back to the patch of frondy yarrow. He hadn't realized that they'd been walking at all.

They reached the yarrow and sat down again. Master Nikko gazed into the distance and then at the ground. After too many agonizing moments he spoke again. "The beggar was wall-eyed, hare-lipped, club-footed, and filthy."

"And he was a god," breathed Brother Arcadius. "Even, maybe, God."

"Not at all," said Master Nikko. "I learned later that he was the twenty-sixth child of a family that was miserably poor. So poor and so desperate that they'd never even bothered to give him a name. In any event, I didn't want to know his name or anything about him. I just wanted him to get out of my way. Brother Arcadius, I should emphasize here that in all these years, I've never told this story to anyone else—and that includes the head of your monastery. You don't have to be a chess master to see why."

"No, you don't," Brother Arcadius said. Father Julian would think this story very...unreasonable. He himself just wanted to hear the rest of it. What had happened, what had happened? "I won't tell anybody ever, Master." Not even to his Mam, if she were to appear by some magic, would he say one word.

"That's a promise that has to be kept," Master Nikko said. "Now that you know that, I'll go on. As the beggar and I approached each other, he didn't step off as he should—as I felt that he should—to the side of the road. I decided to teach him a lesson. I slashed at him with my riding whip. When I did that, my new horse took fright and ran away with me. I had always prided myself on my horsemanship, but I couldn't control him. There was a deep gorge not far from the road, a terrible drop, twice as high, at least, as the one over there. We went over the edge."

Master Nikko looked off once more into the far distance and cleared his throat. "When I looked round after the fall, I saw my horse's broken body there on the rocks. My own broken body lay some distance away. I don't need to describe to you what a fall from that height does to bodies. My gold nose clip had come off and was caught on a bush. Then came the heavenly judges."

"The heavenly judges!" Brother Arcadius was glad he was sitting down, for he felt that otherwise he might have lost his balance. The story had carried him over the edge of that gorge, had made his sandals, in the absence of any nose clip, go flying—had broken his body. Now he was facing judges from Heaven. "What did they look like?" he whispered.

Master Nikko's voice dropped low. He nodded toward Saint

George's grotto. "They looked like the saint that Brother Zossimus gave me," he said. "Unfinished, with just markings for features. They were somewhat taller than I, though, and there was some sort of light within them. I wouldn't say they glowed brightly, but they did glow."

"And what did they do?" Brother Arcadius asked. Whatever oddness he'd thought the day might bring, he never could have imagined that there'd be anything like this. That he'd hear a story like the one he was hearing now, and believe it absolutely.

"Mind you, they weren't the first rank of heavenly judges," Master Nikko said. "Not for the likes of me, a spoiled princeling who couldn't even calm a nice horse. But judges they were. They said they were very disappointed in me. They said that with somebody else, they might have just issued a warning, or issued an ordinary penalty and let it go at that. But in view of all the great gifts I'd been granted—good looks, a good mind, great wealth, loving parents, every advantage—they'd expected much more of me. So they made their decree."

Master Nikko stared unseeingly toward the unfinished saint. Grasses stirred in the afternoon breeze. Along the horizon clouds still drifted eastward in their stately line. From down by the stand of pine trees where Atalf and Ziegmunt were working came the occasional sound of an axe. Brother Arcadius held his breath, waiting to hear of the heavenly judges' decision.

Master Nikko turned toward him. "They said I would be sent back to take to the road," he said. "Not in the handsome form that I'd managed to destroy, but pretty much as you see me now—an unlovely old man. They said that I'd have to travel the road for seven centuries, times the age that I'd reached, fifteen. Travel it alone for all intents and purposes, and mostly on foot, and try to do good if and when I got the chance, and think things over. And that's what I've done ever since, Brother Arcadius."

Master Nikko smiled a smile that was somewhat twisted. "I'm not allowed to die. Once in a while, I do die—I can't help it. When that happens, they add more years to my time. It's been my misfortune to die five times over the whole span. But I'm very close to being done now. If everything goes all right, I should square my accounts at last in a hundred years. A hundred years!" Master Nikko's eyes gleamed, and his smile became his regular smile again. "Dear young man, you can't imagine how much I look forward to a peaceful rest."

"You'll have to be very careful, then, and not let anything happen to you," said Brother Arcadius in a rush. If he'd known all this beforehand, he would have had that branch in the water from the very beginning. And wasn't there suddenly a chillier feeling to the breeze? He'd better make sure that Master Nikko stayed warm. He hurried out of his robe and thrust it into the old man's arms.

"Well, that's a problem," Master Nikko said, but he draped the robe over his shoulders. "I'm not supposed to court danger, and I'm not supposed to avoid it. I've been given penalties on both counts time and again. The guidelines are anything but clear. I more or less do whatever seems right at the moment, and hope for the best. If I tried to arrange things so that nothing was likely to harm me, the penalties would pile up so fast that your head would spin."

Brother Arcadius's head was already spinning. "I'm wondering...if you have to keep to the road, how did you get to be Father Julian's teacher? Did he go along with you, or what?"

"They let me do it," Master Nikko said. "That's all I can say. Sometimes they let me stay a good long while in places, I never know why. They let me teach in Padua for a year, and live like a regular person. That was the only year Julian studied there. But when he left and my time as his teacher was ended, I took on another student, a promising lad, and I got a warning. It was the only time that they ever gave me a warning. I appreciate the kindness more than I can say."

"Well, I appreciate *you*," cried Brother Arcadius. If it hadn't seemed so disrespectful, he would have thrown his arms around the old man and held him close.

Master Nikko didn't seem to have heard him. He pulled the robe more closely around him, but said nothing. After a moment, Brother Arcadius ventured a final question. "If you're not an angel or anything like that, Master Nikko, then how...."

"How do I know things before anyone tells me about them?" Master Nikko gave his quick laugh again, but there didn't seem to be any amusement in it. "When you've been around as long as I have, Brother Arcadius, a good many things become very obvious. Not all of them, though. Far from all of them. The chains of actions and consequences are often very much longer than we can comprehend. The most intricate games of chess played by the greatest masters are child's play in comparison."

Once again he fell silent, and a good many moments went by. The sun sank lower in its journey around the—round?—earth, and cloud shadows drifted over the land. Just when it seemed that his silence would never end, the old man spoke again. "Anyway, that's my story," he said. It was clear that he didn't intend to tell any more of it. "And that's what I am—no king, no angel, no god. And anyway"—he laughed a little—"we're all just clouds, when you come right down to it."

He pointed into the distance, where a darkish cloud had stayed put in the sky for a good long while now, without ever moving or changing its shape. "That's me, doing my penance and living on and on seemingly forever, but it won't be forever. Nothing here is forever. And the ones that are moving along so nicely, one after the other...." Master Nikko tracked them one by one with a pointing finger. "The first one, that's Father Julian," he said. "And there behind him is Father Arcadius, and the next one after that is Father Keti, although Father Keti will want a more dignified name...."

He's wandering now, thought Brother Arcadius. He felt very much moved by great pity and great respect. Even men of great wisdom had a right to wander sometimes, when they were that old and had been so many years on a perilous way, and had died five times into the bargain. Even so, there was never going to be any Father Arcadius. Never in all time would that happen, and never should it happen. A Father Keti, now.... He could see a Father Keti, all grown up and come into his own, games of chess and all. Except that Keti did not belong to the Julian family, and the Fathers of Spiritus Sanctus had to be Julians....

"Life is change," said Master Nikko distantly. "Things come to pass, things pass away."

He slid the robe from his shoulders and laid it carefully down on the grasses beside him. An air of great formality had come over him. He crossed his legs tailor-fashion and then, in one easy motion, rested his feet on his thighs. He pressed his hands together, palm to palm, and closed his eyes. He murmured strange words that were beautiful and peaceful to hear. He seemed lost to the world. He breathed slowly and deeply, in and out, in and out, in a steady rhythm. Then, as slowly as a slow-changing cloud might take on new forms, his body took on new postures, one after the other. And somehow all of this strangeness seemed natural and right.

Not knowing what else to do, Brother Arcadius crossed his own legs tailor-fashion and breathed deeply too. He barely managed to get his crossed feet up past the ankles, but the breathing went fairly well, or so he judged. And he pressed his hands together, palm to palm, and made up for the prayer that he'd slighted earlier, and slow thoughts drifted through his mind, one after another, of all that he'd been told that afternoon....

In and out, in and out, slow thoughts drifting.... The far-off sound of axes striking wood....

In and out, in and out, no thoughts drifting, no axes ringing....

No thoughts at all, just a slow white silence, like being inside a cloud....

And thoughts again, slow and drifting....

Keti and Pangur Ban and the kitchen garden.... The sound of axes again from down below.... The tale of how Pangur Ban's life had been saved, there on that wave-tossed boat... So one hunter had rescued another, Master Nikko had said, down there in the kitchen garden. Yes, Pangur Ban was a hunter and he, Brother Arcadius, was a hunter too.... A hunter of words, a hunter of poetry.... Someone could write a poem about something like that....

In and out, in and out.... Soft thoughts, no thoughts...no sound of axes ringing...a stirring of poetry...Pangur Ban....

"We should go back now," said a voice. Brother Arcadius's eyes flew open, and he came back into the world. His robe was over his shoulders again and Master Nikko was standing there, smiling down at him. "But first there's something we'll want to see." He'd put on his tunic and robe and his bag was over his shoulder. He patted the bag. "Saint's back in it," he said. "Soap too." He looked like nothing more than a merry old man, a lake-washed, wind-dried, merry old man.

Brother Arcadius smiled too and got to his feet. He was curious about what Master Nikko wanted him to see, but more than anything he felt peaceful, peaceful and pleased. It had felt good, thinking those slow breaths, breathing those slow thoughts, or whatever it was he'd been doing. But now the time for slowness was past. Master Nikko had already reached the grotto and was beckoning him to follow. Together they came to the knoll's sheer edge. Brother Atalf and Brother Ziegmunt were standing down there, waiting. Groaning and creaking, the towering pine slowly leaned forward. For a breathless moment it stayed steady, at a slant. Then, with a great swaying of its own branches and the branches of the trees around it, and an outcry of birds, it crashed to the ground.

"It calls for poetry, doesn't it," Master Nikko said. "*Incedunt arbusta per alta, securibus caedunt*.... Those two big fellows, down there among the high trees...."

"But that's my poem!" cried Brother Arcadius. "You know my poem!"

Brother Arcadius and Pangur Ban

"*Percellunt magnas quercus, exciditur ilex*.... The trees of the forest falling, the great oaks falling.... I do know it, Brother Arcadius—that is, what's left of it. And what better time or place could there be to say it to you? Let it be a gift from the day for your good breathing, and a tribute to the fallen tree. You found two lines of the poem, and I herewith present you with three more." And Master Nikko spread his arms wide and recited:

> Fraxinus frangitur atque abies consternitur alta,
> Pinus proceras pervortunt: omne sonabat
> Arbustum fremitu silvai frondosai.

Brother Arcadius breathed in the glorious words, the words he'd already known, the new words he hadn't.

"The poet Ennius wrote those lines, just as you guessed," Master Nikko said. "Wrote them over a thousand years ago, for his friend, Hannibal's conqueror, Africanus."

Brother Arcadius recited the whole thing again to himself. In the poem, people were felling mighty trees in an unknown forest. The new lines told of the rustlings of leaves and then the whole forest resounding as the great trees came down, among them a pine. But who the people were and why they were cutting the trees down—of that, nothing was said. The missing parts of the poem must have explained all that. "What is it about?" he asked Master Nikko. "Do you know? And is there more of it?"

"A lot of goats happen in a thousand years," Master Nikko said. "Ennius's work survives only in bits and pieces. I have a number of those fragments by heart, and I'll write them down for you before I leave. But as for what these particular lines are about, I can only guess. Roman heroes, I think, mighty warriors of old, are felling trees to make a funeral pyre. Beyond that, I couldn't say." The old man's eyes narrowed. "Brother Arcadius, imagine, if you will, a picture to go with the poem. What would those heroes look like?"

"Why, they'd be great strong fellows like...." Brother Arcadius paused for a moment in wonder. "They'd look like Brother Atalf and Brother Ziegmunt." The faces, he supposed, would be noble and Roman, but the bodies...the bodies would be Atalf's and Ziegmunt's, for sure. Not even in Rome could there have been two heftier men. From now on, whenever he thought of his poem, he was going to see them in it, two mighty heroes with Roman faces, striding along.

"And there you are," said Master Nikko. "Things do come round in ways that can surprise us." But suddenly his whole manner changed. "We should go back now," he said. He turned to the long slope they'd ascended so many clouds and worlds and centuries and breathings ago and began to walk down it in silence, as if he were trying to reach a painful decision. Brother Arcadius, now greatly worried, kept pace with him.

At the foot of the knoll the old man came to a sudden stop. "Brother Arcadius," he said, "you've done nobly today. Faced with all sorts of strange things, one after another, you've kept a courteous and an open mind. I'm sorry to say that there has to be one thing more." He offered his hand, and Brother Arcadius took it. Master Nikko's grip was firm, his expression solemn.

Brother Arcadius squared his shoulders, waiting. Whatever was coming, he told himself that he'd take it. After all, he was almost twenty. And great gifts had been given to him all his life, not least today. Could he or could he not stand up to some trouble? He told himself that he could. But he also hoped, deep inside, that whatever this was would turn out to be just a joke, as when Brother Silvanus put on a pretense of sternness.

Master Nikko looked steadily at him—steadily, and kindly. "There are times," he said, "when it's best for people to speak in general terms, to say things like, 'All people must eat or die.' There are other times when we need to be very specific. This is one of those times. If you were not Brother Arcadius, and did not come from Dublin, and did not have ties with a brickyard, and did not have that nice fringe of curly red hair or a poetic mind, and if you were not going to be twenty on the day after the return of spring, and if obedience were not your first nature, most of the time, I would not say a word of this to you. But because you are who you are, and you'll be who you'll be, it is imperative that you hear and come to terms with what I'm going to say. Can you listen to words you'll dislike, not just with an open mind but with an open heart?"

"I don't know!" said Brother Arcadius, perplexed and alarmed.

Master Nikko looked at him keenly. "It's clear to me that you can. You need to know then that Father Julian, every moment of every day, year in, year out, detests being here at Spiritus Sanctus, and wishes he were somewhere else."

Brother Arcadius now felt as if he were in a dank cellar, with cold waters rising around him, slowly, slowly. "Where else would he want to be?" he asked.

"He'd like to be in the land of the next farthest song, playing perpetual games of chess with that great master."

"He doesn't like us? He doesn't care about Spiritus Sanctus?"

"He does like all of you—in various ways. And he does care very much about Spiritus Sanctus. He just doesn't want to be here."

"But he has to be here!" cried Brother Arcadius.

"Yes, at this time he does, and for a good long while yet," Master Nikko nodded. "You couldn't be more right. All the same, you need to remember that he doesn't like it. He truly and absolutely doesn't like it."

"Is it a penance he's doing? Did the heavenly judges tell him he had to do it?"

"If he were derelict in his duty, the heavenly judges might get into it," Master Nikko said. "But I doubt that they have. I see no dereliction of duty here, and that's part of the point I'm making."

"I think he does like to be here," Brother Arcadius said. "In his way."

"Well, for his sake I'd like to think so, but it's not true," Master Nikko said. "When his father decided to place him with the church, he was in anguish. That was at the end of my term with him, when he was fifteen. At the same time, his sister was betrothed to a count she detested – you've met him, I believe."

Brother Arcadius nodded. He had.

"The two young people stormed against these decisions," Master Nikko continued. "They raged, they wept. Of the two of them, the sister was more justified, by far. It was a painful time. I played no part in the sister's life and couldn't help her. As Julian's teacher, I might just possibly have been able to help him, but I refused to try. I could not see him wasting his splendid mind and his splendid talents trailing after me on the road and playing chess matches for money to earn his living. That's what he wanted to do. I told him adamantly that he must not. It's a mark of his very good heart that he finally listened, and that he still speaks to me. I adjured him to understand that his work lies here at Spiritus Sanctus. Looking around me today, I know that I'm right."

"It's the best monastery," Brother Arcadius said. It was unmonklike and wrong to make claims like that, but the words came out before he could stop them. He felt almost incapable of thought, and was sure that he couldn't take in another thing. They were walking on now, and Master Nikko was praising the monastery, that much he

318

could tell. He was extolling the lake, the fields, the pastures, the vineyards, the scrublands, the grasslands, the woods, the kitchen garden, as if he could see them all before his eyes.

"It's a place that gives back to the land what's due to the land and takes good care of its water," the old man was saying. "There is no sense here of stupid privilege. The monks who dig out your latrines are valued as highly as those who take care of books, and vice versa, and dung that enriches the soil and books that enrich the mind are rightly held to be equal treasures—or at least that's the clear intention," he said with a smile. "I know that intentions can take a while to be realized. Some of your brethren may not yet be convinced that books have any value at all. But all in all, everything here is as I hoped it would be."

Master Nikko stopped on the path for a moment and looked around him. "Coming here," he continued, walking on again, "when I was still in Rome, many miles away, I encountered a formidable young woman named Beatrice, a very capable and valued manager now of her uncle's weaving business. She didn't have a good word to say for Spiritus Sanctus, but I gathered that she'd been saved here from a terrible fate."

Well, it was interesting to learn what had become of Beatrice. Brother Arcadius had sometimes wondered about it. He wasn't surprised to hear that her uncle's weaving business was now under her thumb. "There was a man who wanted her to be burned as a witch, but Father Julian turned the tables on him," he managed to say.

"Exactly," said Master Nikko. "And I ran into that well-known windbag, Tullius, who said that the library here is a joke, and that Father Julian is an arrogant know-nothing. I rejoiced to hear it. When someone like Tullius dislikes you, that's a very good sign."

"He tried to steal our books," said Brother Arcadius, but his mind was elsewhere. Why, why didn't Father Julian like it here? There were so many good things at Spiritus Sanctus. The library, with its five hundred books, including its beautiful Genesis. Every last one of the brethren, including even Brother Atalf and Brother Ziegmunt. Brother Zossimus's saints. Keti's bed up on the high cupboard. Keti himself. The fish paste. The herbed game stew.

"Yes, Tullius has that streak of larceny in him," Master Nikko said. "I also crossed paths with a pilgrim named Placidus, whom I liked very much, and who says that his whole life was changed for the better here."

"It was a bad life before, for sure," said Brother Arcadius. It was *unreasonable* of Father Julian to be unhappy here.

"That's what the dear fellow told me, although he couldn't remember any details," said Master Nikko. "I also heard tales of two scoundrels, two out-and-out murderers, whose escapade here led to their being put out of commission, and I talked to an excellent magician, who said that here he had reaffirmed his true calling." He smiled again at Brother Arcadius. "I believe you yourself played a great part in some of these things, and so did the cat I met this afternoon."

His words were kindly, but somehow they gave no comfort. Don't you start sniveling now, Brother Arcadius told himself. Grow up. You're almost twenty. But he felt as bad as he would have felt if somebody suddenly told him that his own Mam didn't want to be his Mam. Oh, if only he'd worked harder at chess. He *would* work harder at chess. Father Julian must never, never, never get so disgusted with things that he suddenly gave it all up and went away.

Master Nikko laughed softly. "He'll never do that," he said. "You can count on him to be steadfast. He gave his word. Spiritus Sanctus is his life's work, done very much against his will, but done well all the same. As for growing up...well, that's an endless task, Brother Arcadius. I'm still working at it myself, and Julian too is just a beginner at it. Even the heavenly judges looked quite unfinished, if you'll recall. Brother Zossimus doesn't know it, but for once he did catch a very close likeness of something. Now, square your shoulders yet again, Brother Arcadius"—Brother Arcadius did so—"and let's march on. But let's remember that all of this is between us. Julian confides in your medicus, I'm pretty sure. But Salix keeps his own counsel, and so will you."

Side by side they went forward. It was an effort, but Brother Arcadius kept his shoulders squared. They followed the path into the courtyard and entered the refectory. They passed the image of Charles Martel. Going out through the farther door, they saw Father Julian coming toward them, eyes alight. Brother Dietrich, bewilderment on his face and a wrinkle in his robe, slunk along two paces behind.

"Solved it," said Father Julian joyfully. Student and teacher met in a heartfelt embrace. Student led teacher to the rooms for distinguished guests. It had to be hoped that the heavenly judges allowed this. Crossing his fingers, Brother Arcadius returned to the library.

At supper that night, Father Julian's strange guest sat beside him on the dais. He was wearing a proper monk's robe that had been brought out of storage and quickly hemmed up for him. Proper sandals had been found for him also. He ate sparingly but appreciatively of everything, and clearly enjoyed his helping of barley gruel. Father Julian's delight was evident to the whole monastery. Brother Dietrich still looked as if he'd been hit on the head, but seemed to be slowly coming back into himself.

The next day Father Julian took Master Nikko everywhere about the grounds. The dark Julian look was the thinnest of disguises for an eagerness that kept shining through. Brother Arcadius couldn't follow them about, but he caught frequent glimpses of them through the library window. Father Julian might hate being here at the monastery, but he very obviously enjoyed showing it off to a revered teacher, and getting that teacher's beaming approval. Brother Arcadius noted also that Pangur Ban kept steady watch from the garden wall. Pangur knows, thought Brother Arcadius. Somehow he knows how different Master Nikko really is.

That evening Master Nikko fell deathly ill. Right after mass, leaving the church at Father Julian's side, he leaned slowly forward like a tree getting ready to fall, and then he did fall. Brother Salix was at his side instantly, loosening the borrowed robe, pressing his ear to a chest that seemed not to be moving. "There's a heartbeat, but only barely," the medicus said. The old man's eyes were closed, his face was dead white, his mouth was slack. Brother Atalf carried him to the infirmary.

Unable to stay away, Brother Arcadius ate a token supper and then went there too. A side door was ajar and he slipped through it. He found a dark corner and knelt down with a breaking heart. Don't let him die, he prayed. Don't let him die and then give him a penalty. Just let him live out these last hundred years and then take him. Be kind to him. He's been good. He is good. Be kind, be kind, be kind!

The long room was lit by only a single candle. Master Nikko's bed was the only one in use. The old man lay unmoving under a linen sheet. His face was drained entirely of color, his features stark, the skin molded tight to the bone. Now and then, at long intervals, his chest heaved. Otherwise he might have been a wax figure. It was strange to be praying for him to live so that he could die. Father Julian stood by the bedside, keeping vigil. If he'd noticed that Brother Arcadius was in the room too, he gave no sign of it—or of knowing, even, that Brother Salix was also nearby.

It seemed then that a long time passed, but it was hard to be sure. The candle, a fine one of beeswax rather than tallow, burned down slowly. From time to time Brother Salix moistened the patient's lips with some liquid that smelled of wine and heart's-ease and honey. From time to time the old man took a labored breath. At those times it seemed that he might be reviving. He always sank back at once into stillness again. Father Julian remained standing, motionless, for what must have been hours. But at last, with a sudden movement, he dropped to his knees and searched out the old man's hand, and clutched it tightly. Once, when Brother Dietrich came warily in with a question, he murmured an answer. Otherwise he was still.

Brother Arcadius kept vigil from his dark corner.

> Incedunt arbusta per alta, securibus caedunt
> Percellunt magnas quercus, exciditur ilex,
> Fraxinus frangitur atque abies consternitur alta,
> Pinus proceras pervortunt: omne sonabat
> Arbustum fremitu silvai frondosai.

He gave me this gift, he gave me so many gifts. He gave Father Julian to this monastery. Be kind to him, be kind!

The candle burned halfway down, then a quarter more. Nothing else changed, except that there was a promise of far-off dawn in the air. On his knees all this while, Brother Arcadius concluded that sometimes he must have been sleeping. He admonished himself to forget about sleeping and stay awake. He fell asleep again.

Moments later he woke to see that now things were changing. Master Nikko's mouth had fallen helplessly open. His chest, the next time it moved, barely rose at all. Brother Salix was moving quickly back and forth with cloths and remedies. Tight-jawed, tight-lipped, Father Julian's head was bent low over the hand that he gripped.

Another presence was in the room now as well.

Pangur Ban.

When had he come in? And did Brother Salix and Father Julian know he was there? They had to know he was there. Right there on the stand at the foot of the dying man's bed, there he was, rounded, cloud white, unmoving, alert. Wasn't it at least an hour too early for him to quit mousing? What had brought him here, to stare and stare and stare at the old man in the bed the way he was doing? The others were paying no attention to him. Maybe he wasn't there at all. But he seemed to be, and maybe he ought to be carried out. Brother Arcadius admonished himself to get up and do so, before anyone ordered him to. *Arcadius, will you attend to that cat?* His resolve lasted only a moment. Sleep took him again.

A half doze, rather, a sort of waking sleep. A vision formed in it, a half-waking dream. A strand of silver, thin almost to invisibility, was floating from the dying master's open mouth. Now came another, and then another. And now came many more. And Brother Salix, swift-moving and fiercely intent, had turned away to mix another remedy. And Father Julian's face was pressed tight to the hand he was clasping. But Pangur Ban....

The big cat had risen up on his haunches, and was quietly reaching his forepaws into the air. Quietly, quietly, with sure and purposeful motions, he was gathering up the silver strands as they came by. Gathering them, and sending them back with quick pats to the dying man.

Brother Arcadius woke up with a sudden start. No, Pangur Ban wasn't reaching for anything. He still rested there in quiet repose on the little stand. But Master Nikko's chest heaved largely, once and then again. The hand that was clasped in Father Julian's two hands moved. Father Julian was bolt upright now. There was moisture on his tightly drawn cheeks. The whites of his eyes were very red. Their dark centers were fiercely alive with shock—and hope.

Master Nikko opened his eyes and raised his head from its pillow, just barely. Brother Salix bent down to help him, but he whispered, "No." His full attention was fixed upon Pangur Ban. Eyes gleaming brightly, Pangur gazed steadily back at him, alert and calm.

Master Nikko's head sank back to the pillow. He whispered something that couldn't be heard, then whispered it louder. "Catmint," he whispered. "In a decoction...a tea.... Hurry...." His eyes closed again. His breathing faltered.

Brother Salix and Father Julian stared at each other. "Catmint can't help him," the medicus said, low-voiced. "But if he wants it, it might give him some comfort."

"I'll get some!" Brother Arcadius leaped from his corner. Rushing by the two men at the bedside, he took note of their startled faces. So they hadn't known he was there, or if they had, they'd forgotten. It didn't matter. He ran headlong, as he'd once run to save his beautiful poem. A sandal fell off and he ran lopsidedly then, but did not slow down. When it became hard to breathe, he forced himself to run even faster. He'd been too late to save the poem. He prayed that he'd not be too late to give Master Nikko the healing potion he asked for—the drink that might save him, if Brother Salix was wrong.

When he reached the door in the garden wall, he tugged it open. Brother Marcus and his crew had already started their day's work, so Brother Homelius was out there gathering marrows. "They need catmint at the infirmary, quick!" Brother Arcadius cried. "I'll explain later! Hurry!" Oh, if in spite of all this speed he failed once more!

Brother Homelius blessedly wasted no time. In moments Brother Arcadius was clasping an armful of great leaf-heavy stalks of catmint, roots and all. Lopsidedly running, robe flying behind him, he returned to the infirmary with his treasures—he prayed they'd be treasures. Master Nikko lay white-faced and speechless, just as before. Pangur gazed steadily at him, just as before. There was no need to wait for Brother Salix to heat up water. The kettle in his fireplace was already simmering. In moments the decoction was ready. The aroma of steeping catmint filled the room. Pangur Ban watched from the stand. Looking close to despair, Father Julian raised Master Nikko up just a bit on the pillow. A spoonful of liquid was pressed gently to the old man's lips. They opened, and the spoonful was slowly taken. "More," whispered Master Nikko, and more was offered....

Offered, and taken.

Master Nikko's eyes fluttered open, and he looked round. "Hello, Julian," he whispered.

"Hello," Father Julian whispered back, but his face suddenly crumpled. Bother Salix tossed him a towel. He mopped his eyes. Then he handed the towel back to the medicus and sniffed twice. The hands that had clasped Master Nikko's were now clasped in turn.

"You're a churchman, Julian," whispered Master Nikko. "You're not supposed to take it so hard when people die." He took another sip of the offered decoction. He took in a great breath of the catmint-scented air. Color began to flood back into his face. He patted Father Julian's shaking hands. He said, "You were always a good boy, Julian." He said, "When can I get up?" Brother Salix said, "We'll think about that tomorrow." Father Julian returned to being Father Julian. "Should the cat be in here?" he asked. But Pangur Ban had already slipped out through an open window.

By noon the next day Master Nikko left the infirmary on Father Julian's arm—not because he needed support, but because Father Julian insisted. By day's end the medicus had to take Father Julian aside and explain to him firmly that cured was cured, and that worry alone never made anyone stronger. He confessed himself mystified, though, by the whole thing. Yes, Master Nikko had caught sight of the cat, and seeing the cat must have made him think of catmint. That much was plain. But under no circumstances could a decoction of catmint have cured him. Something else had done that, but what? He'd clearly been dying.

Brother Arcadius kept wondering about it too. There'd been all that talk about catmint in the kitchen garden on the way to the lake, and the power that maybe it had, and all of that. So Master Nikko had already been thinking along those lines. And just in time he must have decided to test it, and maybe in time he'd explain how it was that it had worked. As for the dream about Pangur Ban and those silver threads— well, that had been a dream. But it wasn't an assistant librarian's place to start chatting about things like that, and maybe vex Father Julian further. So he didn't.

Master Nikko said only that he was bewildered too. He agreed with Brother Salix that the whole thing was a mystery. Under Father Julian's anxious eyes, he went on with the business of admiring Spiritus Sanctus. And he copied out, for the library, no fewer than twenty-five bits and pieces of the works of Ennius.

Within the week he said goodbye to the monastery and went on down the road in the short patched robe and the tunic and breeches that he'd arrived in, heading south. The bag slung over his shoulder was stuffed with catmint. He'd asked to take plenty with him, and was bound to find plenty of it growing wild, also, along the way.

There were three who watched until his dwindling figure passed from their sight: Father Julian, Brother Arcadius, and Pangur Ban. And then they all went about their business again, the same as they were before...or maybe not....

* * *

"It was coincidence," said Brother Salix to himself for the hundredth time. "He saw the cat, he thought of catmint, he got well. But as for what really cured him, we'll never know."

* * *

"Something funny was going on," said Brother Atalf to Brother Ziegmunt. "The cat was in on it."

* * *

"There's no point in having you continue with chess or lessons in reasoning, Arcadius," said Father Julian. His voice was calm, his dark eyes were unreadable. "They're simply a waste of your time."

"Yes, Father." Brother Arcadius bowed his head to hide his leaping thoughts. Yes, he wanted to be free of chess and lessons in reasoning. No, he didn't want to disappoint Father Julian—in fact, he *feared* to disappoint Father Julian! Disappoint him and make him hate being at Spiritus Sanctus more than ever—that must not happen! Yes, it was a compliment of sorts to be told that chess and lessons in reasoning were wasting his time, instead of being told that he was wasting Father Julian's time. No, being almost twenty was no easy business, what with all the things he had to worry about. But a new letter had come from his Mam, all full of good cheer....

> Dir Tammis, Yir broders and sisters all got marryed. they are all ekspecting. All with the brick works and all doing gud. Kng Edw vry pleased with our gud bricks. Tammis I hope yir lerning a lot at Sp. Sanc. and not speking out wen yu shudden. All vry proud of yu Tammis and all luv yu be gud Mam

His Mam was steadfast too, like Father Julian. And he himself, Tammis Scholar of Dublin, Brother Arcadius of Spiritus Sanctus, must be steadfast also. And march on. And keep his shoulders squared. And use the time freed up by not playing chess or studying reasoning to do more for the library and more for Spiritus Sanctus, and not fret too much about people being unhappy, or that there were a thousand and one ways that an old man could die and then have to live more years of unwanted life, of weary wandering on the endless road.

Let it not be so, let it not be so, let it not be so!

* * *

"Brother Arcadius?"

"Yes, Keti?"

"Brother Kongro just got a message for you. He sent me over with it."

"A message! A message from whom?"

"Brother Kongro doesn't know," said Keti. He handed over a small piece of parchment, rolled up and tied. "They gave him the message and left. They said they don't want an answer. Anyway, they're gone."

"Well, I guess you can go then too, Keti. Thank you very much."

Keti hurried back to the kitchen, and Brother Arcadius unrolled the message. It was printed neatly in Greek, in tiny letters. "Time reduced," it said. "Thirty more years, not 100. No penalties for mishaps. And I can settle down and teach. I'll be seeing you soon. But keep it a surprise. N."

Brother Arcadius read this amazing missive again and again. It was all he could do not to kiss it. If only he could tell Father Julian that he'd be seeing his teacher again very soon! Not just seeing him, either, but having him here at Spiritus Sanctus, year after happy year! For if Master Nikko could settle down again, wouldn't here be the right place to do it?

* * *

Pangur Ban, the invincible mouser of Spiritus Sanctus monastery and cat of Brother Arcadius's own heart, curled up in a sun-filled corner of the courtyard and let his thoughts drift out over the world. The very rounded world, although there were straight things in it, here and there—people's things such as shelves and corners, but also things like sheared-off rocks, or a cat's leg thrusting against its natural curve, or a mouse fleeing headlong to shelter.

But overall the world was a great curved place of enormous beauty, wrapped up in rich earth and shining water and blue air and clouds. Cats knew very well that it spun dizzily around and around like a kitten chasing its tail, and that, spinning, it circled the sun in a mighty rush that went on and on and on, as if some giant paw had swatted it into motion. Over it, among much else, sages sometimes walked, and sages sometimes collapsed, and when that happened, it was good if a wise cat was there to help them. For wise cats knew that sometimes it was best to think in general terms—"Cats tend to be smarter than people." But sometimes it was necessary to be very specific....

To know, for instance, that if a sage had once been a very foolish boy, with a new bay horse and a gold nose clip.... and if that sage had paid dearly for his foolishness, and had walked a long, lonely way many thousands of times, between the lands around here and the land of the next farthest song...and if he had jolted his soul out of place by swimming back and forth too vigorously in a very cold lake...and if he had then climbed up a long grade rather too quickly...and if, after all that, he'd sat down like a tailor and moved like a cat—then the only remedy would be a decoction of catmint. Restoring sages like that was the one and only great power that catmint had—but it was so very great, that power, that it was extremely important to show it respect. Aside from that, catmint mainly served to make cats who happened to be foolish more foolish still.

Pangur Ban rolled onto his back and gave his curving shoulders a refreshing rub against the warm straightness of the stones beneath him. A refreshing rub was much needed. It had taken a great deal of very serious, tiring gazing to put the idea of a drink of catmint into that old man's mind. But it wasn't sages alone that cats should attend to. Cats should be cats and mostly keep to their place in the world, but sometimes they had to reach out and help their people. Keti...Brother Marcus...Brother Salix...Father Julian...Brother Atalf and Brother Ziegmunt and Brother Silvanus and Brother Zossimus, and many more...but ever and ever and always his rescuer and first friend, Brother Arcadius....

These were his people. And the people they worked with and also the people they loved, those were his people too. And when a cat's people were sad or in trouble, then a cat should help them whenever he could, whether they understood they'd been helped, or not. One thing caring for another—that's what kept the world round and wrapped in its sky, so that up and down remained in their proper places, growing up could happen, and life could breathe.

With a quiet "mmrrwwr" Pangur Ban rose from his corner, and stretched hard. He raised a forepaw and regarded it closely. Yes, he could see it as well as feel it—a piece of one of those silver things, caught between two of his toes. He worked it loose with his tongue and watched it catch the breeze and float away. The old sage would never miss it. He had a great abundance of silver things, that sage. Pangur Ban yawned mightily, again and again. Then he padded off to the library of Spiritus Sanctus, to say hello to his first and foremost person, Brother Arcadius, and to catch a quick snack of something, and to be himself.

"Mrrm," said Pangur Ban to himself alone. "Mmrrwwm."

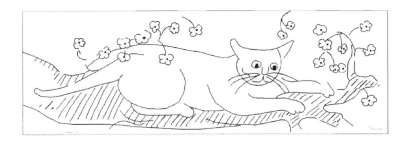

EPILOGUE

In which, as always, the end is just the beginning

AD 902

Brother Arcadius paused in his library work for a moment to think contentedly about this and that. It was a good world he'd come to, this world of Spiritus Sanctus, that was for sure, and just about everything in it gladdened his heart. The spring sun shone agreeably down through a thin veil of clouds, and the cherry tree outside his cell window was in bloom, and he was twenty.... Twenty years old and a month, to be exact.

He didn't usually do library work in his cell, but Master Nikko was using the library today to teach one of his classes. Brother Atalf, Brother Ziegmunt, and several other beginners were going to take turns reading a story that Atalf himself had composed, and that Master Nikko had copied out in large letters on a beechwood plank. "Saint George killed a dragon" is what the story said, and Atalf was thrilled to see it there in writing. After that, and after everyone's hands had been carefully cleaned and dried, the class would look at the pictures in the library's beautiful Genesis.

That was all very good, and Keti the kitchen boy just yesterday had played Father Julian to a tension-filled draw in chess, and the unreadable look in Father Julian's eyes, although just as dark as ever, was brightly so.

A rustling in the cherry tree claimed Brother Arcadius's attention. It materialized into a form he knew well. Pangur Ban, the sensible, sociable master mouser of Spiritus Sanctus monastery, was gazing benignly at him from among the blossoms. It was amazing how a cat—

a personage, really—could blend in with petals and branches, and with the clouds in the background, as if he were part of them.

Brother Arcadius sighed with happiness. "Don't you start gloating now," he told himself. Grown-up people weren't supposed to gloat, and although he was certainly not grown up and never could be for a long, long time, he was heading in that direction. And he was starting to blend in for sure at Spiritus Sanctus. People still said that the wind might blow him away, but it didn't seem like an insult anymore. Even Brother Atalf, these days, was starting to get his name right, and calling him "Arcaderus" instead of "Arcaperus." In a tone that was friendly, too, or almost so.

And the poem, his own poem, was taking shape. It was not a grand poem such as Ennius would have composed. It wasn't in Latin, either, but rather in Irish. Down-to-earth Irish, too, that his Mam and his six older brothers and two younger sisters and the people they'd married would feel at home with. It wasn't right yet, it would need changes, it was just a beginning, but it was coming along. To himself, and to Pangur out there on the branch, he murmured it softly:

> Pangur Ban, my cat so true,
> You're a hunter, I am too.
> Mice you hunt, and voles, and birds.
> I myself hunt thoughts and words.

Another idea came to him and he paused, considering it.

> When I was pent in fearsome cave—

He shuddered at the memory.

> Pangur's hunting did me save.

Something like that ought to be part of the poem, and yet it couldn't be. For what if somehow, in some unimaginable way, his Mam got to read it? It would be wrong to worry her about things like caves. No, he'd better not allude to anything dangerous, or cast aspersions on anybody, or say anything that might give a secret away. Best to stay with mice and learning, mice and learning. Keep to the trail, he told himself, and smiled again, remembering himself as a know-nothing creature of sixteen, and how alarming those words of advice had seemed to him then. It hadn't been such bad advice after all.

> You're a master at your skill,
> I myself am not, but still!
> Trying harder every day,
> May I match you, in my way....

"It's just a start," said Brother Arcadius to the cat gazing at him from the tree. "I'll have to change it a lot. But what do you think about it, my dear friend?"

"Meow," said Pangur Ban.

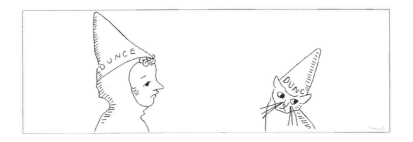

AN APOLOGY TO ACTUALITY

In which the author tries to set a few things straight

CE 2016

The benign Neverland of Spiritus Sanctus is not meant to be a guide to matters of fact. Readers who check it against the record of things that are so (or are thought to be so) will find much to complain about. For instance, it is highly unlikely that Brother Arcadius's Dublin or King Alfred's Wessex would have supported a brickyard. Charles Martel was never an actual king, although he ruled like one. The notion that Saint George rode a horse and killed a dragon came in with the later Middle Ages. And Arcadius's accounts of Danish depredations in Ireland vastly oversimplify a very complex situation.

On the other hand, quite a few of the background details are actually true. The two forced marriages of King Alfred's young stepmother, Judith, and her eventual happy elopement with Count-to-Be Baldwin of Flanders, aka Iron-Arm, took place pretty much as Lady Aurelia says they did. The Romans and Roman politics of that era were turbulent, so much so that in 799, a political faction attacked Pope Leo III in the open streets and gave him a savage beating. Saracens and Christians did seek to form alliances with each other sometimes. And learning, as we know, did find havens in Constantinople, and among the Arabs and the Jews, and in monasteries here and there throughout the shattered West.

One more thing that is true should be noted here. Sometime during the ninth century or thereabouts, a monk living in Alpine regions wrote a poem in Irish about his cat—a cat named Pangur Ban. The name (properly Pangur Bán) is indeed Irish and "signifies whiteness"—or fairness, or prettiness, or general appealingness. The poet tells us that just as his cat zealously hunts mice, so does he zealously hunt words and ideas. Just who this person was remains unknown, but as far as I'm concerned he was Brother Arcadius.

Since its rediscovery by the wider world in 1903, "Arcadius's" poem has won many admirers. It has been set to music by the renowned composer Samuel Barber. Its many English translations include one by Nobel laureate Seamus Heaney. It has appeared in numerous anthologies and continues to provide inspiration for readers and for artists working in many fields.

The poem that appears in the epilogue of this book is my own invention. Among the many English translations of the real poem, the one I first encountered can be found in *Poems and Translations*, by Robin Flower, published by Lilliput Press in Dublin (www.lilliputpress.com). Four stanzas of Mr. Flower's translation also appear in *Alfred the Great*, by P.J. Helm (New York: Thomas Y. Crowell Co., 1965). That's where I first learned about Pangur Ban and his monk, and the adventures of young Judith, and the attack on Pope Leo III, and much more. Concise, zestful, and eye-opening, at least for me, this biography is an excellent introduction to Brother Arcadius's times, and a good antidote to the vagaries of fiction. And so,

> Pangur B and Brother A
> Bid you farewell and go their way,
> Bypassing reality's rockier trails,
> To their rightful home, the realm of tales.

Acknowledgements

I owe whole-hearted thanks to Vickie Nagel and Tom Hahne, for all that they do; to Bonnie Mutchler, for designing the cover of this book with skill and care; to Sarah Hahne, Milton Nagel, Jane Woolley, and Paige Temple, for their indispensable encouragement and on-target suggestions; and to Mary Kim, whose stellar editing has been a writer's dream.

About the Author

Margaret Nagel is a native and long-time resident of Western New York, and formerly taught there. She received degrees in English and education from the State University of New York at Fredonia. She has three children, and presently lives in Evanston, Illinois. This book took shape and gained its final form partly in Evanston and partly in Three Mile Bay, New York, where she spends much of the summer.

.

Printed in Great Britain
by Amazon